Merry Me

C.R. JANE

Podium

Copyright © 2025 by C.R. Jane
Cover design by Mayhara Ferraz
Editing by Stephanie H./Hannotek, Ink

ISBN: 979-8-3470-0769-1

Published in 2025 by Podium Publishing
www.podiumentertainment.com

Podium

ALSO BY C.R. JANE

Merry Me

For my ho, ho, ho's.
You know who you are.

Dear Reader,

This is a story about love found, love lost, and love that refuses to stay buried under fear or time. At its core, this is a sweet romantic comedy with a guaranteed happily ever after—complete with festive chaos, grand gestures, sharp banter, and one very feral fictional man. But while the laughs and swoons are abundant, this book also brushes up against deeper emotional threads. Because sometimes the holidays come wrapped in more than just ribbon . . . they carry heartache, too.

If you prefer to know what you're stepping into, here are a few possible emotional triggers to be aware of:

- Parental abandonment
- Estranged parent-child relationships
- Mentions of emotional neglect and childhood trauma
- Sexual content (consensual, emotionally charged, and explicit)
- Brief mention of a loved one with cancer

If any of these themes are sensitive for you, please take care of yourself and skip as needed. Above all, I hope this book makes you laugh when you need it, cry when you least expect it, and believe—just a little—in the magic of second chances.

With love,

CR
Jane

Merry Me

PROLOGUE

Natalie

You never think you're going to lose the love of your life because of a Walmart run. But here we were.

"Are you seriously breaking up with me?"

Easton stood in front of me, his six-foot-something frame silhouetted by the warm orange glow of the streetlamp. He looked every bit the heartthrob the modeling scout had promised he'd become that day in the store—the sharp angles of his jaw, the dark tumble of his hair, those piercing green eyes that had once been solely mine. And now they stared at me, wide and confused and *devastated*, like he couldn't process the words I'd just said.

"Nat." His voice cracked slightly at the end.

I folded my arms tightly across my chest, digging my nails into my elbows to keep my voice steady. "Yes, Easton. I'm breaking up with you."

"Why?" He took a step closer, his hands gesturing helplessly. "We've been together for four years, Nat. You're my *everything*. Why now?"

Because you're leaving, I thought. *Because you're destined for bigger, shinier things, and I still have senior year to finish. Because I refuse to be the girl left waiting by the phone while you conquer the world. Because it hurts too much to imagine you forgetting about me while everyone else falls in love with you. Because I saw what waiting did to my mom—and I swore I'd never let myself become her. I already know what it feels like to be left behind by a man who said he loved us.*

But I didn't say any of that.

Instead, I threw up a shield of sarcasm, my oldest defense mechanism. "Because dating someone famous sounds exhausting. I'm not cut out for red carpets and groupies, Easton." I gave a shrug that I hoped looked breezy instead of brittle. "Besides, we both have things we want . . . dreams, college, careers. I don't want to be the reason you stay, and I definitely don't want someone holding me back, either."

His brows furrowed. "That's not—" He cut himself off and shook his head. "You're not even giving me a chance to prove to you that nothing's going to change. That *I'm* not going to change."

There was a flash of hurt in his eyes, and it dug deep inside me. I hated the way my chest twisted at the sound of his voice . . . that he was looking at me like *I* was the one leaving him.

"You think I don't know what's coming?" I said a little too sharp, a little too scared. "You'll go to LA, or wherever they decide to turn you into the next big thing. And I'll be stuck at school, trying not to check your Instagram at two a.m."

"Natalie—"

"No. Look, this"—I gestured between us—"was magic. High school magic. But we both know it doesn't survive out there."

He stepped forward, closing the space between us, close enough that I could feel the warmth radiating off him, close enough that I wanted to bury my face in his chest and take it all back.

But I didn't. I wouldn't.

"You'd think I'd give this all up just to play pretend?" he asked, quieter now, but still not backing down. "That it would be possible to just walk away and forget you?"

I opened my mouth, but the truth was sitting like a stone in my throat.

His voice softened, and his hands lifted like he wanted to touch me but he wasn't sure if he was allowed to anymore. "Natalie, I *love* you. You're my girl. My soulmate. People say you can't meet your forever person when you're young, but we know that's not true. You're my *everything*. I don't care about any of that Hollywood crap. I care about *you*."

The cicadas hummed a discordant melody, their persistent song mingling with the low rumble of a passing truck. The air was thick with the scent of freshly cut grass and the faint, sugary sweetness of melted snow cones from the carnival down the road. A classic small-town summer night. The kind of night that used to feel like ours.

A lump formed in my throat, but I swallowed it down. "You think you care about me now," I finally said, my voice wobbling despite my best efforts. "But give it a year, Easton. Maybe less. You'll realize you don't need me. You'll have everything you ever wanted, and I'll just . . ."

"Just what?" His eyes were pleading now, bright and desperate. "You'll just what, Nat?"

"I'll just be the girl who held you back."

He blinked, stunned, and I took the momentary silence to slide past him, turning toward my car. I felt his hand wrap around my wrist, gentle but firm.

"Don't do this," he said, his voice a low rasp that almost broke me. "Please, Nat. Don't walk away from us. I won't go if that's what it takes. I'm not going to lose you."

I pulled my arm free and kept walking, every step heavier than the last. When I reached my car door, I turned back, one hand gripping the frame like it might hold me upright.

"You're wrong, Easton. No one finds their soulmate in middle school. We're done." The words tasted like poison on my tongue. "I hope LA knows how lucky it is."

I turned before he could see the tears prickling at the corners of my eyes.

And then I got in the car, closed the door, and drove away. Pretending that I didn't hear him yelling *This isn't over, we'll never be over* as he ran after the car.

It was over.

Even if it felt like I was dying as I drove away.

Even if I cried the entire drive home and then for days and weeks after.

He went west the next day—to bright lights and red carpets and dreams so big they barely fit inside movie screens. And I stayed. Quietly. Hollowed out. Pretending I hadn't just let go of the only real thing I'd ever felt.

People said I'd move on. That I was young, that I'd fall in love again.

But I knew better.

What we had . . . that kind of love didn't come around twice.

And I was the one who'd let it go.

I told myself it was for the best. That I needed space to grow, to find myself, to become someone on my own. But watching him become famous, watching the world fall for him while I stayed behind—still aching, still hollow—that was a kind of punishment I hadn't prepared for.

Because the truth was simple and cruel:

I didn't think I'd ever find anything like that again.

CHAPTER 1

Natalie

ONE YEAR AND ELEVEN MONTHS LATER

t wasn't just loud . . . it was apocalyptic. The kind of roar that made your ribs buzz and your brain short-circuit. A sea of orange and white screamed from the stands, like they'd all decided to collectively lose their minds in unison. Tennessee's colors bled into everything: the field, the stands, the shirts, the painted faces, and apparently the bra the girl a few seats down was wearing like she thought ESPN might zoom in for a half-time segment titled "Spirit Gone Wild."

"Get it together, Davis! My grandma could make that throw, and she's blind in one eye!" My voice cut through the noise like a rogue trumpet blast, drawing a few laughs and more than a few glares from the die-hard superfans around me, decked out in full body paint and beads like this was Mardi Gras in Knoxville.

But I had no regrets.

Parker Davis, golden boy of the college football world and my best friend Casey's personal Ken doll, was currently playing like he'd forgotten what team he was on . . . and *somebody* had to hold him accountable.

If these people were really die-hard fans, they would be yelling, too.

Maybe a little heckling would light a fire under their asses.

Jace, Tennessee's star wide receiver and Parker's best friend, somehow heard me out on the field. He turned his head, giving me a salute and a smirk so obnoxious it should be illegal.

Casey nudged me with her shoulder, her cheeks pink from the cold—or maybe secondhand embarrassment from how bad her fiancé was playing. "Is your grandma really blind?"

"No," I said, straightening up and crossing my arms. "But they need me out there, so I'm trying things out."

"They definitely need you," she muttered, and I side-eyed her.

"Are you being sarcastic? Because I'm a critical component of Tennessee's game-day strategy, I'll have you know."

"Of course," she said with a grin. "You're their secret weapon."

"Exactly. You may be Tennessee's lucky charm on account that Parker Davis can't breathe unless you are in the stands," I continued, gesturing vaguely toward the field. "But everyone knows that I'm like the unofficial mascot. If they lose this game, it's because I didn't yell enough."

"Or because you insulted every offensive starter," Riley, Jace's fiancée, chimed in, appearing next to us with a hot chocolate that looked like it had more whipped cream than liquid.

"Constructive criticism builds character," I said solemnly.

"You sound like the coach I had for my one and only year of swimming," Casey said, sipping from her water bottle. "She once told me to channel my inner dolphin and then screamed when I didn't shave a second off my time."

"Dolphins are overrated," I said. "Do dolphins have SEC rings? No, they do not."

Casey just shook her head, her smile soft. She had that look she always got when Parker was on the field, all gooey and dreamy, like she wasn't freezing her ass off right now with the smell of hot dogs wafting around us.

I was also freezing my ass off, I hated hot dogs, and I did not, in fact, have a hottie out there on the field waiting for me.

But I had been raised a Tennessee fan from birth, and these kinds of games were the ones we lived for.

"You haven't told me yet what you're doing for the holidays," Casey said suddenly, her tone a little too casual, like she was trying to sneak it in past my defenses.

"Oh wow, is that Ophelia over there warming up for halftime?" I asked in a bold attempt to deflect, pointing at a completely random person who looked nothing like our friend—and was also very clearly holding a nacho tray.

Casey raised an eyebrow. "We both know that's not her. And now I feel like you're avoiding my question on purpose."

My happy mood immediately dropped ten degrees. All the good juju I'd felt after that five-yard gain abruptly disappeared. "Oh, you know," I said vaguely, doing a little jazz hand like that would cover my tracks. "This and that."

"'This and that'?" Riley asked, raising an eyebrow. "What does that even mean?"

"Exactly what it sounds like," I said with a grin. "This. That. The other thing. Possibly a covert mission to the North Pole. The usual."

Casey didn't look convinced. In fact, she started to look suspicious, like she was two seconds away from dragging the truth out of me with an interrogation lamp and a clipboard. "Nat . . ."

"I'm staying on campus, okay?" I said, cutting her off before she could suggest something sweet, like inviting me to spend Christmas with her, Parker, and his ridiculously hot brothers. "I've got projects. Plus, I hate Christmas anyway."

I added that last part really fast as I popped some red-and-green Nerds Gummies in my mouth, hoping the sugar could neutralize the emotional vulnerability I'd just spewed. Before Casey could say anything, I reached over and popped some in her mouth, too, just so I could delay whatever she was about to say.

Casey choked and sputtered for a second before she remembered she knew how to chew, and we watched as Tennessee finally got a first down.

The crowd surged, and I nearly forgave Parker for being tragically mediocre this quarter.

"You hate Christmas?" Casey finally said, sounding genuinely horrified, like I'd just confessed to hating puppies or stealing from the Girl Scouts.

"Hold that thought for one second, Case," I said before cupping my hands around my mouth so my voice could be louder. "Hey, Thatcher, did you forget how to catch, or are you just morally opposed to touchdowns?"

"That was a hard catch. He had two defenders on him!" Riley said indignantly.

"No excuses. Play like a champion," I muttered.

"Did you get that from *Wedding Crashers*?" Riley drawled.

"They got it from me," I mumbled around another handful of gummies.

"So," Casey said, turning back to me as Tennessee lined up again, because evidently my angel baby of a best friend could not take a hint. "Are you going to explain the Christmas hatred? I feel like that's a betrayal of everything I know about you. You wear sparkly boots. You own an Advent calendar with perfume samples. You basically *are* Christmas in human form."

"Because I'm blonde, enjoy Starbucks every day, and shop at Target like it's a full-time job? That's so judgmental, Case. I happen to be *very* against the glitter of commercialism, actually."

She snorted. "You literally *love* commercialism."

"It's still profiling," I muttered back.

Her expression softened, and I could see the gears gently turning in her head, already planning how to fix me with some kind of cinnamon-scented-candle holiday intervention.

I had to redirect. Fast. Casey was a fixer, a nurturer, the kind of person who probably couldn't hear someone say they hated Christmas without deciding it was her personal mission to make them love it.

"So," I said loudly, pointing at the field. "Think Parker's gonna pull off this Hail Mary, or are we all gonna die cold and disappointed?"

She blinked, startled out of her planning of Operation Holiday Healing, and turned back to the game.

"He's got this," she said firmly, her voice full of that unshakable faith she had in him.

I leaned back in my seat, watching her watch him. For all her blushing and shyness, Casey had a steel core when it came to Parker. It was nice seeing her like this. Happy. Very different from the quiet, sad girl who I'd roomed with for part of freshman year.

But me? I was going to spend Christmas exactly how I wanted: alone, on campus, with no mistletoe, no eggnog, and no made-for-TV miracles involving hot cocoa and emotional breakthroughs. No pretending the holidays were merry and bright when, for me, they never really had been.

Because Christmastime was when my biological father had left. Second grade. A tree still standing in the living room, lights blinking like they hadn't gotten the memo. He walked out of the house, and he never came back.

I stopped believing in Santa and fathers on the same day.

So if anyone needed a Hail Mary, it was me. But it wasn't coming from a quarterback.

I'd ruined my chance at that kind of happiness a long time ago.

CHAPTER 2

Natalie

The phone buzzed in my hand, vibrating and scaring the living shit out of me since I'd obviously been in a half-asleep, half-scrolling daze because it was eight-fucking-o-clock in the morning.

My sister was calling—a rare thing as of late—which meant that whatever she had to say was going to be important or something I wasn't ready to hear.

"Hey, Paige. What's up?" I asked, doing my best to sound like I'd been awake for hours because my sister was one of those people who woke up at the crack of dawn to work out . . . like a psychopath.

"Nat!" she screeched, and I winced. "I have the best news!"

"You won the lottery?"

She paused. "No."

"You got someone to pay for that boob job you've been wanting?"

"Also no," she said, beginning to sound annoyed.

"Well, then I can't think of anything you would have to tell me that would be exciting."

"I'm getting married!" Her shrieking was so loud that it took me a second to comprehend what she was saying.

Then it clicked.

"What do you mean you're getting married?" I asked, faintly aware of the fact that my voice was coming out equally screechy.

But in my defense, I hadn't even known that my sister was dating anyone seriously, so forgive me if my voice had lost its usual, very pleasant tenor.

"Levi asked me to marry him, and I said yes!" she squealed.

"Well, yes. That's generally how these things work," I said, still sound-ing frantic. "But who the fuck is Levi?"

"You know who Levi is . . . He's Levi."

I blinked at the phone, trying to recall who Levi could possibly be.

Until it hit me.

Levi Martin.

My high school boyfriend's best friend.

My insides clenched like I'd just swallowed an entire lemon.

"You're marrying *Levi*?" I blurted, a little too loud and a little too horrified-sounding.

"Yes!" Her voice sparkled through the phone like she was announcing she'd just won a cruise. "Isn't that crazy?"

"*Crazy* is one word," I said, clutching my phone like it might stabilize my nervous system. "We're talking about Levi 'lit a microwave on fire try-ing to make a grilled cheese' Martin, right?"

She giggled like I was exaggerating. I wasn't.

"That was forever ago. He's matured. He does CrossFit now."

"Oh well. Obviously that's the same as therapy," I deadpanned. "Tell me you didn't say yes to a man who once thought wearing a backwards snapback made him deep."

"He's not like that anymore! He's thoughtful and focused now."

"Thoughtful? Paige, he once ate seventeen mozzarella sticks at our house and then threw up in our dryer."

"That was also forever ago," she said, unfazed. "People grow up. You of all people should know that."

I paused, trying to reconcile the image of Levi Martin doing deadlifts and saying things like, *emotional accountability*.

I went on Facebook and started frantically scrolling through Levi's pictures, past the few of him and my sister, desperately searching to see whether he had any recent pictures with *him*. My heart was thumping like I'd just been caught cheating on a pop quiz by a nun with a ruler.

"So, when's the big day?" I asked belatedly, feeling marginally better after I'd scrolled back at least a year and found zero evidence of Easton and Levi still being in each other's lives. No recent selfies. No bro-hugs. No golf outings or barbecue reunions. Easton was firmly ensconced in Hollywood and, more importantly, firmly away from me.

Ensconced. That was a big word. I gave myself a mental high five. It was good to reward yourself for literacy.

"Christmas Eve!"

"Christmas Eve?" My voice jumped an octave. "As in *this* Christmas Eve? Paige, that's two fucking weeks away!"

"I know; isn't it romantic? Snow, Christmas lights, everyone together for the holidays . . ."

Her words blurred into a festive, tinsel-covered buzz saw as my brain conjured the nightmare that awaited me.

"You mean everyone *forced* together for the holidays," I grumbled.

I could already picture it: an entire weekend filled with Christmas activities, endless happy couples, and the looming possibility of running into *him*.

Easton's face popped into my head uninvited—his dark hair, those piercing green eyes, the lopsided grin that used to make me feel like the center of the universe. My stomach twisted again.

From the pictures of him I'd seen online . . . he'd only gotten hotter. Leaner. Sharper. Like someone had taken the gorgeous boy I'd fallen in love with and added about seven layers of smolder.

"Natalie?" Paige's voice yanked me out of my spiral. "You still there?"

"Yeah, sorry." I scrambled for an excuse. "Look, I'm really happy for you, sis, but it's so last minute. Finals, work, you know how it is—"

"You're coming," she interrupted firmly. Her voice was tinged with amusement, like she'd been waiting for me to try that exact excuse.

"Paige, really, I—"

"I know what this is about," she said pointedly.

"It's not about anything—"

"We don't even know if he's coming."

"Who's *he*?" I asked, wincing because that weird squeak was back.

There was silence on the other end of the line. A weighted one. Like Paige was holding back an eye roll.

"Natalie," Paige said softly, "it's hilarious that you would even pretend you're not coming. You know you're my maid of honor."

I got all weepy at that, which was rude of her. I didn't ask to have emotions.

"I am?" I asked, suddenly sounding like a soft marshmallow of a human.

"Nat," she groaned, exasperated. "Like you didn't know that."

I exhaled sharply, trying to get myself under control.

"Of course I knew that," I finally said, sounding much more like my usual, fabulous self. "Who else in your life could compare? But if you make me wear one of those hideous Christmas sweaters at any point during the wedding festivities, I'll never forgive you."

"Throw away the llama sweater I'm holding. Got it." She snorted.

A guy's voice called her name. *Levi*, I assumed. "'Kay, sis. I've got to go! Love you. See you soon."

"Let me know if—" Paige hung up before I could finish my sentence. Also rude.

I flopped back onto my bed, staring at the ceiling like it held answers. I started mentally calculating the odds of Easton being there. He'd been Levi's closest friend in high school . . . but that had been a long time ago. Things change. People grow apart. Especially when one of those people becomes a literal movie star and the other—Levi, obviously—still lives in a town where the biggest news last week was the church potluck catching fire.

But what if he *was* there?

That question dug into me like a splinter.

Who gives a fuck, though? I told myself with a little more venom than necessary. I was the one who had ended things. I'm sure he had long forgotten about me. He'd probably see me and shake my hand like we were old business associates. Maybe even thank me for not dragging it out.

Cool. Great. Fabulous.

For the rest of the day, I pretended to care about finals, pretended to pay attention to my group project meeting, pretended I wasn't internally screaming.

But all I could think was:

What if he's there?

CHAPTER 3

Easton

The bright lights were harsh against my face, and the sticky layer of makeup didn't help. I was supposed to be gazing into my costar's eyes like she was the love of my life, but my jaw was clenched so tight I could feel a headache forming.

"Take twenty-eight, people. And action," Paul, our director, called out.

Take twenty-eight. That meant we'd done this exact same scene twenty-seven other times. Twenty-seven other lip-locks. Twenty-seven other failed attempts to capture something that wasn't there and never would be.

I leaned forward, brushing a hand against her cheek like I'd practiced in the mirror a hundred times, and our lips met.

Don't flinch, I coached myself as her overeager mouth moved against mine like she was trying to devour me in front of the whole movie set. Her lip gloss tasted like synthetic cherries, and the whole thing felt about as romantic as kissing a corpse.

Not that I knew firsthand what that felt like.

But this had to be close. Somewhere between embalmed and disinterested.

I forced myself to hold the moment, camera-ready and stone-faced, but all I could think about was the last time a kiss had meant something.

Really meant something.

Natalie.

Her name slammed into me like a sucker punch.

She'd tasted like mint and mischief, like strawberry lip balm and too many memories. Kissing her had never been rehearsed. It had never needed staging. It was messy and real and electric in a way that couldn't be manufactured under studio lights. With her, I never had to fake it. Never had to pretend I was in love.

Because I was.

"Cut!" Paul bellowed, his voice ricocheting across the set. "What the fuck is going on? Easton, you're supposed to look like you *want* to kiss her, not like you're being forced to at gunpoint. What the fuck is going on with your face?"

The crew chuckled, but I didn't crack a smile as I pulled back from Vanessa, who was blinking up at me like she'd actually felt something. Which was awkward. She was a rising star whose name was plastered all over the tabloids . . . and she happened to be annoying as fuck.

"I'm acting," I said dryly.

"Well, stop," Paul snapped. "Try pretending you like her, not that she's your dental hygienist. Reset for take twenty-nine."

I stepped back, swallowing down a sigh as the makeup artist swarmed me again with powder and blotting papers, dabbing the sweat from my temples like it was a crime scene.

This was the part that I hated most about this job—and what I was the worst at.

Paul rubbed his temples. "We need this scene done today, Easton. It's one little scene. And then you're done. And we're all off for Christmas. Please, get your fucking head in the game."

I was pretty sure that *please* came out more like a threat, thank you very little . . . but I couldn't really blame him. This had to be torturous to watch.

"You know what, let's take a break for fucking lunch," Paul announced, muttering to himself as he walked away.

Vanessa gave me a sly little smile and leaned in close. "Maybe we could practice," she murmured, low enough that the boom mic wouldn't pick it up, "in my trailer." Her voice was dripping with suggestion as her hand brushed against my chest.

I forced a polite smile, the kind that said *not in a million years.* "No thanks," I said quickly as I stepped out of her reach.

Fuck, that came out aggressive. That was going to make the rest of the day a real treat.

Her face froze in a mixture of irritation and disbelief. I imagined she wasn't rejected very often, but there had to be a first time for everything, right? Judging by the way she was suddenly snarling and baring her teeth like a rabid wolf—she didn't agree with that assessment.

"I've gotta make a few calls," I said soothingly, trying to sound charming since I did have to get through at least the rest of the day with her.

"Sure," she snipped, spinning on her heels and walking off set to her trailer, her hair whipping behind her like she was auditioning for a shampoo commercial directed by Satan.

I rubbed a hand down my face and let out a slow exhale . . . before immediately realizing I now had a sticky layer of makeup smeared on my palm. *Great. Now I look like a sweaty raccoon. Could this film be over already?*

Reaching my trailer, I shut the door behind me and flopped back onto the small couch.

Kissing scenes. Sex scenes. Anything romantic was the bane of my existence. The only way I'd managed to get through any of them was by thinking about *her.*

Which was the exact opposite of what I wanted to be doing.

Natalie.

Natalie Fucking Bennett. The girl who'd been living rent-free in my head since the moment I'd seen her face in middle school.

Her honey-blonde hair. The soft way her lips used to part against mine. The little gasp she made when I tucked a hand under her chin and kissed her like the world had gone quiet around us.

Her laugh that had always felt like summer.

What the fuck did that even mean? Was I writing poetry now?

I groaned and leaned back, letting my head thump against the wall. Almost two fucking years without a word, and she was still the first thing I thought of when someone said *love scene* or *love,* or anything remotely resembling soulmates and the person you were obsessed with.

Fortunately, that silence—our exile—felt like it was finally coming to an end. The distance. The wondering. The ache of not knowing if she ever thought of me, too. I was finally going to have the chance to look her in the eye and say all the things I hadn't been allowed to say.

Maybe then, I could finally get my sanity back.

Grabbing my phone off the tiny foldout table, I unlocked it to check for the text I was waiting for. I'd been sneaking glances at my phone all day like a maniac. And there it was.

Holy fuck.

Right at the top. A text from Levi, my best friend from high school, whose wedding I was supposed to be in. The wedding that, if all went to plan, was going to fix my life and change everything.

Levi: She's in.

A slow grin spread across my face, and for the first time in longer than I could remember, it felt real. The first real smile I'd worn since . . . well, since she'd walked away.

She's in.

This day had just turned around.

Because I was going to the wedding.

Because Natalie was going to be there.

Because, for the first time in almost two years, I had a shot at getting back what I'd lost.

This time, I wasn't giving her space to run. I wasn't letting her talk herself out of us, out of what we had.

This time, I was going all in.

I'd already lost her once. I wasn't going to make the same mistake again.

Not when I'd waited this long. Not when every part of me still wanted her.

This time . . . I wasn't going to take no for an answer.

Natalie

The bar was loud, packed, and exactly where I would normally want to be . . . if I wasn't currently spiraling over my sister's wedding and the fact that I had to leave for it tomorrow. The kind of spiraling that made tequila seem like a viable medical solution.

But I could never say no to Casey, Riley, and Ophelia—they were my ladies—so here I was.

"Are you excited for Paige's wedding?" Casey asked, looping her arm through mine as we shoved our way through a wall of people who all smelled like beer, bad decisions, and too much cologne.

The knot in my stomach tightened just thinking about it. The wedding. *Him.*

"At least get me drunk first before you go digging into my deepest, darkest secrets," I drawled.

She snorted. "I'm pretty sure you spilled one of your darkest secrets last month over two margaritas and a plate of cheese fries."

"See, that doesn't count," I said, raising a finger. "That was a very emotionally vulnerable week. Also, the cheese fries were aggressively salty."

"You told me you accidentally sexted your pastor thanks to autocorrect."

"I meant to say *feeling blessed*, not *feeling breast*. It was an honest mistake!"

Casey smirked. "I'm not sure that I expected you to label your sister's wedding as a platform for your dark secrets, but I'm intrigued now."

I scoffed, because evidently the cheese fries hadn't been enough to throw her off the scent.

Before she could dig any deeper into my wretched past, we reached the back of the bar, where our group had staked out a couple booths like pirates laying claim to treasure. Parker, Jace, Riley, Matty, and Ophelia were already there, laughing and shouting over the music like they were hosting a frat party on karaoke night.

"I was about to come find you!" Parker purred, reaching out to take Casey's hand and pulling her into the booth.

"As if you weren't watching me the entire time," Casey said, sounding amused as she slid in beside him.

Parker looked entirely unbothered by the callout, and I didn't doubt the statement at all. Parker Davis was *obsessed* with my bestie. And that wasn't an exaggeration. He'd literally seen her in class last year, and that was it. He was all in.

Every time I was around them, I felt this weird longing in my chest.

Because I wanted that.

I'd had that once.

And then I'd thrown it all away.

"Sit down," Riley urged, and I slid into the booth next to her, accepting the red-colored concoction she immediately pushed into my hand.

"Drink," Riley commanded with a grin. "You look like you need it."

"Bless you, bartender goddess of my heart," I said and downed half the glass in one go.

The burn was instant. But effective. The weight in my chest lightened by just a fraction.

By the time I finished my second drink, I was actually starting to feel better. Or at least drunk enough not to care about my problems and the slow-motion car crash that was my emotional life.

"Okay, I've got one," Jace announced, lifting his beer in the air like he was about to give a toast.

"No," Matty said, shaking his head.

"What do you mean, 'no'?" Jace asked, mimicking Matty's voice with an unholy amount of sass.

"I'm saying we're having a great night, let's not ruin it."

"I actually think Jace's jokes would only improve the night," Riley said, batting her eyelashes at Jace, because like Parker and Casey, she and Jace were madly in love.

Sickeningly, actually.

"You would say that." Matty sighed. "You're blind to actual humor because of Jace's hair."

I snorted at that one. Jace had dramatic, long blonde hair that he refused to cut because he believed he would lose his football superpowers—his words, not mine.

"Actually, I think it's because of my big c—" Parker slapped a hand over Jace's mouth.

"No talking about your cock in front of my lady," he hissed.

Jace grinned beneath Parker's hand. "Well, now *you're* talking about my cock, so technically . . ."

"Don't get him started on the quarter of an inch." Ophelia sighed as she batted her eyelashes at Matty.

Another couple sickeningly in love.

Matty growled at her all cute-like.

"Don't you mean an inch?" Jace said, wagging his eyebrows up and down as Matty groaned loudly.

"Tell your joke," Parker growled, a small smile on his lips because it was impossible not to smile in the midst of Jace's antics.

"Why does Mrs. Claus always pray for a white Christmas?" Jace said smugly, because he obviously thought this one was going to be a good one—even though his jokes rarely were.

"I don't actually want to know the answer to that," Matty drawled, his face looking pained.

"She's married to a guy who only *comes* once a year."

There was an elongated pause, and Jace scoffed. "You know, a *white* Christmas, like the color of cu—" Parker slapped another hand over Jace's mouth, and Jace rolled his eyes. "Is anything not off-limits, Parkie-Poo?" he drawled.

Riley was the first to break, giggling like a madwoman as Jace wrapped an arm around her shoulders and beamed down at her. Matty looked vaguely traumatized, but I at least laughed for a second.

It wasn't his worst joke.

Ugh. There was that pang again. I really needed to find a way to carve a hole in my chest and take out my heart because this amount of feeling was unacceptable.

The fun of the night continued until Casey leaned over and whispered, "Okay, spill. What's up with you lately? And this time I'm requiring you answer the question."

I froze, my glass hovering midair. "What do you mean?"

Casey rolled her eyes. "Oh please. You've been moping for days. Is it the whole holiday thing? Your sister's wedding? Or is it something else . . . perhaps someone else, if we're being technical?"

"It's not . . ." I trailed off, glancing around to make sure the others were still wrapped up in their conversation about why Tennessee was going to win the national championship again this year. "It's just that my sister's fiancé . . . His best man might be someone I know."

Her brows furrowed. "Someone you know?"

I took a long sip before answering. "My ex."

Casey's confusion deepened, and she leaned forward. "Okay. And? You're not the type to spiral over a guy. Did he cheat on you or something?"

"No." I laughed bitterly. "He never would have. At least not back then . . ."

She blinked at me, her beautiful brain obviously still confused. "Okay?"

I threw back a peppermint schnapps–flavored shot that was basically Christmas in a cup. This was the part of Christmas I liked.

"Because my ex is Easton Maddox," I blurted out once I'd gotten a little more of that liquid courage.

Casey blinked. Tilted her head.

"Wait . . . like . . . the barista from that coffee shop on Fifth?" she asked, brows furrowed in concentration.

I stared at her. "No. I'm pretty sure that guy's name is just Maddox. And also, he spells *latte* with a *y*, so I'm insulted you think I would date him."

Then her eyes went wide. *Too* wide.

"Okay, wait. No. There's no way. But I'm just going to ask just in case . . . Do you mean *movie star* Easton Maddox?"

There it was. Her jaw dropped like someone had unhinged it. She looked like a cartoon character mid-fall. I cocked my head, vaguely impressed that eyes could even get that big.

She pointed at me with her drink, already sloshing. "Easton Maddox? As in *Easton Maddox*, the hottest young star in Hollywood right now? *That* Easton?"

I rolled my eyes. "No, Casey. I meant the Easton Maddox who sells Bibles out of the back of a van in Missouri."

She ignored me completely, spiraling into open-mouthed disbelief.

I sank lower in my seat, miserable. "Yes, that Easton."

Casey let out a screech that turned a few heads. "Natalie! What the hell? You dated *Easton Maddox* and never told me? Are you kidding me right now?"

"Would you keep your voice down?" I hissed, glaring at her.

Parker was watching us like a hawk now, looking unamused that another man's name had come out of her mouth.

"Go back to your conversation, QB," I growled.

He smirked and kissed Casey's shoulder possessively, as if to remind everyone in the bar that she was taken and he was still the hottest guy here.

Second-hottest if Easton had been here, obviously.

Ugh.

Casey leaned back in, still buzzing with shock and whisper-shouting, "How is that even possible? You dated Easton Maddox, and you're just, what? Casually not talking about it? Is he the reason you don't want to go home?"

"Obviously," I said miserably. "What am I supposed to do if he's there? Pretend everything's fine? Pretend I didn't break up with him and ruin everything?"

Casey tilted her head, considering me like I was some kind of puzzle. "Okay, first of all, you didn't ruin anything. Second, you're going to woman up, Natalie Skye Bennett. You're going to go to that wedding, looking like the hottie you are, and enjoy your sister's day. If Easton Maddox is there? Good. Let him see what he's missing. Make him feel all that hot movie-star regret. Let him eat his heart out."

Parker coughed, his eyes now resembling a cartoon character as well. I was pretty sure Casey was about to get dragged away and taken on the nearest flat surface so that he could remind her of who she was with.

You're welcome, Case.

I sighed. "He won't regret it," I muttered. "I broke it off. I thought I was doing the right thing. I *did* do the right thing."

Casey's expression softened. "Then maybe it's time to find out if it's *still* the right thing . . ."

I sighed. "Fine. I'll go. But if I embarrass myself, I'm blaming you."

"Deal," she said, grinning like the meddling best friend she absolutely was.

As the group around us laughed and toasted, I made a silent vow to myself. No matter what happened, I'd get through this wedding. Even if it meant facing the boy I'd once loved—and the man he'd become.

CHAPTER 4

Natalie

The drive to my childhood home was as familiar as the back of my hand. The roads wound through sleepy neighborhoods and past landmarks that hadn't changed in decades—Mr. Hampton's bait shop, Ms. Alexandra's dance studio, the rusty water tower that boasted a faded painting of the high school mascot. Each curve in the road brought with it a million memories, like ghosts trailing the car, whispering reminders of who I used to be.

I loved my family. Besides the whole being deserted by my biological father thing . . . I'd had a great childhood. Backyard birthday parties, summer nights catching fireflies, snow days with cocoa so sweet it made your teeth hurt. But coming back here since that last night with Easton always felt like digging up something buried. Something better left undisturbed.

Because everything here . . . every cracked sidewalk, every blinking streetlamp . . . It still echoed with him. With us.

I turned onto my parents' street, the old oak trees arching overhead like a tunnel, branches heavy with December frost. And there it was. The white house with blue shutters. My stepdad Steve's old Chevy parked in the driveway. The flower beds, even in winter, were weed-free and neatly mulched, my mom refusing to let them go dormant like the rest of the world. The porch swing creaked in the breeze. It was the picture of home.

And yet, every corner of this place reminded me of *him*.

Pulling into the driveway, I sat there for a moment, gripping the steering wheel like it could anchor me. Like if I held on tightly enough, I could keep the past from crashing into the present.

But it always did.

My mind always drifted, always went back . . . to the first time I'd seen Easton Maddox.

Mrs. Green's homeroom buzzed with the low hum of pre-class chatter as I sat at my desk, doodling swirls and stars on the cover of my notebook. Betsy Meyers, seated beside me, droned on about her older brother's latest reason for being grounded, but I wasn't really listening. The faint smell of pencil shavings and tater tots lingered in the air, even though lunch was hours away.

The door creaked open, and Betsy stopped mid-sentence. A hush fell over the room as everyone turned toward the doorway.

I finally glanced up to see why everyone had gotten so quiet.

And there he was.

Wow.

The new boy walked in like he owned the place.

Tall for a seventh grader, with dark hair that fell in that perfect, just-rolled-out-of-bed way, and eyes so green they seemed to cut through the harsh glare of the fluorescent lights. He wasn't just confident; he was magnetic, like some invisible force pulled everyone's attention toward him.

He glanced around the room, his gaze sweeping over everyone like he was deciding where he belonged. When his eyes landed on me, he smiled. Not just any smile—that smile. It stretched slow and easy across his face, disarming and infuriating all at once. My stomach flipped so hard it was a miracle I didn't fall out of my chair.

I couldn't look away even though I wanted to. My fingers froze on my notebook, the pen hovering mid-scribble.

He walked toward me, his steps purposeful and sure, like he'd already decided exactly where he was going to sit.

Stopping at the desk next to mine, he turned to Charlie Cordweiler, the kid occupying the chair. "Move," he said, his tone more matter-of-fact than rude.

Charlie blinked up at him, obviously confused. "Uh, why?"

"Because I'm sitting there," the new boy replied, flashing that cocky grin again, like he was already king of the school.

To my absolute horror, Charlie shrugged, grabbed his stuff, and moved to another desk. The kid plopped into the now-vacant chair without a second thought, immediately turning to me.

"Hi," he said, extending a hand like we were grown-ups meeting for a business deal. "My name's Easton Maddox, and I'm going to marry you someday."

Laughter erupted around the room, and my face ignited. Heat rushed to

my cheeks, and I stared at him, mortified, like he'd just announced he was an
alien from another planet.

"You're insane," I blurted, willing the floor to swallow me whole.

He didn't flinch, didn't even blink. "Probably," he said with an easy shrug.
"But that's okay." He leaned back in his chair, his grin as self-assured as ever.
"Are you going to tell me your name?"

"I don't provide that information to clear psychopaths," I said primly,
beginning to organize my pencils on my desk like it was of utmost importance
that they be in a straight line.

I didn't know it was possible, but I could feel his smirk burning into the
side of my face. "That's fine," he said, and I finally sneaked a glance at him to
see what he was doing.

He was indeed smirking, and he was still leaning back in his chair like he
was some kind of king instead of a seventh-grade boy. "We've got the rest of our
lives for me to get you to trust me."

I was torn between running out of the room and smacking him upside the
head, but instead I stayed frozen in my chair, watching him like he was some
kind of exotic animal that had wandered into the classroom.

Easton Maddox. The name stuck in my head like a song I couldn't shake.
And from that moment on, he was impossible to ignore.

I shook off the memory, blinking back to the present.

The rest of our lives. Funny how that had turned out.

With a deep breath, I got out of the car and grabbed my bag from the
back seat. The cold air stung my cheeks, the kind of chill that cut right
through nostalgia and straight to the bone.

My mom's voice rang out from the front porch as I walked up, warm
and welcoming.

"Nat-bug, you're home!"

I forced a smile and headed right into her arms, trying to get comfort
from her hug like I used to. She still smelled like vanilla and dryer sheets,
her arms strong, her embrace solid.

But as I sank into her warmth, I couldn't shake the weight of the memories that seemed to cling to my skin.

And the fact that all of them led back to him.

The pizza was greasy and delicious—the kind that left a sheen of oil on
your fingers and a warm, happy glow in your belly.

And possibly indigestion.

It was the kind of dinner that I preferred over anything else I could have been eating, including whatever gourmet nonsense my more put-together friends swore by. Some moms were really good at cooking homemade meals, others were good at ordering food. My mom had always been the latter, and I loved her for it. She never once pretended to be something she wasn't unless she was playing Bunco with the neighborhood moms and trying to win them over with store-bought potato salad she "doctored up."

My parents, Aunt Kathy, and I were gathered around the kitchen island, holding greasy paper plates and swapping stories while trying to out-yell one another over the Christmas music playing from my dad's Bluetooth speaker. It was chaotic and weirdly cozy and almost enough to forget why I'd been dreading this trip home.

Almost.

The screen door slammed against the frame, rattling like it was holding on for dear life.

"Look what the wind blew in. The party has arrived!" a voice crowed, and I didn't even need to look. A smile was already on my lips as I glanced toward the entry and saw MeMaw walking in.

Wow.

I bit back a laugh as I took her in.

There she stood in all her yuletide glory.

MeMaw was decked out in a bright green sweater featuring the Grinch tangled in Christmas lights that lit up every time she moved. She'd paired it with neon green leggings covered in what I could only describe as dancing candy canes—candy canes that were, judging by their poses, *definitely* meant to be sexy.

Her earrings were two oversized Christmas bulbs, dangling precariously from her ears, and her glasses—Lord help us—were red and bedazzled with tiny rhinestones shaped into snowflakes.

She looked like Mrs. Claus's chaotic cousin who drank spiked eggnog year-round and judged everyone for not embracing Christmas hard enough.

She looked like home.

"Well, don't all jump at once." MeMaw sniffed, eyeing everyone like we were a disappointment because we hadn't broken out in applause at her appearance. She set a leopard print purse shaped like a Christmas tree on the counter. "Honestly, the silence in here is downright rude. I should've gotten a standing ovation or at least a slow clap."

"We were blinded by that sweater," my dad muttered under his breath.

"And don't even pretend you weren't all just sitting around, waiting for me to show up and liven this place up."

MeMaw's lipstick was a bright red that bled just outside the edges of her lips. She did that on purpose she'd told me once because it made her lips look "more fuckable."

Yes, I had thrown up a little at that one.

MeMaw pulled the sprig of holly from her cloud of teased silver curls and flung it at my mom. "Where's your holiday spirit, young lady? I taught you better than that."

My mom rolled her eyes so hard I thought they might get stuck. "You also taught me how to get into bars with a fake ID. So thanks for that."

"And did it serve you well?" MeMaw asked sweetly.

"I'm not answering that in front of my daughter."

I enjoyed the fact that my mom had someone to keep her in line. All I had to do was tell her she was acting like her mother, and she shaped right up.

It was a blessing in my life.

"Come here, my girl," MeMaw said as she caned her way over to me. She reached for me with her bedazzled talon-like nails, and I threw my arms around her, breathing in that unmistakable mix of floral perfume and powder—her signature scent since the dawn of time. A scent she said that had always brought lovers to her in droves.

Something I preferred not to think about.

"You've been gone for far too long, baby girl," she murmured, squeezing me with surprising strength. "Still gorgeous, though. Your mother can thank me for those genes."

"I heard that, Mom." My mother sighed.

MeMaw sniffed. "You were supposed to."

She kept one arm wrapped around my waist as her sharp blue eyes surveyed the kitchen like a general preparing for battle. "There'd better still be pizza left. I didn't come all this way to starve. And by the way, that driveway of yours is a death trap. Nearly broke my hip getting out of the car."

My mom shot my dad a look. "Did you actually make it into the driveway, Mom?" she asked. "Or did you use the lawn again?"

"Well, where else was I supposed to park? The neighbor's kitchen? Heavens, Emily, use your head."

Mom snorted and pinched the bridge of her nose, but out of the corner of my eye I saw Dad grab MeMaw's keys from her purse and head out to move her car.

MeMaw's gaze landed on the Christmas tree in the living room next, and her eyebrows shot up so high they nearly hit her hairline. "Is *that* what y'all are calling a tree? Looks like a squirrel dragged in a branch and gave up halfway through decorating."

If it wasn't obvious, MeMaw was a big fan of Christmas. She considered it her Valentine's Day and said that the men in her fifty-five and up community were extra *in the spirit* this time of year.

I wasn't sure what that meant, and I was also sure I didn't want to know.

"She's going for minimalist," I whispered.

"She's going for tragic," MeMaw whispered back.

"We're keeping things simple this year because of Paige's wedding," Mom said, setting a tray of cookies that she'd just pulled out of the oven down on the counter.

The scent of them instantly filled the kitchen—store-bought cookie dough baked to perfection. If there was an Olympic category for baking preportioned dough, my mom would medal every time.

"Simple is for funerals, Emily, not Christmas," MeMaw declared, plucking a cookie right off the tray and biting into it like it wasn't burning hot. "And these better not be any of that gluten-free bullshit, or I'm walking right back out that door."

Aunt Kathy was gluten-free, and MeMaw had happened to come over for a meal my mom had attempted to cook for my aunt. MeMaw had taken one bite of the brown rice pasta and actually spit it back onto her plate, coughing like she was dying.

Good times.

"They're not, Dorothy," my dad said as he came back in with MeMaw's keys. He leaned in close as he passed by. "She'd made it all the way into the bushes this time," he whispered in my ear.

"Good. I don't trust anyone who doesn't eat real cookies," MeMaw announced, chewing loudly as her ornaments swung wildly under her ears like wrecking balls. "Back in my day, we didn't waste time with all this organic nonsense. We ate what we wanted and then handled the consequences like adults—with a shot of whiskey and a good lie."

"Wise words, Mom," my mother drawled.

MeMaw ignored her completely.

"And speaking of men," MeMaw said suddenly.

"She wasn't," I cut in, but it was too late.

"It's my understanding you're still single."

I grimaced. "MeMaw . . ."

"What?" she asked, blinking innocently. "I'm just saying. A girl as pretty as you ought to be snatched up by now. The men should be tripping all over themselves. I blame these boys today. No grit. No guts. Not like your Papaw. Or Ronald from next door. They knew their way around a woman's hoo-ha, that's for sure."

My dad made a choking sound.

"Don't act like you weren't impressed by his Corvette and those calves. That man knew how to use a resistance band."

He started choking again and wandered off to refill his drink.

"I think I'm good on the dating advice," I said quickly, grabbing a cookie to stuff in my mouth before she could push further.

"Well, fine," she said with a sniff. "But don't come crying to me when you end up alone with twenty cats."

"Maybe I like cats," I muttered.

"You don't," she shot back without missing a beat. "Now, someone pour me a drink before I say something rude."

"You just said something rude," Aunt Kathy pointed out.

"I meant ruder," MeMaw replied sweetly as she glided . . . okay, clomped . . . toward the living room, muttering about the tree and "these bland cookies."

I was grinning as I watched her go.

That was tame for her.

At least she hadn't brought up Easton.

Yet.

With my luck . . . it was only a matter of time.

All was going shockingly well until I heard the front door creak open, followed by the familiar *thunk-thunk* of boots on tile and the soft murmur of voices. A few seconds later, Paige swept into the kitchen with . . . Levi.

I had to swallow down the weird twist in my stomach when I saw him. Good to see time had been kind to him. His floppy brown hair was still falling perfectly into place like some Pantene commercial gone rogue, and his bright brown eyes still looked perpetually amused. Levi's broad shoulders and muscular frame made it clear he still spent a lot of time at the gym, but his easygoing smile softened him—made him look like the kind of guy who'd rescue kittens from storm drains *and* remember your birthday.

He was perfect for my gorgeous, charming, annoyingly flawless sister.

Paige, with her auburn hair cascading in cinematic waves down her back, practically *glowed*. Not even in a bridal way. Like, in an "I was touched by an angel and moisturized with fairy tears" kind of way. She wore winter white like she'd invented it, her cheeks flushed from the cold, and her lips were naturally pink and glossy.

She and Levi were all smiles, looking disgustingly happy. Like they shared secrets and playlists and a private language only the hot and in love could decode. It was very sweet. But I also hadn't actually ever seen them speak in high school since Paige was two years older than us, so it was a little weird to see them wrapped around each other now.

But, evidently, no one else was having that problem.

Mom swooped in for a hug from Levi, squealing like she'd just been reunited with a long-lost son. Dad clapped Levi on the back like they shared beers on weekends. And even our dog, Frederick Von Licktenstein, came charging over, tail wagging furiously like *he* hadn't decided last week that he only liked people who gave him rotisserie chicken.

Traitor.

Paige's brown eyes scanned the kitchen, and when she spotted me, they lit up even more. "Natty-kins!" she exclaimed, gliding over to throw her arms around my neck like we were in some kind of reunion special.

It was good to know that my childhood nickname was indeed going to follow me for the rest of time. I'd always wondered if it would die out with maturity, but no. Apparently, it was here to stay. I could rest easy now.

I gave her a tight but warm hug because, for all her dramatic flair and bridal sparkle, I did love the brat. And then there was Levi, arms open like we were long-lost siblings instead of—well, whatever weird Venn diagram our history fell into. Someone who would have been privy to all the no doubt *terrible* things Easton had to say about me after we'd broken up.

I hesitated. Hugging Levi felt a little like hugging a land mine. One that also might talk.

But I went through with it, stiffly, and he gave me a brief squeeze like this was just another holiday get-together and not a ticking emotional time bomb.

"Hey, Nat," he said, his voice as easy as ever, but his eyes held that tiny, knowing edge.

"Hey," I mumbled, avoiding his eyes and grabbing another slice of pizza, hoping to bury the awkwardness under cheese and pepperoni. If my mouth was permanently stuffed, then no one could expect me to talk, right?

That was the plan anyway.

Everyone launched into small talk about the wedding . . . what time everyone was heading to the resort tomorrow, how beautiful the venue was going to be, blah, blah, blah. I probably should have been paying close attention—maid of honor and all that—but my patience wore thinner with every passing second, the anxiety buzzing under my skin like electric eels had attached themselves to my arms.

Finally, I couldn't take it anymore. "Is he going to be there?" I blurted out, interrupting Levi mid-sentence.

The room froze.

Everyone knew who *he* was. The *he* to end all *hes*. The *he* my brain had refused to let go of for the last almost two years.

Except MeMaw, who, of course, let out a little snicker like this was her favorite soap opera and someone had just dropped a shocking paternity twist.

Paige winced, her gaze darting to Levi like she was silently begging him to handle it.

"Uh, yeah," Levi said, shifting his weight awkwardly. "He's actually on his way here now."

I stared at him, my brain rebooting like a computer from 1997. "What?"

"He texted me like ten minutes ago. He's almost here," he said, tone casual, like we were talking about a UPS delivery and not the fucking ex love of my life.

"What?" I repeated again. My voice came out as a shriek this time, louder than I'd intended. "Here? Now?"

And that's when the knock came.

Right on cue. Like some cruel sitcom moment written by the gods of cosmic mischief.

I went into full-body panic mode.

"Nope. Nope. I'm out," I said frantically, dropping my plate like it had burned me and backing out of the kitchen as everyone stared at me like I was crazy.

It wasn't even a graceful retreat. I knocked over the coatrack, almost tripped on the dog—Frederick barking once like he approved of the drama—and I barreled down the hallway toward my childhood bedroom.

"Nat, come on," Paige called out after me, but I didn't turn around.

Once I got there, I quickly slammed the door, locking it for good measure like I was barricading myself from a zombie apocalypse. I pressed my ear against the wood, trying to hear what was going on out there.

Muffled voices. Laughter. Footsteps. More laughter.

Traitors. Every last one of them.

I couldn't do it. I'd been coaching myself since Paige had called to tell me about this magical Christmas wedding. I'd gone full *Rocky* montage, complete with mirror pep talks and themed playlists, telling myself this wasn't going to be a big deal.

Lies. All of it.

This was a big deal. It was a *fucking* big deal.

I needed Nerds Gummies. Where were my emergency Nerds Gummies?

Or vodka. I'd even take the cheap peppermint kind someone always brought to college parties and called *festive*. Anything to numb the growing flood of *oh no, oh no, oh no*, currently rising in my chest like I was about to barf emotions everywhere.

I pushed away from the door and started pacing in a crazed circle, trying to figure out what to do while also avoiding the boxes my mom had all over the room because, obviously, she didn't love me anymore and was trying to erase all evidence by making my room into a storage facility.

I finally stopped, hunched over, bracing my hands on my knees like I'd just finished running a marathon—or maybe like I was trying not to throw up. Either way, I was seconds away from a full-fledged meltdown.

I couldn't face him. Not yet. Maybe not ever.

My gaze darted to the window.

Oh no.

No.

But also . . . yes.

Before I could talk myself out of it, I was sliding it open with a sharp squeak and pulling one leg over the sill, adrenaline pumping as I prepared for a good old-fashioned sneak-out.

Just like I used to do.

Just like I used to do *for him*.

Because we'd been so disgustingly, stupidly in love that twenty-four hours in a day had not been enough. I would sneak out in pajamas, barefoot, just to lie on the hood of his truck and talk about life. Or climb into the passenger seat of his beat-up Ford and drive until the road ran out.

Fuck. He really was everywhere in this house. In this town. In my godforsaken, traitorous head.

This was not acceptable.

With a frustrated grunt, I grabbed onto the window frame and hoisted the rest of myself out the house. The ground didn't seem that far. I'd just land gracefully like I had a few years ago and slip away before anyone even realized I was gone.

Except . . . I didn't.

I slipped on the wet grass the *second* my feet hit the ground and went flailing, arms and legs pinwheeling until I crashed into the thorny, overly aggressive bush just below the window. Branches scratched my arms, something distinctly slimy grazed my ankle, and I was *pretty sure* a bug flew into my mouth mid-yelp.

I was still flailing when a deep, maddeningly familiar voice cut through the night air.

"Need a hand?"

The voice froze me mid-struggle.

No. No, no, no.

But also, kill me now. Why wasn't he in the fucking house already? That knock had been *ages* ago. Hadn't they all just been laughing and stabbing metaphorical knives in my back?

I looked up through the tangle of leaves and regret, and there he was.

Easton Maddox.

Just standing there. Like a fucking Calvin Klein ad, or whatever other kinds of ads movie stars were doing nowadays. His hands were in his pockets, his dark hair tousled, an unruly grin on his ridiculously handsome face. His green eyes sparkled with amusement as he took in my predicament.

Why had he gotten hotter over the last couple of years? Why wasn't he at least *pretending* not to be perfect?

Hadn't life heard of karma?

A wart. That's all I was asking for. A wart. Or a receding hairline. Or one of those unfortunate chinstrap beards.

Even bushy eyebrows would have been nice.

Or something.

Not the overwhelmingly delicious specimen that I suspected no one was ever going to live up to for the rest of my life.

I knew I'd been right to compare every man to him.

"Oh, for the love of . . ." I muttered, trying to untangle myself without giving him the satisfaction of helping me.

"You know," he said, his tone far too smug, "most people use the door."

I glared at him as I struggled to untangle myself, my cheeks on fire as I tried to ignore the fact that my panties were suddenly soaked from him muttering one sentence.

It was the Hollywood effect. I was sure of it. They probably gave their actors magical powers that somehow gave them a direct line to a girl's pussy.

"Why are you here?" I finally growled, trying to discreetly pick out the leaves and twigs that were currently tangled all over my hair.

"Levi invited me," he said, crouching down so we were eye level. "But you already knew that."

I scoffed, because he sounded like he used to when faced with my antics—attractively amused, like I was some charming hurricane he'd just been waiting to get caught in again.

Absolutely unacceptable.

"Not here, *here*," I hissed. "Like, here at this exact moment." I attempted to discreetly flick a beetle off my sweater. "Watching me fall out of a window."

He grinned wider, leaning forward like he was enjoying every second of this. "And miss you making a dramatic . . . exit, Trouble? I would never."

My stomach flipped. *Trouble.* Heaven help me.

"Ugh, don't call me that. Just go inside and pretend this never happened." I groaned, finally freeing myself and scrambling to my feet. What was with these people and old nicknames?

And why the fuck did I *feel* something every time someone called me one of them.

Easton didn't move. Just stood there, watching me with that same maddening, handsome smirk. "Not until you say please."

I narrowed my eyes at him. "Notice I'm not laughing."

"Only thing I've noticed is that you're covered in leaves," he shot back, brushing a twig off my shoulder. His touch lingered for half a second too long, sending an unwelcome shiver down my spine.

"I hate you."

"You used to say that *a lot* right before you kissed me."

I scoffed, ignoring the bolts of thunder spreading through my thighs.

"And how beautiful you look. I'm definitely noticing that," he muttered suddenly, a pained expression crossing his freakishly hot features as he took me in. "Pretty hard not to notice that when you're still the most gorgeous girl I've ever seen."

Oh hell no.

Fuck. It was happening.

I was swooning.

Someone call 9-1-1. This was not supposed to be in the picture. He reached up to touch my hair again, and I quickly stepped out of reach, almost falling back into the bushes in the process.

I was spiraling. Full-on, sparkly, emotionally destabilizing spiral. The kind where your brain whispers *Just one kiss for nostalgia* while your body yells *Jump him! Feel those hands . . . and that dick for a second for old times' sake . . .*

This was bad.

Really, *really* bad.

Look, I was a pretty confident gal who believed the sight of me should be celebrated by all mankind . . . but having him stare at me with those green eyes that I'd possibly fallen in love with the moment I'd seen them . . .

Well, I was in a danger zone.

I'd wondered if there was something wrong with me the past two years, if every guy I'd met was just not doing it for me because I was building Easton up in my head. Making up a picture of him that wasn't real.

But standing in front of him right now, it was obvious that my head had been just fine. What had been wrong with me was that I happened to date the gold standard for all men in high school, and now every guy I met would never measure up.

Fuck me.

Why did Paige have to find true love and decide to get married?

This was really inconvenient.

I had to get out of here. Now. His radiuses were going to be trouble all week, though. I wasn't sure that I could get far enough to escape his sexiness.

"I need to go," I muttered, sidestepping him and nearly tripping again in my haste.

"Where are you going?" he asked, laughing now. The *sexy* laugh. The one I used to feel all the way down to my toes.

I didn't answer. Just power walked like I was on a mission, muttering curses under my breath as I made a beeline for the side of the house, determined to avoid him—and everyone else—for the rest of the night.

I climbed the rickety wooden ladder one careful step at a time, the familiar creak of the boards beneath my weight bringing a weird kind of comfort.

I would think about the fact that I'd been reduced to hiding in my childhood treehouse at a later date. For now, I was just going to be hiding.

The treehouse had been here since I was little—Steve had built it when Paige had insisted on one in sixth grade—but of course, as was my nature, I'd taken it over from her, and it had become the sacred space for every big feeling I'd had growing up. Joy, heartbreak, anger, confusion—this place had seen it all.

I hoisted myself up through the hatch, brushing the dirt off my jeans as I stood inside and celebrated the fact that I'd made it to the top without dying or thinking about his arms wrapped around my waist.

It smelled like old wood and memories.

Unlike my poor room, which had been taken over by my mom's random stuff, everything up here was just as I'd left it. The worn cushions on the floor, the small desk in the corner with my name carved into it from the summer I'd been obsessed with carrying around a pocketknife.

A weird stage, admittedly, but I'd made it cool.

Dropping onto one of the cushions, I let out a deep breath and pulled my phone from my back pocket. I needed my people. Well, my people minus Ophelia, who was morally opposed to technology unless it was mirroring Matty's phone like the gorgeous little stalker she was.

> Me: Mayday. Mayday.

> Casey: This sounds serious.

> Riley: As serious as I am about these Nerds Gummies.

A second later a picture of her and Ophelia eating a bag of them popped up on the screen.

> Me: Focus. And tell FiFi hi.

> Me: Actually, maybe I should get some gummies, too. They would probably make this situation tolerable.

> Casey: Did he immediately pin you against the wall and kiss you?

I blinked at the phone as an errant image of Easton's lips filled my head. Followed by his perfect dick.

> Me: Hey . . . none of that. This is the exact opposite direction for how this convo should be going. I'm currently in my childhood treehouse in the backyard, hiding like a rat because he's in my house right now.

> Riley: I don't know . . . sounds like against the wall is exactly where this conversation is supposed to be going.

> Me: . . .

> Me: The problem is that he's hotter.

> Casey: Not seeing the problem, Nat. Were you hoping that they'd been putting makeup over new facial warts he'd developed since you last saw him?

I tried to picture that for a second, but it was impossible because the man was hotter than Hades.

> Me: Well, yes.

> Riley: Someone send me a pic. Every time I try to look him up, Jace puts his hands over my eyes and confiscates my phone.

A second later . . .

> Riley: Do not send my flutter muffin a pic. This is Jace.

Casey: Like we couldn't tell.

Casey: Moral of the story. Maybe you should jump your hot ex's bones. Get him out of your system.

Me: Who are you and what has Parker Davis done to you?

Me: Because I kind of like it.

Riley: Phew. I'm back. I also think you should jump your hot ex's bones. And so does Ophelia.

Me: NOT HAPPENING.

Casey: Ok, well what's the plan?

Me: Plan? I don't have a plan. I'm hiding in a treehouse in the freezing cold, texting you guys.

Casey: Well, you can't stay up there forever.

Me: Watch me.

Riley: You're going to be fine. You've handled worse. Remember that time Jace accidentally set your kitchen on fire?

Me: How is this relevant?

Riley: It's not. But you survived that, so you'll survive this.

Me: If only that made any sense.

Snorting, I leaned my head back against the wall, the knot in my chest loosening just a little. I was Natalie Bennett. I could survive anything. Even Easton.

Maybe.

Easton

Was I having a heart attack? Because that's what it felt like. As I hovered at the entry of Natalie's house—a place that was almost as familiar as mine was growing up—it was all I could do not to lose my shit completely. My pulse was hammering, my hands slightly shaking . . . and it wasn't because I was nervous to be Levi's best man. It was because I'd just seen the love of my existence fall out a fucking window.

And I'd never wanted to catch someone so badly in my entire life.

It was like time slowed the second I laid eyes on her again. And yeah, she was covered in leaves, cursing under her breath, and her hair looked like it had been in a battle with a squirrel—but I'd never seen anything so fucking beautiful. Even when she was trying to disappear into a bush, she somehow managed to look like the center of the universe.

I'd never felt like acting was hard until now.

I felt dazed. Hungover. Not the kind that came from too many drinks, but the kind that came from too many emotions hitting you all at once. She was here. Natalie.

My Natalie.

She was real, not just some dream I kept replaying in my head every night for almost two years. Not pictures that I'd stared at until it felt like my eyes were going to bleed out.

And she was perfect. More than perfect.

The second I saw her, it was like someone had punched me in the gut. She was even prettier than she used to be . . . How was that even possible? She had that same wild energy in her eyes, the same way she carried herself, like the whole world could either worship her or go to hell. But there was something new, too. A confidence that hadn't been there before. It made her dangerous.

I was already a fucking goner, so it really wasn't fair for her to be even better than I remembered.

I winced as I adjusted my dick, wondering how I was going to walk into her house, with her parents inside, when my dick was trying to break through my jeans. My need for her was painful . . . like I'd been dropped back into high school, unable to think straight around her because I couldn't wait to get in her pants.

I'd kept waiting for the moment when I'd stop missing her. When I'd wake up and not feel the need to check her socials, or scroll through old photos on my phone like some lovesick loser. But that moment never came. No matter how many auditions I booked or how many flashing cameras I faced, she was still the only person I ever wanted to see at the end of the day.

And now that I was finally here, finally back, I felt like I was on the edge of a cliff, hoping like hell that when I jumped, she'd be there to catch me.

The only way to survive was to remind my dick that our sabbatical was almost over.

Almost two fucking years.

I was pathetic—or at least that's what my friends all said. I hadn't been with anyone since she'd walked away.

I'd tried, and I probably had a whole bunch of rumors out there about me having erectile dysfunction or not liking women because my dick took one look at someone else and . . . completely stopped working.

The only time I could get it up had been if I was thinking about her, or looking at a picture of her, or . . . staring at her.

My friends didn't understand, though. My dick knew something they didn't.

No one ever could have compared to her. Not even close.

Think of bananas, I coached myself as I willed my dick back in my pants. Nothing could get me limper than that disgusting fruit. A few more seconds . . .

The door flew open, and there was Natalie's mom, Emily. "Easton!" she cried, pulling me into a warm hug.

Fuck, I kept my hips far, far away, but evidently a mom hug had the same effect as bananas because I was blissfully, thankfully, limp as a fish.

She released me from her boa constrictor hug and squeezed my shoulders for a second before taking a step back. "It's good to see you," she told me, and I could tell she meant it. And fuck, she looked like she was about to cry.

Me too, Mrs. Bennett. Me too. I'd thought I'd prepared myself for what this was going to be like, coming back here, but evidently that hadn't actually been possible.

I followed her inside, still trying to get a grip on myself. Levi came around the corner, greeting me with a grin and a clap on the back. "About time, man," he said. "Thought you got lost, Mr. Hollywood."

"Better late than never," I said, proud at how normal and steady my voice sounded. He grinned knowingly at me, well aware that it was killing me to be in here—without her. Levi had been one of the only friends I'd kept in touch with after leaving town, and unfortunately for him, he'd also been my sounding board for how miserable I was without Natalie.

Possibly every time I got drunk. Which was quite often in the early days after she'd broken up with me.

The rest of Natalie's family was gathered in the kitchen, and I tried to be my most charming self—after all, these people were going to be my family again in the near future if I played my cards right.

My eyes locked with Natalie's grandmother, MeMaw, and I winced. Her eyes had taken on a glint that was half bat-crazy and half furious. I knew what that was all about. I'd come over the day after Nat had broken up with me, and MeMaw had met me at the front door.

I was on her porch before the sun had fully risen, still wearing the same hoodie from the night before. My hands felt clammy, and my heart pounded like it was in my throat. I'd been up all night, going over all the words I was going to say to change her mind.

I raised my fist to knock, but before my knuckles hit the door, it flew open. MeMaw stood there, dressed in some kind of oversized sweatshirt with a glittery HOT GIRL SHIT *winking from the front, and large hoop earrings that jingled when she moved. She squinted at me from beneath her red glasses like she'd caught me trying to steal the family silver.*

"Easton Maddox," she said, her southern drawl as sharp as a whip. "What on God's green earth are you doing skulking around my granddaughter's porch at this hour?"

"I need to talk to her," I said, trying to push past her, but MeMaw stepped squarely in my path. For someone so small, she had the stance of a linebacker.

"She doesn't want to talk to you right now, sugar," she said, crossing her arms and tilting her head like she had all the time in the world. "But I do. Take a walk with me."

I didn't have a choice. MeMaw had that way about her—like she'd already decided what you were going to do before you did it. She grabbed her coat and stepped out onto the porch, nodding toward the dirt road that led toward the woods.

We walked in silence for a few minutes, her pace unhurried, mine stiff with nerves. My chest felt like it was caving in, and I wanted to break the quiet, to plead my case.

But MeMaw spoke first. "You love her, don't you?"

The words hit me like a punch to the gut. "Of course I do," I said, my voice breaking. "I've loved her since the second I saw her."

MeMaw stopped and turned to face me, her bright red glasses catching the light. "I believe you, darlin'. But sometimes loving someone means letting them fly."

"She doesn't want to fly," I said, my frustration boiling over. "She's just scared."

"Maybe," MeMaw said, her voice softer now. "But Natalie's like me. She's got a free spirit. You try to cage that, and it'll break her." She put a hand on my arm, her grip surprisingly strong. "This first year of college? She needs to figure out who she is without wondering what you're doing or feeling like she's letting you down or holding you back."

"She could never hold me back," I protested, feeling the ache of my own words.

"I know you think that," MeMaw said, her eyes studying me like she could see every corner of my soul. "But it doesn't matter what you think, sugar. It's what she feels. And right now, she feels like she needs space."

I swallowed hard, the lump in my throat threatening to choke me. "What if she never comes back?"

MeMaw smiled then, a small, knowing smile that didn't reach her eyes. "If she's yours, she'll find her way back. And if she doesn't . . . well, you'll just have to come get her, won't you?"

The words cut deeper than I wanted to admit. I hated her logic, hated that it made sense, but more than anything, I hated the idea of letting Natalie go.

MeMaw patted my arm and started walking again. "Now go home, Easton. Focus on your movie and let her focus on herself. She's got to fly, and you've got to let her."

I didn't go back to her porch that day. I didn't beg or plead or try to change her mind. But as I walked back to my car, a hollow ache settled in my chest, and I knew something had shifted.

Because MeMaw was right. I couldn't cage Natalie. But that didn't stop me from hoping she'd fly right back to me.

And if not, I'd just have to convince her that a life with me was better than anything she could find out there.

I snapped back to the present, deliberately keeping my gaze away from MeMaw's disapproving stare. Evidently, her idea of letting Natalie fly free and *my* idea of what that meant had been different.

But it was okay. I was here to remedy it all now.

Everyone started talking about the wedding, and I should've been paying attention. But my attention kept slipping, pulling toward the window. Toward her.

I could imagine how she looked sitting in that treehouse. Her legs dangling through the hatch, her hair catching the soft glow of the backyard lights. She was up there, probably freaking out, probably fuming about me being here.

Fuck, just being near her, knowing she was close, it was like I could finally fucking breathe again. For almost two years, I'd been suffocating, drowning under the weight of missing her. And now she was here, and I wanted to crawl through that window, up that damn tree, and tell her everything I hadn't been able to say back then.

But I couldn't. Not yet.

So instead, I stood there in the kitchen, pretending to care about whatever Levi was talking about, pretending I wasn't shaking with the effort it took to keep myself in check.

Because as much as I wanted to fix this—to fix *us*—I couldn't lose her again. And rushing her? That wasn't an option.

I'd play it cool. For now.

Even if it killed me.

CHAPTER 5

Natalie

The screen door creaked as I stepped onto the porch, the morning air biting at my skin like it held a personal grudge. I was half human, half bed gremlin, still wearing the leggings and hoodie I'd tossed on after my restless night in the twin bed from hell. That mattress was a relic of my middle school years, and it felt like it had a personal vendetta against me. I was convinced there was a spring in there sharpened to impale dreams.

Or at least that was the excuse I was giving myself for the fact that I hadn't slept a wink.

I'd stayed in the treehouse for most of the night. Paige had come out eventually, laughing like it was the best thing she'd ever seen, until I reminded her that I still owed her for the time she cut my hair in my sleep in first grade. I told her I may not have had scissors right then, but I had adult-level pettiness and access to bleach.

That had shut her up.

Needless to say, I hadn't gotten a lot of sleep last night.

When I finally dragged myself out of bed this morning, I'd tripped over a box of dog toys right out of the gate. Because apparently this house had become booby-trapped since I'd left it. Frederick Von Licktenstein's squeaky pizza slice had launched me face-first into a pile of decorative pillows that hadn't been decorative in at least ten years. I would have loved to blame my mother for this chaos, but she had the audacity to text me before I could:

> Mom: We're all headed to the venue! Come when you're alive. 🤍

Thanks for the empathy, Mother. Remind me to nominate you for humanitarian of the year.

I made my way to my car, keys in hand. The sooner I got to the B and B, the closer I would be to all this being over.

Had I been tempted to get off in my childhood bedroom thanks to the nonstop Easton montage that was going through my head?

Yes.

Had I successfully managed to stop myself from such a thing?

Also yes.

But only because I knew from experience how thin the walls in the house were.

I'd get in my car and drive, blast music that had nothing to do with love or heartbreak, suck down three coffees, pretend I wasn't two seconds away from a full meltdown . . . and then I'd hide out in my room until it was time for me to do maid of honor things.

It was a solid plan, I thought. What could go wrong?

Sliding into the driver's seat, I shoved the key into the ignition and turned.

Nothing.

Not even a sputter. Just dead, lifeless silence.

"You've got to be fucking kidding me," I muttered, smacking my forehead against the steering wheel.

Again. I turned the key harder, as if that would help.

Still nothing.

It was dead. My car was dead. And the venue? A solid two hours away. Of course.

Evidently, *this* was what could go wrong.

I leaned back in the seat, staring up at the sky like the answers might be up there. They weren't. Just a family of squirrels mocking me from the branches.

This was fine. Everything was fine.

I was still muttering to myself as I popped the hood, more out of habit than hope. This car—Old Bessie, may she rest in unpredictable peace— had already had a hundred thousand miles on it when I'd inherited her at sixteen. She'd lived through my Easton heartbreak, two flat tires, a rogue raccoon incident, and exactly one regrettable road trip to Florida.

She was my ride or die.

Until apparently . . . today.

When she'd decided to die.

As I climbed out of the car and stared at the engine like it might miraculously come back to life, I heard the sound of a vehicle approaching.

I turned just as a shiny, lifted truck pulled into the driveway, tires spitting pebbles from the road. My stomach sank when I saw the driver.

The sexy-beast, gird-your-loins, handcuff-yourself-to-a-pole-so-you-don't-jump-him, driver.

Easton.

He was wearing a backwards hat and a cocky grin that should be illegal before ten a.m. Something that happened to be an issue for my kind—aka every girl with a freaking pulse.

He stepped out like sin in denim. Worn jeans that clung in all the right places, a thermal shirt that looked spray-painted onto his stupidly sculpted chest, and that hat—fuck, that hat—that made every rational thought I'd ever had do a nose-dive off a cliff.

I wasn't wearing makeup. Or a bra. I was in leggings that were one sneeze away from betraying me and a hoodie that may or may not have pizza sauce on the front.

How dare he look so hot this morning?

Especially when I didn't think my shower had actually gotten all the leaves out from my fall yesterday evening. I was planning on getting super-hot once I got to the bed-and-breakfast. I wasn't ready for this so early in the day.

"Need a ride?" he called, doing some kind of sexy prowl that had me gritting my teeth.

I crossed my arms and glared, pretending my heartbeat wasn't punching itself in the face. "What are you doing here?"

"You keep asking me that, Trouble," he said with a smirk, adjusting his hat in a way that made his forearm muscles flex. Not fair. Muscles should not flex like that without warning.

"You keep popping up in places," I retorted, yanking my gaze away from him and staring at the engine of my car like it held all the secrets to the universe. "And not like a cute groundhog, might I add. Like a mole."

"Oh, are groundhogs known for being cute? I wasn't aware of that." I could hear the stupid smile on his lips.

"Well, now you know," I said haughtily. Even though I had no idea if they were cute or not.

Easton stepped closer, his presence warming the air around me like he had a personal force field of cologne and body heat. "Regardless, it looks like you might need a lift."

I could feel his body next to mine, close enough that my brain went offline for a second and started writing poetry I was never going to admit to. There was something about the curve of his jaw and the scent of him that apparently was still calling for my destruction even after all this time . . .

Ugh, there was my stupid heart again.

It was freaking pining.

I groaned inwardly, swiping a hand down my face. "I'm fine. I was just on my way."

Easton tilted his head, looking at my dead car with exaggerated skepticism. "Yeah, sure. Looks like you're all set."

I glanced from my sweet, stubborn Old Bessie to his truck. It gleamed in the morning sun, a big upgrade from the beat-up one he'd driven in high school. Figures even his truck would be sexier.

I, evidently, was cursed like that.

Easton leaned against my car, crossing his arms in a way that made the muscles in his forearms flex again. "You can sit here all morning and wait for a tow, or you can hop in and let me save the day."

"I don't need saving," I said, my voice clipped, even as I shivered and immediately regretted not wearing real pants.

Easton raised his eyebrows, his grin widening. "You're awfully stubborn for someone who's *stranded*."

I opened my mouth. Closed it. Tried again.

"I'm . . . evaluating my options."

"Uh-huh." He scratched his jaw like he was thinking real hard. "Would one of those options be accepting a ride from the guy who's offering, no strings attached?"

My eyes narrowed. "Do you even know how to do 'no strings attached,' Maddox?"

His grin widened, and damn it, it was still the most devastating thing I'd ever seen. "Not when it comes to you."

Boom. There went my ovaries. I didn't need them. Not for this trip anyway.

I wanted to argue, but my family was already gone, and asking them to come back and get me with all the wedding stuff going on would just be rude. I also didn't have the time to wait around for a tow truck to take my car to a mechanic to get fixed, as the first wedding event was in just a few hours.

Not to mention I didn't want to have to pay for what a cab ride would cost.

"Fine," I muttered, stalking toward his truck. "But we are not doing the thing."

"What thing?"

"The thing," I said, gesturing vaguely. "Where we rehash old memories or talk about what we've been up to the last couple of years."

"You mean the last twenty-three months, twenty days, and twelve hours," he offered casually.

I tripped over my own feet. Literally. Because my brain had short-circuited at his disturbingly accurate math. "That was oddly specific."

"Mmm," he said vaguely, winking at me like he was actually trying to kill me. "I like to be precise about the important things."

Like the date I dumped him. Great.

Why was I like this?

He opened the passenger door like a gentleman—or a man who was secretly trying to ruin my life with his good manners—and I stood there debating if I could vault into the truck without flashing him or tearing something.

Spoiler alert: I could not.

"Ah," I cried out as Easton's strong hands gripped my waist, lifted me up like I weighed nothing, and set me in the cab.

"That's also not allowed, Maddox," I managed to comment after I finally collapsed in my seat, sparks lighting up my veins from where he'd been touching me.

I took a deep breath. Well, that was a mistake. The truck smelled like new leather and cologne—his cologne—aka my favorite scent in the world.

"What's not allowed?" he asked, cocking his head, that same smug, hot, annoying smile on his lips as he watched me desperately take in hits of his scent like it was the only oxygen my body recognized.

"Touching," I said pointedly. "No *touching* allowed."

"Phew, I thought you were going to say that I wasn't allowed to stare at your perfect ass. And then I would have to say no, and it would be this whole thing."

He closed the door in my face before I could say anything.

The audacity.

Easton got behind the wheel, a grin on his face like he'd won some kind of competition.

"Natalie?" he asked, sounding amused. It took me a second to realize words had come out of his mouth, I was so entranced watching the muscles in his forearms move as he turned the steering wheel. I blinked and casually wiped my face, making sure no drool had slipped off.

If I had an addiction, it was arm porn.

And possibly abs.

And definitely the backwards hat thing.

And the smell that was currently drowning me in pheromonal despair.

"Yeah?" I finally squeaked, because apparently my voice had joined my brain in abandoning me.

A problem I seemed to be having lately.

"I asked about Old Bessie," he said, tossing me a side-glance. "I'm surprised you're still driving her."

"Don't say her name like that," I snapped instantly, regretting all my life decisions that had led me to this wedding and the sexual way he'd just said my car's name that was doing terrible, *wicked* things to my insides.

Old Bessie had been the site for *a lot* of sex, and just hearing him say her name was sparking a flashback of Easton's and my hottest moments.

Weird but true.

"Such a greedy pussy," he growled, his hot tongue licking through my core.

Natalie, get a fucking hold of yourself.

"Well, unfortunately most of my money goes to clothes, Nerds Gummies, and alcohol . . ." I stammered, only being a little sarcastic on account of the need thrumming in between my thighs. "Bessie hasn't had a checkup in, like, a year, but she's loyal."

"But not tuition," he inserted smoothly, staring out the driveway with that same annoyingly hot smirk on his lips. "Your money hasn't been going to that."

I blinked at his statement, a frown on my lips. How had he known that?

"No . . ." I said slowly. "It hasn't been going to tuition."

It was true. I hadn't paid a dime toward tuition since going to school. A miracle, really—one I hadn't questioned because I'd assumed it was some obscure scholarship or university glitch sent from the heavens. The grant email had been vague, the name on it unfamiliar. I'd never questioned it too deeply because . . . well, I *needed* it.

But what if . . .

Surely not.

Fuck.

A horrible, gut-sinking suspicion was gnawing its way through my insides. Paying for my college was never going to be an option for my parents. I'd known all along I was going to have to take out a buttload of school loans and then spend the majority of my adult life trying to pay them off.

I side-eyed Easton, trying to study him as closely as I could without making it obvious. I used to know his every expression like the back of my hand. The twitch of his lip when he was holding back a joke. The crease between his brows when he was annoyed but trying to be chill about it. The way his jaw flexed when he was nervous.

But I was finding this new version of him was a lot harder to read.

"Easton," I finally began cautiously. "How did you know that I haven't been paying tuition?"

His smirk turned into a full-fledged grin that threatened to take my breath away.

"Because *I* paid for it, obviously," he said, completely unrepentantly, might I add. As if it were perfectly normal to pay for your ex's tuition from your big Hollywood contract after she brutally stabs you in the heart.

My entire body locked up. My breath snagged. My ovaries simultaneously tried to riot and slap me.

I choked. Like, actual sputtering, gasping, about-to-die choking.

He didn't even flinch. Just lifted one hand and casually placed it on my knee. Right on the soft black cotton of my leggings. His thumb started doing this soft, slow, comforting stroke like I was some kind of panicked bunny who needed to be calmed.

Another spoiler alert: it did *not* calm me.

"Breathe, Trouble," he said softly, like I was being dramatic for having a *full-blown existential crisis*.

"Easton," I wheezed. "Why—why would you do that?"

His thumb kept stroking, and I had to resist the urge to throw open the truck door and roll into traffic.

"After everything," I continued, my voice rising. "After I—after we— Why would you do something like that?"

Now that my initial shock was wearing off, there was a strange ache spreading through my veins instead. One that was unwelcome and unacceptable and . . . fucking agonizing.

His eyes went back to the road, but his face was suddenly serious. No teasing. Just . . . Easton. The one who used to tuck my hair behind my ear and say he wanted to know all the ways I was broken so he could love every single one of them.

"You should know me better than that to think that just because you said you were done . . . that it meant I was done, too," he said, his voice quieter now. "Although, I guess the reason you broke up with me in the first place indicated you didn't actually know me that well, huh?"

I rubbed at my chest, trying to get the aching sensation to go away. "I'll pay you back. It might take a while . . . okay, a long while. Unless I win the lottery, which could happen. I knew a girl at school who went to a random gas station on a family vacation in Wyoming and won twenty thousand dollars . . ."

"You're not paying me back," he said, cutting off my word vomit mid-sentence.

I was very aware that I was rambling, but what else were you supposed to do when you found out your ex-boyfriend, your very famous ex-boyfriend, had paid for your tuition . . . after you had broken up with him?

I sat back against the seat, huffing, trying to decide if I should be mad or just . . . drown in whatever the hell this was.

Generosity? Love? Guilt?

Or maybe all three wrapped in a six-foot-something, unfairly hot Hollywood package?

I needed answers. I needed clarity.

I needed to stop fantasizing about climbing into his lap.

"I'm *going* to pay you back," I insisted, pulling my phone out of my legging pocket—thank fuck for that particular invention—and sending an SOS to Casey and Riley.

Easton hummed noncommittally and then mercifully stopped talking as I tried to come to terms with what he'd done.

My phone buzzed in my hand, and I pulled up the message like it was a lifeline while trying to ignore the fact that Easton seemed to be paying a lot more attention to me than he was to the road.

Casey: He kissed you!

I gaped at my phone before quickly angling it so that Easton couldn't see the screen. I definitely didn't want him seeing the texts since they were obviously going to be about him.

"Something wrong?" Easton asked, entirely too innocent.

"Nope," I lied, gripping my phone tighter.

> Me: Why would you say that?

> Riley: Well, what else would be an SOS?

> Me: A lot of things, actually. If he kisses me, it will be more than an SOS situation.

> Casey: What exactly constitutes being worse than SOS?

> Me: Constitutes. Big word, Case-face. But, I don't know. How about DEFCON 3 or maybe 10? I feel like you guys don't even know me right now.

> Riley: I'll just make a note in my phone to ensure I have these rankings right for next time.

> Me: Good girl.

> Me: But also . . . focus. This may not be a DEF-CON 3, but it is an emergency.

> Riley: We're ready.

> Me: Are you, though?

"What are you typing so furiously about?" Easton asked as he touched my shoulder, his thumb grazing bare skin this time where my oversized hoodie had slid to the side.

I jerked like I'd been shot, and that choking sound came out of my mouth again. He laughed like this was all very funny, and the sound of it ripped through me . . . absolutely drenching my panties.

Fuck.

Just when I thought I might combust from the sheer volume of pent-up lust coursing through me . . . a sprawling mountain lodge came into view, rising from the snow like some kind of rugged fairy tale. This had to be the bed-and-breakfast.

Easton moved his hand back to the steering wheel as we pulled into the driveway, and I melted into my seat in relief. Maybe I was going to live after all. Maybe I'd survive this car ride without spontaneously combusting. Maybe.

The lodge stood nestled against the slope like it belonged there, its stone-and-cedar exterior dusted with snow and trimmed in pine garland. Frost clung to the dark wooden beams, catching the light like glitter, and a soft layer of snow blanketed the grounds. Twinkling lights were strung along the sloped roofline and wrapped around thick log columns on the porch, casting a golden glow against the silvery stretch of the late morning sky.

Lanterns lined the drive, their flames flickering warmly despite the chill, like the whole place had been pulled from the front of a winter postcard. Beyond the lodge, snow-draped pines stretched toward the mountains, and a frozen pond mirrored the string lights above it—calm, perfect, and almost too magical to be real.

Paige and Levi had done well. Really well.

This was exactly the kind of place where you'd want to get married. Not that I was thinking about that. Obviously not. I wasn't thinking about weddings or rings or what Easton would look like in a tux or what our hypothetical children might inherit from him besides the jawline of death and the ability to smirk with weaponized charm.

Nope. Not at all.

There was a valet waiting outside the double doors of the building, bundled up in some kind of bushy brown fur coat like we lived in Antarctica or something. I'd never been more relieved to see someone in my life.

My phone was vibrating like it had just snorted espresso, but I'd have to update my ladies later. Right now, I had one mission: escape the truck before Easton could say something else with that infuriatingly hot voice of his.

I threw open the passenger door like I was being chased by a bear, taking in gulps of the smell of wood smoke that lingered in the crisp air as I desperately tried to get his cologne out of my nostrils.

The valet flinched as I nearly collided with him. The guy caught me right before I toppled onto my face on the cobblestoned drive. Because, of course, this place had cobblestones. It couldn't have been cuter if it tried.

"Wow. Are you okay?" he asked, his brown eyes wide.

"She's fine." Easton's voice came from behind me, smooth and growly and entirely too territorial . . . And then I was being yanked out of the valet's arms. "The bags are in the back," Easton added as he tossed the keys to the poor man, who was now giving Easton that squinty do-I-know-you-from-somewhere look that probably haunted Easton's life nowadays.

"You're being rude," I hissed under my breath, glancing back at the valet who was definitely starting to connect the dots.

Easton shrugged, still gripping my arm like I was his date and not someone two seconds away from spontaneously combusting into a flaming pile of unresolved sexual tension. "He was *flirting* with you."

"Well, duh—" I began, ready to launch into an explanation of all my wonderful qualities, but I didn't get the chance.

Because the moment we stepped through the door, I lost the ability to form coherent thoughts.

CHAPTER 6

Natalie

We had walked into a Christmas explosion.

Twinkle lights wrapped around every railing, staircase, and potted plant. Garlands were laced with velvet bows. A literal twelve-foot Christmas tree stood in the center of the lobby, decked out in what had to be a thousand ornaments.

The smell of cinnamon, pine, and cookies assaulted me like some festive drug, and the fireplace—because, of course, there was a fireplace—was crackling like it was auditioning for a fireplace commercial.

"Wow," I whispered.

Next to me, Easton leaned in with a cocky grin. "Bet you a gingerbread man, there's mistletoe somewhere in here."

The insinuation in his voice was heavy, and I gave him another glare.

"If I see mistletoe, I *will* light it on fire, Easton Maddox."

"'Tis the season," he said, all smug and amused like my barely contained breakdown was his favorite show on Netflix.

Yanking my arm from Easton's grip, I hustled over to reception, where a woman in her sixties stood behind the polished mahogany check-in desk decorated with a glimmering garland, her round glasses perched on the tip of her nose as she peered over the lenses at me with an aggressively cheerful smile. A red-and-green plaid scarf was wrapped around her neck, and a festive pin in the shape of a tiny Christmas wreath was fastened to her cream-colored cardigan. Everything about her screamed "holiday spirit."

"Welcome to the Pinewood Bed-and-Breakfast!" she chirped. "Where the beds are cozy, the cocoa is bottomless, and the Christmas magic never runs out!"

I blinked at her. That was . . . a lot.

The woman beamed, clearly expecting some kind of enthusiastic response, so I forced a smile. "Sounds . . . great."

Easton, of course, was beside me now, oozing charm like a freaking peppermint mocha with legs.

I leaned over the counter. "Natalie Bennett," I said, trying not to sound as crazed as I felt at the moment. "It should be under the wedding block."

The woman—Margaret, according to her name tag—typed away with festive purpose. I blinked at the fact that her keyboard was red with little green LED lights. That was what you called going all in.

"Hmm . . ." she said, her smile dimming. "That's strange, dear."

I knew that tone. Fuck. That was the there's-been-a-horrible-mistake-but-I'm-going-to-deliver-the-news-like-a-Christmas-angel tone.

"What's strange?" I asked in a tight voice.

"It seems there might have been a glitch in the system. I don't have a room under your name."

I blinked, leaning over the counter to look at the screen, too, as if that would somehow conjure up my name. "That can't be right. Maybe my sister put it under her name when she reserved it. She's the bride, Paige Bennett," I said quickly.

Next to me, Easton was checking in with a man who was the closest thing to a living, breathing Santa Claus I'd ever seen. Margaret's husband—at least, I assumed that's who he was—was straight out of a Christmas card. He had a full, snow-white beard that spilled down his chest in a soft, cloudlike mess, rosy cheeks that looked like they'd been pinched by angels, and a round belly that stretched the buttons of his red-and-black flannel shirt like it had hosted one too many gingerbread cookies. If the man let out a *ho ho ho*, I was going to drop everything and become a true believer.

"Donald Humphries," Easton drawled, flashing Santa his most devastating smile as he slid a sleek black wallet out of his coat.

I blinked.

That was the name of our old high school football coach.

The same Donald Humphries who had smelled like mothballs and wore athletic shorts pulled so high he could've smuggled his lunch in the waistband, paired with a whistle he never stopped blowing and a visor that seemed permanently glued to his forehead. Not exactly the suave alias I would've gone with.

I steadfastly ignored how much I loved the sound of Easton's voice. It was too bad I couldn't have enjoyed it more on the drive here, but obviously that hadn't been possible.

Santa's eyebrows raised, and then he nodded as Easton handed him an ID that clearly wouldn't have that name. Obviously, this had been arranged beforehand.

He was smirking at me, of course. Probably because I was staring like I'd forgotten how eyes worked.

I forced myself to look away and pretend to be normal. The effort was herculean. I focused on the Christmas tree. The garland. The twinkle lights. Anything but the fact that Easton was giving a fake name. Because that's what celebrities did, right? They used fake names. I'd seen that in gossip columns. You know, the ones I definitely didn't read late at night in bed while pretending I was *so* over him.

Gird your loins, Natalie.

This was why I'd left. This. Exactly this. His life was fake names and assistants and glossy premiere photos. And mine was . . . Nerds Gummies and a beat-up car named Old Bessie.

Easton's frown deepened slightly as he glanced over at me; he could always read my moods like a flipping road map, and for one traitorous second, I thought he looked . . . sad. But then Santa let out a hearty chuckle.

"Ah yes! One of the groomsmen, I assume? We've got you in the Evergreen Suite—top floor, best view of the mountains. A fan of Christmas, are ya?"

"Something like that," Easton said with a chuckle, his eyes still on me.

"I'm so sorry, darlin'," Margaret said, breaking Easton's and my much too heavy eye contact. "But there's only one room coming up under your sister's name."

"Do you have your reservation number?" Easton asked oh so helpfully as he leaned one elbow on the counter.

I turned and glared at him like I might bite him.

"Well . . . no. I thought Paige and Levi were taking care of all that," I said slowly.

Easton tilted his head, looking positively entertained. "It was in the email. There was a link to book the rooms. My assistant did it that day."

Now I was panicking. I vaguely remembered some kind of email, but I'd been finishing up finals and existing on caffeine, stress, and an unreasonable amount of Nutella, and everything was so last minute and . . .

Fuck. I definitely hadn't read that email.

"We were responsible for booking our own rooms?" I said, that weird squeak back in my voice.

Margaret winced. "I'm so sorry, sweetheart. But we're at full capacity right now. We don't have any other rooms available."

I sighed, dragging a hand through my hair. "Okay, you have double occupancy, right? My grandmother is staying here. I'll see if I can room with her."

Before Margaret could answer, a familiar voice piped up from behind me. "Oh, honey, I'd love to help, but I can't."

I turned to see MeMaw standing in the middle of the room, wearing a sweater so aggressive it could have blinded me. It had a massive blinking Rudolph nose smack in the middle, and her bedazzled red glasses made her look like a Christmas ornament come to life. Her earrings—Santa riding a candy cane, naturally—jingled as she gave me an exaggerated shrug.

"Why not?" I asked, half expecting an excuse like she needed her beauty sleep or something equally inane.

She leaned in, dropping her voice to a conspiratorial whisper, though it was loud enough for the whole lobby to hear. "Because I'm expecting to hook up this week."

I blinked, my brain short-circuiting. "I— What?"

"You heard me," she said, her grin wicked as she patted my arm. "I've got a good feeling about this place. A woman has needs, Natalie."

Margaret coughed, clearly trying to suppress a laugh, and I wished the floor would open up and swallow me.

"Great," I muttered under my breath. "Fantastic. Just what I needed."

MeMaw winked. "If you get desperate, you're welcome to the cot in my room. It folds out right next to my bed."

I blinked at her. "You mean the cot *you* will fold someone out on next to *your* bed."

She winked. "It's Christmas, baby girl. Miracles happen."

As MeMaw sauntered off to inspect the cookie tray, I turned back to Margaret, praying she had some miracle solution. "So . . . just to confirm . . . there are *no* other options?"

She offered me a sympathetic smile. "I'm really sorry. We could put you on the waitlist if someone cancels?"

There were a lot of problems with this situation. I didn't have a working car, there weren't any other hotels nearby, and paying for an Uber for a four-hour round trip drive every day until the wedding was going to be astronomical. There was also the fact that I had paid enough attention to know that Paige had planned events every night, and the idea of dragging my ass two hours back home in the middle of the night was less than ideal.

Maybe they had a stable I could sleep in. That had worked out for someone in the past.

"You can stay with me," Easton said oh so casually, slipping his key card into his back pocket like he hadn't just detonated my last shred of chill with five casual words.

Margaret gasped, clapping her hands together like he'd just invented Christmas itself. "Oh, that's a *wonderful* idea!"

I gaped at her, because why was this stranger trying to ruin my life? "That's actually a *terrible* idea."

She waved off my panic with a dismissive flap of her hand. "Oh, don't be silly! It's a suite, dear. Plenty of space! One of you can take the couch—" Her lips twitched. "But why *would* you?"

I choked on air. My soul literally left my body.

Easton had the audacity to grin like it was the best thing that had ever happened to him.

"No, absolutely not," I snapped, shaking my head so hard I probably looked like a bobblehead. "There's gotta be another option."

Margaret pursed her lips and turned back to her computer, clearly humoring me. "Well, let's see . . . your grandmother said she needs her own room—"

"For hooking up," I muttered under my breath, already knowing that was a dead end.

Margaret continued scrolling on her screen. "Your parents are in the Mistletoe Lodge—romantic suite, big bathtub, very cozy. Not ideal."

Rooming with my parents while they reenacted their second honeymoon. No. *Not ideal* was an understatement.

"I assume you don't want to stay with the groom's parents . . ."

I tuned her out as I mentally went through the list of people I knew were staying at the B and B this week. The other bridesmaids were all married. Aunt Kathy snored like a freight train. Uncle Clayton had weird rules about temperature control and made everyone sleep with the windows open, even in the snow.

I was officially out of options.

"Oh!" Margaret perked up like she'd just remembered a winning lottery ticket in her apron pocket. "You could stay in Santa's Bunkhouse!"

I leaned forward. That sounded . . . better than a stable. I could get behind quaint.

"It's where the flower girls and ring bearers are staying," she finished with a proud smile. "It has plastic sheets, in case of accidents . . . and hot cocoa on tap!"

I groaned, rubbing my hands over my face.

Margaret grinned like she'd solved world peace. "Well, then!" She gestured between us with delight. "Looks like you two are roommates!"

I turned toward Easton, my mouth already open to tell him exactly where he could shove that smug little smile—only to catch him mid–*fist pump*.

A *fist pump*. With an actual arm flex and everything.

Like a *child*.

Like he'd *won*.

I narrowed my eyes. "I don't know why you're celebrating."

Easton tilted his head, still grinning. "You say that now . . . but wait until you see how good I still am at sharing a bed."

I sucked in a breath. My pulse betrayed me, thudding like it was trying to beat its way out of my chest and leap into his arms.

Margaret *giggled*. Giggled like this was the best rom-com she'd ever seen, and she had front-row tickets.

"I'll be sleeping on the *couch*," I said, glaring daggers at him.

He smirked, utterly unfazed. "Sure, Trouble. Whatever you need to tell yourself."

This was going to be a *nightmare*.

And not the fun, sexy kind where you wake up flushed and panting.

No. This was going to be the kind of nightmare where your ex is still stupidly hot, smells like a daydream, sleeps *six feet away* from you, and makes your panties combust every time he so much as breathes.

Awesome.

Merry fucking Christmas.

CHAPTER 7

Easton

I pushed open the suite door, motioning for Natalie to go in first, and the second she stepped through the threshold, she whirled around like she'd just walked into a crime scene.

"This is not romantic. So don't get any ideas," she declared immediately, her blue eyes wide and accusatory, as if I had personally laid out the rose petals and queued up the soft jazz.

I leaned against the doorframe and surveyed the room. "I don't know, Trouble . . ." I gave her a slow once-over before letting my gaze sweep the suite. "Seems awfully romantic to me."

The B and B had gone full Hallmark Channel in here. Vaulted ceilings, twinkling lights on a pine-scented tree tucked into the corner, a fireplace crackling beneath a garland-draped mantel, and a bed so big and plush it could've moonlighted as a marshmallow. Add in the floor-to-ceiling windows and the fur rug and—yeah. Whoever designed this suite wanted people to get naked and emotional.

And judging by the way Natalie's mouth had parted slightly as she looked around, she agreed.

She spun toward me, hands on her hips. "I'm sleeping on the couch," she spat out.

I smirked, dropping my bag on the bed. "As I said downstairs," I drawled, kicking off my boots, "I don't mind sharing."

Natalie made a sound that I could only describe as a rage-gargle. "Not. Happening."

I held up my hands, all faux innocence. "Hey, your call. Although, if memory serves, you did once say I was the human equivalent of a weighted blanket."

She glared so hard I half expected the tree lights to short-circuit. Honestly, it was impressive. That kind of fury? Still hot.

I stretched my arms over my head, letting my shirt ride up just enough to tease. She noticed. Oh, she definitely noticed. Her eyes flicked—just for a second—then snapped back up like she hadn't just taken a mental screenshot of my abs. Victory.

"But since we're clearly setting boundaries," I said casually, already walking toward the bathroom, "you should know I'm about to take a shower."

Her arms were still crossed, her lips pursed. "Thank you for that information. That is good roommate behavior." She sniffed. "I'll expect that level of respect for the remainder of the week."

I bit my lip to keep from laughing. "Of course," I said smoothly. "I'll try to be as good a roommate as Casey."

The sound she made was somewhere between a gasp and a wounded animal. She knew I'd been keeping tabs. Not everything. Not yet. But the breadcrumbs? I was dropping them with calculated precision. Maybe one day I'd tell her how many hours I'd spent clicking through photos of her and her friends. How I knew what coffee shop she studied at. How many times I'd come close to jumping on a plane just to see her face in person.

How I was the one who'd temporarily disabled Old Bessie so I could have more time with her . . .

But for now?

This was way more fun.

Stepping into the bathroom, I left the door open. *Just a crack.* Just enough to let the steam creep out. Just enough to drive her insane.

I knew her too well.

Natalie might claim to hate me. She might fight me every step of the way. But she *loved* my body.

The second the water started, I imagined her out there—arms crossed, legs curled up under her, probably pretending to scroll on her phone while doing everything in her power not to listen. Not to think about me. Not to picture me naked.

But she would.

I braced a hand against the tile, my head falling forward as the hot water pounded against my back. Steam rose like smoke from a fire I couldn't put out, and the ache that had been pulsing since she landed in that bush—since her eyes locked with mine like she hated how much she still wanted me—intensified to something feral.

I palmed my dick, exhaling sharply through my nose as the pressure surged through me. My hand closed tight, stroking slow, deliberate.

My brain went straight to her. Always her. Her lips parted. Her thighs spread. That sweet, soft gasp when I pushed inside her tight pussy.

I hissed, gripping tighter, moving faster.

I wasn't just turned on . . . I was possessed.

"Fuck," I muttered under my breath, hips rocking as I imagined her slipping into the bathroom, whispering my name, dropping to her knees. Her mouth hot and wet, her eyes locked with mine.

Grabbing some more soap, I slid my fist up and down my shaft, gasping at how good it felt. This was way better than usual. Fucking my hand while my metaphorical dream girl was just outside . . . much better than doing it alone.

My balls tightened, the coil snapping with an almost violent rush.

"Natalie," I groaned loudly as an orgasm crashed through me, my cum splattering against the tiled wall. I wasn't going to wash it off, either. That spot was sacred now. It was practically a shrine. It would give me spank-bank material for weeks, picturing her naked body in this shower with my cum all over the wall.

I stood there a minute longer, trying to pull myself together. The after-shocks still hummed through my body, my hand braced against the slick tile as I took slow, deep breaths.

It had never been like that before. Not once since she'd dumped me.

Because she hadn't just been in my head.

She was twenty feet away.

That changed everything.

When I finally felt like I could walk without falling over, I shut the water off and reached for a towel, making sure it hung low on my hips. I knew what my V did to her. I'd seen her brain short-circuit over it more than once. And now, after almost two years of personal trainers, meal plans, and shirtless photo shoots . . . it had only gotten better.

Weapons-grade abs, thank you very much.

I stepped out of the bathroom like I was walking into battle, and there she was, curled up on the couch with her phone clutched in her hands like it might protect her.

I smirked.

There was no way she hadn't heard me say her name in there.

She didn't look up right away, but I saw her eyes flick—just for a second—before she snapped them back to her screen like she hadn't noticed I was only wearing a towel and all her fantasies.

"Something wrong, sweetheart?" I asked, my voice dipped in velvet and sin as I raked a hand through my damp hair.

She whipped her head up. Her pupils dilated. Her cheeks flushed. Her lips parted for just a second before she snapped her mouth shut like it was a trap and turned away so fast that it was a miracle she didn't give herself whiplash.

I bit back a laugh, sauntering over to my bag on the floor near the fireplace. I bent at the waist, slowly, purposefully, knowing she was looking. Even if she swore she wasn't.

Out of the corner of my eye, I saw her shifting—legs crossing tighter, body tensing, her knuckles white around her phone.

Time to up the stakes.

I stretched.

And let the towel drop.

It hit the hardwood with a soft, innocent little *thud*.

She made a noise.

It wasn't a word. It wasn't even a full gasp. It was a tiny, strangled *squeak*, like a startled chipmunk.

I straightened slowly, rolling my shoulders like my ass wasn't visible right now, and turned my head just in time to see her eyes widen, huge, round, full-on Disney-princess horror—and then her hands slapped over her face.

"Fucking hell!" she screeched in a strangled, *crazy*-sounding voice. "Nope, nope, nope."

And then she bolted.

Straight for the door.

Natalie hated running. So I was kind of mad at myself for not filming such a rare occurrence.

Although, I guess she could have picked up running since she'd left for college. I frowned at that thought.

"Natalie," I called, grinning now, not bothering to move. "Come back. I was going to offer you the bathroom next."

She smacked into the frame on her way out—actually bounced off it—before recovering and disappearing into the hallway, the door swinging shut behind her.

I smirked, bending down to pick up my towel, *very* pleased with myself. Natalie could say what she wanted.

But that girl was not over me.

Natalie

I didn't stop running until I made it down to the lobby, and then I whipped out my phone as I gasped for breath because exercise . . . Turns out it was hard.

> Me: DEFCON 10!

> Riley: Oh good, I was wondering when we would hit that level. Although, I'm pretty sure there are only 5 levels.

> Me: One of you has to come get me.

> Me: Immediately.

> Casey: Now, why would we do that when you're having so much fun.

> Me: . . .

> Riley: The boys have taught you so well.

> Me: I saw his ass.

> Casey: . . .

> Riley: . . .

> Riley: No talking about asses with my flufferkins.

I scoffed. Jace would be reading over her shoulder.

> Me: Go away, Jace. This is a DEFCON 10.

Riley: Sorry about that. Proceed with talking about asses.

Me: I saw it.

Casey: Ok, well, yes, you said that.

Me: And we might be sharing a room.

Casey: WHAT????

Me: Hey, don't be so shouty.

Riley: IT FEELS LIKE A SHOUTY SITUATION!

Casey: How did this happen?

Me: Well, you know how I sometimes don't read my emails?

Casey: You mean you never read your emails. Go on.

Me: Well, I may have missed the email that told me to book my room.

Riley: Did you see if there was anyone else you could room with?

I scoffed, eliciting a look from Margaret at the front desk, who was eyeing me like she knew exactly what had happened upstairs.

This was all her fault.

Me: Of course I tried to find a different roommate. The choices were a bunkhouse with toddlers and plastic sheets or Easton. I did my best. You know how I feel about toddlers.

Riley: What about your grandma?

Casey: The grandmother who's blind?

I blinked at the phone before remembering the football game where I'd said that.

> Me: No, remember. She's not blind. And no, she's not an option.

> Riley: Why not?

> Me: Once I tell you, you're never going to be able to unremember it.

> Riley: Ophelia said to tell you that unremember is not a word. But alrighty then.

> Casey: This is where you woman up. So you saw a hot guy's ass. Cry me a river, Bennett.

I huffed again, and this time Margaret started over with cookies like she could tell I was on the verge of a mental collapse.

I typed out one last hurried text as she got closer.

> Me: This was the energy I needed.

Riley sent a GIF of some guy mooning me, a cartoon one, thank fuck, and I choked on a laugh that came out more like a wheeze. I texted back a skull emoji because I was, in fact, dead.

I took a deep breath and glued what I hoped looked like a composed, friendly smile on my face. Margaret, ever the holiday hostess, swooped in with her bottomless tray of sugar cookies like a well-meaning fairy godmother fueled by butter and flour.

"Here, sweetheart," she said, wiggling the tray in front of me like she knew I was seconds from imploding.

I took one. And then another.

Because if sugar wasn't necessary for this situation, then I don't know what was. Honestly, the only thing that might've helped more was wine, and considering it wasn't even noon yet, cookies would have to do the heavy lifting.

A bell rang as a familiar broad-shouldered figure walked through the front door of the B and B, brushing snow off his jacket, his eyes scanning the room. My stomach unclenched the second I recognized him . . . and then promptly clenched again in a totally different, relieved way.

His face broke into a smile the moment he saw me.

"Natalie-girl," my stepdad, Steve, said, already opening his arms. "I barely got to talk to you last night."

I didn't hesitate.

I launched myself forward, crashing into his chest and melting into his embrace. His arms wrapped around me, strong and familiar, warm and solid. Just . . . Dad.

He smelled like cedarwood and the faintest trace of motor oil, which, somehow, still clung to him even though I knew he hadn't touched an engine in weeks because of all the wedding prep. It was his signature scent. The smell of home. Of scraped knees and science fair projects and late-night heart-to-hearts on the porch swing.

My dad had never been the kind of man to hold back affection, not with me, and not with my sister. He hugged like he meant it, like he was trying to protect you from the world, if only for a moment.

I squeezed my eyes shut and pressed my face into the soft flannel of his jacket, blinking fast. It didn't matter that I was a grown woman, I was always going to need my dad.

I didn't tell many people that Steve wasn't actually my biological father. My real father, Terry—my birth dad, I guess—had once been the picture of perfection. Smiling in Christmas photos, camping with us in the summer. Until one day, he got stationed in Hawaii for work. And three months in, he called my mom in tears, drunk and confessing to a hookup in a bar.

As if that wasn't enough of a gut punch, the woman got pregnant. My mom tried to forgive him, God bless her, but it unraveled everything. He left that Christmas before she could even file for divorce.

My perfect father who'd once been part of my *perfect* family—he'd never come back. He'd never called. He'd never sent a card. He'd simply disappeared.

Enter Steve.

He married my mom when I was nine, after a year of being the kindest, most patient man in existence. He was there for everything—every scraped knee, every missed bus, every ridiculous school talent show.

He never acted like he was filling someone else's shoes.

He just built us a whole new pair.

From then on, he became the only man I would ever call Dad. He'd adopted Paige and me, and I carried his name proudly. He'd never once made me feel like I was anything less than his. Not for a second.

But . . . the lessons from my bio father had stayed.

Like tiny paper cuts I kept reopening without realizing. I think it's why I'd pulled the rip cord on Easton the second LA had become a reality. Like I'd seen warning signs that didn't actually exist. I'd convinced myself it was better to leave than get left. Better to tear it down myself than wait for someone else to light the match.

I knew for a fact that Steve and my mom had a rule in their marriage about no overnights . . . and I was pretty sure that one had *Mom* written all over it. Because if a man was close by, he was less likely to forget who he was coming home to. Or at least that would be her thinking.

"I don't think you should go back to school," Dad said with a wink, even though he was as rabid of a Tennessee fan as I was. He'd painted the garage orange and white one summer, and he refused to let anyone park in it until football season ended.

"We miss you too much," he added, tugging me into another quick squeeze.

"Missed you too, Dad." My voice came out muffled against his chest, thick with emotion. Honestly, way too much emotion, considering the number of inflatable reindeer staring at me from the window display over there.

He pulled back, his hands firm on my shoulders as he studied me. "You been eating enough? You look too skinny."

I rolled my eyes, the smile creeping back onto my face. "I'm fine. You're the one who needs to lay off the protein shakes. You're starting to look like you're trying to fight Thor."

He snorted, pleased with himself. "Hey, old man's gotta stay in shape. I've got to keep your mom interested somehow."

"Please stop talking," I begged, pretending to gag as I backed away. "There are Christmas cookies here. I don't want to associate them with . . . that."

His expression sobered a bit, and he gave me the *dad look*—part concern, part curiosity, and one part the overwhelming urge to fix something he wasn't sure was broken. "You sure, sweetheart? School and work going okay? I've been picking up extra hours at the shop just in case . . . you know, if you need anything."

That familiar ache flared in my chest, the one that always showed up when he tried to do more than he had to. He'd stepped into our lives and hadn't stopped trying to prove himself since . . . like loving us wasn't enough on its own.

"Dad, I promise. I'm good. The grant covers everything."

Even as I said it, the words tasted like a lie. Not because the grant *didn't* cover everything. But because I now knew exactly who was behind it.

For some reason I didn't tell my dad about that, though. Nor did I tell him about the fact that I was trapped in a bed-and-breakfast with my movie-star ex-boyfriend who I'd just seen naked in our shared suite.

Nope.

That little nugget was getting shoved into a box and duct-taped shut until further notice.

"I'm good," I repeated, louder this time, like I could force it to be true.

Dad studied me for another beat, and for a second I thought he might push. But then his eyes crinkled at the corners, and he nodded, ruffling my hair with one calloused hand.

From across the lobby, a high-pitched cackle echoed like a warning bell.

My head whipped around just in time to see MeMaw perched on a velvet love seat by the fireplace, sipping cocoa from a mug shaped like Santa's butt and eyeing me like she knew *everything*.

Which, honestly, she probably did.

MeMaw had powers. Unspoken, terrifying, possibly telepathic grand-mother powers.

I turned back to Dad and forced a laugh. "I'm fine," I said, my voice wobbling like a busted ornament.

But I wasn't.

I definitely wasn't.

CHAPTER 8

Natalie

The bar was buzzing with holiday energy, all glitter and jingle and very loud Mariah Carey. Twinkling Christmas lights were strung across the ceiling like a net of cheer and poor electrical decisions, and garlands wrapped around every beam like the building itself had gotten stuck in a tinsel tornado. A DJ in an ugly sweater that read SLEIGH ALL DAY was spinning upbeat remixes of Christmas classics, and everyone was in such a good mood it was actually starting to feel suspicious.

My sister looked like a literal heroine, glowing with post-engagement sparkle and bridal glee as she clung to Levi, who had the dreamy smile of a man in love and was also slightly buzzed on eggnog. Their joint bachelor/bachelorette party was officially in full swing—the first stop on the weeklong wedding train to matrimony. Everyone was disgustingly festive. Disgustingly in love. Disgustingly perfect.

And me? I was on the verge of needing a full-body exorcism just to stay upright.

Because Easton was here.

Somewhere.

Lurking. Like a sexy, brooding Christmas spirit of heartbreak past.

I hadn't seen him yet, but I *felt* him. Like some kind of soul-splitting sixth sense that whispered *You're about to humiliate yourself again—run.*

And I wasn't nearly drunk enough to deal with it yet.

I'd spent the rest of today successfully avoiding him while I helped Paige with wedding stuff. I was pretty sure, though, that I wouldn't be able to avoid him tonight.

"Come on, Nat!" a bubbly voice called, and before I could escape, Ellie, one of our high school friends, slid a sparkly red cocktail into my hand like she was passing me a grenade.

"It's called Jingle Juice," she chirped, winking. "Basically Christmas in a cup. Drink up!"

I pasted on my *I'm fine* smile, nodded like a bobblehead, and threw back almost the entire glass like it was NyQuil on a sick day.

It tasted like cranberry juice, peppermint vodka, and maybe cinnamon? And definitely regret. A lot of regret.

Then I heard it.

The giggle.

Not just any giggle. *That* giggle. The one that sounded like high-pitched fairy bells of female thirst. It was the giggle that followed Easton Maddox around like a parade of desperate puppies.

Which meant . . . he had entered the building.

Mayday. Mayday.

That giggle was an obnoxious sound that also came out of my mouth when faced with his perfection, so it was best that I didn't look over at him.

Wouldn't want to embarrass myself any more than I already had running out of the room after I'd seen his ass.

It was a really good ass, though.

I did what any mature, grounded adult woman would do in that moment. I fled.

Okay, not *fled*, exactly . . . but I did speed-walk to the nearest bar like my heels were on fire and the bartender had a fire extinguisher.

The man behind the counter looked up as I approached, offering a smile so dazzling I felt like I should be paying admission. Blonde, tan, and clearly someone who'd rehearsed his smolder in front of the mirror, he leaned forward with practiced ease.

"What can I get you?" he asked, his voice like melted caramel and confidence.

Under normal circumstances, I would've flirted. At least a little. I might've tossed my hair, bitten my lip, leaned in. But right now? He might as well have been a decorative reindeer.

Absolutely nothing.

No spark. No flutter. Not even a flicker.

It was like Easton had short-circuited my entire romantic operating system and left nothing but static in his wake.

"Whatever has the most alcohol," I said dryly, throwing back the rest of my original cocktail before propping my elbows on the bar.

He chuckled, the sound low and smooth, clearly not deterred by my lack of enthusiasm. "Rough night already? I thought you just got here?"

He winked, and it wasn't even a subtle wink. It was one of those Hello-I-have-been-watching-you-since-you-entered-the-premises winks.

Normally I would love that kind of stalker behavior . . . It was kind of my brand. I mean, the fanfic I used to write in middle school . . . A lot of stalkers in those pages.

But clearly Easton Maddox had broken me in ways I hadn't fully accepted yet. Because I felt *nothing*. Zero. Zilch. Nada.

The flirting bounced off my very dry, very unimpressed vaginal region like rubber bullets off a tank. There was a tumbleweed rolling through my pants. My hoo-ha had packed a bag and moved to another zip code.

"You have no idea," I muttered as I stared at the rows of liquor bottles behind him, pretending to inspect them while really just avoiding everything else.

"Well," he said cheerfully, reaching for a laminated drink menu with the sort of practiced flair that told me this wasn't his first rodeo with sad girls in sequin dresses. "The bride and groom really went all out with the Christmas spirit. Let's see what's on tonight's festive hit list."

He cleared his throat like he was preparing to perform at Carnegie Hall. "We've got Santa's Slushy Surprise, Reindeer Rum Punch, Nog on the Rocks, and my personal favorite"—he paused dramatically—"the Ho-ho-ho-tini."

I blinked at him. "Are . . . are those real?"

He tapped the menu solemnly. "Straight from the bride's brain to this laminated piece of art."

Of course. It was all very Paige. Only she could find a way to combine eggnog, puns, and alcohol into a theme.

I blinked at him, wondering how long it had taken my sister to come up with those names. "Which one will make me forget my life the fastest?"

He didn't hesitate. "Reindeer Rum Punch." The conviction in his voice was almost unsettling. "It'll take you to the edge of oblivion and then back again just in time for 'All I Want for Christmas Is You.'"

That . . . actually sounded perfect.

"As long as it doesn't end with me sobbing into a plastic wreath or flashing the valet, we're good," I muttered, sinking onto the barstool like my feet had declared a mutiny. These shoes were not made for walking. They were made for standing still and looking hot.

Another reason why I needed to ride that fine line between drunk and wasted.

He winked again. Maybe something was wrong with his eye. He was doing that an awful lot.

He smirked as he grabbed a shaker and started working his mixology magic. "So," he said, tilting his head as he tossed in a splash of something bright red and alarming. "Why's a girl as pretty as you looking like she's carrying the weight of the world? Hate the bride and groom? Hate Christmas? Secretly afraid of tinsel?"

I snorted. "None of those. It's . . . just one of those nights."

"Ah," he said knowingly, tossing in another liquor with a little extra flourish. "Let me guess—man trouble?"

I didn't respond, but I felt my lips twitch despite myself. He was persistent, I'd give him that.

A minute later, he set a bright red drink in front of me. "Here you go. One Reindeer Rum Punch. And there's a bonus that comes with this drink."

I lifted an eyebrow as I brought the glass to my lips and took a sip. Wow. That was *a lot* of rum. And some other sweet flavor I couldn't really identify but was actually delicious. I kind of loved it.

"What kind of bonus?" I finally asked, lifting the glass to my lips and taking another long sip. Honestly, I only wanted a bonus if it came in the form of a tranquilizer dart or three more shots of tequila.

The bartender leaned in like he was about to whisper sweet nothings into my soul. "My number."

I snorted. Loudly. In a very unsexy, very nasal kind of way. He flinched like I'd just slapped him with a snow-dusted tree branch.

His hopeful face fell. "You're not even going to pretend to flirt back?"

I sighed, tapping my fingers against the sticky bar. "Sorry. It's not you. It's me."

"Classic line," he said, trying to turn his pout into something charming. Bless his heart, he was trying so hard. But I wasn't biting. And not just because my ovaries were still on a full-blown strike.

I needed to get out of here. Unfortunately, the other bar—the one without the overly ambitious flirting—was all the way across the room.

Where he was.

And then it happened again. The sound. That unmistakable, shrill, hormone-laced giggling.

I froze. My fingers tightened around my drink.

Don't do it, Natalie.

Don't be that girl.

But I was already glancing over my shoulder before my brain could tell my neck *no*.

And there he was.

Easton. Fucking. Maddox.

Leaning against the opposite bar like he'd been sent straight from every erotic dream I'd ever had. He was wearing a dark green sweater that hugged his body like it had taken an oath to ruin lives. And it was succeeding. The sleeves were pushed up just enough to show off the veins in his forearms . . . veins that had absolutely no business looking that good.

He laughed at something someone said, his stupid jawline doing that thing where it flexed and made me irrationally angry. His hair fell into his face, artfully tousled and just the right amount of *I didn't try but look at me being perfect anyway.* Unlike the bartender's gelled mess, I knew for a fact that Easton's version was real. Real and dangerous.

My fists tightened in his hair, holding him to me as his tongue licked through my folds. He forced two fingers inside me, and I whimpered as my orgasm approached . . .

NOPE.

I threw back the rest of my drink like it was holy water and I needed to exorcise the memory of that particular orgasm immediately.

Fuck.

I looked around the bar, trying to find a distraction, but all I saw were a bunch of wide-eyed girls clustered around Easton like they were auditioning for *The Bachelor: Mistletoe Edition.* They were giggling and flipping their hair, glancing over their shoulders like one seductive glance would unlock the key to his heart and his . . . assets.

Idiots.

Okay, no. That wasn't fair.

I was a girl's girl. I was. And I supported all women in all their pursuits of hotness and happiness.

But I was also *human*.

And watching those women fawn over him—after knowing what it felt like to have him in my bed, in my life, in my soul—it hit a nerve. A frayed, raw, I-cried-into-a-Blue-Bell-ice-cream-container-the-night-we-broke-up kind of nerve.

This exact scenario was why I had broken things off in the first place. Because no matter how much Easton said I was the only one, I'd always worried . . . *what if he looked back?*

And then . . . he did look.

But not at them.

His gaze swept lazily across the room, like he wasn't about to set me on fire with a single glance.

And then it landed on me.

Direct. Steady. Devastating.

Like I'd been the only one in the room the entire time.

I stiffened, trying to pretend I was fully focused on the half-melted ice cube in my glass. But I could *feel* him watching. Like an actual heat wave was passing through my body.

Every time I peeked? Yep. Still looking. A small, maddening smirk curving those stupid lips like he could *see* what he was doing to me. Like he *knew* how hard I was trying not to care.

Which, of course he did.

Because as much as I wished it wasn't true, besides being heartbroken, I hadn't changed that much in the last couple of years. And if there was anyone who knew me . . . it was him.

I groaned under my breath. "Why can't he have hairy warts?"

"Because that would be too convenient," Paige said, popping up beside me like a gremlin.

She was grinning at me, already holding her own festive cocktail—some sparkly thing with a rosemary sprig and actual glitter floating in it. She was wearing a sparkly white cocktail dress, and she looked like the smuggest little shit I'd ever seen.

"You should just give in," she said casually, sipping her drink like she wasn't the devil incarnate.

"Aren't you supposed to be circling the room, thanking guests, doing the bride thing?" I asked, nodding at the crowd of people milling around with their matching Christmas-themed drink cozies.

Paige raised one perfectly groomed brow. "Why would I circle the room when the entertainment is *right here*?"

My eyes narrowed.

"I've already exchanged five bets that you crack tonight," she added gleefully, swirling her drink with a flourish.

I rolled my eyes, not surprised in the least that she'd done that. "That's rude. At least allow me to be in on the bet."

"*Everyone's* betting on you," she said brightly. "Aunt Kathy has fifty bucks on a full makeout by the bonfire, and Levi thinks you'll fake trip and fall into his arms like you're in one of Easton's movies."

"I *should* trip," I muttered, "just to take him out."

She didn't even bother responding to that, just took a slow sip of her drink and gave me a pointed look.

"Don't look at me like that," I snapped. "You're the one who invited him."

"Levi invited him," she said with a shrug. "It's not my fault your unresolved sexual tension is the most entertaining part of the evening."

"I hope you get glitter in your eyes."

She snickered, entirely unfazed, as if the threat of ocular sparkle damage meant nothing to her. "I hope you get laid. We all have our holiday wishes."

Before I could come up with an appropriately scathing retort, the DJ's voice boomed through the speakers, sounding way too cheerful for someone in charge of ruining lives. "All right, folks! It's karaoke time! Who's ready to get onstage and embarrass themselves in the name of Christmas?"

Paige let out a little squeal, immediately bouncing like she'd just been told Taylor Swift was about to enter the building. "Oh! We're doing 'Baby, It's Cold Outside!'" she declared, practically lunging over to where Levi was standing and grabbing him by the arm. He looked alarmed but also resigned in the way men in long-term relationships often do.

Levi, bless him, let himself be dragged. "Can we do the version where she *definitely* wants to stay and it's not creepy?" he asked as he stumbled after her.

"That's the one I queued up," Paige called over her shoulder, her drink still somehow intact. "We're the progressive couple everyone wants to be!"

I blinked after them. "Great. Feminist Christmas karaoke. That's . . . fine."

As they climbed onstage and the crowd started cheering, I turned back to my drink like it held the answers to life's deepest questions.

Maybe drinking myself into oblivion really *should* be the game plan tonight.

*   *   *

Karaoke was still going strong . . . which was to say, it was as wildly enter-taining as it was an outright assault on the ears. I was equal parts impressed and deeply horrified.

My family and friends were not just *bad* at performing . . . they were offensively, enthusiastically terrible. If there were an award for Most Likely to Shatter a Champagne Flute with Their Voice, we would've swept the category. And that might've been generous.

MeMaw had already brought the house down with her deeply disturb-ing, pelvis-thrust-laden rendition of "Firework" by Katy Perry. There were hand gestures. There was a wind machine someone had dragged in from who-knows-where. There were sparkles involved, and I'm still not sure from *where* on her body they originated.

After that, the night had turned into a slow, glorious train wreck.

At the moment, Susie Cummins—who was, yes, still as unfortunately named as ever—had just finished what I *think* was supposed to be "Jingle Bells." Somewhere between the second verse and the chorus, though, she'd gotten confused and started belting the lyrics to "Tubthumping" with such slurred conviction that the whole room joined in. Now there was serious talk about adding Chumbawamba to every holiday playlist from here on out.

And for a moment . . . I was actually kind of enjoying myself.

I'd even smiled once.

And then it happened.

Easton stepped onto the stage.

And every molecule of joy in my body screamed and fled.

There were cheers, naturally; he looked like a god among mortals in that damn sweater. A few gasps followed, mostly from the people who hadn't grown up with him and were just now putting two and two together. Judging by the way they were grabbing one another's arms and pointing at him like he'd descended from Mount Olympus instead of driving here from town, they'd just realized *Easton Maddox*—actual movie star, human panty melter—was in the room.

He didn't grab the mic and sing like a normal human.

Oh no.

Instead, he looked right at me.

Don't do it, Easton. Don't do it. Save yourself from being murdered.

"Natalie," he said into the microphone, all low and smooth, because

Hollywood had obviously taken his self-preservation skills from him. "Come up here."

I almost dropped my drink. I clutched it to my chest like it was a holy relic. Surely he didn't just—

"Come on, Trouble," he said again, and his grin widened into something dangerous. "Don't make me beg."

Trouble?

He said that out loud. With sound. In front of *people*.

I shook my head with slow, dramatic defiance.

The crowd, the traitorous masses, did *not* appreciate my resistance. They began to chant. Yes. *Chant.* "Na-ta-lie! Na-ta-lie!" Like this was a gladiator ring and I was about to go fight for my dignity's life.

And, of course, Paige, my beloved, evil sister, was no help. She appeared at my elbow like a drunk Christmas fairy, cheeks pink, eyes shiny, and beaming like she'd just won the lottery.

"Come on, Natty-kins," she slurred gleefully, yanking on my arm like she'd just called dibs on humiliating me first. She jostled my drink—the *fifth* one, probably? Maybe sixth?—and I shot her a look of betrayal.

"Paige," I hissed. "This is the kind of thing people never recover from. I will die up there. My soul will leave my body and haunt you forever."

"You'll be fine," she chirped. "And if you're not, I'll play this at your funeral!"

That was not the comfort she thought it was.

"Natalie," Easton drawled, and the crowd cheered again like he was announcing free puppies.

I flipped him off. Then downed the last of my drink like it was courage in liquid form and rose to face my doom.

"This is how people end up on viral YouTube compilations," I muttered as I stomped forward, wobbling precariously on my heels.

Easton winked at me as I stumbled onstage. Unfortunately, it was much sexier than the bartender's eye twitching. And *unfortunately*, it did far different things to my panties.

"I hate you," I whispered, which came out more breathy and less full of loathing than I meant. Which frankly meant that the alcohol had kicked in . . . and I might be in trouble.

"Looking sexy when you're angry is not helping your case," he murmured back, just loud enough for me to hear.

I gave him a glare that would've killed a lesser man. Unluckily for me, Easton Maddox was not a lesser man.

Easton handed me the second mic, making sure that his fingers dragged against mine as he did so. Completely unnecessary if you asked me. I tried to move to the other side of the stage because distance seemed really important right now, but he grabbed my hand and kept me next to him.

I didn't understand how it could still feel like this, like his hand was my home, even after all this time. Maybe I had been cursed that day when he'd walked into my middle school class, and I was going to feel like something was missing for the rest of my life.

Natalie, pull yourself together. Now's not the time to go all morose.

The crowd hooted. The lights twinkled. Somewhere in the back, MeMaw whooped and yelled, "Take it off!" which I was praying wasn't directed at either of us.

The music started, jingle bells with a jazzy undercurrent, and my stomach dropped.

Oh no. No, no, no, no.

"Santa Baby."

He'd picked *"Santa Baby"*?

"I swear to all that is holy, Easton," I muttered under my breath. "I will deck your halls."

"Looking forward to it," he murmured back, his voice dangerously close to my ear.

The intro came and went, and like a true professional, or maybe just a woman on her fifth . . . or sixth drink, I lifted the mic.

"Santa baby . . ."

My voice was breathy, low, borderline sultry—and yes, I regretted *everything*.

I could feel Easton watching me, no doubt a slow grin spreading across his face. He hadn't even sung a note yet, but the smug bastard was already winning.

I continued the song, doing my best not to shrivel into dust under the weight of a hundred pairs of staring eyes—and his. I kept my gaze on the ceiling, knowing one look at him would melt me straight into the floor.

I was halfway through the second verse, cheeks on fire, when his voice joined in—smooth and deep and so unfairly confident it made my knees wobble.

I actually stumbled. *Stumbled*. I forgot the lyrics. I forgot my name.

Easton. Was. Singing.

And he sounded like some kind of Christmas angel who'd had too much whiskey and sin. I wasn't sure how all Hollywood actors seemed to know how to sing . . . but he sure could.

He crooned into the mic like he'd been born on a stage, his grin full of wicked promise as he glanced sideways at me . . . like he knew exactly how unhinged I was going to be after this.

The room was in *shambles*.

Paige was crying with laughter. MeMaw had pulled out her phone and was recording. Someone yelled, "Kiss! Kiss!" which I was going to assume was ironic and not a direct order from the gods of holiday mayhem.

I turned back to the mic, my face on fire, my brain doing everything except cooperating.

Easton leaned in beside me, his voice smooth as silk and full of mock innocence as he delivered his next line. His tone was all charm and wicked suggestion, his eyes practically glowing under the stage lights.

Then he glanced at me again, sideways, sly. His green eyes lit with mischief as his hand slid to the small of my back.

I nearly forgot how to breathe.

Because of course he wasn't just singing.

He was *performing*.

And I was the stage.

I nearly combusted.

We were inches apart now, singing into each other's space, the crowd forgotten, the music just a vehicle for this ridiculous tension that had been steadily smoldering since I fell into that bush.

Easton's voice slid against mine like velvet ribbon, and I hated how much I liked the way it sounded. Smooth, sinful, a little smug. He wasn't just singing . . . he was seducing me. In front of *everyone*.

His fingers ghosted along my bare arm again, like he was testing how many light touches it would take to unravel me completely.

Spoiler alert: we were close.

"Santa baby . . ." I sang, trying to keep my tone light and cheeky, as the lyrics demanded, but the truth was I could barely breathe. My body was screaming *danger*, my brain was buffering, and my ovaries were sending up flares.

He leaned in, his lips barely brushing the mic. "Beeeen . . ."

I almost dropped the mic. Not because I forgot the words. But because his voice had dipped into this husky register that made my thighs clench like he was the lead singer for the boy band I'd crushed on all growing up. I risked a glance at him . . . and immediately regretted it.

Green eyes. Locked on mine. Full of heat and history and the unmistakable spark of a man who *knew* exactly what he was doing.

I snapped my gaze forward again. *Focus, Natalie. You're here to sing and survive, not combust onstage.*

And then he touched me again—just the small of my back this time, as if to "guide me" into the final chorus like he was some kind of chivalrous holiday menace. I knew that touch. Knew how it had once made me feel safe and on fire all at once. Knew that it would haunt me later.

"Santa cutie . . ."

My voice cracked. He smiled.

This was public foreplay, and he was *thriving*. Meanwhile, I was seconds from jumping off the stage and hiding behind the bar with nothing but a bottle of vodka and a plate of reindeer-shaped cookies to comfort me.

The song slowed, our voices blending on the final verse. He turned to face me fully now, like we were alone in this little holiday hellscape. His voice softened, deepened.

"Hurry . . . tonight."

It was criminal. That note. The way he held it. The way he held *me*—not with his hands, but with every inch of his stupid, perfect presence.

The room *exploded* in applause, hoots and hollers filling the air, and someone in the back shouted, "GET MARRIED ALREADY!"

Before I could turn and bolt, Easton *dropped to his knees* like a literal Christmas rom-com hero, his eyes shining, his mouth curved into a grin that could melt the North Pole.

Mic still in hand, he lifted it like he was serenading me personally. "Please, baby," he crooned with a wink. "Hurry down the chimney tonight . . ."

Laughter burst through the crowd. MeMaw screamed, "I'LL OFFICI-ATE RIGHT NOW!" which really didn't help my blood pressure.

My knees wobbled. My chest heaved. And I stared down at him, the world spinning just a little too fast.

"Easton," I whispered because it was the only word I could summon. I wasn't sure if it was a plea or a warning or just me being delirious with lust and nostalgia.

He grinned up at me, all dimpled charm and underlying devastation. But something flickered behind it. Something raw. Something *real*.

"Going to give me what I want, *baby?*" he asked, low and private and almost unsure.

I swallowed hard, the ache behind my ribs blooming into a full-blown ache in my soul. That touch of vulnerability . . . of realness. It caught me off guard. It twisted something inside me that had already been stretched too thin.

"Say something," he murmured, the humor fading from his face, his voice rougher now. "Anything."

I opened my mouth.

Nothing came out.

The crowd was still cheering. Someone somewhere was yelling, "Kiss him!" and I was 99 percent sure MeMaw had climbed onto a chair. But none of it mattered. All I could feel was him. All I could *see* was him.

And that was the problem.

I shoved the mic into Easton's hands, ignoring the way his fingers curled around mine like he didn't want to let go—and *bolted* off the stage.

I needed air.

CHAPTER 9

Natalie

I pushed through the throng of bodies, ignoring the high fives and teasing comments like I hadn't just fled a karaoke stage like it was on fire. My hand found the door to the alley, and I shoved it open, welcoming the slap of cold air like it was salvation. It stung. Good. Maybe it would freeze the chaos boiling beneath my skin.

The night bit at my exposed arms, but I didn't care. I leaned against the cold, unforgiving brick wall, gulping air like it might smother the ache in my chest. Like it might cool the flush in my cheeks or the memory of *his* voice crooning Christmas lyrics like he meant every word.

Would it always feel like this? Would there ever be a time when I could be near him without it cracking open every carefully sealed scar? When I could hear that voice . . . *that name* . . . without feeling like my heart was trying to claw its way out?

"You're a badass bitch, Natalie," I whispered to myself. "You don't cry in alleys over boys. You cry in bathrooms like a *lady*."

And then, because fate was clearly a drama queen, the door behind me creaked open. A gust of humid bar air rushed out, carrying the scent of beer and sugar cookies and the sound of my impending emotional doom.

My stomach dropped.

It was him.

"Natalie."

Just my name. Three syllables, soft and gravelly and rough like it had gotten caught on something on the way out of his throat. I didn't have to turn around to feel the heat of him, standing just a few feet away.

I didn't move. "What do you want, Easton?"

My voice came out sharper than I intended, but maybe that was good. Maybe sharp would keep him at a distance. I wrapped my arms tighter around myself, focused on the twinkling Christmas lights reflecting off a puddle like they might hold the answers to this cosmic disaster of a reunion.

"Why did you follow me?"

"I'd follow you anywhere."

His words were a sucker punch—gentle but powerful, soft but devastating. They hit like a snowball to the chest. The good kind. The worst kind.

His boots crunched softly on the gravel as he took a step closer.

I blinked hard, the world swaying slightly. "What did you just say?" I finally whispered hoarsely, more to the shadows than to him. My fingers pinched my forearm, hard enough to leave a mark, because this *had* to be a dream. A glitch in the simulation. A Christmas movie hallucination brought on by too much rum punch and sexual frustration.

When he didn't answer, I turned toward him, unable to stop myself.

Easton was leaning against the wall a few feet away, hands shoved into the pockets of his coat, his jaw tight, and those stupid, breathtaking green eyes fixed on me like I was something he was afraid to blink and miss.

I couldn't help it, I traced the stubble on his face, a brief thought flickering through my head, wondering how the man in front of me would compare with the boy he'd been.

How much more experience he had . . .

Don't think about that, Natalie!

Easton looked out of place in the cold, grungy alley, like now he could only belong under stage lights or on a movie screen. Except those eyes? Those were mine. They always had been.

And they were burning me alive.

"Don't say things like that," I said, my voice cracking under the weight of it all. "You don't mean them."

His brow furrowed, that cocky grin nowhere in sight. He pushed off the wall and stepped toward me, each movement slow, deliberate—like I was a deer about to bolt and he didn't want to spook me.

"What if I do?"

I instinctively stepped back only to be stopped by the wall behind me. The cold seeped through my clothes, but I barely felt it. He was too close now. Not quite touching . . . but close enough that I could feel the tension crackling in the space between us like static before a lightning strike.

"We're over, Easton," I said, trying to sound firm. Like I believed it. "Remember? We agreed it was for the best. It's been a long time. We don't need to do this. We don't need to rehash things just because of this wedding."

He tilted his head, eyes narrowing. "*We* agreed?"

The sarcasm hit hard, sharp as sleet.

"I don't remember getting a say in it at all, actually."

My breath caught, shame threading through me like smoke. I looked away, but that only made it worse . . . because now I could feel his gaze travel across my face, lingering at my mouth like he could still taste me there.

"Regardless, Easton. We've been over for a long time."

The words came out stronger than I felt, because if I had one more second to breathe him in, I was going to forget how sentences worked.

"Then why do I feel like this?"

His voice was low now . . . rough, frayed around the edges like it had been rubbed raw by years of silence. He moved closer, slow and deliberate, like he was stalking a truth he didn't want to admit.

"Why can't I stop thinking about you? Tell me when this is supposed to leave my system, Natalie, because fuck knows I've tried."

My heart thudded so hard I was sure he could hear it. Maybe the whole damn town could.

The rawness in his voice knocked the breath from my lungs, scraping away every wall I'd spent the last two years trying to build. His gaze locked on mine, searing and desperate, and so heartbreakingly real it felt like a punch straight to the soul.

He was too close now. His scent, pure temptation, wrapped around me like a cloak, dragging old memories out of their shallow graves.

"We've both moved on," I forced out, but the words sounded tinny. Weak. Like I was trying to convince the wrong audience. Namely, myself.

"You have a whole other life now."

"A life that feels like nothing when you're not in it," he said, stepping even closer, his voice like fire wrapped in silk. "Guess what, Trouble? I was right. None of it matters if you're not there."

I blinked up at him, my pulse hammering. An alarm screamed in my brain. *Danger, Natalie, danger.* But my body wasn't listening. It had gone rogue the second he'd said my name.

He was everywhere. His heat, his breath, the brush of his coat against my shirt, the way his eyes didn't look *at* me, but *into* me. I felt stripped down to my most vulnerable layer.

"You don't mean that," I whispered, even as my voice trembled. Because I wanted so badly to believe he did. That this wasn't just a heat-of-the-moment confession or some whiskey-laced nostalgia.

He reached out, his fingers brushing my cheek, and I felt it all the way to my knees. I shivered . . . not from the cold, but from the soft reverence in his touch.

And then I leaned into it. Just a little. Just enough.

I shouldn't have.

An image flashed in my mind. Him on the red carpet beside his first costar, Raylyn Lareux. Her perfect hair, her even more perfect collarbone, his arm slung casually around her like he belonged there. I'd stared at that photo for an hour, trying not to crumble. Then I'd gone out and let some faceless guy kiss me, trying to drown out what I'd seen.

Just in case you were wondering . . . I'd still felt everything.

"We'll get it out of our systems," I blurted, the idea crashing into me like a drunk wedding guest. Desperate, messy, maybe genius.

Easton blinked. "What?"

"There's clearly . . . something. Lingering tension. Leftover feelings. Ghosts of orgasms past. *Whatever*. But it's obvious that this—us—it could never work again."

He scoffed, and I immediately pressed a finger to his lips.

"Don't." I narrowed my eyes. "Don't say anything romantic or sweet or funny. We are being *logical*."

His lips twitched under my finger, and he kissed it. *Kissed it.*

Like he was trying to destroy me with that mouth alone.

I snatched my hand away like he'd burned me. "You've officially lost your mind."

"And yet," he murmured, inching even closer, "you're still here."

I realized, suddenly, that his hand had found its way to my waist. His fingers had slipped beneath the hem of my dress, where they now brushed slow, hypnotic circles against my skin. My stomach fluttered like it had swallowed an entire flock of nervous pigeons.

"I don't know, Nat," he said, voice low and frayed like something unraveling. His hand tightened on my waist, fingers digging in just enough to make my pulse stutter. "I don't know how I'm supposed to play at pretending this is casual."

I froze.

He leaned in, his breath brushing the shell of my ear, his body a whisper away from mine.

"When I've already gone years starving for . . ."

My mouth went dry. "Starving for what?"

He leaned in more, his chest brushing against mine, the contact so light it felt like a promise. His eyes, those devastating green eyes, pinned me in place.

"A taste," he said, his voice like a caress. "Of you."

His words settled into my skin like heat, like a threat, like a promise. And then his hand slid up, cupping my jaw, his thumb brushing just beneath my cheekbone with the kind of gentleness that made something inside me break. His fingers pressed into my skin—not roughly, but firmly, like he was holding something precious, like if he let go, I'd disappear into the cold night air.

I'd been missing that. The one-night stands I'd collected like sad trophies to try to forget him . . . the football player who had cheated on me without a thought. None of them had touched me like this. Like they couldn't believe I was real. No one had ever kissed me like they were both worshiping me and punishing themselves at the same time.

Easton's lips touched mine . . . and the world stopped.

I forgot the cold. I forgot the party. I forgot the past and the future and the part where I was supposed to have moved on. All I knew was *him*. The soft press of his mouth against mine. The heat of his breath. The way he tasted like mint, whiskey, and something unreasonably addictive.

It wasn't just a kiss.

It was a slow, soul-level detonation.

His mouth moved against mine with maddening control . . . soft and coaxing, then suddenly demanding. His tongue teased at my bottom lip, licking into my mouth with long, deep sweeps that had my knees quivering. A low sound vibrated in his chest, and the noise shot through me like thunder.

"Fuck," he groaned, pulling back just far enough to look into my eyes, his voice wrecked. "I can't believe you made me live without this."

The words hit me like a sucker punch to the chest, but I couldn't make myself pull away. I couldn't make myself tell him to stop. Not when my entire body was begging me to do the opposite.

He tilted his head and kissed me again, deeper this time, his thumb brushing the corner of my mouth like he was savoring the taste of me. Like he'd missed it, too. Like he'd counted every day since he last had it.

And fuck, I wanted to scream *Me too.*

My arms wound around his neck before I could think better of it, my fingers slipping into his hair like I was starving. His other hand dropped to my hip, and he tugged me flush against him, molding to mine, heat pouring off him in waves, and then—oh. Oh.

There it was.

His dick.

Hard. Massive. *Dangerous.*

The pressure of it against my stomach made my breath hitch. I froze, barely daring to glance down.

Dear Santa, I take back everything bad I ever said about Christmas.

My mouth went dry. My brain short-circuited. Because Easton's dick—*the dick*—wasn't just good. It was weaponized. Like, certified large-scale emergency, evacuate-the-building kind of weaponized. It was very much not exaggerated by memory. It was *worse*. Or better. Depending on your survival instincts.

And apparently, mine had left the chat.

I'd tried to convince myself I'd just been remembering it wrong. Everything must have felt huge as a virgin with zero experience with any dicks but his. But nope. I hadn't been imagining anything. The huge pole trying to find its home was like a giant boa constrictor.

And I was thirsty for it.

Easton smirked against my mouth like he *knew*, the arrogant bastard, and I felt the low, lazy roll of his hips, like he was deliberately letting me *feel* what I'd been missing.

When he pulled back, I chased his lips, whimpering in a blind, lust-driven haze.

"Fuck," I whispered, eyes fluttering. "You're still ridiculously big."

"You're still ridiculously sexy," he shot back, his lips brushing mine like he couldn't stay away for more than a second. "We all have our curses."

I whimpered, *actually whimpered*, like some kind of Victorian ghost with a corset problem. My fingers tightened in his hair, and when he pulled back again, just slightly, I followed him instinctively, breathless and wild.

"I need . . ." I didn't even know what I was about to say. A glass of water? A fire extinguisher? A lobotomy?

"Don't worry, baby. I'm going to give us both what we need," Easton murmured, the words rough and reverent as he dropped to his knees in front of me.

Time fractured.

The brick wall scraped against my back, grounding me in the here and now, but everything else, the cold air, the noise from the bar, the ache in my chest that hadn't eased since I walked away . . . faded to nothing.

He looked up at me like I was something holy.

"Easton." I gasped, already trembling as his hands slid over my thighs and pushed up my dress. His palms were warm and steady, anchoring me even as they made me feel like I might fall apart. He leaned in, dragging the bridge of his nose up the center of my panties, inhaling like he was starved for the scent of me.

"Fuck," he groaned. "You're even better than I remembered."

Easton shoved my panties aside, his fingers dragging over my smooth skin before he slid them through my folds.

"So fucking wet for me, sweetheart," he breathed, a smug smile on his lips.

The way he said it—like he was wrecked with the knowledge—shouldn't have sent a shiver down my spine, but it did. It was the honesty in it. The ache.

"I . . ." I tried to say something, anything. But my body was louder than my voice, already rocking against his touch.

"Tell me what you want," he said, fingers teasing, hovering just shy of where I needed him.

I was literally shaking against the brick wall of the building as I tried to focus on not collapsing into a puddle. The cold didn't seem to exist as I stared down at him, flames licking across my skin.

"Do it," I rasped. "Make me come." The words fell out before I could catch them.

"Fuck, I missed you," he murmured, sliding two fingers inside me like he'd never stopped knowing how to touch me. I bit down on my lip, my head falling back against the wall as he rubbed against that perfect spot inside me. His thumb circled my clit in slow, devastating strokes, and I sobbed.

He pressed a kiss to my inner thigh, his stubble scraping my skin in the way I used to crave. "You're so tight," he groaned as his fingers fucked in and out of me in the perfect rhythm.

Had it always felt this good? This right?

Fuck. It had.

"Such a greedy pussy," he murmured, pulling his fingers out and lightly slapping my core.

"Easton," I panted, my body bowing toward him as he thrust his fingers back inside me. I felt like I was flying and unraveling at the same time.

"I fucking love it." He forced another finger inside, and I thrashed against him, my body trying to stretch the way he wanted me to. Easton ripped my underwear off like it had offended him, throwing them somewhere behind him before he caught my thigh and lifted it over his shoulder.

"Fuck." I gasped as he buried his face against my sex, his tongue sucking and flicking as it moved through my folds. I gripped his hair, holding him against me, well aware how intimate this was.

I'd never admit this, but I hadn't let anyone go down on me since I'd broken up with him. It had felt too personal . . . too much.

And now here I was giving it to my ex in the back alley of a bar.

Classy, Natalie. Real classy.

That thought slipped away as his hand squeezed my ass and his lips sucked hard on my clit.

Fuck being classy. This felt far too good.

I squeezed my thighs, crying out at the sensation of his fingers and his tongue and his rough stubble scratching against my skin.

"Missed this, baby. You taste like fucking heaven," he growled as his tongue replaced his fingers in my core, lapping in and out of me for a moment before he pulled away. I watched wide-eyed as he unbuttoned his jeans, his giant cock springing out, the tip angry and hot-looking. I was in a fever dream as pre-cum dribbled from his head, dripping on the concrete beneath him.

My mouth was literally watering staring at it.

"Can't have me coming in my pants when we're going to have to go back in there after this," he rasped.

"Right." I gasped, feeling like I might be able to come just from watching him start to jack himself off.

Hearing him in the shower today . . . another thing I'd never admit, it had almost broken me.

This, though, this was *definitely* going to break me.

Easton went back to work, and my hands fisted in his hair as I thrashed against his face. Fuck. This was another reason that I hadn't even bothered.

I was quite sure that no other guy could ever eat me out like this. Easton gave me head like it was his favorite thing in the world. Like he actually craved it. He was moaning as he licked through my folds, tonguing my clit as his hand that wasn't fucking into me pulled at his dick.

I panted, arching against his face as he forced another finger inside me.

Sucking and licking, he pushed me closer to the edge.

"Yes, yes, yes," I chanted, about shrieking when his finger suddenly grazed *there*.

The bar door started to open, and he ripped his face out from between my legs. "Get the fuck out of here," he growled, sounding a little . . . crazy. The door slammed shut so fast I wasn't even sure who'd tried to come out—who might've seen what we were doing.

But Easton didn't care.

He got right back to work, like he needed to worship me to stay alive, tonguing my clit as everything in me tightened.

"So close," I breathed.

He growled against me, and that sound alone might've tipped me over the edge. But then his fingers curled just right, and the orgasm crashed through me so violently that my scream was swallowed by the night air. My body thrashed against his mouth, every muscle seizing as the world turned white.

Tears were sliding down my cheeks from how good it felt.

Easton didn't give me time to think. "On your knees," he suddenly commanded, and without a thought I dropped to the cold ground, still shaking, my heart hammering against my ribs like it was trying to warn me of what I already knew—this was dangerous. This was everything.

Easton's hand was tight around himself, his chest rising and falling in hard, ragged pants. His eyes were wild, burning with something too bright to name. "Open up, Trouble."

I did. Obediently. Like I always had for him.

A strangled gasp erupted from his chest as he came, ropes of cum hitting my tongue and my face and my neck as he fucked his fist. I swallowed what I could, moaning at the flavor of him. It was so much better than I'd remembered. I licked my lips, trying to capture each drop as my fingers scooped up the sticky mess on my chin and chest.

Easton just watched.

His gaze burned. His breathing ragged.

We stayed like that, our gasps filling the air around us, our eyes tangled in a silent war as he watched me taste him.

Then sense started to return, slowly, like creeping frost.

I froze, my finger still pressed to my tongue.

What the hell had just happened?

I had thought, stupidly, that maybe this would *get him out of my system.* That I'd finally feel closure. Like I'd scratched the itch and could walk away clean.

But no. I wanted him.

Even more.

My whole body still ached for him, my skin burning where he'd touched me, my heart pounding with the echo of everything we hadn't said.

Fuck. Fuck. Fuck.

I grabbed the front of his shirt, yanking him toward me, and frantically used the fabric to wipe the remaining slickness from my chest.

"Natalie," he murmured, but I couldn't stay to see what he wanted to talk about. I scrambled to my feet, practically sprinting up the alley to where the street beckoned me like a safe haven.

The cold air burned my lungs as I ran, my heels slipping on the wet pavement.

"Natalie, wait—"

Nope. Not happening. Because if I waited, I might look back. And if I looked back, I might *go back.* And if I went back . . .

We all knew how that story ended.

I shoved through the front doors of the bar like I was storming a battlefield, weaving around a couple pressed against the wall in a sloppy, open-mouthed embrace. The music was louder now—too loud—the bass thumping so hard it vibrated in my chest, but none of it could drown out the noise in my head.

I beelined for a different bar across the room. New bartender. New location. New identity, maybe?

Because the last one? The one who'd let her ex kneel in front of her like a sinner in a confessional and *come undone* in an alley behind a karaoke bar? That version of her needed to go into witness protection.

"Whiskey," I barked, sliding onto the barstool like a woman on a mission. "And make it a double."

The bartender, a guy with tattooed forearms and an eyebrow piercing, barely blinked before pouring.

I grabbed the glass and knocked it back in one go, relishing the burn. It chased down the taste of him still clinging to my lips, my tongue, my soul.

Fuck.

What was wrong with me?

I tapped the bar for another, throat tight, stomach twisted, and lifted the second drink to my lips just as the hairs on the back of my neck rose like a warning flare.

I didn't have to turn around.

I knew he was there.

Easton's presence rolled over me like a fog . . . thick, suffocating, laced with memories I didn't want but couldn't forget. I could feel him at my back, feel the weight of his stare burrowing into the soft, cracked places I'd spent years patching up.

I swallowed hard, then took another sip. Slower this time. Like it made me seem more in control. Like I wasn't completely falling apart on the inside.

The stool next to me scraped across the floor, and my sister—because of course—slid in beside me, her face flushed with alcohol and a little too much *glee*.

She propped her elbows on the bar and gave me a once-over.

Then she glanced over her shoulder. To him. Still standing near the back exit, arms crossed, jaw tight, eyes trained on me like I was some fragile bird he'd broken and didn't know how to fix.

And then her gaze slid back to me.

Her smirk was slow. Sharp. A dagger dipped in glitter.

"Guess I won my bet," she said casually, like I hadn't just emotionally combusted behind a dumpster.

I scowled and threw back another shot.

The warmth spread through my veins, but it wasn't enough to erase the truth—

I was screwed.

CHAPTER 10

Natalie

Pain.

That was the first thing I registered. A dull, throbbing ache that pounded behind my eyes like a sledgehammer. Every muscle in my body had apparently filed a formal complaint, and I wanted to burrow under the covers and never emerge again.

The second thing I noticed?

I wasn't alone.

The realization slithered in slowly, creeping through the fog of my hangover. A heavy arm was wrapped around my waist like it had a right to be there, fingers resting low on my hip in a way that screamed possessive and delicious and deeply unhelpful to my sense of self-preservation. My limbs were tangled around him like I was some kind of desperate, drunk octopus. My leg was tossed over narrow hips like I'd been practicing for a gymnastics event in my sleep. My cheek? Firmly planted against smooth, naked man-chest.

Oh no.

Oh no, no, no.

I cracked one eye open.

Easton.

His name flashed in my brain like a neon warning sign. My stomach flipped—possibly from the hangover, possibly from the sheer hotness of him lying there looking like a *GQ* spread. Hair a mess. Eyelashes obnoxiously thick. Jaw shadowed with stubble that had definitely done things to me last night.

My brain short-circuited.

Fuck.

This was not how the morning after was supposed to go. There was supposed to be a healthy amount of regret and maybe a hasty escape wrapped in a comforter. There was definitely *not* supposed to be cuddling. And definitely not *this much touching.*

His hand flexed in his sleep, gripping my hip tighter like even unconscious Easton wasn't ready to let me go.

Memories from last night came rushing back. The alley. His mouth. My mouth. The way we'd devoured each other like we were starving, like we were trying to make up for all the lost time in one night.

And then?

The bar.

I had gone back to the bar and promptly started to drink. Possibly a hundred of those devil drinks, aka Rudolph's Nose, or whatever they'd been called. And whiskey. So much whiskey. I remembered lifting a glass like I was toasting to my own destruction.

Apparently, I'd succeeded.

Fuck. It hurt to think.

At some point I'd obviously blacked out.

I groaned internally, squeezing my eyes shut as if that would somehow rewind time and undo the absolute disaster I had walked into on my own two feet.

Or my vagina. I was pretty sure that my traitorous vagina had been steering last night's ship, and clearly she'd decided to go down with it. In spectacular fashion.

I should move. I needed to move.

I would move.

Any second now.

Except the second I tried to shift away from him, my body revolted like I was betraying it. My head pounded in angry pulses, my stomach twisted in a way that did not feel promising, and everything, *everything*, felt like it had been run over by a Mack truck.

I felt gross. Hungover and sticky and in dire need of a shower.

Easton let out a low sigh in his sleep, his chest rising and falling against mine in the rhythm of someone completely at peace.

Must be nice.

I stared at the ceiling, debating whether I should try to sneak out or just die right here. But the warmth of him, the safety I hadn't felt in *so long*, it wrapped around me like a blanket I didn't remember missing until it was back.

Just for a second, I told myself.

Just one, tiny, hungover second.

I'd lie here.

Let the room stop spinning. Let the nausea fade. Then I'd escape this tangled mess of limbs and lust and lies with what little remained of my dignity.

That was the plan.

The very solid, very reasonable plan.

But instead of eventually moving . . . I melted.

The tension drained from my shoulders. My fingers relaxed their death grip on the sheet. My head dropped back against his chest like it had always belonged there.

And before I could talk myself out of it, before I could remind myself of the million reasons this was a bad idea . . . I drifted off again.

Warm. Sated. Safe.

Curled in the arms of the one man I had *absolutely* sworn I was over.

Easton

I wasn't going to let her avoid me.

She was trying. I'd give her that. Like her life depended on it. Like eye contact might actually kill her. Frankly, it was adorable.

We were at some post-party event Paige and Levi were calling a Hangover Brunch—complete with a Bloody Mary bar, mimosas in the hands of toddlers—*Okay, not really, but it felt that way*—and whispers of a Santa appearance. The whole thing felt like a fever dream of holiday chaos, but it was a good call. Nearly everyone who'd been at karaoke last night had been *obliterated*. Including Natalie.

My Natalie.

Fuck, she'd been cute last night . . . just soft and tipsy enough to stop pretending she didn't want to hold my hand. Her head had rested on my shoulder like it had always belonged there. I'd even snuck a couple selfies of us while she wasn't looking—nothing scandalous, just her tucked into my side with the kind of peace on her face that made my chest hurt.

I'd wait to show her those, though. Timing was everything. Right now, she'd probably scream and launch her mimosa at me if I even hinted at them.

Speaking of mimosas . . . Natalie was currently sitting as far from me as physically possible in the room. Her focus was laser-pointed on the glass in front of her like it held the answers to all life's mysteries. Or, more likely, like she could manifest it into a shield and block me from her memory entirely.

I watched her, taking a sip of my coffee and pretending to care about the guy in a reindeer onesie making balloon animals. She was flustered.

And she *hated* that she was flustered.

I knew her too well—her tells, her habits, the way her foot tapped when she was anxious or overstimulated. She was at war with herself right now, and I'd be lying if I said it wasn't entertaining as hell.

But I wasn't here to play. I was here to win her back.

I smirked to myself, strolling over to the buffet and loading up a plate—not for me. For *her*. The plate practically looked like it had been curated by a personal chef who'd spent years studying her exact taste buds. Blueberry pancakes. Crisp bacon. Scrambled eggs with a ridiculous amount of cheese. I even made her a coffee exactly how she liked it, a splash of milk, two shots of espresso, and five tablespoons of sugar . . . because I wasn't above playing dirty.

The second I placed the plate in front of her, she narrowed her eyes at me like I'd just handed her a proposal on bended knee instead of breakfast. Her cheeks went pink, which only made me grin harder.

She was so fucking beautiful it actually hurt to look at her.

I winked before sliding into a chair a few spots down . . . close enough to watch her squirm, but far enough to give her the illusion of space. I stretched out, all fake nonchalance, like my heart wasn't thudding in my chest every time she looked at me.

"You looked hungry, Trouble."

She stared at me with that look that made men flinch and wait for objects to be thrown. "Did you poison this?"

I leaned forward, voice low, just for her. "If I wanted to kill you, I'd just kiss you again."

Her fork froze halfway to her mouth, eyes wide like she'd forgotten I was capable of weaponizing charm.

And then—then—she took a bite of the pancakes.

Her lashes fluttered.

Her lips parted just slightly.

For half a second, she forgot to be mad.

And *that*, that tiny flicker of pleasure on her face, was everything. My own little Christmas miracle.

I adjusted my dick under the table because apparently some things hadn't changed over the years . . . like the fact that I was still painfully attracted to *everything* Natalie did. Chewing? Turn-on. Sipping a mimosa? Somehow erotic. Literally just existing? Torture. She could be reading a cereal box, and I'd be halfway to losing it.

I dug into my own food, doing my best impression of a man with chill, and pretended not to notice how her shoulders relaxed just a fraction. How the tight lines around her mouth eased as she took another bite of pancake, the tiniest sigh escaping her like the food had knocked down at least one of the walls she kept barricading between us.

If this was what it took to break down her walls—one carefully planned breakfast at a time—I was willing to play the long game.

I just needed to keep pushing.

I took a sip of my coffee and decided to keep the momentum going. "You look beautiful," I said smoothly, like it was just a casual observation and not the culmination of twenty-three months of deprivation.

Natalie snorted into her mimosa, coughing a little as she swallowed. "Well, obviously. What do you want?"

I grinned at the sass, loving her more in that moment than was probably healthy. "What, a guy can't compliment his—" *Ex-girlfriend? Soulmate? Girl who had broken his heart but still owned every inch of it?* "Girl?"

She arched a brow, her expression somewhere between amused and mildly homicidal. Her mouth opened, probably to tell me I had absolutely lost my mind, but before she could get the words out, the double doors burst open behind us.

An obnoxious, booming "HO HO HO!" rolled across the room like thunder.

Every head turned as "Santa Claus" made his grand entrance.

Except, not just any Santa Claus.

Brian. Fucking. Sanders.

Natalie groaned under her breath, dragging a hand down her face like she couldn't believe her life had sunk this low. "Oh, you have *got* to be kidding me."

Brian. *Of course* it was Brian.

He'd spent all of high school trailing behind Natalie like a sad golden retriever, acting like if he just flexed hard enough in gym class, she'd magically realize he was her soulmate. I'd blocked his number from her phone *twice* junior year. Once because he "accidentally" sent her a shirt-less pic. The second time because he made a playlist called "Songs That Remind Me of Natalie's Smile."

And now here he was. Playing Hot Santa. Jingle balls and all.

I watched as his gaze went straight to Natalie's, a slow, eager smirk spreading across his stupid face.

Natalie's eye twitched.

Mine did, too.

Fuck.

I wasn't sure what was worse—the obnoxiously cheerful Christmas music playing in the background or the fact that Brian Sanders was practically drooling over Natalie right in front of me.

Scratch that. It was Brian.

Definitely Brian.

I was hungover. I was pissed off. And I was exactly five seconds away from stabbing him with the decorative peppermint stir stick in my coffee.

It wasn't enough that Natalie was avoiding me like I was a particularly clingy Christmas ghost. That she was dodging every compliment I tossed her way like she had a deflector shield and responded to most of my comments with grunts, glares, or outright threats involving hot coffee.

The universe wasn't done humiliating me.

It had to throw Brian into the mix.

I hadn't seen him since school, but the sight of him sauntering into brunch dressed as Santa was enough to make my entire mood nose-dive.

Brian, who had spent every second of junior year trying to wedge him-self between Natalie and me.

Brian, who I knew deep in my soul had been lying in wait for the moment I was out of the picture.

Brian, who was now grinning at her like he'd just been given a personal Christmas miracle.

I clenched my jaw as he plopped into the seat beside her, draping his arm over the back of her chair like he belonged there.

Natalie stiffened, but she didn't push him off.

Blood pounded in my ears as I stared at them, my fork clenched so tightly in my hand that I was 90 percent sure I could bend steel now. My pancakes sat untouched, getting colder by the second as I watched them.

He leaned in toward her, whispering something stupid in her ear with that same grin that used to make girls in high school swoon and guys in locker rooms roll their eyes.

Natalie wasn't laughing. Thank fuck. She was giving him that same unimpressed stare that used to make teachers, coaches, and rogue homecoming DJs shrivel in fear.

It was the you're-on-thin-fucking-ice look.

The one she'd given me once when I'd called her dog ugly.

But Brian? He was too stupid to be scared.

"Damn, Nat," he said, shaking his head like he couldn't believe his own luck. "You look better than ever. Seriously, if I'd known Santa was delivering gifts this early, I would've left out some milk and cookies last night."

My jaw clenched. "Milk and cookies"? This dumbass.

I was going to commit a crime. A very festive, red-and-green-tinted crime. There would be carolers singing in the background as I ended him with a plastic reindeer antler.

Natalie huffed a small laugh, stabbing a piece of bacon with unnecessary force. "Right. Because that's not the creepiest way you could've said that."

Brian just grinned, clearly proud of himself.

"I mean it," he went on, undeterred by her lack of interest. "You ever sit on Santa's lap, Nat? 'Cause I've got a sleigh big enough for two."

I nearly snapped my fork in half.

Natalie closed her eyes and massaged her temples like she could physically remove the trauma he was causing. "Brian, are you drunk?"

"Not yet," he said smoothly, leaning closer with the world's most confident smirk for a man in a fake white beard and jingle-bell suspenders. "But I'd love to jingle your bells later if you're free."

That was it.

That one didn't even make sense.

It was time for him to go.

I shoved back my chair, the legs scraping against the floor so loudly that at least four people flinched and turned. Including Natalie.

"Easton?" She blinked, surprised.

But I wasn't looking at her.

I was looking at Brian.

Brian, who was still grinning like this was some charming spectacle and not a public humiliation countdown.

I didn't say a word. Just casually tossed my napkin down on my plate like I wasn't seconds away from committing a misdemeanor.

Natalie barely spared me another glance, too busy trying to annihilate her breakfast like it had personally offended her entire bloodline. Which was fine. Perfect, actually. She didn't need to be a witness.

I waited until Brian got up—probably to go admire himself in the bathroom mirror or rehearse his next horrifying holiday innuendo—and then I followed him. Quietly. Calmly.

Kind of like a psychopath.

He had just pushed open the bathroom door when I picked up my pace, shoving in right behind him before he even knew I was there.

"Dude, what the—"

He didn't get the rest of that sentence out because I grabbed him by the shoulders and spun him toward the utility closet next to the sinks.

Brian barely had time to blink before I yanked the door open, shoved him inside, and slammed it shut.

"What the hell?!" His voice was muffled through the wood. "Easton? What the fuck, dude, let me out!"

I snapped the lock on the outside, just to be safe, and grinned like the unhinged ex-boyfriend rom-coms had warned Natalie about.

I knocked twice on the door for good measure. "I'd love to, Bri. But Santa's got a schedule to keep."

"Easton, you crazy bastard, let me out!" he shouted, pounding like he was in a horror movie and not a cleaning supply prison of his own making.

I adjusted my sleeves, took one last satisfied look at the vibrating door, and strolled out of the bathroom like I had all the time in the world.

Brian was going to be busy with a mop for a while.

And me?

I had a girl to win back.

CHAPTER 11

Easton

When I got back to the main room, the cozy brunch vibe was being seriously threatened by one very concerned B and B owner. Margaret was pacing in front of the buffet with a plaid clipboard and a frown deep enough to ruin tinsel.

"Where did Brian go?" she asked, scanning the room. "It isn't time for his break yet. The children are starting to sense something's wrong. I can feel it."

I followed her gaze to where two toddlers were arguing over a candy cane, while a third kid poked suspiciously at the empty velvet throne by the fireplace.

Yeah. They looked . . . concerned.

I stepped forward, slipping into my most dangerous weapon: my innocent charm.

"Don't worry, Margaret," I said smoothly. "I'll do it."

She blinked up at me, startled. "You?"

I nodded solemnly. "Wouldn't want to let Christmas down, now would I? It'd be a shame to disappoint all these lovely people. The children. The elderly. The mimosas. All counting on Santa."

Margaret's brows pulled together like she was trying to decide if I was sincere or secretly plotting something.

"I . . . I don't know . . ." she said slowly. "It's just that Brian's done it for the last two years. He knows the script. The tone. The *jingle*. And the suit—"

"I'm a fast learner," I said, placing a hand over my heart in mock sincerity. "And I've been told I've got natural jingle energy."

She hesitated for one more moment, but then beamed like I'd just solved world hunger.

"That's the Christmas spirit!" she said. "There's an extra Santa suit in the back. Go change, dear."

I turned, shooting her a winning smile over my shoulder. "You got it, Margaret. Operation Save Christmas . . . commencing now."

Behind me, she beamed like I was the second coming of Kris Kringle himself, completely unaware that Brian was currently locked in a supply closet yelling about mop buckets and betrayal.

Not my fault he couldn't keep his jingle bells in his pants.

Besides, it wasn't about revenge.

It was about . . . giving.

And today, I was *giving* Natalie a Santa she'd never forget.

Natalie

Ten minutes later, Brian still hadn't come back from "checking his phone," and I was relieved.

Until a *new* Santa walked into the room.

I froze.

The red velvet clung to his stupidly broad shoulders like it had been tailored for sin. The white gloves were stretched over his hands, and the hat sat just so, pushed back far enough to reveal a peek of tousled dark hair that had no business looking that good under felt.

And the boots.

The *boots*.

Santa, it turned out, had thighs.

But the worst part? The part that truly undid me?

Those green eyes locked on to mine the moment he entered, like he'd known exactly where I was without needing to look. Like I was the only person in the room.

I froze, mimosa halfway to my lips, my entire soul screaming a very definitive *nope*.

"Where's Brian?" I demanded as he reached me, suspicion already blooming.

Easton shrugged, all casual mischief. "Busy."

"Busy?" I repeated, narrowing my eyes.

He leaned in slightly, the corner of his mouth quirking into that lazy, cocky smirk I hated loving. "I might've . . . locked him in a closet."

My jaw dropped. "You did *what*?!"

Across the table, Paige choked on her drink, laughing so hard her mascara was already halfway down her cheeks. "Holy fuck."

"Relax," he drawled, lowering himself into the seat beside me like he hadn't just committed a holiday-themed felony. "It's not like I murdered him. Just gave him some alone time. Very important during the holidays."

"And who," I snapped, "made *you* Santa?"

"Margaret," he said proudly. "She seemed thrilled. Said I had jingle energy."

I gaped at him. "You have *felon energy*."

He grinned wider, leaning in until our faces were way too close for comfort. I could smell the cinnamon from the cookies, the peppermint of his breath, the faintest trace of my favorite cologne he knew drove me insane. "I make a better Santa, don't you think?"

I blinked at him.

Murder. That was still on the table. Very much on the table.

Although . . . there was a tiny, traitorous voice in my head whispering, *Or you could sit on his lap.*

Nope. That voice needed therapy.

I opened my mouth to retort, something scathing and brilliant no doubt, but Easton didn't wait.

He reached out and grabbed my hand, tugging me out of my chair.

"Where are we going?" I hissed, trying to plant my heels against the floor even as my heart did a dramatic Broadway leap inside my chest.

"I have a present for you," he murmured, pulling me out of the dining hall and down the empty corridor toward the staircase.

The sounds of clinking glasses and off-key caroling faded behind us as we slipped into the hallway, lit only by twinkle lights woven through garlands like they were trying a little too hard. My hand was still in his, fingers laced like a promise—or maybe a dare—and I wasn't exactly trying to pull away.

His Santa costume must be driving me crazy. His shoulders were filling out the red velvet in a way that no one else's ever could, I was pretty sure. I bet Mrs. Claus didn't feel like jumping Santa when she saw him.

But I certainly was right now.

"Where are we going?" I asked, breathless, barely keeping up with him, my heels clicking against the polished floors.

I mean, I kind of knew where we were going, okay, maybe not where . . . but what we were about to do. I'd had a long talk with my vag about being a hussy, but she didn't seem to be listening . . . She seemed to be actively humming like a Christmas caroler, actually.

I'd need to have another talk with her.

At some point.

Easton looked over his shoulder, his lips tugging up in a smirk beneath the white curls of the beard he'd shoved down around his neck. "Someplace quiet. You deserve a . . . Christmas surprise."

His voice was low, roughened by something that sent a shiver darting straight down my spine. It was the kind of sound that didn't belong in a festive hallway. It belonged in bedrooms and fantasies and that tiny corner of your brain where all your dignity goes to die.

He stopped near the end of the hall, pushed open a door, and led me inside.

It was an office, empty except for a worn maroon couch and a desk covered in wrapped boxes. Lights twinkled softly in the windows, casting the whole space in a glow that felt stolen—like this moment wasn't meant for anyone else but us.

He closed the door behind us.

Click.

I jumped slightly.

It wasn't like there was a perfectly acceptable room in this building we could be using.

The beard. His mussed hair. His expression?

This wasn't Easton. This was *Santa with benefits.*

And apparently, my ultimate weakness.

Every woman's secret dream. According to that one song at least.

Staring at Easton as he turned around to face me . . . it was perhaps my secret dream as well.

Fuck.

"We can't stay long," I said, my heart thudding against my rib cage at how close we were.

"Then I guess we better not waste any time," he murmured. "Let's get your surprise started."

Before I could respond, his hands found my waist, tugging me forward until I was pressed against him, Santa suit and all. The plush velvet was soft against my skin; the gold buckle of the belt was cold where it met my stomach.

He kissed me, slow and sure, coaxing rather than demanding, his mouth soft and warm and somehow tasting faintly of peppermint. I wasn't sure if he'd popped a mint on the way here or if he'd actually gone full method actor, but I had questions. Later. Definitely later.

Right now, all I could do was melt.

I gasped as his hands slid down my waist, squeezing gently, then dipping lower to cup between my thighs. Ugh. Yep, my girl, aka my lady, aka Ms. *Hussy*, evidently lit up like the Fourth of July as his fingers pressed against my core.

With a low grunt, he lifted me easily, setting me down onto the edge of the desk as the kiss deepened.

"I'd just like to state for the record," I huffed against his lips, breathless. "This is a new kink I'm discovering, so bear with me as I come to grips with the fact that I am apparently . . . into Santa Claus."

Easton leaned back just enough to look at me. His green eyes sparkled, that grin of his tipping toward wicked. "Didn't think I'd ever hear *that* come out of your mouth, but I gotta say, I'm very into it."

"Shut up," I laughed, heat flushing my cheeks as I tugged him closer by the front of his coat. "You are not allowed to use this against me later."

"Oh, baby," he murmured, voice thick with heat as his mouth hovered over my skin. "I'm framing this moment and putting it on our mantel."

I almost snorted. Almost. But I was too busy trying not to combust like a string of faulty Christmas lights.

This means nothing, I told myself. This is what sad, lonely people do during the holidays when thrust together with their emotionally complicated, unfairly hot exes. I was basically living in a Taylor Swift ballad, thank you very much. Probably "Evermore" if we're being specific. This was totally natural.

This meant *nothing*.

His lips found the sensitive curve of my neck, trailing fire with every kiss. His beard scratched just right, making my breath hitch in the most humiliatingly obvious way. I arched into him without meaning to, my fingers fisting the lapels of his Santa jacket like I was trying to keep myself from floating away.

I could practically hear the inner sirens wailing. *Danger! Danger! You're slipping.*

But they were also saying *We ride at dawn.*

So the situation was complicated.

"You remember what you said that first time we were together at Christmas," he murmured, his lips brushing my ear, his voice like smoke and secrets.

I blinked, trying to keep up. "You mean . . . when I drank that peppermint schnapps and tried to make out with a snowman?"

He laughed low against my skin, the vibration of it tickling down to very inappropriate places. "No, not that time. The *other* first time."

I shook my head, breath catching. My brain cells were currently on sabbatical. But also, he was being very talkative for Santa. I wanted more ho ho ho and less reminding me that he was the best I'd ever had.

"You told me you wished you hadn't fought me for so long," he continued, his voice suddenly softer, rawer. "That we could've just been together from the very beginning."

Oh. *That* first time.

His hands slid beneath my sweater, fingers brushing over the bare skin of my stomach. I sucked in a breath.

"That must've been drunk me," I said, attempting a light tone as panic nudged at my rib cage . . . even though I'd said that way before I'd ever tried alcohol. "She's a bit of a romantic and can't be trusted. Honestly, she's embarrassing."

Maybe I should quote those Taylor lyrics to him so he would understand what was supposed to be happening here.

Might drive the point home, right?

He grinned against my neck. "She's my favorite version of you."

"Well," I muttered, "she's definitely not here today."

But even I didn't believe it.

Easton pulled my sweater over my head, revealing the lacy red bra I'd worn on a whim . . . a hoochie mama whim, obviously. His gaze roamed over me, dark and heavy. "This is what you wore for brunch?"

I lifted my chin. "Maybe I wore it for Santa."

He groaned low and guttural, and suddenly I felt like the most powerful woman on earth.

With a reverence that made my breath catch, he lowered his mouth to my chest. His hands spanned my back, undoing the clasp like he'd been born with the skill. I gasped when his lips wrapped around one aching nipple, his tongue flicking, teasing, worshiping like I was something holy.

"Easton," I breathed, head falling back.

He growled softly, trailing his kisses lower, down the curve of my stomach, pushing my skirt up around my hips.

"I feel like this might break some kind of North Pole code," I whispered.

"Pretty sure the only pole Santa's worried about right now is mine," Easton muttered as his fingers slipped beneath the waistband of my thong, sliding through my slick folds. I gasped, my hips bucking toward his hand.

"So ready," he murmured, his voice almost reverent. "Always so damn ready for me."

He dropped to his knees, lifting one leg over his shoulder as my dress slid up my thighs. I gasped as his mouth found me, licking and sucking with lazy, devastating precision, like he had nowhere else to be. My fingers tangled in his thick, tousled hair, grounding myself as the storm of him built around me.

"Fuck," he growled, pausing just long enough to rip the fake beard from his face and toss it across the room.

"Hey," I breathed, only half kidding. "I was kind of into that."

I whimpered as he dove back between my thighs, his tongue licking through my slit before he sucked hard on my clit.

He glanced up at me, his green eyes dark with heat and mischief. "I'll grow the beard later, baby. But I'm not walking into brunch smelling like your perfect pussy unless you want me to start breaking noses. That scent?" He grinned, wild and wicked. "That scent's *mine*. And God help anyone who thinks otherwise."

"There's a lot of things wrong with what you just said." I gasped, and then promptly forgot how to speak as he dove back in.

"I—" I tried again, but my words vanished as he slid two fingers inside me, curling just right, just as his mouth closed around the sensitive bundle of nerves that made me see stars.

My back arched off the desk as the orgasm slammed through me, fast and blinding.

I was still trembling, still trying to catch my breath, when he rose and crushed his lips to mine.

He kissed me like he'd missed it, like he was trying to memorize me with his mouth. I moaned at the taste of him, of me, of everything we'd ever been and everything we still could be . . . and tried to ignore how much it undid me.

"You always taste like heaven," he murmured, his voice low and wrecked with need.

Easton shoved the Santa pants down, his erection springing free. I reached for him, wrapping my hand around his length, stroking him slow and deliberate . . . trying not to think about the fact that he had the most perfect dick on the planet.

"Fuck," he hissed under his breath.

Before I could catch my breath, he growled and flipped me over, pressing my breasts against the cool surface of the desk.

Very un-Santa-like.

I tried to pretend like this room was never used and that Margaret and her husband never came back here to do paperwork. If I pretended that, it wouldn't be so weird later on when she inevitably tried to shove a Christmas cookie down my throat.

I barely had time to brace myself before I heard the sound of fabric rustling, the soft *thud* of boots hitting the floor. I turned my head just in time to catch sight of him—gloriously bare, his body lean and strong and every inch of him tattooed into my memory already. He was still wearing the Santa hat. Of course he was.

Fuck. Forget Santa-kink. My unfortunate real kink was everything Easton Maddox.

"Hope you've been nice this year," he said as he rubbed my ass, his gaze focused on where the head of his cock was pressed up against my soaked slit.

"Define nice," I shot back, breathless.

He responded by spanking me. Once. Sharp and delicious. The sound echoed, and I gasped, the sting fading into warmth as my body responded with a traitorous rush of slickness.

"Look at you," he rasped, dragging his fingers through my arousal. "My perfect, dirty girl. Soaking wet for Santa's cock."

I moaned, because I was only human, and this was extremely fucking hot.

His hands had a possessive touch as they moved across my skin, reverent and teasing all at once.

Then, a beat later, he started pushing in.

"Fuck. Wait just a sec—" I moaned, because no matter how wet I was . . . it was always going to be a tight fit when a cock that big of a monster was trying to get in.

It needed a warning label. Something like: PLEASE STRETCH RESPONSIBLY.

Easton thrust in with a growl, burying himself to the hilt in one smooth, devastating motion that had me seeing stars, stripes, and everything in between.

Count me out. I'd just been sliced in two . . . or at least that's what it felt like. Had he gotten bigger since high school? Because it felt that way.

He groaned behind me, the sound vibrating down my spine. "Still so tight, Trouble. Like your body remembers I'm the only one who's ever really filled it."

I tried to think of a witty comeback—maybe something involving a traffic jam or a construction permit—but my brain was currently being jackhammered by pleasure.

Easton gripped my hips, his fingers digging in, his rhythm quickening, each thrust rougher than the last. The desk creaked underneath us, my nails scraping across the polished surface as he took me hard, deep . . . relentless.

"You can pretend this means nothing," he panted, leaning over me so that his mouth brushed my ear. "You can lie to yourself all you want. But you're mine, Natalie. You always have been. And I'm not walking away this time."

His words hit harder than the thrust that followed, and I nearly buckled.

I bit my lip so hard I tasted blood, staring at a roll of Christmas-themed packing tape on the desk and briefly, *seriously*, considering the logistics of duct-taping his stupid, beautiful, infuriating mouth closed.

"Don't talk," I gritted out, already breathless. "Just—"

He slammed into me again, hitting that perfect spot with merciless precision.

"Just *what*?" he asked, smug and wrecked and glorious.

"Just keep doing *that*," I moaned as the world blurred at the edges.

He chuckled darkly, then did exactly that, pounding into me relentlessly, each thrust sending sparks of pleasure racing up my spine. I could feel the intensity building, my body trembling beneath him. He wrapped a hand around my waist, pulling me back to meet every drive of his hips.

"You feel so fucking good," he groaned. "Like you were made for me."

I blinked at those words, and suddenly I was in the past.

We were seventeen, lying on our backs in the bed of Easton's truck out on the ridge, the stars stretching endlessly above us like someone had spilled a jar of glitter across the velvet sky.

The air was crisp, sharp enough to turn our breaths into fog, but neither of us minded. Not with the way the flannel blanket was tucked around us, or the way our bodies had inched closer and closer, sharing warmth that had nothing to do with the weather.

The world was quiet up there, like it had taken a breath and held it just for us.

"Do you think there's one person for everyone?" Easton asked, his voice low, almost reverent, like he was afraid that speaking too loud might scare the stars away—or maybe me.

I didn't answer right away.

I thought of my parents. Of how my mom used to look at my dad like he held the moon in his pocket, only for him to vanish one day like none of it had mattered. One suitcase. One voicemail. No apologies. Just . . . gone.

She'd believed he was her soulmate. She'd said it with certainty, like it was a fact, like gravity.

And then she'd cried for a week straight. Screamed his name into the sink one night when she thought we were asleep. Said it like it was a curse.

So, I didn't know what I believed. Maybe I didn't want to believe in something that fragile.

As much as it felt like love with Easton, I always reminded myself that love could crack. That it could wither under pressure or bleed out slowly and quietly when no one was watching. That it left.

"I don't know," I said finally, staring up at the constellations. Orion. Cassiopeia. Shapes that had been there forever, even when everything else fell apart. "I guess . . . maybe. But if there is, it's probably rare. And people mess it up all the time."

There was a long pause. Then I felt his hand reach for mine, our fingers tangling together, warm even through our gloves.

I turned to him, heart thudding like it was trying to speak for me, but I didn't know what it would say.

His eyes caught the starlight, and I swore they looked brighter than anything overhead.

"I think you were made just for me," he said, his voice so sure it scared me more than anything else in the world.

My breath caught. My heart stuttered and then thundered, slamming against my ribs like it wanted to leap right into his hands.

"Easton . . ."

He didn't give me time to say more. Maybe he knew I'd try to ruin it with logic or fear or something else that had nothing to do with him.

"You're my one, Natalie. I've always known it. And I won't mess it up."

I hadn't said anything then.

But I'd never forgotten it.

Not his voice. Not that night. Not the way his hand held mine like it belonged there.

Not for a single heartbeat since.

I blinked, and I was back, and the memory shattered something in me.

I cried out, my release crashing over me like a dam finally giving way. It wasn't gentle. It wasn't sweet. It was raw and relentless, rolling through my body like it had been waiting years to escape.

He followed moments later with a strangled groan, his body stiffening as he thrust deep one final time. I felt the rush of him inside me, the heat, the way he muttered my name like a curse, like a prayer, like he'd never meant anything more in his life.

For a long beat, neither of us moved.

Thank fuck I was on birth control . . . because that was definitely *a lot* of cum dripping down my thighs. Holy hell.

We were still wrapped around each other, skin slick with sweat, breath coming in uneven pants. I trembled in his arms, the aftershocks pulsing through me as if my body were unwilling to let the moment go.

He wrapped his arms around me, pulling me up against his chest, his mouth finding my shoulder . . . soft, reverent kisses that stole the last bit of fight I had left.

"Still think this doesn't mean anything?" he whispered, and this time, it wasn't teasing. It was quiet. It was vulnerable. He kissed my shoulder again. And again. Like he could *will* the answer out of my skin.

I didn't reply.

I couldn't.

Because the truth was already unraveling inside me, slipping through the cracks in my denial like light through a broken window.

He pressed a kiss to my temple, then murmured almost to himself, "No one else could ever come close."

The words didn't register at first—just a quiet rumble in the haze of the afterglow.

But then my brain snagged on them, turning them over, examining them under a light that was far too bright.

I blinked. My stomach did a slow, swoopy somersault, one of those queasy-giddy-nauseous flips that only came when you were in serious,

serious trouble. Emotionally compromised. Teetering on the edge of falling all the way back in.

I stared at the ceiling. Willed the words to leave me alone.

But then I did the worst thing imaginable.

I opened my mouth.

"So . . ." I said, my voice raspy.

He loosened his arms, enough for me to roll and face him. His green
eyes were heavy-lidded but alert, his brows raised in anticipation.

"Yes, Natalie," he said patiently, like he already knew I was about to
be annoying.

I cleared my throat, trying for breezy. "I mean, it kind of just sounded
like I'm . . . still number one on your list. Which—don't get me wrong—
isn't surprising. I'm excellent. Like, if I were a Yelp review, I'd be five stars.
With photos. And a waiting list."

His mouth twitched.

"But," I added quickly, "it's maybe . . . *slightly* surprising. I imagine all
those Hollywood girls are pretty good in bed." The last part of the sentence
came out in a whisper, barely audible over my mortification. I stared at the
wall behind him, pretending to be fascinated by a festive garland that was
definitely not worth dying over.

His mouth did an amused smirking thing that I personally did not
like, but which my lady parts did. A lot.

Ugh.

"Hmm. I wouldn't know," he finally said.

I blinked again. "What does that mean?" I asked slowly, like maybe I'd
misheard him. Like maybe the post-orgasmic fog had translated it all wrong.

He hesitated, his expression shifting. That teasing glint in his eye
dimmed, replaced by something unreadable—guarded, but not cold.
Something almost too sincere. He shook his head a second later, shrugging
it off. "Forget it."

Because clearly, he was messing with me. That had to be it. Right? It
was just some flirty post-sex nonsense. A joke. A throwaway comment to
keep the mood light.

Except . . .

"Okay," I said, trying not to sound as thrown as I felt. "It kind of sounds
like you're trying to say you haven't been with anyone else." I rolled my eyes
and added, "You can tell me the truth, you know. I'm a big girl. I can take it."

There was a pause. A long one.

And then I noticed I'd closed my eyes, like I was bracing myself for a blow. Like I'd rather not see his face when he laughed and told me I was being ridiculous.

But the laugh never came.

Instead, there was silence. And more silence. Thick, tense, electric.

I opened my eyes.

And promptly forgot how to breathe.

Easton was staring at me. Really staring. His gaze pinned me like a butterfly beneath glass—open, raw, stripped of all the glossy charm I'd come to expect from him. There was no smirk. No smug grin. Just heat. And something else that terrified me more than all of it.

He reached up and gently tapped under my chin, nudging it closed. I hadn't even realized my mouth had fallen open.

"I'm not joking," he said, his voice rough . . . his words rasping against the quiet like sandpaper.

Time slowed.

No. Time *stopped*.

A thousand things crashed through me at once. Shock, obviously. But also disbelief, panic, confusion . . . and underneath all of that, a dangerous swell of longing that made my chest feel tight.

He meant it.

He hadn't been with anyone else. Not since me.

My mouth went dry. My stomach twisted, and suddenly the room felt too small, like the walls were inching closer with every heartbeat.

I wanted to laugh, to toss out something biting and sarcastic, to pretend like none of this mattered. But I couldn't find my voice. Because beneath all the heat still simmering in my body, beneath the walls I'd rebuilt over and over, something fragile cracked open.

Why would he do that? Why would he wait—hold on to this . . . whatever *this* was—for *me*?

I swallowed, hard, and a hitched gasp came out of me because evidently I'd been holding my breath for this entire fucking time. "Easton . . ." I said finally, my voice barely above a whisper. "Why?"

He exhaled, slow and steady, but there was no calm in it. "Do you really want to hear the answer to that?"

And that did it.

Panic flared so violently in my chest it nearly knocked the breath from my lungs. It was like someone had lit a match right under all the carefully stacked reasons I'd built to protect myself from this very moment.

I could feel it rising, tight and furious and uncontainable. I didn't *want* the answer. Not really. Because I already knew. I'd known it from the moment he'd kissed me in that alley like I was air and he'd been drowning for years. I'd known it from the moment he touched me like no one else had ever touched me, from the way he said my name like it was sacred.

I didn't want the answer because it wasn't casual. It wasn't temporary.

It wasn't nothing.

And that terrified me.

Because if this was something . . . if this was *everything* . . .

Then what the hell did that make me, for walking away once?

My breath hitched as I hurriedly righted my clothes, mourning the loss of my panties. I looked at him—at the boy who'd once held my hand under the stars and whispered promises into my hair like he meant every single one of them—and I bolted.

No words. No clever quip to soften the blow. Just me, running.

Again.

This was coming awfully close to becoming a habit . . . this whole running thing.

The sound of the door shutting behind me was too loud, too final, and it echoed down the hallway like a countdown clock.

Because I wasn't ready.

And deep down, I wasn't sure I *ever* would be.

Easton

She ran.

I just stood there, dumbfounded in the glowing aftermath, the echo of the door slamming reverberating like a gunshot in the silent office. The only thing louder than that echo was the sound of my own heartbeat—too fast, too loud, still thudding like it was trying to catch up to hers.

Everything was still warm. The desk. My hands. My skin.

The air was thick with her. Her perfume, her moans, the ghost of her fingers clawing at the wood for leverage while I held her hips like a man possessed.

I could still feel the imprint of her body against mine, the way she trembled, breathless, as I buried myself inside her.

And she'd run.

I stared at the closed door like it had betrayed me. Like it should've locked itself before she could escape.

What the hell had I been thinking?

I wasn't supposed to *say* it. Not like that. Not now. I had a plan. A whole careful, stupid, slow-burn plan. Win her back one small, gentle step at a time. Feed her breakfast. Make her laugh. Be the guy she remembered, the one she once loved, before I let the distance and the months and the career take all that away.

I wasn't supposed to just lay my heart out, raw and bloodied, and ask her to step over it.

But she looked at me like she wanted to believe it. Just for a second. And that second? It broke me. Because I remembered what it was like to have her believe in me.

I tugged my hat back on, letting the red velvet slouch over my brow, the stupid white puff bouncing like it didn't realize it was now sitting on the head of a man who'd just emotionally detonated all over his ex-girlfriend in a random office.

And yeah. I didn't bother cleaning myself up.

I *wanted* to smell like her.

That lotion she always wore—something with vanilla and citrus and sin. The perfume that clung to my jacket like a ghost whenever we used to say goodbye. I wanted all of it soaked into me, branded on me, because maybe if I held on to it long enough, I could pretend she hadn't looked at me like I was the biggest mistake she almost made twice.

I walked back into the hallway with all the grim enthusiasm of someone heading to their own execution—or worse, having to play a jolly Santa when I was feeling the opposite of jolly at the moment.

"'Bout damn time."

I nearly jumped out of my velvet pants. Her grandmother, *MeMaw*, popped out from behind a fake snow-dusted wreath like some sort of yuletide goblin. A terrifying one. Wearing orthopedic shoes and a necklace made of glowing Christmas bulbs that blinked in time with her judgment.

"For fu—fudge sake, MeMaw," I wheezed. "Are you trying to give me a heart attack?"

"You should be so lucky," she said dryly, squinting at me like she was trying to set my eyebrows on fire through sheer force of will.

I tried not to fidget. She had the kind of stare that could curdle milk.

"You gonna mope all the way through Advent, or are you planning to fix what you just broke with my granddaughter?"

"I didn't break anything," I muttered, not at all sounding convincing. "I told her the truth. That should count for something, right?"

MeMaw kept giving me that long, squinty-eyed look. Then, without a word, she reached for the oversized plastic candy cane leaning against a nearby entry table and whacked me across the head with it.

"Ow!"

"You deserved that."

"How did I deserve to be assaulted by Christmas decor?"

"I have a ceramic nativity in my purse. Don't tempt me," she snapped. "That girl has been through enough without you bungling this all up. You tell her you love her?"

I ran a hand down my face, my palm dragging through sweat, regret, and a healthy dose of self-loathing. The Santa hat slipped sideways again, like even it was disappointed in me.

"Not . . . in so many words."

She leveled me with a look so blistering, I half expected the hallway tinsel to catch fire. "Then you're a fool."

"Thanks for the emotional support," I said, deadpan.

"I'm not here for emotional support. I'm here for action." She crossed her arms. "Now go faster. Get her back before it's too late."

I hesitated, the weight of everything pressing down at once . . . Natalie's silence, her eyes when she ran, the confession I couldn't take back.

"And button your damn pants, Easton. No one needs to see Santa's gingerbread."

I blinked. "Fucking hell."

"You'd better hope that guy's not listening," she barked, then spun on her heel and stomped off like a tiny, tinsel-wrapped general muttering about men and their tragic inability to use their mouths for anything other than getting into trouble.

I stood there, processing for a long beat.

Then I looked down.

Yeah. Pants. That would be good.

I yanked them up with what was left of my pride, squared my shoulders, straightened the Santa hat one last time, and marched toward the hallway.

Because for Natalie?

I'd go to war in a Santa suit.

And I'd win. Or die trying.

CHAPTER 12

Natalie

As soon as I staggered down the hall, my phone was out and I was texting my girls.

Me: 911

Casey: . . .

Me: Don't . . . me. This is a real emergency.

Riley: I'm not sure that you know the meaning of that word, Nat.

Me: I JUST HOOKED UP WITH SANTA CLAUS!

Casey: What?

Casey: What do you mean?

Casey: What does that mean?

Riley: Are you being serious right now?

Me: DO I SOUND SERIOUS?

Riley: Well . . . no. Obviously.

Casey: Right now I'm picturing you and a mall Santa banging it out in those fake workshops they set up.

Riley: That was oddly specific. You and Parker act that out or something?

Casey: If anyone is going to act out that particular fantasy, it would be you and Jace. Just saying. Or . . . evidently Natalie.

Me: OK, I may not have hooked up with actual Santa.

Casey: I'm not sure you actually had to tell us that.

Riley: Yeah, I'm not sure Mrs. Claus would have allowed that. Oh, and I have one for you.

Casey: Have what for us?

Riley: Why does Santa always come through the chimney?

Me: I'm not sure this is the appropriate time for this, but I'll allow it.

Casey: . . .

Riley: Because he knows better than to try the back door!

Casey: OK, tell Jace that one was funny.

Riley: Hey! That could have been from me.

Casey: OK . . . we can pretend to live in that world.

Me: Can we focus? Less ho ho hoing and more fixing my life!

Casey: I would like to point out again . . . that the only one ho ho hoing is . . . you.

Riley: She's probably preening right now.

Me: I HOOKED UP WITH EASTON DRESSED AS SANTA!

Casey: Now this is getting good.

Me: It was the costume. One look and I turned into one of those he-can-sleigh-me-anytime kind of girls.

Casey: I'm not sure I know what you're talking about.

Me: Think of Parker in his football uniform and how you get all wild and crazy. That's what happened to me. One second, he was saying "Merry Christmas." And the next second, I was on his lap. And the next-next second, I was saying "Yes, Saint Nick. Yes."

Me: I am not OK. Just in case that wasn't obvious.

Casey: You just made me choke on my tea. Rude.

Me: DO NOT LAUGH! I AM SPIRALING. MY HOLIDAY WREATH IS CROOKED. I LOST A FAKE EYELASH. AND I THINK I YELLED "JINGLE MY BELLS" MID-CLIMAX . . .

Riley: Honestly, this is peak you, Santa-seducing queen.

Me: I need a deep cleanse. Like sage, a shower, and three hours of silence. Also a cookie. Possibly a nap. SEND HELP.

Casey: Sending cookies. And a therapist.

Riley: I don't think you need cookies. I think you need a fire extinguisher. Because apparently, Santa's lap is flammable.

Me: That's not the worst part, though . . .

Riley: OK, what's the worst part?

Me: I don't want to tell you. Because I don't want to tell myself.

Casey: Just do it.

Riley: We're literally your emotional support group. You can tell us if you moaned *stocking stuffer*.

Me: It's worse.

Casey: . . .

Riley: . . .

Me: I think I might still . . . like him.

Casey: Wait.

Riley: HOLD UP!

Me: Not like like-like. Just . . . like. With extra feelings.

Casey: Nat.

Me: OK FINE . . . MAYBE I NEVER STOPPED.

Riley: OK, everyone breathe.

Casey: Are you saying you're catching feelings for your ex . . .

Me: I KNOW HOW IT SOUNDS.

Casey: What are you going to do?

Me: I don't know. Maybe run away. Join a gingerbread convent. Change my name to Holly and never wear red again.

Riley: OK, before that . . . maybe talk to him?

Me: Ew. Gross.

Casey: You're already emotionally compromised. Might as well finish the character arc.

Riley: We'll be here if you need backup. With jokes. And possibly snacks. And like . . . emotional tasers.

Me: I hate how supportive you both are about this. You're supposed to be telling me this is the worst thing ever.

Me: But also, thank you.

I was still trying to decide if I needed a priest, a therapist, or a vat of holy water when I turned down the hallway and heard it.

Crying.

At first, I thought maybe someone was laughing too hard. Holiday brunch had that effect on people—too many mimosas, not enough shame. But then I heard it again . . . softer this time, raw, like someone was trying not to be heard.

I stopped mid-scroll on my phone, Riley's latest text blinking up at me:

Riley: Moral of the story, though . . . you're fine. You just got sleighed. Happens to the best of us.

I didn't laugh. I couldn't.

Because just up ahead, tucked in the shadow of a side corridor near the library room, was Paige.

Sitting on a bench with her knees pulled up to her chest, her red waves a mess, her face blotchy and streaked with mascara.

And she was crying. Hard.

Panic flipped in my stomach. Not because I didn't care . . . but because I had no idea what to do. Emotional comfort was not exactly my area of expertise. I could juggle sarcastic banter like none other, but crying?

I was out of my depth.

Still, I slipped my phone into my pocket and took a step closer. "Hey . . . uh. You okay?"

She jerked a little like she hadn't realized anyone was there. Her eyes found mine, red-rimmed, shining. "Oh, hey," she croaked, quickly wiping her face with the sleeve of her sweater. "I'm fine. Totally fine."

My brows rose. "Right. Because nothing says fine like hiding in the hallway outside your wedding brunch and leaking tears onto your heels."

She let out a watery laugh that turned into a hiccup. "I didn't mean for anyone to see me like this."

I dropped onto the bench beside her with a dramatic sigh, ignoring the uncomfortable feeling of Easton's cum leaking down my thighs. "Well, I just panic-texted my friends that I might be falling for Easton again . . . *after* having sex with him while he was wearing a Santa suit. So honestly? Neither of us is winning today."

Her mouth twitched. "That makes me feel a little bit better, actually."

I scoffed and side-eyed her. "What's going on?"

She bit her bottom lip. Then she said it. Quietly. Almost like she regretted it the second it left her mouth.

"I invited him."

I blinked. "Invited who?"

"Terry. Our *father*. I invited him to the wedding."

Everything inside me slammed to a halt, like someone had yanked the emergency brake straight through my rib cage. "You what? Why would you do that?"

"I don't know," she said quickly, wiping at another tear. "I wasn't thinking. I just— I got caught up in the moment. I was looking at old pictures, and I . . . I missed him."

My mouth was dry. My lungs felt tight.

"You missed *him?*" My voice cracked somewhere between disbelief and betrayal.

She nodded miserably. "I know I shouldn't want him there. I know. But I *do*. I don't want to. I just . . . do."

I swallowed hard, a rush of memories hitting me all at once.

The year he left and all the pain that had come with it.

The birthday where I waited on the porch for hours in my best pink dress.

I thought of how Mom went quiet for months—*not angry*, just . . . empty. Like the air had been sucked out of her and she didn't have the strength to try anymore.

The way Paige had pretended not to care. Even though she'd been sitting on that porch with me.

And now she wanted him *here*? At her wedding? Like nothing had ever happened?

I blinked fast, forcing myself to look away before the heat in my chest spilled down my face. "Do you think he'll come?"

She gave a helpless shrug. "I don't know. Maybe. Probably not."

We sat in silence for a long moment.

And then finally, I spoke. Each word measured, held between gritted teeth and a heart that still remembered how to break. "He doesn't deserve to walk you down the aisle."

"I know," she whispered.

"But if he does show up . . ." I swallowed hard, forcing the words out through the lump in my throat. "I'll be there."

Her head turned, eyes wide. "You will?"

I nodded. "I'll be standing right beside you. Holding your bouquet or your purse or the emotional shrapnel when it all hits the fan. Whatever you need."

Tears welled again in her eyes . . . but this time, they were softer. Quieter.

She leaned her head on my shoulder, and I let her.

Because sometimes sisters cry in hallways, and sometimes ex-boyfriends wear Santa suits, and sometimes life throws you curveballs that hit you square in the heart.

And sometimes, just sometimes, you don't have to have the right words.

You just have to stay.

We didn't speak for a while. I didn't reach for her hand. I didn't move her head from my shoulder. I just sat there beside her in that quiet little alcove, the scent of pine and sugar cookies still lingering in the air, and stared at the rug on the floor like it might suddenly rearrange itself into a map that told me where the hell to go next.

But it didn't. Nothing did.

I could hear Paige breathing . . . those soft, stuttered inhales that came after a cry so big it felt like it scraped something out of you. And under it all was the sound of my own heartbeat, thudding out a rhythm that felt hollow. Unsteady.

Something had cracked open in me, and I didn't know how to close it.

Even now, years later, I could still see my father's back as he casually walked away down the driveway, unaware he'd already put his suitcase in the car. I remember standing at the window with sticky fingers from gingerbread icing, watching him go. Waiting for him to look back.

He never did.

The memories of him always ended the same: with someone I loved disappearing while I stood there frozen, trying to figure out what I'd done wrong.

That—*that*—was the future I'd convinced myself was inevitable if I let Easton in again.

Another beautiful beginning doomed to the same, crushing end.

I didn't tell Paige more about what had happened with Easton. I couldn't. Because if I opened my mouth, I wasn't sure if I'd cry . . . or explode. Or admit that maybe the reason I ran out on Easton had nothing to do with the timing and everything to do with the fact that I'd never actually let myself heal.

Maybe I was scared—terrified even—that no matter how real it felt when he touched me, no matter how honest he looked when he said I was the only one . . . it would all disappear.

I would open my eyes one morning and he'd be gone.

And I didn't know if I could survive that again.

So, I sat there in that hallway next to my sister, our silent grief braided between us, and I wondered how the hell you're supposed to love someone when you don't even know how to trust that they'll stay.

CHAPTER 13

Natalie

I knocked gently on the door of room 204, the hallway quiet except for the absolute riot happening in my chest. The light over the door flickered faintly, casting a weird halo around the gold-plated numbers. Somehow that made the whole thing feel even more dramatic, like I was about to deliver news that would change the course of history—or at least the wedding. The door opened a few moments later, and it wasn't my mom standing there.

It was Steve.

"Hey, kiddo," he said with a smile before looking me over and frowning. "Whoa. That's a face."

I gave him a sheepish half smile. "What kind of face?"

"The kind that says you need girl talk, chocolate, and maybe a small, controlled fire in the woods," he said, stepping back to let me in. "Possibly in that order."

Despite myself, I let out a quiet laugh. "You're not wrong."

He ruffled my hair like I was still a kid. "Well, your mom's in there with a mug of tea and terrible *Real Housewives* commentary. I was just headed down to see if MeMaw is hustling anyone in the lounge again."

"She already took down a bridesmaid and a groomsman," my mom called from inside.

His face lit up like a man who knew he'd married well. "I love that woman."

Then he looked at me for a long moment, eyes soft, warm with that fierce kind of love only a dad—the real kind—could give. "You okay?"

I nodded. It wasn't a lie. It just wasn't the full truth.

He didn't push—just wrapped me in one of those rib-cracking hugs, the kind that made you feel safe enough to fall apart if you needed to. Then he gave my mom a wink and headed down the hall with a casual, "If I'm not back in an hour, MeMaw's won my credit card."

The door clicked shut behind him.

And then it was just me and my mom . . . and everything I was finally ready to ask.

She sat on the bed, wrapped in a robe and a blanket, tea in hand and a Housewife mid-monologue on the muted TV, waving a champagne glass like it was a weapon. Mom looked at me, eyes warm and knowing. "What's going on, sweet girl?"

"I just . . ." I tried to find a light version of the truth. Something casual. Something that didn't feel like the world cracking open.

But all I could say was, "I couldn't sleep."

Even though I hadn't exactly tried to sleep on account of the fact that I'd been avoiding anywhere that Easton could be after the whole Santa office thing this morning.

She turned off the TV and patted the bed beside her. "Come here, baby."

I sat, curling my legs beneath me. We sat there for a moment in silence, and I could still feel the warmth of my dad's hug wrapped around my middle. My mom waited patiently beside me, her fingers absently tracing the rim of her mug as if she could feel the weight of what I wanted to say.

I stared down at my lap.

"I think I push people away before they get the chance to leave me," I began.

Her fingers paused mid-circle, resting against the ceramic like the thought had frozen them in place.

"I know, it's dramatic. But it's like—I get this warning siren in my chest the second someone gets too close. Like my heart's yelling *Abort! Abort! Pull the rip cord before we crash*."

My mom didn't interrupt. She just listened. Like she always had.

"It's like I think if I break it off first," I continued unsteadily, "it'll hurt less. Like I'm somehow in control of the damage."

"And does it?" she asked gently. "Hurt less?"

I shook my head, tears already stinging behind my eyes. "No. It just hurts longer. Quieter. And I still end up alone."

Her hand reached over and squeezed mine. "You've always been strong, Nat. But somewhere along the way, I think you started thinking that being strong meant being alone. And it doesn't."

"I keep thinking about him," I said after a long pause. "About my— about *him*."

My mom didn't need clarification.

Her expression didn't change. She simply nodded, folding her hands in her lap. "Terry."

I looked down at my fingers, twisting the hem of my sweater. "I haven't thought about him in years, not really. But now . . . with Paige inviting him and the wedding in a few days, I don't know. I feel like I'm a kid again. Waiting on the porch with mittens and hope, thinking maybe this year he'd come."

Her eyes softened. "He didn't deserve you."

"Maybe not," I whispered. "But that didn't stop me from wanting him."

My throat tightened. I hated that it still had power over me. The ache. The wondering.

She exhaled, and it was slow . . . probably full of memories. "Do you want to know what I remember most about when he left?"

I looked up, my voice tight. "What?"

"You. Sitting on the stairs. Your face crumpling when you realized he wasn't coming back. Crying so hard you couldn't breathe. And I remember the way you looked at me and asked if he left because of *you*."

I closed my eyes. "I was obviously deranged even at that age."

"No. You were just a kid. And heartbroken. And already trying to shoulder blame that wasn't yours." Her voice was firm but not harsh.

I swallowed hard. "It just . . . It felt like maybe there was something wrong with me."

"Oh, sweetheart." She reached over, placing a warm hand on mine. "There was never anything wrong with you. There was something wrong with *him*." Her voice was fierce now, the kind of fierce that could punch holes through doubt. "He was the problem. He was a coward. And he missed the best parts of your childhood."

I blinked, and the tears that I hadn't known were there slid down my cheeks. I swiped at them quickly. Because how dare they.

"He left," I said quietly. "And I spent years convincing myself it didn't matter. But now the idea of him showing up to the wedding like

he belongs—like he deserves to watch Paige's happiest day—it makes me
feel . . . off-balance. Like I'm that little girl again."

My mom nodded slowly. "I understand that."

"Do you?" I asked, looking at her, my voice sharper than I meant.

She didn't flinch. "More than you think."

She brought the mug to her lips, took a sip, then set it back down.
"When he left, I thought I would never trust anyone again. I was angry.
Not just at him. At myself. For believing him. For loving him."

I watched her closely. "But then you met Dad."

Her lips curved gently. "Yes, then I met Steve. And I realized that loving someone isn't what hurts. Loving the wrong person—that's what leaves
the bruises."

I exhaled shakily.

"I didn't love him right away," she went on, her voice quieter now. "But
he was patient. Kind. He didn't push. He just . . . stayed. Through the
hard days. Through the guarded silences. Through me needing to *believe*
he wouldn't leave."

She paused.

"And eventually," she said, "I realized that love isn't proven in the grand
gestures. It's proven in the staying. In the showing up. In the choosing to
be there. Again and again."

I looked down at my hands, her words stirring something deep and
unsteady inside me.

"Does it still hurt?" I asked. "What he did?"

She thought for a moment. "Less now. But back then, yes. I thought it
would break me. But then life gave me something better. Someone better.
A love that made the pain feel like it had a purpose."

My throat tightened. "So, you're not mad Paige invited him?"

She sighed. "I wish she hadn't, only because I don't think she under-
stands how deep that scar runs. But I also understand why she did. He's
her dad, too, even if he wasn't much of one."

I hesitated, then asked, "Do you think he'll actually show?"

My mom shrugged lightly. "Maybe. Or maybe not. Either way, it
doesn't change what came after. He left. But that opened the door for
someone better. For a man who loved you like you were his own. Who
raised you with patience and pride and a fierce, unwavering love."

Maybe. Or maybe not.

It was almost exactly what Paige had said earlier.

I wasn't sure that it made me feel better.

I nodded slowly. "Remember how nervous Dad got before father-daughter dances?" I said, wiggling my eyebrows up and down.

She smiled, her eyes shining. "I definitely jumped him afterward."

"Ugh. No. We can't talk about that."

She winked at me like scarring me for life was funny.

We both laughed, each of us blinking away tears, and then we sat in silence for a long moment.

"Are you thinking about Easton?" she asked softly.

I looked up, startled. "What makes you say that?"

She gave me the patented mom look—the one that said *Please, child, I made you with my body and have known your soul since it was the size of a walnut.*

"You look like you're standing in the middle of the road trying to decide whether to leap or run."

I swallowed hard. "I'm scared."

"I know."

"What if it ends the same way?" I asked. "What if I let him in, and he leaves, and it breaks me all over again?"

My mom reached for my hand again, her grip firm and warm. "Then you heal. Then you grow. But love doesn't always mean pain, sweetheart. Not if it's the right kind."

I stared at her.

She smiled softly. "What if it *doesn't* end the same way? What if it's the beginning of the best thing that ever happened to you?"

I didn't know how to respond.

"He's not your father, Natalie," she said gently. "He's not that man. And you're not that little girl anymore."

My chest ached. I let her words settle around me, into me, deeper than I realized I needed them to.

"Easton was always the one who could make me feel everything. Back then, it felt too big. Too real. Like if I really gave into it, there'd be nothing left of me."

"And now?"

"Now it feels even bigger," I said quietly. "But not like it'll destroy me. More like . . . if I don't let myself have it, I'll never stop wondering what it could have been."

My mom's face softened. "That's love, sweetheart. The real kind. It's not supposed to make you smaller. It's supposed to show you how much more there is to feel. How much more you're capable of."

I blinked hard, willing myself not to cry. "But what if I'm not ready?"

"Then go slow," she said. "You'll be scared. You'll question it sometimes. But real love can take that. It can hold the messy parts. It doesn't need to be perfect. It just needs to be true."

I let her words settle. Let them find the broken places in me and start stitching.

She smiled, brushing a strand of hair behind my ear the way she used to when I was a kid. "You know what Steve told me right after our first date?"

"What?"

"That he didn't care how long it took. He just wanted the chance to be the one I didn't have to be brave with."

My throat caught.

"I hope you let someone love you like that, Natalie," she whispered. "You deserve to be loved without armor."

"You said love is proven in the staying," I murmured. "But what if I'm not sure I believe in that anymore?"

My mom looked at me, her eyes warm and steady. "Then let someone show you it's still real."

I felt something shift then. A door cracking open. Not wide. But just enough for light to peek through.

"I'm not sure I know how," I whispered.

She squeezed my hand. "You don't have to know. You just have to try."

Silence fell again, but it wasn't heavy this time. It was full of something else—something like peace.

I leaned my head on her shoulder, and she rested hers gently against mine.

"You were never hard to love, you know," she said softly.

I closed my eyes.

And for the first time in a long time . . . I tried to believe.

The hallway was quiet, wrapped in the kind of stillness that only settles in late at night—blurred at the edges, almost reverent. My footsteps were barely a whisper against the old wood floor as I walked toward the suite.

I stopped in front of the door, heart thudding a steady rhythm that echoed in my chest.

The key card was cool between my fingers.

I stared at the door for a long time, chewing on my bottom lip, the silence between heartbeats stretching thinner with every second. The words from my mom still echoed in my head.

What if it's the beginning of the best thing that ever happened to you?

I swallowed hard, then slowly slid the card into the reader.

A soft *click*. A green light.

The door swung open with a whisper.

The room was dim, lit only by the warm glow of the bedside lamp. It smelled like cedar soap and the faintest trace of my perfume, clinging to the sweater I'd left thrown over a chair.

And Easton was there. In bed. Propped up on one elbow, shirtless, the blankets rumpled low around his waist. His dark hair was messy, his jaw shadowed with scruff, and his green eyes were heavy lidded but locked on me the second I stepped inside.

He didn't say anything.

Neither did I.

We just looked at each other, the silence between us thick with everything unsaid. With everything we'd been. Everything we still could be.

After a long moment, he shifted, his expression softening.

Then, slowly, he reached for the covers and pulled them back, exposing the empty space beside him.

"Come here, Trouble," he said, his voice low and raw.

It was just three words. But they pushed that door inside me open a little wider . . . the one that had started to crack the moment he walked back into my life.

I didn't speak. I didn't joke or deflect or run.

I walked.

I slipped off my shoes, crawled beneath the covers, and let him pull me into the warmth of his chest. His arms wrapped around me like they'd been waiting, like they knew how to hold all the pieces.

He didn't kiss me.

He didn't ask questions.

He just held me.

And for the first time in longer than I could remember, I let myself be held.

No armor. No walls.

Just me.

Just him.

And the quiet, trembling beginning of something that might just be real.

CHAPTER 14

Natalie

That night I dreamed . . .

The air was thick with summer . . . heavy with pine and the scent of lake water, warm enough that our skin stuck where it touched, but neither of us moved. We were stretched out on a quilt by the shore at Lakeview Park, tucked away from the world in a little pocket of night that felt like ours.

Easton lay beside me, one arm behind his head, the other brushing lazy patterns against my hip. His T-shirt had ridden up slightly, and my hand rested on the sliver of bare skin just above his jeans like it had found a home there.

We'd started sneaking out a few weeks earlier—when the heat made it impossible to sleep and the world felt too big to stay inside. My parents thought I was at Sarah's house, and Easton had muttered something to his dad about a football meeting. But really, we were here, every night if we could help it, wrapped in stolen time and the illusion that nothing would ever change.

He was talking softly, something about the stars and how that cluster above the horizon looked like a heart—if you tilted your head just right—but I wasn't really paying attention. Not to the sky anyway.

I was watching him.

His mouth. His profile. The way his lashes flickered when he looked up as if the universe had personally invited him to dream.

"Do you see it?" he said, his finger outlining a cluster of stars just above the horizon, his tone bright with excitement.

I squinted, following his finger, trying to see what he saw, but all I could make out was a random scattering of lights, twinkling against the dark. "A heart?" I teased, turning my head to look at him, a playful smile tugging at my lips. "I think you're making that up, Easton. It looks more like . . . a lumpy potato."

His laugh rumbled through me, warm and unfiltered. "A potato? You wound me. No vision at all."

"None," I said, grinning as I rolled onto my side to face him.

He was already watching me. Not the stars. Not the sky. Me.

The way he looked at me then . . . I don't think I'll ever forget it. Like I was something cosmic. Like I was the constellation. His eyes were reflecting starlight again, distracting me from anything else, but it was the way they softened that nearly undid me.

"Come on," he murmured, brushing a piece of hair from my cheek, his fingertips lingering. "It's totally a heart. It's our heart."

"Our heart?" I repeated, amused.

"Our star," he said, correcting himself, quieter now. "We found it together. So it's ours."

I swallowed around the sudden tightness in my throat. It was such a dumb, sweet thing. A made-up star, a teenage boy with a wild imagination and a crooked grin. And yet, I knew I would carry it with me forever.

"What should we call it?" I asked, because I already knew this moment was one I'd come back to in the quiet.

He didn't answer right away. Just looked at me, really looked at me. His thumb continuing to brush those slow, lazy circles on my skin. The air between us felt charged, like something was about to happen. Something important.

"The Promise," he finally whispered.

My breath caught.

"Because I promise, Nat. No matter what happens, I'll find you. Always. Even if we're on opposite ends of the world. Even if we lose touch or get lost or . . . or hurt each other. I'll come back. I'll always come back to you."

There was a beat of silence, thick and fragile, hanging between us like glass.

And then I reached for him. My hand cupped his cheek, my thumb brushing over the faint stubble he'd been trying to grow. I felt my chest squeeze, something blooming painfully behind my ribs.

"Easton," I whispered, my voice trembling as I searched for the words, my heart pounding so hard I thought it might burst. "I . . . I promise, too. I'll always find you. No matter what."

I swallowed hard, my eyes filling with tears as I let the words I'd been holding back spill out, the words I'd known were true for years but had been too scared to say.

And then, like it was the most natural thing in the world . . . I said it.

"I love you."

His eyes widened just a little, and then his whole face transformed. The grin that spread across his lips was slow and breathtaking and so full of wonder that I felt it down to my bones.

"I love you too, Nat," he whispered, his forehead dropping to mine.

Then he kissed me.

It wasn't our first kiss. But it was the first one that felt like more.

His lips were soft and sure, coaxing rather than claiming, like he wanted to give me every chance to run—and every reason to stay. And I did stay. I kissed him back, my arms wrapping around his neck as the world slipped away.

For a while, it was just us. Two teenagers in love beneath a summer night sky, sealed together by a promise written in stars.

Eventually we lay back down, his arm a warm anchor around my waist, his chest the rhythm I fell asleep to. I remember thinking that the world could fall apart, and I'd still have this night. This memory.

"Our star," I whispered as my eyes began to drift closed.

"Forever," he murmured, pressing a kiss to my temple.

And in that moment, under the eternal sky and the flickering promise of constellations, I believed him. With everything I had.

I woke with a start, my breath catching in my throat like it had nowhere else to go. For a second, I didn't know where I was.

The dream still clung to me, wrapping around my limbs like lake water—warm, heavy, impossible to shake off. I could still feel the damp summer air, the scratch of quilted fabric beneath my back, the weight of Easton's promise echoing in my chest like it was still a teenage me lying under the stars.

I sat up too fast, the blanket slipping down around my waist. My heart was racing for reasons that had nothing to do with this soft, cozy room and everything to do with a memory I hadn't let myself visit in years.

The other side of the bed was empty.

The pillow was warm, though, and the dent from his head was still there. My hand slid across it before I realized what I was doing, like I was searching for something to hold on to.

And that's when I saw the note.

Folded neatly, tucked under the edge of the pillow like a secret he'd wanted me to find.

*Out with Levi—he dragged me hunting. I think he might actually
be a morning person?? Pray for me. Can't wait to see you when I get
back. —E*

I stared at the note for a long moment, my chest aching in a way that
was both too much and not enough. The handwriting was familiar, even
though it had gotten slightly messier since high school. The swoop of the
E at the end still looked like a flourish he'd practiced just to sign my year-
books with something cool.

I lay back down slowly, the sheets cool against my bare skin, and stared
up at the ceiling.

The dream wouldn't let go. The way he'd said *forever*. The way I'd
believed him.

Maybe I still did.

That was the scariest part.

My eyes had just drifted shut again—only half-heartedly, like my brain
knew I wasn't really going back to sleep—when my phone buzzed on the
nightstand.

The shrill ring that accompanied the vibrations shattered the quiet,
slicing through the morning hush like it had a personal grudge.

I reached over, bleary-eyed and half-draped in the comforter, and
squinted at the screen.

Unknown Number.

My heart gave a little stutter.

I stared at it, a frown tugging at my mouth.

It could've been a spam call. Some cheerful robot trying to offer me a
new car warranty or tell me I'd won an all-expenses-paid cruise to somewhere I'd never asked to go. But something about the timing . . . something about the way my stomach clenched on instinct, made me freeze.

I didn't answer.

I let it ring until it stopped, the silence that followed somehow louder
than the ringtone.

Still frowning, I set the phone back down and pushed the covers off.
My feet hit the floor with a soft *thud*, the hardwood cool against my skin.
I padded toward the bathroom, rolling my shoulders, shaking off the rem-
nants of the dream, of the ache in my chest, of the call I hadn't picked up.

It was time to face the day.

Whatever it decided to throw at me.

Easton

The suite was dark when I walked in.

No sign of Natalie.

No coat on the hook. No heels by the door. No light left on.

My chest tightened instinctively, the calm I'd finally found somewhere during hunting in the snowy woods with Levi and the rest of his grooms-men—and swearing at frozen bootlaces—vanishing in a heartbeat.

She wasn't here.

The echo of our last conversation replayed in my head. Her avoidance of me all day yesterday. The pain in her eyes when she'd come into the room last night. All of it twisted into something too loud in my ears.

I set my gear down slowly, tugged off my gloves, and scanned the room again like she might suddenly materialize from behind a lamp.

She didn't.

Then I noticed it—her phone was on the nightstand.

A rush of relief hit me hard and fast. She hadn't left for good. She wouldn't go anywhere without that thing.

She was still here. Somewhere.

I exhaled, my fingers tightening on the doorframe as I turned back around.

Everything had that late-night stillness to it—like even the walls had gone to sleep. The only light came from the holiday garland strung along the railing, the tiny white bulbs casting soft halos intermittently across the hallway like breadcrumbs.

And then I heard it.

A quiet *clink*. A soft shuffle. Something subtle but familiar.

The kitchen.

Of course.

I followed the faint spill of light stretching into the corridor and pushed open the half-closed door.

And there she was.

Standing near the stove in one of those oversized sweatshirts she lived in—this one some faded shade of blue that might've once belonged to me. Her hair was pulled into a messy bun with strands falling loose around her face, her posture slightly hunched like she'd been lost in thought. She was biting her lip as she poured something into a mug, steam rising in curling ribbons from whatever she was making.

Mmm. Hot cocoa. Her favorite comfort drink. Beyond tequila.

Her back was to me, but the sight of her, the soft slope of her shoulders, the quiet way she moved . . . it hit me square in the chest. Every instinct pulled me forward, like my body knew before my brain did that I needed to be closer to her.

I didn't say anything. Not yet. Just leaned a little against the doorframe and watched her for another beat.

She didn't notice me right away. Her hands were moving slowly, carefully, as if she were trying to do something—anything—that didn't require too much thinking. Or too much feeling.

Which meant she was probably doing both.

And then she turned.

Her eyes lifted, soft and startled, but not surprised. As if part of her had expected me to find her.

We just looked at each other for a second. No words. Just the quiet recognition that even with everything messy and unspoken between us, somehow, we'd still found our way to the same place.

And maybe that meant something.

Or maybe it didn't.

But either way . . . I stepped fully into the kitchen.

The old floorboards creaked softly under my boots, and Natalie's gaze dropped for half a second, like she wasn't sure whether to smile or brace herself.

She didn't move.

Neither did I.

The warm light overhead cast her in soft amber, catching on the edges of her hair, the curve of her cheek, the faint shadows under her eyes. She looked tired. Beautiful, but tired in that bone-deep way that comes from thinking too much and sleeping too little.

Still, she held my gaze.

"Hey," I said quietly.

"Hey," she echoed, equally soft. Her voice wasn't cold—it was cautious. That was worse.

I looked at the mug in her hands, filled to the brim with hot chocolate, and then at the second mug on the counter beside it that was empty.

"You making one for me?" I asked, trying to keep it light.

She gave me a shrug, holding up both mugs. "If I drank two, it'd feel sad. But if I *held* two, it might just look like holiday spirit. Or pathetic . . . hard to tell, honestly."

I stepped closer, not touching, but close. Close enough to smell the vanilla in her shampoo. Close enough to feel it again—that *pull*. Always the pull. "You've never looked pathetic in your life."

Her eyes lifted to mine, and for a moment, we just . . . stood there. Wrapped in quiet and all the things we weren't sure how to say.

"Levi kept you out late," she said eventually, turning back to the stove to stir the cocoa again.

"Yeah," I muttered. "Apparently, he thought it was a good idea to get lost on purpose and 'see where the trees took us.'"

She laughed under her breath, and that small sound loosened something in my chest.

"I came back, and you weren't in our room," I said, not accusing. Just honest.

"I needed to think," she replied, just as honest.

"About last night?"

A pause. "About everything."

I nodded, stepping to the counter beside her, careful not to crowd. I leaned my hands on the edge, facing the opposite wall, breathing in the warm chocolate-sweet air like it might ground me.

"Can I ask what conclusions you came to?" I urged after a beat.

Natalie didn't answer right away. Instead, she filled the second mug slowly, set the saucepan aside, and slid the mug toward me.

I took it, my fingers brushing hers.

"I don't have any conclusions," she said finally. "Just . . . feelings. Conflicting ones."

That hurt more than I wanted it to, but I kept my voice even. "Okay."

"I wasn't expecting . . . anything," she said, clutching the edge of the counter. "And I definitely wasn't expecting you to say what you said."

"That I haven't been with anyone else?" I asked quietly.

She nodded. "It kind of knocked the wind out of me."

"I didn't say it to make you feel guilty."

"I know."

Her voice was quiet but steady, like someone walking a tightrope in the dark—careful, measured, trying not to slip.

But I felt it. She wasn't just talking about what I'd said. She was talking about *us*. About the weight between us. The ache of time. The fear that maybe too much had happened to go back.

A beat of silence passed—thick, but not cold. Just real.

And beneath all of it, I felt the sting of what I didn't ask:

Who held you when I didn't?

Whose name did you say when I couldn't hear it?

The pain lodged like a splinter in my chest.

Another beat of silence passed between us.

Then she took a breath—small, steadying—and added, "I just didn't know how to sit with it. And maybe I still don't."

"That's okay," I said, and I meant it. "You don't owe me anything. Not even an explanation."

She gave me a look at that, one of those sharp, half-skeptical stares she used to give me in high school when I'd say something too profound for someone who'd once used duct tape to fix a broken shoe. "Don't do that," she said. "Don't make it too easy."

"I'm not," I said, keeping my voice low and steady. "I'm not trying to get credit for showing up. I'm just . . . trying to show up. For real. The way I've wanted to for a long time."

Her gaze dropped again, this time to the surface of her cocoa, where she'd started stirring slow, mindless circles with a spoon, like she was hoping the swirl would sort her thoughts for her.

"Do you ever think about how things might've gone if we hadn't broken up?" she asked, her voice soft but clear.

"All the time," I said without hesitation.

Her head snapped up, like she hadn't expected the answer to come so easily, so honestly. Her eyes searched mine like she didn't want to believe it but also needed to.

I didn't flinch.

"But that's not why I'm here," I added, holding her gaze. "I'm not asking to rewind the clock. I'm not trying to force us back into something we were just because it feels good to remember it."

She waited, silent, still, but everything about her posture said she was listening with both her ears and every inch of her heart.

"I'm here," I said simply, "because I still care. Because I want to know the woman you've become. Because no matter how much time has passed . . . being near you still feels like home. Like I've been holding my breath for years and only now remember how to breathe."

Her breath hitched—just a little. She blinked fast, like she was trying to will away the emotion threatening to spill over. "Easton . . ."

"You don't have to say anything," I said gently. "You don't have to decide anything. I just . . . needed you to know that."

She didn't speak.

Not right away.

She looked down at her mug again, like maybe if she stared long enough the steam would rise and write a clear answer in the air.

I didn't rush her.

Didn't fill the silence with anything but my presence.

And finally, after what felt like forever wrapped in one soft, glowing kitchen, she exhaled.

"I'm not ready to jump back into anything," she said, her voice barely more than a breath. "I don't even know what I'm ready for."

"That's okay," I said again.

"I'm scared," she admitted. "Not just of you. Of me. Of falling again and not knowing if I can catch myself this time."

The honesty in her voice hit like a punch and a prayer all at once. She wasn't building walls—she was laying herself bare.

My heart ached, not in that teenage-heartbreak way, but in that adult, deep-down, soul-level ache that came from seeing the person you loved trying to protect the most tender parts of themselves.

"I get that," I said. "You don't have to fall. Not all at once."

I took a step closer.

"Just . . . walk with me. That's all I'm asking."

It was a lie.

Because I didn't just want a walk.

I wanted everything. Her hand in mine, her voice in my ear, her forever folded into mine like it was the only way either of us made sense.

Her eyes lifted to mine again, and something in them softened—not a green light, not a promise. But maybe a chink in the armor. A flicker of warmth in a room that had stayed cold too long.

"Walk?" she repeated, as if testing the word in her mouth.

"Walk," I said again, quietly.

She hesitated. And then, without a word, she reached out and offered me her hand.

I didn't hesitate.

I took it.

Warm. Steady. Familiar.

And mine.

Not in the way I wanted—not yet.

Because what I wanted was to kiss her until her knees gave out, to pull her into my chest and never let her go again, to burn down every second we'd lost and start over from the ashes.

But I didn't do any of that.

We didn't kiss.

We didn't say forever.

We didn't fall into each other like every instinct in my body was screaming to do.

Instead, we walked out of that kitchen side by side, our hands intertwined like a lifeline. Like a promise no one had said aloud yet—but one I already felt sinking into my bones.

And for now?

For this fragile, borrowed second?

That was enough.

But fuck, I wanted *more*.

CHAPTER 15

Natalie

There were only a few things I truly feared in life.

One: spiders. Because—obviously.

Two: embarrassing myself at karaoke. *All right, I conquered that one this week.*

And three: mistletoe.

Yes, mistletoe.

Specifically, mistletoe hung by bed-and-breakfast owners in dimly lit hallways when I was trapped with my infuriatingly sexy ex-boyfriend who was actively campaigning to reclaim my heart *and possibly destroy my sanity.*

Which was precisely how I found myself now—standing there like a deer caught in festive headlights—beneath a deceptively innocent sprig of green, staring up at it like it might explode in a puff of glitter, while Easton lounged beside me, leaning casually against the wall like this was just another day in paradise.

He looked annoyingly perfect, of course. Tousled hair. The hint of scruff. That one rogue curl flopping over his forehead like it had been sculpted by a rom-com god. And the grin. That smug, sparkly-eyed, full-of-trouble grin that promised chaos and kisses and at least three types of regret.

"Mistletoe," he observed unnecessarily.

"You planted it here," I accused immediately, narrowing my eyes at the offending greenery.

He had the audacity to look faux-offended. "Planted? Like I'm out here gardening with holly and wire in the middle of the night?"

"Don't play innocent, Elf Boy," I muttered. "I see the glint in your eyes. This was not here last night."

He laughed softly, the sound curling deliciously down my spine.

"You absolutely did this," I said, crossing my arms. "This is like the third ambush in forty-eight hours. First the karaoke duet. Then the weirdly intimate hot cocoa moment. And now this."

"First of all, I hit all my notes in that duet, so you're welcome. Second, I did not plant this. I merely . . . noticed it. And appreciated its timing."

I snorted. "You're laying traps."

"I'm improvising opportunities," he said, inching a little closer. Not touching me. Just . . . hovering. Which somehow felt worse. Or better. Depending on whether you asked my brain or my hormones.

"What's the endgame here?" I asked, chin lifting like I was preparing for battle. "Is this the part where I spontaneously fling myself into your arms?"

He shrugged with zero shame. "I wouldn't say no to that."

"You are ridiculous."

"I've been called worse. Usually by you."

I attempted to sidestep him and the cursed mistletoe. He mirrored me like we were doing a weird, sexy two-step.

"Easton," I warned.

"Nat, if I'd known mistletoe worked this well at making you flustered, I'd have bought the entire stock at the craft store."

"I'm not flustered," I lied, casually clutching the front of my shirt like it was the only thing anchoring me in this dimension.

He raised one perfect eyebrow. "Your cheeks are literally the color of Rudolph's nose right now."

"It's hot in here."

"It's snowing outside."

"Holiday stress."

His mouth tilted in a grin that had no business being legal. "Or maybe it's because you're thinking about kissing me."

"Actually," I said primly, crossing my arms and hoping my armpits weren't visibly sweating, "I was thinking about the fastest way to remove mistletoe without being noticed. Preferably with fire."

His smirk widened. "Sorry, sweetheart. You're stuck with tradition."

"Tradition says kiss—not annoy—me into submission."

He tilted his head, and his eyes darkened just enough to make my breath catch. "Submission, huh?" he echoed, voice rougher now. "Interesting word choice."

Heat instantly swamped my entire existence. Face. Chest. Knees. Libido. All on high alert. Easton was too good at this—this teasing, magnetic I'm-too-hot-for-common-decency thing.

"Not what I meant," I muttered, wishing a snowdrift would conveniently appear inside the building and bury me.

Easton stepped closer. Not touching me—but the space between us had officially reached dangerously intimate territory. His voice dipped, low and coaxing. "Just one kiss," he said. "For tradition's sake."

I glanced nervously down the hallway. Voices and laughter drifted from the kitchen and living room, the B and B filled with family, friends, and a whole host of people who didn't need front-row seats to my emotional regression.

"One kiss?" I repeated skeptically, my voice laced with suspicion and not nearly enough resolve.

"Promise," he said solemnly, placing a hand over his heart like we were signing a legal contract. "Scout's honor."

"You were never a Scout. That's not even the Scout sign."

He gave a roguish grin. "Then I'm honor bound by mistletoe law alone. It's sacred. Can't break tradition."

"You're impossible," I groaned, stepping closer despite myself. "One kiss. Quick. Like, peck-level quick. Like blink-and-you-miss-it quick."

He didn't move. Just smiled that slow, cocky smile . . . the kind that made me want to kiss him and punch him in equal measure. "So do it, then."

I blinked. "What?"

He tilted his head, infuriatingly smug. "You said one kiss. Sounds like a dare to me. Go on, Trouble. Take it."

Oh, he was the worst. The absolute worst.

So obviously . . . I did.

I leaned in, trying to ignore the flutter in my chest and the heat of his breath against mine. His scent—peppermint and something woodsy and infuriatingly *Easton*—wrapped around me, softening every edge of my resolve.

And then I kissed him.

Soft. Teasing. Barely there.

It wasn't what I expected . . . not a fireworks-and-exclamation-point kind of kiss. More like an ellipsis. A breath. A sentence that wasn't finished.

But he didn't move, didn't lean in. Just stood there, letting me take it. And somehow, *that* rattled me more.

When I pulled back, my heart doing something uncoordinated in my chest, he was smiling. Still smug. Still annoyingly gorgeous.

But there was something gentler in it now. Something that made my breath catch.

"That wasn't so terrible, right?" he murmured, still far too close.

"You didn't even kiss me back," I said before I could stop myself—then immediately wishing I'd swallowed my tongue.

His eyebrows rose, that infuriating sparkle back in his eyes. "Oh. So *now* you want participation?" he asked, pointing upward. "Because technically . . . we're still under the mistletoe."

I narrowed my eyes. "You're a full-time problem with part-time charm."

"And yet, you haven't walked away."

I hesitated, biting my lip. He was too close. Too familiar in all the wrong ways. And the ache in my chest reminded me exactly why this was so dangerous.

Because Easton Maddox still had an irritatingly strong gravitational pull, and I was dangerously close to orbiting. One more second in his presence, and I was going to need NASA to extract me from his stupidly magnetic field.

I took a steadying breath, trying to convince myself I was in control of this situation and not, in fact, one ill-timed look away from launching myself into his arms.

I met his gaze. "Fine. One more. But just to prove I'm not flustered."

His smile deepened, turning wicked and slow, like he already knew how this scene ended. "Sounds fair."

I stepped back into him—only because I had something to prove, obviously—and braced my hands on his chest, trying not to notice how solid it was beneath my palms. His head dipped, his breath warm and mint-tinged against my mouth. And then he kissed me.

Properly.

No teasing this time. No skimming lips or breathy flutters. This was a kiss built to undo me . . . slow and thorough, his tongue brushing the seam of my mouth until I gasped, and he slid inside like he owned the place.

I melted.

There was no other word for it. My entire body sighed into him like it had just remembered what it felt like to be touched like this. My fingers curled in the fabric of his shirt, tugging him closer as he deepened the kiss, coaxing my mouth open wider, stealing breath and logic and every ounce of common sense I had left.

"Mmm," he murmured against my lips, the sound low and pleased and thoroughly unfair. "Not flustered, huh?"

"Shut up," I mumbled, too breathless to sound convincing.

His mouth trailed to my jaw, brushing kisses along the edge, softer now, more intimate. Like he was tracing old memories across my skin. I tipped my head back against the wall, unable to stop the involuntary whimper that escaped when he reached that sensitive spot just below my ear.

Fuck, I hated him. Okay . . . maybe I didn't hate him. But I did hate how good he was at this. At *me*.

"Easton," I managed weakly, breath hitching as his mouth skimmed the hollow of my throat, "someone could see us."

"No one's looking," he whispered, lips ghosting just beneath my earlobe. "They're all too busy arguing over eggnog ratios and whether *Die Hard* is a Christmas movie."

"It's not," I said automatically, though my voice was breathless and my brain was barely functioning.

"Agreed," he murmured, placing a featherlight kiss just below my jaw. "It's just a winter action film with festive lighting."

"This is a terrible idea," I said, my hands fisting in his shirt, pulling him closer anyway.

"Awful," he agreed, nuzzling the curve of my neck. "Disastrous, really. But . . ."

I felt the smirk before I heard the words.

"Tradition."

"Your favorite excuse." I gasped, shivering as he nipped playfully at my collarbone.

He grinned, completely unrepentant, his fingers still curved lightly around my waist. "Can't argue with sacred holiday laws."

"Oh, I can definitely argue," I muttered, even as my hands clutched at his shirt like a woman thoroughly compromised.

He thought he'd won. That one kiss—okay, technically two—was enough to knock me off-balance.

And . . . fine. Maybe it *had* rattled me.

Maybe it had melted a few brain cells and made my knees feel suspiciously like pudding.

But I still had something to prove.

I wasn't just going to fall back into orbit like some swoony little satellite. I had control. I had logic. I had a plan.

I reached up without breaking eye contact and yanked the mistletoe clean off the ceiling.

He blinked, caught somewhere between amused and impressed. "You realize that's cheating, right?"

I didn't answer. Just stepped forward—slow, deliberate—and lowered the mistletoe until it hovered right above the zipper of his pants.

Easton went utterly still.

"Nat—"

"You dared me, didn't you?" I said softly, lifting one eyebrow tauntingly. "Still think I'm scared?"

Easton's breath hitched. His usual smug grin faltered for a second, replaced by something darker, more reverent. "Okay," he rasped, his voice suddenly hoarse. "Point made."

"Good," I whispered, the word floating between us like the brush of a fingertip over bare skin.

I sank gracefully to my knees in front of him, my eyes never leaving his, the mistletoe still dangling between my fingers . . . held like a crown or a dare or both. His gaze tracked me the whole way down, and when I looked up at him through my lashes, something inside him snapped taut.

"Nat," he said quietly, as if he didn't know whether to worship me or haul me to my feet and kiss me until the walls fell down.

"Shh." I pressed a finger to his waistband, my tone light, teasing. "Unless you want the entire bridal party to come around the corner and see just how seriously we take tradition."

His breathing quickened, and a thrill of power surged through me as I reached out, boldly undoing his pants. His gaze burned into mine, full of stunned desire.

"Fuck," he whispered roughly, sounding beautifully wrecked before I even touched him.

I freed him from his pants, already hard and pulsing beneath my fingertips. He sucked in a sharp breath, bracing a palm against the wall.

"You're unbelievable," he groaned softly, eyes never leaving mine.

I leaned in, my lips barely grazing his tip, teasing softly. "You started this."

His hips twitched involuntarily. "Then finish it."

I grinned wickedly before sliding him fully between my lips, taking him deep into my mouth in one smooth motion. He bit back a groan, the muscles in his stomach tightening visibly.

His fingers slid into my hair, gripping lightly, a silent plea. His voice was a hoarse rasp as he murmured, "Fucking hell, your mouth feels so good."

I hummed around him, savoring the way his entire body shuddered, my tongue sliding expertly along his length. I moved slowly, deliberately, enjoying every ragged breath, every whispered curse that fell from his lips.

"That's it," he urged softly, guiding me gently with his grip. "You love teasing me, don't you? Driving me crazy."

I pulled back slowly, holding him in my hand, looking up at him through lowered lashes. "I seem to remember you being a fan of torture."

He exhaled sharply, his jaw clenching. "You're playing dangerous games, Trouble."

"I know exactly what I'm doing," I whispered confidently, sliding my tongue along his shaft, making him jerk forward again. "I've been thinking about this all week. How good you'd feel in my mouth."

"Fuck," he choked out, eyes hooded and dark, his chest heaving. "You keep talking like that, I won't last."

I smiled, victorious. "Maybe I don't want you to last."

He groaned softly, hand tightening in my hair. "You're so filthy, Nat. You look so fucking perfect like this."

I took him deep again, increasing my pace, loving the way he struggled to keep quiet. My hand and mouth worked together, pushing him to the edge with each stroke, every slide of my tongue, every flick and tease.

Easton's breathing grew rough, uneven. "That's right, baby," he whispered, gaze locked fiercely onto mine. "Just like that. Fuck, you're gonna make me come right here in this hallway."

I moaned around him softly, encouragingly, desperate to feel him lose control. His grip tightened, hips shifting helplessly.

"Is that what you want?" he asked, his voice tight. "To swallow me down while our friends are right around the corner?"

I looked up at him deliberately, lips swollen, cheeks flushed. "I want you to lose it completely. Right here, right now. Give it to me, Easton."

His eyes darkened, filled with raw need. He guided himself back into my mouth, hips rolling forward, chasing his release.

"You're gonna swallow every drop, aren't you, sweetheart?" he rasped, thrusting carefully, his voice strained. "You always were so damn good at this."

I took him deeper, moaning eagerly, nails digging softly into his thighs, silently begging for it. His breathing turned ragged, his body trembling.

"Fuck, Nat—I'm so close—"

I increased my pace, my tongue swirling, my lips tightening around him. He bucked helplessly, his head falling back against the wall.

"I'm coming," he hissed between clenched teeth. "Fuck. Fuck. Fuuuuck."

Easton's release shattered through him, body tensing, hand gripping my hair almost desperately. I swallowed eagerly, every groan, every broken, breathless curse spilling from his lips making me feel like I'd just cracked open something sacred and secret inside him.

When he finally sagged against the wall, boneless and wrecked, chest rising and falling in hard, uneven pulls, I shifted back slowly. My lips curled into a smug little smile as I licked him clean, my gaze sliding up to meet his. His eyes were heavy lidded and dazed, like I'd just knocked every coherent thought out of his brain.

"Still think I'm scared of mistletoe?" I whispered, my voice playful and sweetly smug.

He let out a ragged laugh, his whole body still trembling slightly. "I mean . . ." he managed, running a hand down his face before dropping it to his side. "You're dangerous. Like, soul-stealing dangerous."

I rose slowly, smoothing my clothes with exaggerated nonchalance as I stepped back, letting the silence stretch just long enough for him to catch his breath. "And you're welcome."

Easton straightened himself with effort, zipping up his pants, eyes bright with laughter and lingering heat. "I definitely underestimated you."

I leaned casually against the opposite wall, crossing my arms and lifting an eyebrow. "Maybe you won't make that mistake again."

Easton moved before I could finish enjoying the moment, stepping into my space like a storm I hadn't braced for . . . quiet, certain, all heat and barely leashed hunger.

One hand slapped the wall beside my head, the other gripped my hip, his fingers tightening just enough to make me gasp. He caged me in like he was claiming me, like he didn't care who saw . . . like he wanted them to.

I could feel the power thrumming off him, thick and magnetic, his body radiating heat that made my legs wobble and my skin tighten in anticipation.

His breath was rough against my ear, the faint trace of peppermint and pine clinging to his shirt—but it was *him* that wrapped around me. The scent of sex and tension and the promise of something obscene just beneath the surface.

My pulse spiked.

"You realize," he murmured, his voice dark and wrecked, "next time I get you alone, I'm going to have you spread out and trembling—so deep, so slow, so fucking thorough—you'll forget everything but my name."

His mouth dragged down the line of my throat, slow enough to burn. "Over and over again . . . until it's the only word you remember how to say."

The words shot straight through me like lightning, and I bit down on a gasp, my body already responding before I could think to stop it. My fingers twitched at my sides. My knees did that traitorous wobble again.

"Promises, promises," I whispered, trying for sass, but it came out a little more breathless than I intended.

His gaze burned into mine, filled with hungry anticipation. "Keep tempting me, Nat. See what happens."

Before I could answer, before I could melt into him or kiss him again or drag him back to the suite, the sound of footsteps clattered from down the hall, followed by the unmistakable voice of my sister.

"Guys?" Paige called, cheerful and unaware. "You two hiding from us?"

We froze. I inhaled sharply. Easton's mouth twitched into a smirk that said he was anything but sorry.

"Shit," I whispered, frantically flinging the mistletoe down the hall.

He leaned in again, pressing a chaste kiss to the corner of my mouth. "Nope," he called in an annoyingly steady voice. "Just . . . getting some air."

"You sound winded," she called, her voice laced with suspicion—and something that sounded awfully close to older-sister I-told-you-so sparkle.

"Just discussing mistletoe traditions!" Easton answered easily, sounding far too composed for someone who'd just had a very scandalous hallway blowjob moment. His voice rang out like he had *nothing* to hide. And the grin he shot me? Wicked. Absolutely wicked. His eyes sparkled with triumph, like this whole thing had gone *exactly* to plan.

I shot him a look that probably should've set his hair on fire. "You're impossible."

"And you love it," he whispered, leaning in like he didn't already know exactly what he was doing. His lips brushed mine again—soft, quick, maddeningly tender.

My heart did that annoying flip thing, my knees going a little traitorous again. "You're gonna get us caught," I hissed, because clearly *someone* had to be the voice of reason here, and it wasn't going to be the guy who still had a post-blowjob glow in his eyes.

"I know," he murmured, clearly delighted by the threat of scandal. "Isn't it fun?"

He reached for my hand like we were just two innocent people walking into a holiday gathering and *not* freshly making-out fugitives. His fingers wrapped around mine, warm and steady, and he tugged me gently down the hall.

I rolled my eyes, my cheeks still on fire, and begrudgingly let him pull me along.

As we rounded the corner into the dining area where people were eating breakfast, Paige's eyes immediately zeroed in on us. Her brows lifted. "You two look suspiciously happy."

"Mistletoe," Easton said innocently, flashing the grin that had probably gotten him out of three parking tickets and half his high school detentions . . . and made him a famous Hollywood star. "Makes the season merry."

I opened my mouth to deny everything—and then promptly closed it again when I realized I had no poker face left. None. Zilch. My cheeks were still flaming, my lips probably kiss-swollen, and I was 90 percent sure my hair looked like someone had run their hands through it. Because someone had.

"Mm-hmm," Paige said, narrowing her eyes like she was conducting a full forensic sweep. "I see."

I busied myself with the cookie tray, grabbing a snowman-shaped treat I wasn't going to be able to taste because my mouth still remembered Easton.

He leaned over and whispered low in my ear, "That's your trying-to-look-innocent face. It's adorable. But very obvious."

I gave him a sharp elbow to the gut, which only made him laugh under his breath.

But despite the embarrassment coursing through me, despite my every instinct yelling that this was dangerous territory, I couldn't deny the thrill still dancing through my veins. The way my skin buzzed where he'd touched me. The way his smile had settled somewhere under my ribs and refused to leave.

It had been worth every reckless, scandalous second.

And judging by the victorious gleam in his eyes, he knew it, too.

The jerk.

I'd missed him.

And that was the problem.

Because missing him . . .

It was starting to feel an awful lot like falling for him all over again.

CHAPTER 16

Natalie

Me: SOS. I have tragic news. Send chocolate immediately.

Casey: Did you lose your phone in the freezer again?

Me: THAT HAPPENED ONCE!

Riley: Twice. But anyway, spill.

Me: I'm afraid I've contracted a dangerous condition.

Me: Symptoms: accelerated pulse, emotional vulnerability, mild nausea.

Me: WebMD says death is imminent.

Casey: . . .

Riley: Sounds familiar . . .

Me: It's love, guys. I think I'm falling in love. Send help.

Riley: WITH EASTON??? 😱😍

Casey: Finally. I'm tired of pretending I don't know already.

Me: How do you know? You're not even here.

Casey: I can't believe that's a real question.

Riley: It's insulting, actually.

Me: Shut up. This is serious. I didn't sign up for feelings. I signed up for hot guys and tasteful holiday flings.

Casey: Aw, she's malfunctioning.

Me: I swear to fucking hell . . . my chest hurts when he smiles. That can't be normal, right?

Riley: Not normal, but totally on brand for you. Wait, is Easton still wearing those sweaters you told us about? That would explain the symptoms.

Me: Yes. And it's making my brain do weird things. And my vagina.

Riley: RIP Natalie's independence, we had a good run.

Casey: OK, seriously though, why are you acting like love is a tragedy?

Me: Because it is?? Hello, have you ever seen a rom-com? Someone always ends up crying, usually me.

Casey: Yeah, but this is real life . . . not one of Easton's movies.

Me: Real life is worse. People leave. Feelings change. It's not exactly foolproof.

Riley: Easton's not people, though. He's your people.

Me: You don't know that.

Casey: Nat. Be real for a second. Why don't you want to fall in love?

Me: Because if I fall . . . What if he doesn't catch me?

Riley: And what if he does?

Casey: Maybe it's time to stop thinking about the fall and start thinking about the landing.

Me: OK, fine, Yoda.

Riley: For real, though, you deserve happiness. Even if it scares you.

Me: Wow. Thanks for making me have feelings in a group chat named after Santa.

Casey: By the way, we did not approve changing the group name to "Santa's Side Chicks." Parker almost had a heart attack.

Me: And then you got jiggy with it, right? So, you're welcome.

Riley: . . .

Casey: Go kiss Easton and tell him you like him.

Riley: And send pictures or it didn't happen.

Me: I hate you both. Love you. But also hate you.

Casey: She said "love"! It's a Christmas miracle!

Me: You're embarrassing me, Case-face.

Riley: Have fun kissing Easton!

Casey: Tell his sweater we said hi.

Me: GOODBYE FOREVER.

The moment I stepped onto the ice, I knew I'd made a terrible life decision.

Not the kind where you accidentally text your ex at two a.m. because Spotify shuffled to your song and you suddenly forgot how to have boundaries. And not even the kind where you order sushi from a gas station and spend the next twelve hours having a spiritual experience on your bathroom floor.

Yes. Both of those things had happened to me. No, I wasn't proud of either.

This was worse. This was full-body regret. Existential-crisis regret. The kind where your brain is screaming *abort mission*, your feet are sliding in opposite directions, and your dignity is clinging to the railing like it's Jack in the ocean and Rose's stupid fucking door she wouldn't share.

"Are we sure this is a pre-wedding activity and not a secret plot to thin the bridal party?" I asked, arms windmilling as I tried to center myself, which only made me look like a drunk scarecrow attempting yoga.

"Technically," Ellie said, gliding past me like an ice ballerina with a cider in hand. "Paige called it 'festive bonding.' So basically, yes."

"Excellent," I muttered. "I love bonding. Can't wait to break my femur for it."

The skating rink was a pop-up winter wonderland setup just down the road from the B and B. Fairy lights were strung overhead in crisscrossing loops, casting a soft, enchanted glow across the ice like we were trapped inside a holiday snow globe. A vendor cart off to the side was doing God's work serving hot chocolate laced with peppermint schnapps, and someone had the gall to be DJing a mix of Christmas classics and, for some reason, Céline Dion's "All By Myself."

Not that I was complaining. My knees were shaking too hard for me to do anything except mentally cling to her high notes for support.

Around me, other wedding guests skated like they were born on blades—laughing, twirling, holding hands. Meanwhile, I was inching along the wall like Bambi if Bambi had anxiety, schnapps breath, and a mild vendetta against winter sports.

Small mercy? Easton hadn't shown up yet.

He'd been delayed—something about a last-minute call with his agent. Apparently, a new project was being fast-tracked, and he'd needed to step away before the group left for the rink.

Which was fine.

Really.

Totally fine.

Actually, it did give me time to maybe figure out how not to skate like an injured pelican before he arrived and saw me flailing.

Or—I don't know—stage a convincing injury, spend the rest of the night sipping schnapps-laced cocoa, and dramatically sighing about the fragility of the human ankle.

Also a solid plan.

The best part? The entire rink had been rented out for the night to keep the chaos contained to the wedding guests. Which meant no stray paparazzi and, even better, no random fans showing up to witness me biting it in front of my famous ex-boyfriend.

Ex.

Right.

I kept calling him that in my head, but . . . he wasn't really *feeling* like an ex lately.

Not with the way he looked at me.

Not with the way my heart kept acting like we hadn't missed a single beat.

Ugh.

I was halfway through mentally calculating how long I needed to skate before I could "gracefully retire" to the sidelines when I heard it.

That voice.

Low. Smug. Laced with just enough mischief to make me want to bodycheck someone on purpose.

"Hey, Trouble."

Oh no.

I didn't turn. I didn't *need* to turn. My entire bloodstream recognized Easton Maddox the second he entered the rink. It was like my hormones were on high alert. *Code red: panty dropper incoming.*

"Perfect," I muttered under my breath. "Just in time to witness my untimely demise."

He chuckled, the sound far too warm for this much ice. "You look like you're really thriving out here."

"I *am* thriving," I said defensively, just as my left foot slid out like it was trying to disown me. I caught myself on the railing, barely. "This is all part of the routine."

"I figured."

I almost fell again—flailing, wobbling, one ankle dramatically turning inward—and it suddenly felt like way too much effort to pretend I was anything close to a world-class skater.

"I need a new set of legs, actually," I admitted, gripping the railing and wobbling like a baby giraffe. "As we both know, I'm very good at a lot of things . . . but this is apparently not one of them. Makes Lincoln Daniels even more sexy, if you ask me."

Easton's eyes flicked to mine, his jaw tightening just slightly. There was a soft, unmistakable growl from somewhere deep in his chest.

Jealousy. Oh, he hated that.

But he didn't say a word.

Because every warm-blooded human in North America knew Lincoln Daniels *was* sexy. It was a universal truth, like gravity or Mariah Carey owning Christmas.

Instead, Easton wordlessly pulled off his coat, dropped to sit on the nearest bench, and started lacing up his skates with the kind of quiet, efficient skill that made my stomach flip. Which reminded me, unfortunately, of something truly dreadful about him.

He was a *great* ice-skater.

Not just good. *Stupid* good. Like, smooth-as-silk, might've-been-cast-in-a-*Disney-on-Ice*-production kind of good.

He stepped onto the rink and glided a short distance with the grace of a man who had zero business being that smug about it. "Don't worry," he called over his shoulder, like he was some knight in fleece armor. "You've got me now."

"Oh great," I muttered, preparing for death. "Are you going to carry me bridal-style around the rink while I sob into your shoulder?"

He glanced back at me like he was genuinely considering it. "I could. But we both know your pride might not survive."

"My pride didn't survive the moment I took a shot of schnapps and agreed to this, actually."

He skated toward me, fast and smooth, and held out both hands like a damn Disney prince. "Come here."

I glanced around nervously. Paige's future in-laws were sipping cider by the heater. My mom was somewhere on the far end chatting up the officiant. MeMaw was trying to convince the DJ to let her perform a dramatic reading of *'Twas the Night Before Christmas* over a trap beat.

She was already holding the mic. So there was that.

And at least five people were *definitely* staring at Easton like he'd skated right off a movie screen. Because, well, technically, he *had*.

"Nope."

"Nat."

"I value my life," I said, taking a half step back and pressing myself deeper into the wall like I could phase through it and escape.

"Come on," he said, his voice softer now. Less teasing. "Just trust me."

Ugh. I hated when he did that . . . when he dialed the charm down to sincerity. It was disarming. Like a heat-seeking missile aimed directly at my stupid, fluttery heart.

I stared at his hands. They looked warm. Safe. *Deceptive.*

After a beat too long, I sighed and placed mine in his.

Instant regret.

Instant butterflies.

"I hate you for being so good at this," I muttered as he pulled me gently toward him, guiding me away from the wall.

"No, you don't," he said, smiling like he had a secret and I was it. "You love me."

My heart hiccupped at the word. That word.

But I played it cool. I always played it cool.

"I tolerate you," I said breezily. "I tolerate you with fondness."

"That's a dangerous level of affection, Trouble," he murmured—*spinning me*—like I wasn't a sentient panic attack in rental skates.

"Don't get cocky."

I let out a very undignified squeak as I nearly collided with a toddler in a puffy coat, but Easton caught me. Of course he did. His hands gripped my waist, grounding me instantly.

"Okay," I panted, breathless. "You're good. Exactly how are you so good again?"

"I played hockey for five years before I moved to town," he said. "And also, I'm a man of many hidden talents."

"How did I not know you played hockey?" I asked, trying to think if that had ever come up.

"I was always much too interested in finding out everything about you to tell you everything about me," he said with a wink.

But for some reason, the thought of that didn't sit well. And it made me think far too much.

I let him lead me around the rink, trying not to look like I was a malfunctioning Roomba. Every time I stumbled, he caught me. Every time I cursed under my breath, he laughed softly and told me I was doing great.

And I hated it.

I hated how good he felt.

How good *this* felt.

Like we still fit. Like we hadn't been ripped apart, reshaped by heartbreak and distance and time. Like we were still made of the same notes in the same song, even if we hadn't heard the melody in a while.

"You know," he said, voice dropping into something lower, something that curled around my spine, "you're better than you think."

I raised a skeptical eyebrow, focusing on not toppling into a nearby bridesmaid. "At skating?"

He shook his head, a soft smile playing at his lips. "At letting go."

I blinked at him, my heart thudding once, twice, too loud beneath my ribs. "That's a bold observation from someone currently holding me upright."

"And yet," he murmured, his eyes never leaving mine, "you're not fighting me off."

I rolled my eyes to hide the flutter in my chest. "I'm cold and helpless and a little drunk. It's purely survival instinct."

"Of course it is," he said with a grin that somehow looked like it knew every version of me: past, present, and the one I hadn't quite become yet.

He slowed us to a gentle stop near the middle of the rink. The lights above sparkled gold and soft white, like someone had strung a galaxy across the night just for us. Music floated from the speakers—a slow song, something warm and crooning, the kind of track that always hit harder in December.

He reached up and brushed a strand of hair away from my face, the tips of his fingers grazing my temple, my cheek. The touch was light, reverent. Like he didn't want to startle the moment in case it decided to vanish.

"You know what I wish?" he asked, his voice quieter now. Almost careful.

I looked up at him, my throat tightening. "What?"

"I wish you'd stop being so scared of me."

I blinked. The words landed with a strange sort of precision, right where all my doubts lived.

"I'm not scared of you."

"You are," he said without accusation. Just truth. "Not in a big, dramatic way. But in the small, quiet ways. You flinch every time I get too close to the truth."

I tried to laugh it off, to cut the tension before it grew teeth. "You're very full of yourself tonight."

But he didn't smile. He didn't joke.

"I'm full of you," he said simply. "All the versions of you I've ever loved. The girl in the truck bed under the stars. The woman standing in front of me now. All of it. I've carried you with me. And I'm not going anywhere, Nat. No matter how many walls you put up."

My breath caught in my chest like it didn't know how to get out.

I wanted to say something. To tell him he was wrong or right, or that I didn't know which way was up anymore when he looked at me like that. But the words got stuck somewhere in the hollow between my heartbeat and the memories I hadn't dared to touch.

He let the silence sit between us like it deserved space. Then, with a small smile, he offered me his hand again.

"One more lap?"

I nodded, afraid if I spoke, the emotion blooming in my chest would spill out all over the ice.

This time, I leaned into him without hesitating.

Let him guide me.

Let the rhythm of the glide, the hum of the music, the shimmer of lights blur out everything else. The past, the future, the thousand ways we could mess this up again.

Because right now, I didn't want to be afraid.

I just wanted *this*—the steady pulse of his hand in mine, the warmth of him beside me, the soft scrape of blades against ice and the promise of something not yet broken.

And for one perfect lap, I let it be enough.

CHAPTER 17

Natalie

"All right, skaters and future emergency room patients!" Paige shouted from the center of the rink, holding up a thermos like it was a torch. "Who's ready for the official pre-wedding Drinking Olympics: Winter Death Edition?"

"Oh no," I muttered, clutching Easton's sleeve. "This feels like my last night on earth."

"It's festive," Easton said, shrugging with a smirk. "Besides, we've survived worse. Remember the gingerbread rum shooters junior year?"

"Barely," I muttered. "I saw Santa Claus getting into his car that night and tried to confess my sins."

Easton threw his head back and laughed. Loudly. Obnoxiously. Beautifully. And then, without waiting for my consent or my general sense of self-preservation to kick in, he tugged me toward the growing circle of people gathering near center ice.

"Come on, partner. Let's show these amateurs how it's done."

"Excuse me?" I dug in my heels, well, blades, resisting. "Who said we're partners?"

He gave me that look. That Easton Maddox look that was roughly 40 percent challenge, 60 percent cocky affection, and 100 percent trouble.

"Nat," he said, like he was stating a simple fact. "We're *always* partners."

I rolled my eyes so hard I nearly gave myself whiplash, but fine. The man had a point. Team MadNat—or Eastalie, depending on which of our classmates had crafted fanfic about us in their high school notebooks—did have a long and storied legacy of competitive glory.

And an even longer history of questionable judgment.

We joined the circle, which had grown into a chaos spiral of veil-wearing bridesmaids, flannel-clad groomsmen, and at least one elderly relative who looked like they'd been dared onto the rink and were now deeply regretting every life choice that had led them to this moment.

Paige, glorious and slightly wobbly in her bride-to-be glow, wore a sparkly white veil taped to the top of a hockey helmet. Honestly? Genius. Wouldn't be ideal for the bride to suffer a pre-wedding concussion. Maybe I needed one of those, too.

Across the ice, MeMaw sipped aggressively from a bedazzled thermos and hollered "Let's GOOOOOO!" like she was pregaming a football game instead of a wedding skate night, while another guest nearly collided with the DJ booth attempting a pirouette that definitely exceeded their skill level and alcohol tolerance.

"All right!" shouted Jordan—or maybe it was Tommy, it was hard to tell with the puffer jacket and beer scarf combo—as he skated to the center with a megaphone he definitely wasn't qualified to use. "Here are the rules. I'll call out a challenge. If you fail, your team drinks. If you succeed, you pick another team to drink. If *anyone* falls while drinking, *everyone* drinks. And by drink, I mean chug. From your designated flask. Got it?"

Silence.

Then: *DEAFENING CHEERS.*

I clapped my hand to my forehead. "This feels like that time Bobby Joe thought he could rollerblade with the leaf blower strapped to his back."

"Ah," Easton sighed dreamily. "The golden age."

"The age of bad decisions."

"Details," he said, brushing my comment off as he towed me to the starting line like this was the NHL and we were about to win the Stanley Cup.

"First challenge!" Jordan bellowed . . . And yes, I'd committed to calling him Jordan for now. "Couples Skate Relay. You and your partner must skate from this cone to that cone"—he gestured to two traffic pylons that looked suspiciously like they'd been stolen from the parking lot—"without letting go of each other's hands. If you do, or if you fall, you drink. If you win, you choose which team drinks."

I turned to Easton with narrowed eyes. "You've got Olympic ankles. I'm out here like a baby moose on rollerblades. This will end badly."

"Then hold on tight, Trouble," he said, offering his hand with a wink. "I've got you."

We lined up at the start. To our left, Paige was being steadied by Levi. To our right, Ellie and her partner were already arguing over who had better balance while their skates drifted in opposite directions.

"Three! Two! One— GO!"

Easton launched.

I . . . did not.

Or rather, I *launched* in the way one might when yanked behind a speedboat against their will.

"Easton!" I yelped, holding his hand with both of mine now. "Slow down! I'm clinging to life and dignity."

"You're doing amazing!" he called cheerfully, gliding backward while pulling me forward. "Channel your inner Elsa!"

"Elsa had *magic powers*, you maniac."

We skidded around the cone in what could generously be called a controlled spiral and started the return lap. My feet were doing something that felt vaguely illegal, but somehow, by some actual miracle, we crossed the finish line upright and—more importantly—still holding hands.

Jordan blew his whistle. "WINNERS: Easton and Natalie! Choose a team to drink!"

Easton looked at me, smugness radiating off him. "Your call, partner."

I grinned evilly and pointed at Ellie. "You giggled when I fell during warm-ups. Justice is served."

Ellie bowed with a flourish and took her shot like a champ. Her partner followed . . . though definitely not as champ-like.

"Next round!" Jordan bellowed, his cheeks flushed from cold and cider. "Drunken Charades: Ice Edition! One partner acts it out. The other guesses. Failure equals chug. Extra failure equals double chug."

"What exactly qualifies as an 'extra' failure?" I asked . . . because evidently, I was incapable of learning.

Jordan didn't hesitate. He pointed directly at me. "That's a shot for talking back."

"What?!"

"Make that two."

I groaned and grabbed two shots off the tray that had appeared out of nowhere. I winced through the first—it was tequila, and not the good kind. It was more regret, in liquid form. But before I could brace for the second, Easton reached over, scooped it up, and downed it like a damn hero.

He gagged. I felt marginally better.

"Thanks, partner," I muttered.

He grinned, and my heart did a crazy little hiccup in my chest. "Anytime."

That was happening a suspiciously large number of times since he'd popped out of the woodwork.

I blamed it on the alcohol. Or a heart attack. Anything that didn't have to do with unresolved emotions over his stupid, perfect face. And personality. And the fact that we'd slept together. And kept sleeping together.

"Nat?" Easton prompted gently.

"Huh?" I blinked. I had apparently just been standing there, staring at him like a lovestruck raccoon.

He laughed softly. "I said, do you want to act, or should I?"

"Oh please," I scoffed, trying to recover any remaining dignity. "I've seen your acting. Step aside, amateur."

He clutched his chest like I'd wounded him. "I won a Kids' Choice Award!"

I pretended I wasn't impressed. Although, I had seen everything he'd been in, and if there was anyone who deserved any type of acting award . . . it was him.

I couldn't admit that, though.

"All right, but only because you're cute," he muttered, handing me the tiny whiteboard with the prompt, and dragging his fingers across mine in a very *unnecessary* way, let the record show.

I pretended that my breath didn't do anything out of the ordinary. It was a bold-faced lie.

I wobbled my way to the middle of the rink and flipped over the whiteboard: PENGUIN.

Really? I'd spent the last hour waddling like one. This felt like targeted mockery.

I flapped. I wiggled. I made a high-pitched honking noise that would have concerned a few wildlife officials.

I had to take a shot for that since evidently bird noises were against the rules.

Easton narrowed his eyes like he was solving a cryptic crossword puzzle. "Flightless bird? Angry goose? Weird seal?"

Was he serious right now? *Flightless bird* was his first guess?

I flailed harder.

"PENGUIN!" he finally shouted.

I dropped to the ice in victory, arms flung wide.

"Correct!" Jordan yelled. "Winners choose your victims!"

Easton and I pointed immediately at Paige and Levi, who groaned but took their shots, lifting their flasks in a solemn toast.

The night blurred into shrieks and laughter, snowflakes falling steadily as each new game topped the last—Human Curling, "Ice Ice Baby" Karaoke, and a snow angel competition that ended with Easton face-first in a drift and MeMaw yelling, "Suck it, Hollywood!" before flopping down beside him and leaving an angel with a suspiciously aggressive hip placement.

And through it all, he stayed by my side.

Every time I stumbled, he caught me. Every time I laughed until I cried, he laughed right with me.

By the end of the night, we were leaning against the side of the rink, breathless and red-cheeked, our gloves sticky with spiked cider, our knees weak from cold and too much laughter.

He leaned against the wall beside me, his shoulder pressed to mine. "Just like old times," he said softly.

"Only colder. And wetter. And with more alcohol-fueled public shame."

He smiled, slow and warm. "We were always good like this. Laughing. Messy. A little dangerous."

"Speak for yourself. I was an angel."

"You tried to race me down a hill in a sled and launched us both into a pine tree."

"And you caught me before I broke my neck," I said. "So really, that situation was super romantic."

He didn't say anything at first. Just looked at me with that quiet, heart-twisting expression that made everything else fade. "You know," he said, his voice softer now, "you're still my favorite person to fall with."

My heart stuttered. Like a scratched record skipping back to the part that always hurt.

I looked away quickly, focusing very intently on the snow stuck to my glove. Because this had started as a game. As tradition. As fun.

Not in some obvious, cinematic way . . . but in that quiet, breathless way you feel when your heart suddenly realizes it's not alone.

Easton wasn't playing, though. He never had been.

And deep down, I'd always known that.

Every time he caught me before I fell, every look that lingered longer than it should have, every soft laugh we shared like a secret—I felt it. That this wasn't temporary. That this wasn't just a chapter we'd already written.

It was something else. Something still unfolding.

And even though I didn't know where it would lead . . . I knew I didn't want to walk away from it. Not this time.

CHAPTER 18

Natalie

The fire crackled, popping softly as flames licked the edges of the logs, bathing their faces in firelight that flickered like a heartbeat. The whole wedding party was scattered around in a circle, some wrapped in blankets, others holding long sticks over the fire with marshmallows slowly melting into gooey perfection.

Someone passed me a chocolate bar and a graham cracker. I took them absently, still half listening to Paige's dramatic retelling of her skiing disaster from two years ago, complete with hand motions, ski pole miming, and a questionable imitation of a snowplow.

I sat close to Easton, our knees brushing now and then. It was the kind of gentle, unspoken closeness that made my chest ache in that quiet, hollowed-out kind of way.

The kind I'd been missing since the moment I walked away.

His arm rested behind me on the back of the bench we were sharing—not touching me exactly, but so close I could feel his warmth along my shoulder.

The stars were out, clear and sharp and painfully pretty above us, and a speaker sat near the woodpile, someone's phone feeding it a soft stream of acoustic Christmas covers, each one more whispery and nostalgic than the last. It gave the whole night this strange, dreamlike hum, like we were inside a snow globe that hadn't been shaken yet.

"You need help with that?" Easton asked, nodding at my assembled but unroasted s'mores ingredients.

I raised an eyebrow. "I can toast a marshmallow, thank you very much."

He gave me a skeptical look that was entirely unwarranted. "I seem to remember someone lighting hers on fire four separate times that year at the cabin."

"That was intentional," I said, lifting my chin. "I like a little drama with my sugar."

He laughed, and the sound of it, familiar, unguarded, laced with something wistful . . . it wrapped around me like one of the flannel blankets strewn across the benches. "Fuck. I've missed this. I don't know how I've survived without it."

"What? The threat of third-degree sugar burns?"

"No," he said, his smile softening. "Just . . . sitting next to you. Sharing the fire. Talking about nothing. You . . . you weren't just the love of my life. You were my best friend."

The words lodged somewhere tight in my lungs.

I didn't respond right away. My throat felt tight, like something unspoken was pushing its way up through all the defenses I'd carefully rebuilt. The ones that used to hold steady. The ones that had started to crumble the second I saw him again.

"I missed this, too," I finally whispered, the words slipping out before I could stop them.

His eyes searched mine like he could hear everything I wasn't saying. And maybe he could.

He took the stick from my hand with gentle fingers, the graze of his skin electric, then speared a marshmallow onto it with practiced ease. "You know," he said, his voice low and warm, "you used to always do this thing—burn a marshmallow beyond recognition on purpose, take one dramatic bite, and then hand it to me like you were doing *me* the favor."

I smiled despite myself. "Still a valid strategy."

"I fell for it every time."

"You liked it," I said, nudging his knee with mine.

He gave me a look. "I liked you."

The words slipped out so easily, so confidently, like they weren't holding the weight of years between us.

I looked down at the fire, the orange glow flickering across the snow-dusted ground. My heart thudded against my chest in slow, careful beats, like it was trying to decide whether or not to believe him.

Maybe it was the cocoa I'd had earlier. Maybe it was the stars or the way his shoulder kept brushing against mine like he couldn't stop reaching for me in these small, unconscious ways.

But for the first time, I didn't want to dodge the feeling.

I wanted to lean in to it. Let it warm me. Let it burn . . . even if it only lasted the night.

"Hey, Nat," he said, brushing a marshmallow onto a graham cracker and handing it to me like an offering. "Do you ever regret it?"

The question hit like a gust of cold air, unexpected and sharp.

I stared down at the s'more in my hand. My fingers clenched around it too tightly.

"Regret what?" I asked, but we both knew the answer. He didn't have to say it.

He didn't look away. "Ending it."

For a moment, all I could hear was the *snap* of the firewood and the *thud* of my heart behind my ribs.

I stared into the flames like they held the answer, the flickering light catching on the edges of the chocolate bar still unopened in my hand. I turned it slowly, unthinking. Stalling.

"You know, it all happened so fast," I whispered finally, my voice barely audible above the crackle.

"I know," he said.

"I was eighteen. You were going to LA. I knew enough about Hollywood to understand what happens there. I didn't want to be the girl waiting by the phone. I didn't want to hold you back. I didn't want to tie you down."

He was quiet for a moment before saying, "I wasn't asking for strings, Natalie. I was asking for *you*."

His voice wasn't angry. Just quiet. Honest. Like he was gently picking at the stitches of an old wound, not to reopen it, but to understand how it had ever needed closing in the first place.

"I know," I whispered. Shame crawled up my throat, bitter and hot. "But I thought . . . if I let myself need you that much, and it didn't work . . ." I trailed off, eyes stinging. "I wouldn't recover."

He nodded slowly. "So you left before it could break."

I didn't answer. I didn't need to. The truth sat between us, a living, breathing thing. Heavy. Real.

He leaned forward slightly, elbows on his knees, staring into the fire. "I used to think . . . if I just became successful enough, you'd come back. That if I did something *big* enough, you'd regret letting go."

I jerked my head toward him, startled by the rawness in his voice. "Easton . . ."

"I don't mean it to guilt-trip you," he said. "I know we were just kids. But that didn't make what I felt any less real."

I swallowed, my fingers tightening around the melting chocolate in my hand. "It was real for me, too," I said hoarsely. "It was *so* real. That was part of the problem."

He turned toward me again. "So . . . do you regret it?"

He'd already laid everything bare—his hurt, his hope, the ache he'd carried alone. I owed him the real answer. Not a deflection. Not a half-truth. The real one.

So I gave it to him.

I stared at the fire, my voice barely above a whisper. "Yes."

He blinked.

"Not because it wasn't the choice I thought I had to make," I said quickly. "I believed it was right at the time. But I still missed you. Every year. Every birthday. Every time I saw a movie trailer with your name on it and thought, *He's still him.*"

He didn't say anything. Just looked at me like I'd cracked open a part of myself he thought he'd never see again.

"And then I buried it," I admitted. "Because if I let myself regret it too much, I'd have to face what it cost me. And I wasn't brave enough to do that."

The fire hissed. Someone laughed somewhere to my left, completely unaware the ground beneath my feet was shifting like sand.

Easton's eyes were soft, searching, his thumb brushing against the side of his hot cocoa cup like he needed something to ground him. And I knew I wasn't the only one remembering how it felt to be us, back then. Two kids—one already sure, the other too scared to believe it could last.

I turned slightly to face him more fully, my voice quieter, but more sure. "Can I ask you something now?"

He looked over at me, that gentle steadiness in his eyes. "Anything."

"If you felt all of that," I said slowly, heart thudding in my chest. "Why didn't you come after me?"

He didn't flinch. His jaw tensed, but his eyes didn't leave mine. They stayed steady, steady and deep, the way they used to when he was trying to make sure I really heard him.

"I did," he said quietly.

I stared at him, stunned, the *crackle* of the fire suddenly too loud in my ears. "You—what?"

"I came back the next morning," he continued. "Before I left for LA. I hadn't even finished packing. I just got in the car and drove to your house. I had no plan. Just this desperate need to see you . . . to convince you to change your mind."

My breath caught. I felt it like a snag in my chest—sharp and sudden, unraveling everything I thought I knew about that day. "I didn't know that."

"I just couldn't breathe knowing you were really gone." He looked down at his hands, flexing them slightly like he was still holding the steering wheel, still feeling the tremor in his fingers. "The whole drive, it felt like my chest was too tight. Like if I didn't see you, I'd lose something I wouldn't get back."

I stared at him, frozen in the space between then and now.

"But I didn't make it past the front step," he said quietly. "MeMaw opened the door before I could even knock—and then she stepped outside like she'd been waiting for me all night."

The image hit me like a memory half remembered: I could picture her perfectly—arms crossed, wearing that leopard-print robe she always packed when she spent the night, standing at the door like some kind of Southern oracle who already knew the ending and was just waiting for everyone else to catch up.

A lump rose in my throat. "She didn't tell me."

"She told me *you* didn't want to talk," he said thickly. "But she asked if I would walk with her. Just for a bit."

I could see it now—the dirt road that ran alongside the woods, the early morning light slanting through the trees. MeMaw marching down the road like she was headed to deliver a sermon the world didn't know it needed.

"She asked me if I loved you," Easton went on, his voice low. "And I told her I'd never loved anyone more."

He paused, eyes on the fire, like the flames were reflections of that morning, of frost on car windows and the ache of goodbye that never got said out loud.

"She believed me. But she told me that wasn't the question that mattered. Not really."

I held my breath.

"She wanted to know whether I loved you enough to let you figure out who you are without me."

My heart cracked clean in two. A slow, deep splintering I felt behind my ribs. The kind of ache that echoed.

"She said you had a fire in you," he said, the ghost of a smile on his lips. "That if I tried to hold on too tight, I'd only smother what I loved. That the girl I loved needed to fly. Even if it meant flying away from me."

The tears came fast, unannounced, stinging in the corners of my eyes.

"I didn't want to hear it," Easton said, softer now. "Every part of me wanted to argue. But I looked at her, and I knew she was right. You needed to grow into yourself without me standing in the doorway."

His voice faltered, then steadied again.

"I sat in my car for a long time afterward," he said. "Just . . . sitting. Gripping the steering wheel like it could hold me together. Knowing I could walk up to your door and try to fight for you. That I could knock until you opened it, beg you to come with me. And maybe you would've. Maybe you'd have said yes. Maybe we would've packed your suitcase, and we'd be living in some shoebox apartment in LA, trying to make sense of the rest of it."

He paused, his thumb brushing slowly across the top of my hand. That's when I realized—my fingers had found his. Sought him out without permission, without awareness. Just instinct.

"But if I had," he whispered, "maybe you would've come with me. Maybe you would've stayed. But maybe you would've always wondered if you gave up a piece of yourself just to hold on to me."

His words sank into me like soft rain into dry earth, like something my soul had been waiting to hear for years.

"I left," he whispered. "But I didn't stop loving you. Not for one day. And not because I wanted to let go. Because someone wise reminded me that real love isn't a leash. It's a lantern."

My throat thickened.

"You needed space to find your own light," he said, looking at me—not flinching, not looking away. "And I had to believe you'd find your way home."

My heart splintered under the weight of it . . . because I remembered that version of myself. The girl who stood on the edge of everything, terrified that love would make her small. That it would claim too much. That she'd disappear into someone else's story and forget how to write her own.

But this boy . . . this man, he hadn't tried to pull me back. He'd stepped back instead. Lit the road behind me, not to lead me away from him, but to make sure I could see.

I opened my mouth to say something. Anything.

But then his phone buzzed.

It was soft. Just a quiet hum against the bench beside us. The kind of thing that would've been easy to ignore if we weren't both sitting in the stillest, most suspended moment of the entire night.

Easton didn't move.

He didn't look at it. His eyes were still on me. Still holding my gaze like it mattered more than whatever name was lighting up that screen. Still holding my hand like it was a vow.

I might've pretended it hadn't happened, might've written it off as nothing—if not for the second *buzz*.

Then the third.

His lips parted like he was about to apologize for the world intruding.

And then, without letting go of me, he finally picked it up.

He didn't glance at the screen first. Just turned the phone over like it didn't matter. Like it was routine.

I didn't mean to look.

I really didn't.

But I did.

And my stomach dropped, a slow, sinking spiral of nausea that felt like it started in my heart and dragged all the way down.

It was a photo. A nude one, so to speak. Of her.

Vanessa Blake.

Easton's costar. Hollywood's latest obsession.

All glossy lips and effortless curves and a sultry voice that probably came with its own theme music. Golden skin and bedroom lighting and the kind of confidence that only came from knowing exactly what your body did to men. Knowing they'd look. Knowing they'd want.

And she wasn't just his costar. She was the one he'd been filming with for weeks now. The one who'd been interviewed beside him at those press junkets. The one who looked up at him with stars in her eyes and fingers on his arm in every single photo.

The one whose name had been linked to his in *every* damn headline since production started.

"Hollywood's hottest new pairing?"

"Behind-the-scenes sparks—are Maddox and Blake heating up offscreen?"

"On-set lovers or real-life romance?"

I'd seen them.

Of course I'd seen them.

Every link. Every photo. Every blinking, buzzworthy reminder of why getting over Easton Maddox was not as simple as putting away an old hoodie or deleting a number from my phone.

And now, here she was.

On *his* phone.

Naked. Glowing. Posed like she was meant to be framed.

"Fuck," Easton hissed, his whole body tensing. He went immediately to erase the picture, but it was too late.

I looked away, my chest squeezing so tight it was a miracle I could still breathe.

"I didn't ask for that," he said quickly.

I laughed, short and brittle. "You don't have to explain it. It's not like we're . . . anything," I added, waving my hand like I was erasing the last few days from existence. "We're just hooking up for the week, remember? And it's not like we have to do that."

He growled, low and sharp, like he couldn't stand the words even coming out of my mouth. "Natalie."

"It's fine," I said, standing too quickly and absolutely loathing the weird mix of hurt and agony I was experiencing at that moment. My legs didn't feel steady anymore. "She's gorgeous. You're gorgeous. It's not surprising."

"That's not the point," he said, stepping toward me.

"No, the point is, she's clearly comfortable enough to send you that, which probably means she thinks there's a chance you'll appreciate it."

"I don't," he said flatly, his tone carved from stone.

I forced a smile. "I'm not mad. Honestly. It's . . . whatever."

But my voice was too bright, too easy, and we both knew it. I was usually a confident girl, but something about seeing her perfect body had unraveled me in a way I hadn't expected.

Easton's eyes narrowed slightly. "You're doing that thing."

"What thing?" I asked, retreating half a step.

He followed. "That thing where you pretend you don't care. But you do. And I'm not letting you walk away with that look on your face . . . not after everything we just said. Not after what I told you."

I stiffened, trying to protect something inside me that had already cracked. "I'm not walking away. I'm going inside."

"No."

His voice was low and rough, a warning and a plea. "You don't get to walk away from me like this."

Then his hand closed gently around my wrist. Not hard. Not controlling. Just grounding. Just . . . anchoring.

The fire behind us crackled and faded into the background as he stepped into my space, eyes locked on mine, his chest brushing mine with every uneven breath.

"You are mine, Natalie."

My breath caught on the edge of his words.

"You always have been mine," he said, voice a rasp of emotion and steel. "And I don't care if a thousand women throw themselves at me. Strip down. Light themselves on fire. I wouldn't look twice. Because I already found the only girl who's ever mattered."

The world stopped spinning.

I opened my mouth, but nothing came out . . . because what could I possibly say to that?

He reached for my other hand, lacing our fingers together like he was stitching us back together one piece at a time.

"Come with me."

I shook my head, but my fingers were already threading through his, instinct stronger than logic.

"Easton—"

"I'm not doing this here," he said. "Not with people watching. Not with your heart retreating from me like usual."

Someone shouted our names behind us, a question tossed on the wind like confetti, but Easton didn't glance back. His grip on my hand tightened, his stride unwavering as he led me inside the bed-and-breakfast, up the creaky stairs, past the garland lining the railing. He didn't stop until we were inside our suite—our shared, complicated suite—and the door had clicked shut behind us like the sealing of a promise.

The air around us pulsed as he pushed me against the closed door.

"You need to hear this," he murmured, eyes burning into mine. "I've kissed actresses in movies. Held their faces like I meant it. Had fans scream my name like it belonged to them. I've had directors say I've got insane chemistry with women I couldn't pick out of a lineup now."

He leaned closer, close enough that I could feel the words against my skin.

"But you?" His gaze dipped to my mouth, then back up to my eyes. "You're tattooed on my memory. You're not chemistry. You're gravity. You are the standard. The girl every other girl has failed—and will always fail—to be."

A single tear slipped down my cheek, hot and uninvited. I swiped at it, furious at myself for breaking.

"You think I'd risk what I want, what we could be . . . for a nude?" he asked, his voice sharp, eyes searing into mine. "A picture from someone I don't even think about when I'm off set? No. That's not me. That's not who I am. That's *never* who I've been with you."

I tried to speak. But I couldn't. The words were tangled and knotted behind my teeth.

"You think I don't *see* what you're doing?" he said, his voice quieter now, but no less intense. "You're scared. You're looking for any reason to bolt. To tell yourself you were right to leave."

I flinched. It was too honest. Too exact.

He exhaled, like he hated calling me out but hated lying to me more.

He stepped even closer.

"But I won't let you run this time. I'm not letting you go. I let you fly once because you needed to grow. But now you're back. And this time, you're *mine.*"

I was shaking. With anger. With heartbreak. With the terrifying truth of how much I wanted to believe him.

"How do I know it won't happen?" I whispered, my voice thin and cracked. "How do I know that one kiss on set, one late night in a trailer won't spark something you didn't see coming?"

His answer was a vow.

"Because I've seen what life is like without you," he said, pressing his lips gently to my forehead, like I was fragile porcelain he didn't dare drop. "And I'll never live it again."

The wind blew against the double doors that led out to the balcony, rattling the glass. But we didn't move.

We were fire and storm and everything in between.

"I don't want anyone else," he whispered, the words slipping past my skin, carving straight into bone. "And no one else could ever touch what we had. What we still have. And if I have to tell you that every single day until you believe it, I will. I'll break down every wall, every doubt, every scar you've tried to hide behind."

I looked up at him, heart hammering, vision blurred with the tears I refused to let fall. I searched for the lie. For the thing he wasn't saying.

There wasn't one.

There was just Easton. Just his truth.

Just the two of us, suspended in the kind of moment you don't walk back from.

The last breath before the fall.

And this time . . . I wasn't sure I wanted to catch myself.

CHAPTER 19

Easton

Look at me," I said, my voice thick and low, scraping like gravel and heat against the space between us. My hips pressed hers harder into the wall, pinning her there like I was afraid she'd slip through my fingers if I let up for even a second. My erection strained against my denim, throbbing where it pressed into the heat of her.

"No one will ever measure up to you," I said, the words a rough promise between clenched teeth. "Not Vanessa. Not anyone. You hear me?"

Her breath hitched.

"You're mine," I said, slower now, my voice deepening like the words were dragged from the deepest part of me. "You've always been mine. And you always will be."

Her lips parted, her eyes darkening with that beautiful mix of want and disbelief. Her fingers curled into my shoulders, nails digging through the thick knit of my sweater like she didn't know whether to hold on or push me away.

"Easton," she whispered, her voice shaking. "You don't have to say that. I—I'm fine."

"Stop." The word came out like a growl.

I slid my hand up, fingers wrapping gently but firmly around the column of her throat, just enough pressure to make her gasp and tilt her head back. Her eyes fluttered closed for a beat, her body arching instinctively toward mine like she couldn't help it. Like she didn't want to.

"Don't you dare pretend with me, Nat." My voice was low and rough, thick with everything I hadn't been able to say until now. "I saw your face out there. I know you're not fine. But I'm telling you right now—no one else matters. You're the only one I've ever wanted. You believe me?"

She swallowed hard, her eyes flickering with every emotion she tried to bury . . . fear, hope, want. Her lips trembled as she nodded, just barely. "I—I want to," she whispered, her hands sliding up to frame my face, thumbs brushing over the stubble along my jaw with a reverence that gutted me. "It just . . . it reminds me of all the reasons I walked away to begin with. She's . . . she's gorgeous, and I'm—"

"You're everything," I cut in, my voice fierce, shaking, alive. "You're every late night when I couldn't sleep. Every word I wrote but never sent. Every breath that felt too heavy without you next to me."

I kissed her before she could say another word, before doubt could steal the air between us. My lips crashed against hers, possessive and desperate and unrelenting, like I could pour all the years apart back into her in one breathless, soul-deep press of mouths. She moaned into me, her fingers curling at the back of my neck, holding me there like she needed the anchor.

I deepened the kiss, my tongue sweeping in, claiming her, my hand in her hair pulling her head back as I broke away to trail hot kisses down her jaw, her neck, my teeth grazing her pulse point.

"You're fucking *everything*, Nat," I murmured against her skin, my voice rough with need. "No one else gets me like this. No one else makes me burn, makes me this desperate. Just you. Only you."

"Easton." She gasped, her hands sliding under my sweater, her nails raking down my back, leaving a trail of heat in their wake. "I need you. Please, I need you to show me. Make me believe it."

"Oh, I'll show you, baby," I growled, my hands moving to the hem of her sweater, yanking it over her head and tossing it aside, my eyes greedily taking her in.

She was in a white bra, the fabric so thin I could see her hardened nipples through it, and I groaned, my hands cupping her breasts, my thumbs brushing over the peaks. "Look at you," I said, my voice low and possessive. "So fucking perfect. These are mine, Nat. You hear me? Mine."

"Yes," she moaned, her head tipping back against the wall as I unhooked her bra, letting it fall to the floor. My hands immediately returned to her breasts, kneading them as I leaned down to take one nipple into my mouth.

I sucked hard, my tongue flicking over the sensitive bud, my teeth grazing it just enough to make her cry out, her hands tangling in my hair.

"Easton, oh fuck, yes." She gasped, her voice breaking as I moved to her other breast, giving it the same attention, my hand sliding down to grip her ass, squeezing hard through her jeans.

"You like that, baby?" I murmured against her skin, my voice rough as I sucked harder, my hand sliding between her legs, cupping her through her jeans, feeling her heat even through the denim. "You're so fucking wet for me already, aren't you? I can feel it. This pussy is mine, Nat."

"Yours," she whimpered, her hips bucking against my hand as I rubbed her, her arousal soaking through the fabric. "I'm yours, Easton. Only yours."

"That's right," I growled, my voice thick with need as I unbuttoned her jeans, yanking them down her hips along with her panties, leaving her bare before me. I stepped back just enough to look at her, my eyes poring over her flushed skin, her swollen lips . . . her dripping pussy.

"Fuck, look at you," I said, my voice low and reverent as I reached for her, my fingers sliding through her folds, spreading her arousal as I found her clit, circling it with my thumb. "So wet, so ready for me. You want my cock, don't you baby? You want me to fuck you, to make you mine?"

"Yes, Easton, please," she begged, her voice desperate as I slid two fingers inside her, curling them to hit that spot I knew would drive her wild, my thumb never stopping its assault on her clit. "I need you. I need you inside me. Please."

"You'll get me, baby," I promised, my voice rough as I fucked her with my fingers, watching her face as she moaned, her walls clenching around me, her hips rocking against my hand. "But first, I want you to come for me. I want to feel you fall apart on my fingers. Show me how much you need me, Nat. Show me you're mine."

"Easton, I'm—I'm so close." She gasped, her voice breaking as she clung to me, her nails digging into my shoulders, her body trembling under my touch.

"I've got you," I rasped, my fingers driving deeper. "Come for me, baby. Let go. I want to feel it."

Her climax hit her hard, her body shuddering against the wall as she screamed my name, her pussy clenching around my fingers, her arousal soaking my hand as I worked her through every wave of pleasure. "That's it, baby," I murmured, my voice low and encouraging as I watched her, my cock throbbing painfully in my jeans. "So fucking beautiful. All mine."

She was still trembling when I pulled my fingers out and brought them to my mouth, sucking her juices from them, savoring her like a man starved.

"You taste so fucking good," I said, my voice low and rough with want.

Then I reached for my jeans, unbuttoning them with one hand and shoving them down, boxers, too. My cock sprang free—hard, aching, the tip already slick with need.

And then she burst out laughing.

Not politely. Not quietly.

Full-body, slightly wheezy laughter. The kind that made her shake and cover her face with both hands.

I blinked down at her, my cock still very much standing at attention. "Um. You good?"

She dropped her hands just long enough to point at my discarded boxers on the floor. "Easton. Are those *surfing Santas?*"

I looked. Yep. Red trunks. Snowflakes. A repeating pattern of very jacked Saint Nicks hanging ten on candy cane surfboards.

"They were a gift," I said, smirking. "Limited edition. I had to be on a very exclusive list to get these."

She gasped through another laugh. "You're about to fuck the soul out of me, and you've got *Santa shredding* on your junk."

I grinned. "You'll be calling me Saint Nick by the end of this when I *gift* you with my cock. So it seems fitting."

"Fucking hell," she groaned, tossing her head back against the wall, still laughing. "You're completely unhinged."

I leaned in, pressing a kiss just beneath her jaw. "Naughty list. Permanent member."

"I'm never letting you live this down."

"You're about to be too wrecked to speak," I said, my voice dropping again as I grabbed her hips, pulling her tight against me, my cock brushing between her thighs. "So, go ahead and laugh now, Trouble. Because in about ten seconds, you'll be screaming instead."

She was still giggling when I pressed her farther into the wall, her bare chest rising and falling fast, her eyes glossy with desire and mischief. Fuck, she was beautiful like this—flushed and laughing and totally undone.

But the second my cock slid between her slick folds, her breath hitched, the laughter dying into a sharp gasp. Her eyes flew open, locking with mine. That one look? It scorched through every last bit of restraint I had left.

"I need to be inside you, Nat," my voice wrecked with need. "I need to bury myself so deep in your sweet, tight pussy that you forget your own name—forget every man who ever looked at you when I wasn't there. I want to fuck you until your body only knows mine. Until all you can say is my name."

Her eyes were glassy with pleasure as her fingers gripped my ass, rocking her hips up against my cock with a confidence and urgency that made my knees threaten to give. "I need you, too."

I groaned as I lifted her effortlessly. Her legs locked around my waist, and I pressed her back to the wall again, the thick head of my cock pushing into her. We both gasped—hers sharp and needy, mine ragged and barely restrained—as I held us there, letting the tension coil tight, savoring the way she clenched around me before giving her another inch.

"I'm already yours, baby," I growled, my voice rough with need as I finally thrust the rest of the way into her in one swift motion, burying myself to the hilt, her tight, wet heat enveloping me like a glove. "Fuck, Nat, you feel so good. So fucking tight. This pussy was made for me, wasn't it?"

"Yes, Easton, yes," she chanted, her nails digging into my shoulders as I started to move, my thrusts hard and deep, each one a claim as I fucked her against the wall.

"That's right," I growled, my hands gripping her hips tighter, my thrusts growing faster, deeper, the sound of our bodies coming together filling the room, the wet slap of skin on skin mixing with her moans and my groans. "No one else gets to have you, Nat. No one else gets to fuck you like this. No one else gets to feel you come around their cock. Just me. Say it."

"Just you, Easton." She gasped, her voice breaking as I pounded into her, my cock hitting that spot inside her with every thrust, driving her closer to the edge. "Only you. I'm yours."

"Damn right, you are," I growled, my hand sliding up to grip her throat again, my fingers tightening just enough to make her gasp, her eyes darkening with pleasure as I held her in place. "You're mine to fuck, mine to love, mine to keep. No one else will ever have you, Nat. No one else will ever fucking compare."

"Easton, I'm—I'm gonna come," she cried, her voice desperate as she clung to me, her body trembling, her walls clenching around me as I fucked her relentlessly. "Please, don't stop."

"Never, baby," I growled, my voice rough with need as I thrust deeper, my hand on her throat holding her steady, my other hand gripping her hip. "Come for me, Nat. Come all over my cock. Show me you're mine."

Her orgasm hit like a fucking explosion—she shattered in my arms, her body jerking against the wall as she screamed my name, loud and wrecked and perfect. Her pussy clamped down around me like a velvet vice, milking my cock so tight I saw stars. "Fuck, fuck, fuck," she gasped, her nails clawing down my back, her slick soaking my thighs, dripping down to my balls like she couldn't get enough of me.

That was all it took. The sound of her falling apart, the feel of her wrapped around me—mine, completely—and I lost it. I slammed into her one final time and came hard, spilling deep inside her with a guttural groan, my vision going white around the edges. Every pulse of my release branding her from the inside out.

My forehead dropped to hers, both of us gasping for air, her body still twitching beneath my hands.

"You're mine," I rasped, my voice rough, raw, reverent. I kissed her temple, holding her close, still buried deep. "All fucking mine."

We stayed like that for a long moment, our bodies pressed together against the wall, our breath mingling as we came down from the high. I held her close, my arms wrapping around her, my lips brushing against her forehead as I murmured, "It's just you, Nat. It's always been just you."

She didn't respond, her breath still uneven, her body soft against mine, and I could tell she was holding back, not ready to say the words I wanted to hear. I wanted to push, to ask her what she was feeling, to hear her say she loved me the way I loved her . . .

But before I could speak, a sharp knock cracked through the quiet like a thunderclap.

"Well, good to know *one* of us is getting some!"

Jordan.

His voice came through the door with the kind of smug glee only a lifelong friend could manage. "Guess you guys don't want to come back out to the fire, huh? Don't worry, I'll let everyone know you're . . . *occupied.*"

Natalie let out a strangled groan and buried her face in my chest. "Fucking hell, Jordan, go away!" Her voice was muffled, mortified, her hands gripping my arms like she could physically hold back the moment.

I couldn't help it . . . I laughed. A full, smug, utterly unrepentant laugh.

I looked down at her, caught that stormy flush in her cheeks, the way her lashes fluttered against her skin. She looked like sin and softness and the only thing I'd ever wanted. My thumb brushed along the curve of her lower lip, swollen and kiss-bitten, and I tipped her chin up so she had no choice but to look at me.

"Guess the secret's out," I said, my voice still rough with everything we hadn't said. "They all know you're mine again, Nat."

She groaned and swatted at my chest, but there was a smile tugging at the corners of her mouth. Small. Tentative. Real.

It wasn't a declaration.

Not yet.

But her gaze lingered. Her fingers didn't let go. And in the hush of the room, where the only sound was the slowing of our breath and the faint *creak* of old floorboards beneath us, I felt the shift.

A new beginning. A held breath. A promise starting to take shape.

I'd get her there. One step at a time. One truth at a time.

Because she was mine.

And no matter how long it took—she was going to believe it, too.

Natalie

The next morning's group chat was a fun time.

> **Casey:** Don't think we didn't notice the group name change, Natalie. Hot Mess Express? What did you do?

> **Me:** OK, so, um . . . we need to talk about something that happened last night. 😅😅😅

> **Casey:** Was it dick-related or feelings-related. Because I'm prepared for both.

> **Riley:** If it's Easton again, I'm gonna need a towel for my emotions.

> **Me:** He got all growly.

> **Casey:** Define. Because there's lots of ways that could go.

Riley: Are we talking "stay away from my woman" growly or "I just bit your name into this headboard" growly?

Riley: Or was it that special kind—where he sounds like he's about to rearrange your guts and your furniture, then build you a house to recover in?

Casey: What does that even mean?

Riley: . . .

Me: Growly like . . .

Me: He looked me dead in the eye and said "You're mine, Natalie. You've always been mine. You always will be." WHILE INSIDE ME!

Me: There was growling. There was wall pinning. I think my soul left my body and filed for marriage paperwork on its own.

Casey: I just dropped my phone on my face, and I'm not mad about it.

Riley: No because that's not sex. That's a binding ritual.

Me: I think I accidentally said "I'm yours" like I was being possessed by the ghost of every simpering heroine in a telenovela and couldn't stop myself.

Casey: Personally, I'm thriving off this.

Riley: Same. Although Jace wants to know if he drinks iced milk.

Me: He's not a psychopath, Riley. Gosh.

Me: As I was saying . . .

Me: I've never been more turned on in my life.

Me: Also Easton's friend heard everything and yelled through the door.

Me: So my villain origin story is officially LIVE!

Riley: An icon. A legend. A cautionary tale.

Casey: Honestly? At this point, lean in. Put it in the wedding program. "Natalie. Sister of the Bride, Officially off the Market, Bedroom Audio Available upon Request."

Riley: Ophelia says she liked that one, Case.

Me: Tell FiFi that this is serious. What if I can't even look at him without my knees turning to water and my frontal lobe turning to static?

Riley: That's not fear, babe. That's forever.

Casey: He growled "you're mine" and you basically purred in surrender . . . This is not a drill. This is endgame.

Me: I'm reiterating my need for a spiritual rinse and maybe a seven-step recovery plan for my heart. Possibly also for my vagina.

Riley: What you need to do is let him growl at you again. For science.

Me: . . .

CHAPTER 20

Natalie

I knew I was in trouble the moment Easton pulled a baseball cap low over his eyes and slipped on dark sunglasses before stepping out of his truck in front of the mall.

Nobody that ridiculously good-looking ever blended into a crowd—certainly not at Christmastime, when people were already half feral with stress, peppermint mochas, and BOGO sales.

"You realize you look like every celebrity who's trying not to look like a celebrity, right?" I asked as he helped me out of his truck.

He grinned, adjusting his hat with exactly the amount of smugness required to make my knees misbehave. "What do you want me to do? Wear a fake mustache and trench coat?"

"That might actually help," I muttered, falling in step beside him as we headed toward the entrance. "Though, then we'd just look like we were reenacting a live-action *Carmen Sandiego*."

Easton glanced sideways at me, lips twitching. "I think you secretly want me to get mobbed by fans."

"Trust me," I said, clutching my purse like a shield. "Getting crushed to death by overly enthusiastic teenagers waving glitter signs is not how I envision going out. Glitter is the herpes of craft supplies—I've told you this before."

"So you're saying I shouldn't expect any homemade glitter signs from you anytime soon?"

I narrowed my eyes, shuddering dramatically. "Don't even joke about that, Maddox."

He chuckled, reaching out without thinking to tuck a strand of hair behind my ear.

It was such a simple thing.

Barely a breath of touch. But my heart stuttered.

Because *something* had changed.

It wasn't just the echo of his voice in my head—*You're mine, Natalie.* Or the way I'd said *I'm yours* back like I was under some kind of slow-burn spell.

It was everything since.

The way his hand brushed mine now—not an accident, not a hesitant maybe, not some faded ghost of what we used to be. His fingers threaded firmly through mine, as if he'd claimed the right to touch me whenever he wanted.

And the wildest part? I didn't pull away.

And we were in public . . .

We went through the sliding doors, immediately hit by the scent of clove-studded oranges and cinnamon and the cheerful drone of "Jingle Bells" playing for probably the millionth time this season. The mall was pure holiday frenzy: packed crowds, lines snaking from every register, fake snow fluttering from the ceiling in places, and a Santa in the center of it all, who looked desperately in need of retirement.

My phone buzzed in my coat pocket.

I pulled it out instinctively, frowning at the screen. It was the same unknown number that had called before. I hesitated, my thumb hovering over the answer button. A strange twist of unease curled in my stomach again, but I shoved it down.

Not today.

Not here.

I hit ignore, stuffing the phone back into my pocket and forcing a smile as Easton glanced over.

"Everything okay?" he asked.

"Yep, just holiday spam. Probably trying to sell me reindeer-shaped waffle makers or something."

Easton's shoulder brushed mine as he leaned in, his voice low and teasing. "So, do you have a plan, or are we winging this like the absolute chaos magnet you are?"

I glanced down at my crumpled list. "According to Paige's text rants, we still need a gift for Aunt Kathy, something for Paige's murdery cat, and a mystery item she won't name but insists I'll know when I see it."

"Wait," he cut in. "We're shopping for a cat?"

I looked at him deadpan. "You haven't met Lucifer? He's an eight-pound demon. If he doesn't get a gift, someone loses a limb."

Easton burst out laughing. "All right, homicidal cat gift first. Priorities."

We wandered through the mayhem, hand in hand, and I was embarrassingly aware of every time his thumb swept over mine. Easton Maddox—former heartbreak, current maybe-something—was shockingly good at picking out cat toys. He held up a feathery thing on a spring with the seriousness of someone choosing a diamond ring.

"You know a disturbing amount about cats," I said, raising an eyebrow.

"My publicist has three. They've all evil and try to overthrow her house on a weekly basis, but there's one who actually tolerates me," he said, like that was a perfectly normal sentence.

"Let me guess . . . it's the one that knocks over the Christmas tree for fun, isn't it?"

He grinned. "Guilty. That little psychopath thinks I'm cool."

I laughed. "Figures you'd bond with the diabolical one."

"Clearly," he said, nudging me with a flirty wink, "I have a type."

I shot him a look. "You did not just compare me to a sociopathic cat."

"I didn't say *sociopathic*," he replied, all wide-eyed innocence. "There's a subtle difference."

We were rounding a corner by a kiosk selling hot cocoa–scented candles when it happened.

A scream.

High-pitched. Terrifying. The kind of sound that usually accompanied a boy band member taking off a shirt.

Easton and I both turned simultaneously, looking back toward the food court.

A pack of teenage girls were staring at us. Two dozen at least, charging like caffeinated elves on a mission, phones raised high and glitter posters waving wildly—the very ones we'd just been mocking. I wasn't sure how they'd managed to create those in the small amount of time we'd been here. But evidently the gloriousness of Easton's face could create miracles.

I watched as one girl face-planted over her UGG boot, popped back up like it was nothing, and kept sprinting on sheer adrenaline and fangirl determination.

"Oh my gosh," I breathed, panic already fizzing in my chest.

Easton took a step back, eyes wide behind his sunglasses. "I think they recognized me."

"You think?" I deadpanned, heart hammering as the crowd surged closer.

"Run?" I asked, only half joking.

He didn't hesitate. His grip on my hand tightened. "Definitely run."

We wove through crowds, dodging shoppers and blinking reindeer displays, sprinting past a toddler sobbing in Santa's lap, nearly colliding with an inflatable snowman the size of a sedan.

"I blame you!" I gasped, my hair flying, boots slipping slightly on the polished floor. "You and your stupid jawline!"

He threw a wicked grin over his shoulder. "Don't forget my abs. They're also very recognizable."

"I'm actively regretting knowing you!"

"Liar."

We veered left into a narrow corridor, hoping the detour would shake them off. Ducking behind a giant inflatable Santa, we crouched down, both of us gasping for breath.

Or at least I was. Easton looked mildly winded at best. Seriously . . . what was with all the exercise I was getting this week?

Easton peeked around the edge, his hat now askew and his sunglasses completely crooked. "I think we lost them."

I rolled my eyes, wiping hair off my face. "You say that now. Give it ten seconds."

Sure enough, a piercing shriek echoed from somewhere disturbingly nearby. Another. Then another. He swore under his breath and grabbed my hand again. "Come on!"

We bolted down the corridor and burst out into the open again, this time heading toward the food court like it was a finish line. I was half certain someone in a Chick-fil-A visor judged me as we sprinted past, but I didn't have time to unpack that. Easton pointed frantically toward a nearby clothing store. "Quick, in there!"

We dodged past bewildered employees, darting into the maze of clothing racks. I crouched behind a rack of hideous Christmas sweaters, holding my breath, eyes wide as Easton slid in beside me.

He chuckled softly, grinning despite our situation. "Not exactly subtle, are we?"

"I told you that disguise sucked," I hissed, catching my breath. "You look like someone trying *not* to be recognized, and therefore were immediately recognized."

He raised his brows. "You love it."

"Your ego needs therapy," I whispered fiercely.

"You love that, too."

I shook my head, heart hammering. "We're gonna get caught."

"Probably," he agreed, cheerfully casual, like this was a midday stroll through Central Park and not a manhunt.

I stared at him. "Why aren't you panicking?"

He tilted his head, looking at me like I was the one missing the obvious. "Because I'm having fun."

"You call this fun?"

He leaned closer, eyes softening slightly. "I'm with you, aren't I?"

My heart flipped stupidly in my chest, but before I could reply, someone gasped loudly.

"Oh my gosh! There he is!"

We froze.

Both our heads whipped toward the sound. A teenage girl, maybe fifteen or so, stood a few feet away, clutching her phone like it was the Holy Grail. Her eyes bounced between him and me like she couldn't decide who to scream at first.

Easton closed his eyes for half a second. "Time's up."

I groaned.

The girl didn't scream, bless her . . . but she did move, fast. Within seconds, the store filled with the pitter-patter of rapidly approaching footsteps, hushed shrieks, and the telltale glint of camera lenses.

We were surrounded.

There was no more running. No more pretending he wasn't *him*. And certainly no more hiding the fact that he was holding my hand like it was the most natural thing in the world.

Easton stood slowly, pulling me up with him, his sunglasses coming off in one smooth, practiced motion as he led us out of the clothing store and into the concourse so we weren't caged in on all sides. He gave me a small, almost apologetic smile, like he hated dragging me into the spotlight but wasn't letting go, either.

"You ready?" he asked gently.

"Nope," I said, plastering a fake smile. "But I guess we're doing this."

The crowd descended fast, like a glitter-storm of teenage shrieks and phone cameras. Questions exploded from every direction, a frenzy of excitement and disbelief:

"Easton! Are you filming a new movie here?"

"Who is she?"

"Is she your girlfriend?"

I felt my body tense like it had its own defense mechanism, like I could become smaller just by willing it. I wasn't used to this. The stares. The flashes. The demands to *be something* for other people. I could barely make sense of the buzzing in my ears, the pounding in my chest.

Easton threw me a careful glance, gauging my reaction. I stiffened slightly, unsure how to respond. My heart twisted, my nerves fluttering anxiously.

Then, without hesitating, Easton stepped closer, sliding his arm confidently around my waist. My breath caught at his touch, his warmth radiating against me.

"Yeah," he said, his voice clear and calm above the chaos. "This is Natalie."

Just my name. Simple.

But then he added, "She's the love of my life."

And just like that, the crowd *fell silent.*

I stared at him, my mouth slightly open, my eyes wide in disbelief. "Easton . . ."

He squeezed my waist lightly, never taking his eyes off mine. "No hiding, Nat. I can't do it. Not with you."

My throat closed up, something tight and hot coiling in my chest.

One of the girls near the front stepped forward, blinking up at Easton like he'd just rewritten every romance novel she'd ever read. "You mean it? She's really your girlfriend?"

Easton smiled. Not the cocky grin he usually wore. Not the movie-star smirk that lit up a billboard. This was soft. Real. The kind of smile you gave when you were proud of something. Of *someone.*

"Yep. She's the only girl I've ever loved," he said simply. "And the only one I ever will."

Every last scrap of oxygen vanished from my lungs.

My cheeks flamed, my pulse racing wildly. "You're insane," I whispered, barely audible.

"And you're beautiful," he replied simply.

I swallowed, somehow managing to turn toward the crowd of shocked faces. "Hi," I managed awkwardly, lifting a small wave. "I'm Natalie."

I couldn't bring myself to say anything else, because the word all of them were looking for—*girlfriend*—it felt enormous, weighted with meaning and promises I wasn't ready to publicly unpack. Not yet. Not here.

A ripple of delighted gasps ran through the crowd anyway . . . like they'd heard something I actually hadn't said.

See . . . this was how celebrity gossip got a bad name.

"She loves me," Easton said to them, to me, to no one in particular. "She's just stubborn."

And then he dove straight into the chaos like he was born in it—signing autographs, posing for selfies, answering questions like this was all perfectly normal. Like confessing your lifelong love in front of half the mall was just another stop on the holiday shopping tour.

And every few seconds, his eyes flicked back to me.

Checking.

Reassuring.

Making sure I was still okay.

And against all logic . . . against every overthinking impulse screaming in the back of my head.

I was.

Easton

Once I'd signed the last autograph, I turned back to the crowd—only to realize it wasn't the last.

What had started as a small, excitable group of teenage girls had snowballed into a full-on mob. A wall of people stretched from the food court to the atrium, pressing in tighter with every passing second. We were surrounded by a rising tide of shrieks and laughter. "Easton!" was shouted from every direction, some voices shaky with nerves, others bold, paired with their phone cameras held high.

I felt Natalie tense beside me, her hand still in mine, her grip tight enough to make my fingers ache. She'd been quiet while I signed autographs, her blue eyes darting between me and the fans, but I could feel a storm brewing inside her.

I glanced at her, searching her face for a clue to what she was feeling, but her expression was unreadable—a mix of fire and something softer, something vulnerable. I was sure she'd imagined this moment before, but living it was something else entirely.

I shifted closer, curling an arm around her waist and tugging her against me. "Thanks, everyone," I called out, my voice carrying above the swell of noise. "I really appreciate the love, but we're trying to finish some holiday shopping . . . so we're gonna need some space. You guys are great."

For a heartbeat, the crowd seemed to hesitate. A few fans stepped back, nodding sheepishly.

But the spell broke fast.

"Just one more selfie!"

"Easton, wait! What about your new movie?"

"Are you and her really dating?"

Someone grabbed my sleeve. Another person tried to shove a notebook into my hand, their pen bouncing off my chest. A girl lunged closer, clutching my coat. "Please! Just one—"

A mall security guard appeared out of nowhere, wheezing like he'd sprinted from the food court. "Okay, okay, back it up! Everyone needs to—uh—maintain a . . . safe perimeter?" His voice cracked on the last word, and he flailed his arms like he was directing traffic with zero authority.

No one listened.

"Shit," I muttered, grabbing Natalie tighter.

The corridor was swelling with people, a crush of bodies and noise and winter coats closing in from all sides. Phones were raised like torches, fans pressing closer with every breath, their voices climbing above the holiday music.

I tightened my grip on Natalie, my body shielding her from the encroaching mob. The shopping bags in her other hand rustled as she shifted, her breath coming in short, sharp bursts. Fuck.

Her eyes locked on mine, wild and blazing, and I didn't wait.

"Run."

We broke into a sprint, weaving through a tangle of holiday shoppers and glittering decorations like fugitives in a Christmas heist movie. I barreled past a stand of nutcrackers, clipped the edge of a candy cane display, and nearly took out a reindeer-shaped balloon. People were staring now . . . confused parents, wide-eyed kids, a couple of bored teenagers who immediately started recording.

"Sorry! Merry Christmas!" I shouted as we dodged a pack of rogue carolers in matching scarves.

Beside me, Natalie ran without question. Bags flapping against her thigh, hair flying, boots pounding against the tile. I couldn't tell if she was about to laugh or scream.

Maybe both.

Then I saw it. The Holy Grail of retail salvation.

Tucked behind a pretzel stand, half obscured by a display of scented candles and a snowman in a top hat, was a family restroom. The door was slightly ajar, and I didn't hesitate.

"In here," I barked, yanking her toward it. We slipped inside, and I slammed the door shut behind us, twisting the lock hard enough to make it rattle.

The silence was immediate. Jarring.

The only sound was our ragged breathing and the faint *buzz* of the overhead light. The space was small—white tile, pale walls, a sink and mirror, and a folded changing table—and it smelled faintly like lemon disinfectant and whatever scent they thought would calm a crying baby.

It wasn't the romantic setting of my dreams, but it was safe, and there were no fans trying to rip my shirt off.

So that was a plus.

I leaned against the door, my hair sticking to my forehead as I looked at Natalie, my eyes drinking her in.

She was panting, her cheeks flushed from the run, her blonde hair a wild mess around her shoulders. Her blue eyes were blazing, a fire in them that made my pulse race, and I felt a jolt of heat shoot through me at the sight of her.

"For the record," I panted, my eyes locked on hers. "This is *not* how I pictured our Christmas shopping going."

Her laugh was short, breathless, a little hysterical. "You think?"

She dropped the shopping bags to the floor with a *thud*, her shoulders heaving beneath her open coat. The tight red sweater she wore underneath hugged her body in a way that made my mouth go dry. She looked like a fever dream dressed in winter colors . . . and the way she was looking at me now, like she wanted to tear something apart, had every nerve in my body lighting up like the damn Christmas tree in the atrium.

"Girlfriend?" she purred, her voice lower now, dangerous, taunting. The word dripped with challenge, like she was daring me to take it back. Or daring me to back it up.

She stepped toward me, slow and deliberate, every inch of her radiating fire. My back pressed harder into the door, but I didn't move. I couldn't. She had me locked in place without even touching me.

"You told them I'm your girlfriend, Maddox," she said, soft but lethal.

I swallowed, hard, my throat dry. Her scent—sweet, sharp, familiar—slipped beneath my skin like ink bleeding through paper.

"I know," I said roughly. A slow smile curved across my mouth, dark and certain.

I stayed exactly where I was, frozen. There was no moving. Not with her pinning me there like she was carved from every second chance I never thought I'd get. So I let my words do the chasing, my gaze locked on hers like I was daring her to flinch. "You *are* mine, Nat. You said it last night. And girlfriend?" I gave a soft, humorless laugh. "That word's not even strong enough for what this is."

My fingers grazed her hip, possessive and unapologetic. "There's no take-backs. Not now. Not ever."

Her breath hitched, quick, involuntary, the kind of reaction that betrayed everything her mouth hadn't said yet. Her eyes widened for the briefest second, surprise flickering like a spark before that familiar fire surged back in, defiant and unyielding.

That last thread of resistance was still there, taut and fraying. She'd told me she was mine last night, but part of her was still fighting to believe this was just nostalgia. Just heat. Just a memory slipping through her fingers.

But I knew better.

I saw it in the way her eyes burned into mine. Like she was done running, done pretending this didn't mean everything. The way her breathing stuttered again, sharp and shallow, like she knew the fall was coming and had already stopped trying to catch herself.

She didn't need to say a word.

This was her answer.

This was her, charging forward. Raw. Unfiltered. Mine.

She grabbed the front of my coat and yanked me into her, her mouth crashing against mine with a heat that stole every last breath I had left—like she wasn't just kissing me.

She was claiming me.

I groaned, low and rough, as my hands slid instinctively to her waist. She tasted like peppermint gum and something sweeter, something distinctly, painfully her. Her tongue swept into my mouth, bold and possessive, and I nearly lost my balance from how fast my body responded.

She was everywhere. Fingers in my hair. Chest pressed to mine. The need in her kiss wasn't a wildfire. It was pressure, years of it, finally blowing the lid off with nothing left to contain it but my body.

"Fuck, Nat—" I groaned, dragging my mouth from hers just enough to breathe, my hands sliding up beneath her sweater, palms splayed against bare skin. "This isn't a dream, right—"

"Shut up," she growled.

Her hands fumbled for my coat zipper, yanking it down with a desperation that sent a thrill racing along my spine.

"I need you," she said, fierce and breathless. "Right now." My heart jackknifed in my chest.

There was nothing casual in her voice. No hesitation. Just raw, undeniable hunger.

I shrugged out of my coat, letting it fall to the floor in a heap. She was already tugging me back to her, and I didn't fight it. I couldn't.

I kissed her again—harder this time—everything I'd held back since the moment she left pouring into that kiss. My hands clutched her waist, gripping her like a lifeline, my hips pressing forward instinctively as she rolled hers against me.

She reached for my sweater, yanking it over my head with a roughness that I fucking loved. The bathroom's cool air hit my bare chest, but it was nothing compared to the scorch of her palms roaming across my skin.

Her nails scraped down my abs.

I hissed through my teeth, muscles twitching beneath her touch. Her hands were frantic and hungry, like she needed to memorize every inch of me before she lost her nerve.

I didn't wait. I shoved her coat from her shoulders, watched it tumble to the floor, then tugged her red sweater over her head in one quick motion. And damn.

The lacy black bra. The flushed skin. The way she looked under the soft, humming light of this cramped little bathroom—eyes wild, lips swollen from kissing me, chest rising and falling in hard, shallow breaths.

She was a vision. One I'd dreamed about every damn night.

"Fuck, Nat," I murmured, my voice low and reverent as my hands cupped her breasts through the lace. My thumbs brushed over her hardened nipples, and the feel of her beneath my palms nearly knocked the air out of me. "You're so fucking beautiful."

She reached behind her back and unhooked her bra, letting it fall to the floor. My breath caught. Her bare chest rose and fell with every shallow breath, and the soft light painted every curve in gold. Her nipples were tight, peaked, and begging for me.

I leaned down, unable to resist, and took one into my mouth. My tongue circled slowly before I sucked hard, just enough to draw out a gasp that made my cock throb.

"Easton!" she cried, her hands tightening in my hair, hips shifting against me as her body trembled under my mouth. I lavished her with attention, letting my tongue flick over her nipples in a rhythm that had her gasping, moaning, desperate.

I moved to her other breast, giving it the same devotion, while my hand kneaded her first one, fingers rolling her nipple until she whimpered, her whole body alive in my arms.

"More," she breathed, her voice cracking as her hands dropped to my jeans, fumbling with the button. "I need more, Easton. I need you." The desperation in her voice sent a jolt straight to my cock.

Her words were like gasoline on a fire, and I groaned, helping her with my jeans as she finally got them undone, shoving them down my hips along with my boxers.

My cock sprang free, hard and aching, the tip already glistening with pre-cum, and her eyes darkened at the sight, her tongue darting out to lick her lips as she wrapped her hand around me. Her touch was electric, her fingers stroking me with a confidence that made my knees buckle, and I let out a low, guttural moan as she pumped me slowly, her thumb brushing over the sensitive head, spreading the pre-cum down my length.

"Fuck," I growled, my hips rocking into her hand, my eyes fluttering closed for just a second before I caught her smirk. I tugged on her jeans, yanking them down with a roughness that matched hers, taking her panties with them. She stepped out, kicking them aside, and I felt my breath catch at the sight of her, completely bare before me, her thighs slick with arousal, her pussy glistening with need.

My knees hit the tile without a thought.

She opened her mouth like she might say something—maybe a warning, maybe a curse—but the second my mouth met her center, all that came out was a broken moan that ricocheted off the walls.

She tasted like heaven and everything I'd been craving.

I licked slowly, savoring the way she shivered beneath me, then parted those slick folds and circled her clit with the tip of my tongue. A sharp breath hitched in her throat. Fingers threaded through my hair, yanking me closer, thighs quaking as I licked again. And again. She moved with purpose now, grinding against my mouth like her sanity depended on it.

"Oh fuck, Easton." She gasped, her voice broken, hips rolling with a wild rhythm that told me exactly how close she was.

I added a finger, then two, curling them inside her until she cried out, her voice raw with need. She was dripping now, her arousal coating my chin, and I groaned against her, the vibration making her moan even louder.

"Don't stop," she choked out, her voice wrecked, eyes glazed and wild. "Right there. Fuck, Easton, don't you fucking dare stop—"

Her body arched, trembling under my hands, her hips grinding against my mouth like she was chasing oblivion and knew I was the only one who could give it to her. I kept going, relentless, my fingers driving deeper, tongue punishing her clit until she broke apart for me . . . loud, shaking, soaked. She cried out, her pleasure detonating like a fuse lit too long, molten and messy, wringing every last pulse from her body as I held her through it.

She was trembling, her legs unsteady beneath her, and before she could collapse, I stood and caught her. Her legs wrapped around my waist, and I turned us and pressed her back against the door, the slick heat of her dragging along my cock.

Fuck.

That wet slide. That desperate need still clinging to her skin. I felt it all, every breath, every quiver, and it lit something savage inside me—something feral and possessive and absolutely fucking gone for her.

Her eyes locked on mine, dazed and shining, her lips parted on a breathless sound she couldn't quite form. And in them, I saw it . . . something too deep to speak. Too honest to hide.

She swallowed hard. "Are we really calling me your girlfriend?"

Her voice was soft. Not angry. Not teasing. Just . . . bare.

I didn't blink. "I've changed my mind."

Her brow furrowed slightly, confused. "About what?"

I leaned in, the tip of my cock brushing against her slick heat, making us both shudder. "You're not just my girlfriend, Nat."

My voice dropped to a rough whisper as I locked eyes with her, letting her see the truth—unfiltered and absolute.

"You're the love of my fucking life."

Her breath caught, her eyes widening as the words sank in, and for a moment, I saw a flicker of something soft, something tender, beneath the feral intensity.

"Easton," she whispered, her voice trembling with emotion, and then her mouth was on mine . . . soft, desperate, hungry. She clutched at my shoulders like she couldn't bear to let go, and I kissed her back with everything I had, my world narrowing to the girl in my arms.

I pushed into her slowly, inch by inch, savoring the way she stretched around me, the way her tight, wet heat enveloped me like she was made for me. We both groaned at the sensation, and I stilled for a moment, my forehead resting against hers as I tried to catch my breath.

"Nat," I murmured, my voice breaking with the weight of my feelings for her. "You feel so fucking good. So tight. I can't live without this. I can't live without *you*."

A soft sound escaped her, half moan, half sob, and her nails bit into my shoulders as she rocked her hips, urging me deeper.

Her gaze locked on mine . . . wide, wild, wrecked. "Then don't," she whispered, the words trembling out of her like a promise she hadn't meant to say. "Don't ever live without me again."

Something broke open in my chest.

I moved, harder now, deeper, like I could answer her with every thrust, like I could bury every regret, every second we'd lost between the press of our bodies. She met me stroke for stroke, breath stuttering in my ear, her moans splintering into the air, feeding the fire already roaring through both of us.

The door rattled behind her with every thrust, but we didn't stop. Didn't care. The whole world narrowed down to this. Her body tight around me, her fingers digging into my back, her voice raw with need.

"Faster." She gasped, clinging to me like I was the only thing keeping her from unraveling.

I obliged, my thrusts growing harder, deeper, the tension between us tightening with every movement. I could feel her pussy clenching around me, her walls fluttering as I pounded into her, the wet, obscene sound of our bodies coming together echoing around the bathroom.

Her moans filled the air, sharp and broken, each one dragging me closer to the edge.

"Easton," she cried, her eyes wild, her voice shattering. "I . . . I can't. It's too much."

"Come for me, Nat," I rasped, my voice rough with need as I thrust deeper, my hands gripping her hips to hold her steady, my fingers digging into her soft flesh. "Let me feel you, baby."

She shattered.

Her body bucked against mine, her head tipping back as she screamed my name again. Her pussy clenched me in a vise, her nails scraping down my back in delicious streaks as I drove into her, watching her come undone in my arms.

That was it.

Her orgasm tore mine from me like a wave pulling the tide. I groaned her name, my cock pulsing as I spilled inside her, filling her with my cum . . . blinding, blistering pleasure that crashed through me like a supernova, raw and endless.

We stayed like that, locked together, breathless and trembling, as the high slowly receded. I held her, cradled her, pressed kisses to her sweat-damp forehead as I tried to slow the thunder in my chest.

She was still shaking, her body soft and pliant against mine, and I couldn't help it . . . love surged so fiercely in me, it was a miracle I stayed standing.

This wasn't like the other times.

This wasn't just another memory, another mistake for the sake of nostalgia.

This was her letting go, completely, finally, right there in my arms.

"I meant what I said," I whispered, pulling back just enough to cup her face in my hands. Her cheeks were flushed, lashes damp, her lips parted and kiss-swollen.

I brushed a strand of hair from her cheek and met her eyes.

"You're the love of my life, Nat. You always have been."

Riley: UHHHHH HELLO?? NATALIE BENNETT, DO YOU HAVE SOMETHING YOU WANT TO TELL THE CLASS??

Me: Oh no. Whatever it is, it wasn't me. I've been framed.

Casey: What happened??

Riley: Just casually watching TV and EASTON MADDOX HIMSELF popped up on E! News introducing "the love of his life" Natalie to some very enthusiastic fans??

Riley: The fans screamed. He smiled. It was adorable and nauseating and I demand answers.

Casey: NATALIE, EXPLAIN YOURSELF.

Me: I can neither confirm nor deny. I plead the fifth and request witness protection immediately.

Riley: Too late, traitor. You're famous now.

Me: Wait, how bad was it? Did I look okay? Please tell me my fly wasn't down or something.

Riley: No wardrobe malfunctions. But you did turn bright red and wave awkwardly. Like a cartoon character.

Casey: I need video proof immediately.

Me: It wasn't supposed to be public yet!! He sprung it on me out of nowhere!

Riley: Aw, poor Nat. A handsome movie-star boy-friend claiming you publicly. The horror. Thoughts and prayers.

Casey: Are you really complaining right now???

Me: I'm not complaining!! I just wasn't ready. What do you even say when someone calls you his girlfriend in front of a mob of screaming women??

Casey: "I'd like to thank the Academy."

Riley: "And I'd like to thank Riley, Casey, and Ophelia for peer pressuring me into romantic maturity."

Riley: So, are we officially acknowledging he's your boyfriend now?

Me: I mean . . . yeah. I guess we are. The little bathroom interlude kind of solidified that.

Me: Maybe.

Me: Possibly.

Casey: SHE SAID YES! WE HAVE CONFIRMATION!

Riley: Should we alert TMZ or are you handling that yourself?

Me: I hate you both.

Casey: Wait . . . what bathroom interlude?

Riley: Spill the deets.

Me: OK, Jace . . .

Me: But also.

Me: . . .

CHAPTER 21

Easton

Paying off the sleigh driver so I could take over at the last second? A no-brainer. Just like pulling every string I could to make it to this wedding—the only shot I had at winning back the girl who broke my heart. As I stood in the fresh snow, watching Natalie eye the empty driver's seat of the sleigh with uncertainty, it felt like I was making all the best decisions in my life nowadays.

"Where's our driver?" Natalie asked, glancing around the snowy yard in confusion, her lavender scarf snug around her neck, her cheeks flushed pink from the cold.

"You're looking at him," I said, giving her my best confident smile as I took the reins in hand.

She hesitated, then shook her head firmly. "Absolutely not. You don't know how to drive a sleigh."

I raised an eyebrow, feigning offense. "Excuse you—I was in a commercial once where I had to drive one of these. I'm basically an expert."

"A commercial?" She eyed me skeptically. "Was that the same commercial where you stood around shirtless next to a horse, or is there an entirely separate horse-themed incident I should know about?"

I grinned, pleased she'd been paying attention to my career. "Same one. Look at you, keeping track of my shirtless exploits."

Natalie rolled her eyes dramatically, but I caught the twitch of her lips fighting a smile. She sighed heavily and stepped toward the sleigh, brushing snowflakes from her coat. "Fine. But if we crash, I'm leaving you for dead and going straight for the eggnog."

"Harsh," I said, laughing softly as I offered her a hand up.

Her gloved fingers slipped into mine, sending warmth racing through me despite the cold. She settled into the sleigh, rearranging blankets around her lap, clearly doing her best to appear unaffected by the intimacy of the moment.

I climbed in beside her, took a steadying breath, and flicked the reins gently. Mercifully, the horse moved forward smoothly, guiding us down the moonlit path. I released the breath I'd been holding.

"See?" I said gently, nudging her softly. "We're fine."

"We're still within fifty feet of the driveway," she pointed out dryly. "Let's not celebrate yet."

I laughed, and it was kind of crazy how light my chest felt this week. Like every second with her shed something off me.

The sleigh glided through the snow-covered woods, the night wrapping around us like a dream stitched in ink and frost. Trees dusted in white stood tall on either side of the path, their branches bowing gently beneath the weight of the snow. The only sounds were the *crunch* of hooves against the icy ground, the soft *jingle* of bells from the harness, and the steady beat of my heart—which hadn't quite settled since the moment I saw her again.

As the trees thinned and the world grew quieter, Natalie shifted beside me, reaching into her coat pocket. Her phone screen lit up in the moonlight, and I caught the way her expression pinched, subtle but sharp.

"What is it?" I asked, trying to keep my tone casual even as something in my chest went rigid.

She hesitated for a second too long, then turned the phone toward me. A single text blinked on the screen from an unknown number.

Unknown: Call me back.

My jaw tightened. "Is that the same number that's been calling you?"

She nodded, slipping the phone back into her pocket. "Yeah."

"You gonna call it back?"

The growl in my voice surprised even me.

She smirked at that, a teasing glint lighting her eyes as she leaned back in the sleigh. "Please. I already have one overly devoted stalker," she said, shooting me a playful look. "I don't need to add another." I watched as she blocked the number.

Despite myself, I barked out a laugh. "You think I'm a stalker?"

"I think you flew across the country to crash a wedding and win me back," she said with a wink. "If that's not stalker behavior, it's definitely stalker-adjacent."

"Yeah," I said, leaning a little closer, eyes laser-beamed on hers. "But I'm the charming kind."

She grinned, the edges of her smile softening just enough to make my chest ache. "You're not a bad stalker. You haven't locked me in a basement yet, I'll give you that."

"Low bar," I said, deadpan. "But I appreciate the positive feedback."

She laughed, and I loved how it was easy . . . light. The kind of sound that threaded right through me. And she didn't try to immediately put up walls . . . so that was a plus.

Natalie brushed a clump of snow off her knee like we weren't still adjusting to this new-old thing between us. Like we hadn't already said *yes*—to the risk, to the mess, to each other—and now we were just learning how to breathe inside that choice.

The silence stretched again, deeper now. The sleigh drifted forward under the moonlight, and I glanced over, watching her face in the silver glow.

"What are you thinking about?" I asked quietly, unwilling to break the moment but needing her voice, needing her thoughts.

She hesitated, and I felt her shift beside me. Then she looked at me from beneath her lashes, her voice low. "Just wondering if this is weird for you. Being back here after living in Hollywood. We haven't talked about it."

I glanced ahead, guiding the sleigh gently around a curve in the trail. The reins were loose in my hands, but my grip on reality—on her presence next to me—was anything but.

"It's different," I said honestly. "But this . . . this feels nice. Normal."

She gave a small nod, her hand tugging her scarf a little tighter around her neck like she was tucking herself into a memory. "Do you ever miss it? Normal, I mean."

I didn't answer right away. Not because I didn't know, but because I wanted to answer it right—for her. For me.

"Honestly?" I said after a beat, keeping my voice low, the reins loose in my hands. "Yeah. Hollywood's . . . a lot. It's loud and glittery and exhausting in ways I didn't expect. And under all that—it gets lonely."

Natalie didn't say anything right away, just looked over at me, her brows gently furrowed like she already knew where I was going. Because she did. We'd already been peeling back the layers in our conversations this week, one exchange at a time.

"I got caught up in what everyone else wanted me to be. What they *thought* I was. There were moments I didn't even recognize myself. But not once . . ." I paused, my chest tightening. "Not once did I stop missing you."

She reached for my hand, and her fingers slipped between mine—easy, instinctive.

Like it was nothing. Like it was everything.

My heart thudded once, hard. Because she was finally touching me like . . . she'd never stopped.

It was a sign I'd been waiting for.

"You told me that already," she said softly, her voice brushing against me like snowfall. "But I don't mind hearing it again."

That smile she gave me—it did something to me. Knocked the air out of my lungs. Because she wasn't looking at me like Easton Maddox, movie star. She was looking at me like the boy she used to know, and the man she'd decided to choose again.

"I meant it," I said. "All of it. The movies, the premieres, the awards—none of it ever mattered if I didn't have you to share it with."

She gave me a long, thoughtful look. "You don't have to keep proving it, you know."

I laughed under my breath. "I kind of want to, though."

Her mouth curved. "Well . . . you're off to a decent start."

"Excuse you," I said, scandalized. "I risked a lifetime ban from wedding vendors everywhere for hijacking this sleigh. I deserve chocolate. And possibly a statue."

"Let's not get ahead of ourselves, Dasher."

She laughed again, and it wrapped around my ribs and settled there. Easy. Warm. Real.

We rode in silence for a few beats, the soft *clop* of hooves on snow the only sound between us.

And then she said, "You didn't change into someone better, Easton."

I looked over at her, my brows tugging in question.

"You were already perfect," she said, her voice steady. "I just wasn't ready to believe someone could love me like that . . . without it falling apart."

My chest pulled tight.

"I kept waiting for it to break," she added softly. "And when it didn't . . . I broke it myself."

I squeezed her hand, my thumb brushing over her knuckles. "But now?"

She glanced at me, a smile flickering at the corners of her mouth, quiet and sure. "Now I want to see what it looks like when I don't run."

Natalie toyed with the edge of her scarf, not nervously this time—just distracted, thoughtful. Her gaze flicked to the snow-laced trees ahead, then back to me with a smile that tugged something deep in my chest.

"I've watched all your movies," she said casually, like it wasn't a confession. Like it didn't mean everything.

I tilted my head, grinning. "Even the one with the talking dog?"

She laughed. "Especially that one."

That sound—fuck, I'd missed it. Laughter that cracked something open in us both. Easy and unguarded.

"I always told myself it was just curiosity," she added. "But it wasn't. I missed your voice. Your face. Even when it wasn't really you up there."

That stopped me. My grip tightened slightly on the reins, not from nerves—just the force of feeling everything at once.

"I kept thinking," she said, a little softer now, "that you looked like you were trying to be okay. Like you had everything you were supposed to want . . . but you were still missing something."

"You," I said simply.

Her eyes met mine, steady and unflinching. "Yeah. Me."

And there it was.

No deflection. No retreat.

Just the truth, sitting between us like the quietest kind of promise.

"You know," she murmured after a while, "this still feels a little surreal."

I turned toward her, my voice low and certain. "It doesn't to me."

Her brow lifted slightly, amused. "No?"

I shook my head. "I knew the second you let me back in, it was over. For anyone else. For anything else. I've got you now—and there's not a force in the world that's taking you from me."

Her breath hitched faintly, but she didn't look away.

"I mean it, Nat," I said, sliding my hand over hers, holding it tight. "You're mine. You always were. But now? Now you know it, too. And I'm not letting you forget it."

She didn't speak for a second. Just looked down at our joined hands like she was memorizing the shape of us.

Finally, she snorted. "You sound like a caveman who got hit in the head with a Hallmark movie."

"Only for you," I said, dead serious.

And it wasn't a line. It was a vow.

As the soft lights of the rehearsal dinner got closer, I glanced at Natalie again, suddenly unable to look away. Her face was flushed with cold, eyes sparkling in the moonlight. Snowflakes clung to her hair, and when she smiled softly, I felt something inside me shift completely.

I couldn't help but stare—she was beautiful. Breathtakingly, infuriatingly beautiful.

The kind of beautiful that made you forget where you were. Who you were.

"Easton?" she asked, her voice soft and amused, an eyebrow lifting in that signature Natalie way that always told me she knew exactly what I was thinking. "Eyes on the road, Hollywood."

"Technically, there's no road," I replied, dazed and very much not paying attention. I was too busy memorizing every line of her face. Like I could look at her a thousand times and still find something new to want.

"Easton," she said again, more urgently now. "I think—"

That was the exact moment the right runner of the sleigh caught the edge of a hidden snowdrift. Everything that happened next seemed to unfold in slow-motion chaos.

The sleigh tipped sideways, the horse let out a startled snort, and Natalie gave a surprised squeal as we both toppled over the edge. Snow exploded upward around us in a cold, glittering cloud. One second I was warm and romantic and deeply philosophical . . . the next, I was lying flat on my back, buried in a drift, staring up at the winter sky.

"Natalie?" I asked frantically, pushing myself upright, heart hammering in panic. "Fuck. Nat! Are you okay?"

I heard her laugh before I saw her.

Sharp, surprised, and absolutely not the sound of someone mortally wounded.

Still, my heart slammed against my ribs as I scrambled through the snow, slipping once like an idiot before I spotted her—flat on her back in a snowbank, laughing so hard her whole body shook.

"Nat?" I blurted, half panicked, half confused.

She sat up slowly, hair tousled and face dusted in white like some unhinged snow nymph, and the second she caught sight of my face—apparently frozen somewhere between *I think I killed you* and *Should I call an ambulance*—she absolutely lost it.

Tears streamed down her cheeks as she doubled over laughing, wheezing like she'd just witnessed the single funniest thing in recorded history.

I gaped at her, half relieved, half mortified. "Are you laughing right now? I thought I killed you!"

"You should—see your face!" she wheezed between giggles, brushing snowflakes from her eyes. "You look like you single-handedly destroyed Christmas."

"Not funny," I grumbled, even as my lips twitched.

"Extremely funny," she gasped, still breathless. "You crashed a sleigh because I was too pretty. That's, like, top-tier flattery. I'm putting it on my résumé."

I shook my head, slowly starting to grin myself as I helped her sit up. "You realize you look like a yeti, right?"

She gasped dramatically, then pointed at my own snow-covered hair. "And you look like Frosty's long-lost cousin."

"Touché." I chuckled softly, finally relaxing enough to laugh fully. "You sure you're okay?"

"I'm fine," she assured me, her eyes warm and dancing. "But your driving privileges are permanently revoked."

"I can't even argue with you on that," I said sheepishly, brushing snow off my coat. "Okay, full disclosure—there may have been a professional driver just off-camera during that sleigh commercial. I mostly just held the reins and looked emotionally available."

"I knew it," she said, her eyes gleaming. "I knew you'd been trained in brooding, not in basic sleigh logistics."

"Some of us are multitalented," I offered, deadpan. "Just . . . not in ways that involve steering heavy holiday machinery."

She shook her head fondly, still giggling softly as I stood and carefully helped her up, brushing snow off her coat.

"I really am sorry, though," I murmured. "For almost killing you."

She smiled warmly up at me, cheeks flushed. "Well, as far as near-death experiences go, this one wasn't so bad."

"High praise," I said, unable to keep from grinning. "You're giving me a lot of that tonight."

As we continued trying to get the snow off our clothes and tried to rescue the blankets and sleigh, laughter still lingered between us. She shot me a mock-serious look as I tried to steady the sleigh.

"Maybe next time we stick to safer traditions," she said, snorting when she realized there was still snow in her hair.

"Like what?" I asked. "Gingerbread houses and passive-aggressive ornament placement?"

She grinned. "You say that like it isn't a full-contact sport in my family."

"Remind me to bring a helmet next year," I said, nudging her gently. "And maybe body armor. Something festive, though. With bells."

"Obviously," she deadpanned. "We're not animals."

Her laugh spilled out—light, bright, and totally unbothered by the near-death sleigh-riding experience—and it hit me like it always did. Right in the chest.

And in my dick.

We managed to right the sleigh with some teamwork and one very offended horse, clinging to what dignity we had left, and finally made it to the rehearsal dinner. We were windblown, half frozen, and trailed a generous helping of snow through the front door.

No one asked. Not a single person commented on our disheveled entrance. Not when Natalie looked like that—rosy-cheeked, scarf askew, her smile still tugging at the corners of her mouth like she hadn't quite come down from the high of laughing at me.

When I grabbed her hand, she didn't let go.

Not when people looked. Not when a few heads turned and eyebrows lifted. Not even when MeMaw gave us a knowing, smug little smirk.

Natalie stayed right there beside me, steady and sure.

And for the first time, I didn't feel like I was waiting for her to come back.

It felt like . . . she already had.

Natalie

The rehearsal dinner looked like Joanna Gaines and an elf got drunk and decided to cohost a holiday special. Fairy lights draped from every beam, glinting off garlands and place cards with too-perfect calligraphy. It should've been over-the-top. Somehow, it wasn't. It was just cozy enough to feel warm, not forced.

Candles flickered down the long wooden table, casting soft glows over pine boughs and wine glasses filled a little too full. The whole place smelled like cinnamon and cedar—and probably vanilla, thanks to the dessert Paige insisted on adding last-minute because she "didn't think the menu had enough sugar to induce a coma."

Laughter curled up toward the rafters, warm and lazy, the kind that made you feel like maybe, just maybe, life could be good and soft and easy for a minute. I tried to focus on it—on Paige in her cream sweaterdress, glowing with that sort of smug, sparkly joy only brides-to-be get away with; on the way Levi beamed at her mid-story, even though he'd told the same story about their first date approximately eight hundred and sixty-seven times in the past week.

Across the table, my parents sat shoulder to shoulder, their hands brushing as they reached for their glasses. My mom said something that made my dad laugh—really laugh—the kind that lit up his whole face. She smiled like she'd just scored a win, then slid her fingers over his knuckles like she wanted to hold the moment in place.

It was all very sweet.

And I was trying really hard to care.

Really.

But Easton was sitting right next to me.

And Easton Maddox in a suit was . . . a problem.

His thigh brushed mine every time he shifted, which, for the record, was a lot. Like he was doing it on purpose. Like he knew exactly what it was doing to me. Which—judging by the smug curve of his mouth every time it happened—he absolutely did.

His shoulder bumped mine. Once. Twice. A little whisper of contact that felt more like a dare. The navy blazer he wore should've made him look stiff. Corporate. But no, of course not. It hugged him like it had fallen in love and was never letting go. And don't even get me started on the scruff. Or the snow-mussed hair. Or the fact that his scent was making me go feral.

Our knees brushed under the table. Blink-and-you'll-miss-it. Then again. A little longer. A little bolder. The third time, his knee didn't leave mine.

It stayed.

And not just stayed . . . it *pressed*. Firm. Deliberate. Like he was staking a claim.

And it wasn't just a Hey-I'm-next-to-you kind of touch. No. It was a Hey-I-remember-what-you-sound-like-when-I-curl-my-finger-inside-you-just-right-and-I'm-not-done-yet kind of press.

My stomach did a full-on backflip. My breath caught somewhere around my collarbone. And I just sat there, pretending I was still following Levi's story about Paige and the tragic poinsettia incident at his parents' house.

Just in case you were wondering . . . I wasn't.

Easton reached for his wine, and the edge of his sleeve brushed mine—silk gliding against wool, slow and unbothered, like he wasn't setting off tiny explosions along the length of my arm.

I stared at my plate like it might ground me. But all it offered was a Jackson Pollock of roasted vegetables and high-end salad regret.

My brain had fully left the building.

His flirty touches had sent it back to the mall bathroom, while Easton dropped to his knees like a man with a mission and absolutely no shame. My fingers tangled in his hair, my breath stuttering while he looked up at me like I was something to worship. And then he'd smirked—*smirked*—before dragging his tongue over me like he had all the time in the world.

Yeah. That's where my brain was.

Not here. Not at this wholesome rehearsal dinner with cider and candles and emotional vulnerability.

How was I expected to concentrate on dinner rolls at a time like this?

Levi raised his glass, his voice mellow and nostalgic as he continued his toast, now talking about their first kiss. Everyone smiled. Heads turned. Someone might have actually teared up.

I wouldn't know.

Because Easton's hand had started sliding beneath the tablecloth.

His palm found my knee. And the second it had settled on my skin, something low and molten lit up in my bloodstream. Like he'd flipped a switch inside me that was wired to him. My spine went rigid. My breath caught. The world around me blurred into a watercolor smear of flickering candles and soft piano music I wasn't hearing.

He didn't look at me.

That was the worst part.

He just sat there, like he wasn't actively setting fire to every nerve ending I possessed, his expression politely attentive to the toast.

But there was the smallest curve to his lips. Barely there. A private joke only I could feel.

And then . . . because he was evil . . . his thumb started to move.

Slow. Deliberate. Lazy little circles that burned hotter with every pass, like he was testing how far he could push before I combusted.

My fingers curled around my fork in a death grip. I stared hard at my plate, trying to remember what food even was.

My pulse pounded in my ears, drowning out the *clink* of silverware, the sighs of appreciation over the butternut squash ravioli, the way Paige looked like a fairy-tale princess across the table.

His fingers inched higher.

I snapped my eyes to him. "Easton . . ." I hissed.

His head tilted slightly. He didn't even blink. Just let the full weight of that smirk settle into place like it belonged there. "Tell me if you want me to stop," he murmured, too softly for anyone else to hear.

I didn't.

Fuck, I definitely didn't.

"Someone will see," I whispered, glancing nervously to my right, where my cousin was very focused on buttering a roll like it was a performance art piece.

"Then don't make any noise that makes them look," he said smoothly, his voice all warm velvet and bad ideas.

And just like that, Easton's hand was sliding higher.

He leaned in, just enough for his breath to skim my ear, low and warm. He smelled like expensive trouble—cologne and pine trees in the snow and that infuriating brand of confidence that always made my pulse misbehave.

"Enjoying the view?" he murmured, his voice dipped in syrup and sin as he watched me stare at the tablecloth like it was my job.

I lifted my wine glass with a hand that miraculously didn't shake, took a slow sip, and replied in the most neutral tone I could muster.

"It's a very nice tablecloth. Great lace-to-fabric ratio. Really tasteful."

He chuckled low . . . too low. That kind of laugh that rippled under your skin and made a home in all your more dangerous places. "Sure, let's talk tablecloths," he murmured. "But we both know that's not what's got you creaming your panties."

His fingers curled, warm and steady against the inside of my thigh. I felt my whole body go traitorous, tipping forward just slightly, like my bones wanted to chase the touch even if my brain was waving a polite little white flag of panic.

"I'm multitasking," I whispered. "Having a full-blown meltdown and also considering which fork would cause the most damage if I stabbed you with it."

He didn't flinch. Just grinned—lazy and infuriating. "Go with the salad fork. Less surface area, more precision."

His thumb stroked upward again, drawing a line that made my thoughts scatter like skittish deer.

"You're doing great, by the way," he murmured. "If I weren't the one turning you inside out under this table, I'd never guess."

My jaw clenched. "You think highly of yourself."

"I've had almost two years to think about you. To think about all the things I would do once I got you back," he said, all wicked calm. "This isn't arrogance, sweetheart. It's long-term planning."

I narrowed my eyes. "Are you seducing me with . . . military metaphors?"

He grinned, that stupid, infuriatingly sexy grin. "Is it working?"

His hand continued to move higher.

I pressed my lips together, hard. The tablecloth did absolutely nothing to muffle the way his fingers dragged slowly beneath the hem of my dress again, this time pausing just shy of scandal.

"You're the devil," I breathed, barely moving my lips.

"I'm patient," he whispered back, his mouth a hair from my cheek. "But not for much longer."

My heart beat like it was trying to punch its way out of my chest. My thighs tightened instinctively, but his hand stayed right there—steady, possessive, daring me to open. Daring me to give in.

I shifted in my seat. He felt it. His breath caught.

"You keep doing that," I breathed, trying to sound annoyed and not utterly wrecked, "and I'm going to drop my wine glass or say something incredibly unhinged."

His voice came back low and wrecked with heat. "Then maybe sit on your hands, Trouble. Because you're making it really fucking hard to behave."

"I'm literally doing nothing."

"You're blushing, biting your lip, and making those little breathy sounds like you want me to lose control." His fingers flexed against my skin. "You call that nothing?"

I exhaled sharply. "I hate you."

But fuck, he wasn't wrong. I was definitely doing all of that.

Every nerve in my body was tuned to him, strung tight and thrumming. I wasn't pretending anymore. I wanted him—completely, unapologetically—and he knew it.

I could've stopped him. Could've given him a look or brushed his hand away.

But I didn't.

Because I didn't need to test if I was ready.

I was.

Not just for this slow, torturous game we were playing beneath the table. Not just for the way his fingers curled against my thigh like they belonged there. But for all of it. For him. For us.

That certainty didn't scare me now. It thrilled me.

And judging by the way his hand moved—higher now, slower, full of dark confidence—he could feel it, too.

His fingers skimmed the inside of my thigh again, retreating just enough to make me bite down on a gasp, then rising once more . . . teasing, testing, tempting. Every pass edged closer to where I wanted him most.

My thighs shifted . . . subtle, sure. I opened just enough to tell him everything he needed to know. Not an accident. Not an oversight.

An invitation.

He shifted beside me, his breath brushing the shell of my ear, and his voice followed—low, pleased, laced with heat.

"Still breathing, sweetheart?"

"Barely," I managed, my teeth clenched in a smile that was definitely *not* for the toast.

"Good," he whispered. "The moment we're alone, I'm gonna peel you apart, spread you wide, and fuck you so slow, so fucking deep, my cock will ruin that tight, dripping pussy. You'll be a shuddering wreck, choking on filthy moans, begging me to pound you harder 'til you're nothing but a slick, screaming mess, owned by every inch of me."

Holy fuck. I'd never heard hotter words in my life.

I choked on a moan, my core throbbing, slick heat pooling. At least my clothes were still soaked from the snow . . . maybe the damp fabric would hide the fact that my panties were soaked through.

"I'm going to kill you," I breathed in a shaky voice.

His chuckle slid over my skin. "Worth it."

I darted a glance around the table, heart racing, half expecting someone to notice the way Easton's hand was teasing me senseless, his slow, deliberate strokes along the inside of my thigh setting my skin on fire.

But no one looked. No one noticed. The oblivious chatter around us only cranked the heat higher, like we were getting away with something obscene in plain sight.

And fuck, that made it so much hotter.

He leaned back, sipping his wine with that smug, panty-melting grin, like he wasn't unraveling me under the table. But his hand stayed, fingers curling with possessive intent, pressing just enough to make my breath hitch. Each subtle flex screamed *mine*, and I was already so wet, so ready, I could barely keep from grinding against him right there.

His thumb slid higher, boldly slipping just under the edge of my soaked panties—teasing the slick, sensitive skin so close to where I ached for him. My thighs quaked, a soft, needy whimper escaping before I could stop it.

He heard it.

I saw it in the way his eyes darkened, the way his throat bobbed as he swallowed hard, his jaw tightening like he was fighting not to drag me out of that room and fuck me senseless against the nearest wall.

I wasn't the only one unraveling.

His voice dropped, a low, husky purr laced with sinful amusement. "Did I tell you how much I fucking love that dress?"

I tilted my head, lips curling into a sultry smile, my voice a soft, teasing drawl. "Oh, I can tell. Your hand's getting *real* cozy with it."

He gave me a slow, predatory grin, eyes glinting with heat. "Just wait 'til I get it off you."

"You're out of control."

"And you love every second of it, don't you, baby?"

My heart gave a hard, traitorous *thud* at that. Then his fingers slid higher, deliberate and wicked, dipping into my drenched, aching core. His touch was slow, one finger grazing my slick folds, teasing my entrance with a torturous promise that made my hips twitch involuntarily. I bit my lip to stifle a moan, my entire body igniting as he lingered there for a heartbeat . . . before moving away again, leaving me throbbing, empty, and desperate.

The toast ended, applause rippling around us, but the air felt molten, suffocating. My wine glass sat full in front of me, barely touched, and I was suddenly desperate for it—anything to cool the fire crawling under my skin.

He leaned over, his lips brushing my temple, his voice a low, sinful murmur. "Finish your dessert, Trouble."

"Why?" I whispered, my voice shaky, still reeling from the loss of his touch.

"Because after this," he said, his hand grazing the top of my thigh one last time before retreating back down to my knee, "I'm dragging you somewhere quiet."

"And then?" My voice was barely a breath, laced with needy anticipation.

His eyes locked on to mine, burning with raw hunger as he leaned closer, his whisper a dark, filthy promise. "Then I'm gonna fuck you so hard you'll feel me for days."

"Natalie, budge up."

Paige plopped down beside me like a human ice-bucket challenge. Her cream sweaterdress brushed my arm. Easton's hand froze. And then . . . slowly, torturously, he pulled back. Like he knew exactly what he was taking with him.

I blinked at my sister, struggling to remember how to breathe, speak, function. Nothing to see here. Just a maid of honor fighting for her life.

Paige leaned in, her voice low, the sharp scent of her perfume slicing through the lust still thick in my blood. "I never heard from him."

The words hit like a sledgehammer, and I turned to her, the shift in topic jarring enough to snap me straight out of the haze Easton had been weaving around me all night. "What?"

She gave a small shrug, but it was too practiced, too casual. Her eyes flicked to Levi across the room, her expression softening, so much love there, I felt it like a punch. "I thought maybe . . . I don't know. That he'd call. Or text. Something."

She shook her head once, the motion tight. "But nope. Nothing. Zilch."

There was a beat of silence, heavy with the words she didn't say.

"I guess he's not coming."

She tried to sound breezy, like it didn't matter. But the dip in her voice at the end—that pause, like she was still waiting for the story to change—told me everything. She was disappointed. And she didn't know why it still stung. Not after all these years. Not after we'd already trained ourselves not to expect anything from him.

A breath I hadn't even realized I'd been holding eased from my chest. Cool. Quiet. Relief.

That unknown number—the one that kept calling all week, never leaving a message, then texting today with just *Call me back* . . . I'd told myself it was spam.

But part of me had worried—worried it wasn't just a random number. Worried it was him.

I reached under the table and found Paige's hand, giving it a soft squeeze. "It's better this way," I whispered.

And it was . . . because I'd been picturing it all week.

Looking up in the middle of the speeches or the first dance . . . and seeing him there. Standing in the doorway, smiling like he belonged. Like he hadn't left a crater in our lives. Like he hadn't broken our mother. Like I wasn't still haunted by the girl he'd left behind.

I'd imagined sitting through it all with a polite smile, pretending I didn't see him. Pretending I wasn't still waiting for an apology that would never come.

But now? Hearing Paige say she hadn't heard from him . . .

That tight, awful dread I'd been carrying finally let go.

I didn't have to keep looking over my shoulder. Didn't have to brace for a voice I hadn't heard in years, or a face I didn't want to see. That door— the one he'd left swinging open behind him—was finally shut. And for once, I didn't feel like I had to hold it closed.

She nodded, her smile small and tired. It didn't quite reach her eyes, but it was enough. Then she turned, laughing a beat later at something Levi said across the table, like the ache inside her hadn't just opened a little wider.

Easton nudged my knee again.

The touch jolted me. I turned—a dangerous mistake—and found him already watching me.

His gaze was molten, locked on mine, the candlelight catching in those wild green eyes like he was made of trouble and temptation and everything I'd spent all this time convincing myself I couldn't have.

But now?

With that door finally closed . . . I didn't just feel brave enough to want him.

I felt *excited* for what came next.

He leaned in, low and quiet, just for me. "Let's get out of here," he murmured.

His fingers slid up my thigh, one last slow, deliberate stroke, and then they were gone, leaving nothing but heat and a wicked ache behind.

I turned toward him, catching the glint in his eyes, the tension in his jaw like he was hanging on by a thread.

That wild, reckless thing inside me didn't just stir—it *surged.*

I didn't hesitate.

"Yes," I whispered, already breathless. "Please."

I stood up too fast. My chair scraped against the wooden floor with a sharp *screech* that turned a few heads. Easton rose beside me, steady and tall, his hand brushing the small of my back as I reached for balance, like he was already ready to catch me.

I barely looked at him. I couldn't. Not with my pulse already pounding in anticipation, not with the way my body still hummed from his touch beneath the table. I was so ready. He grabbed my hand, and I stepped toward the door, and we were—

The *crash* stopped everything.

Sharp. Sudden. Shattering.

Glass splintered across the wood floor, cutting clean through the soft string music and low chatter like a warning shot. Paige stood frozen, the broken stem of her wine glass still pinched between two fingers, red spilling in slow motion down her wrist like blood in a fairy tale.

And then I followed her gaze.

Straight across the room, past the flickering candles and festive garlands. To the figure standing near the open door, snow clinging to his boots, his shoulders stiff beneath a weathered coat.

My stomach dropped.

My lungs forgot how to work.

He looked older. Of course he did. Gray threaded through his dark hair, his skin pulled tighter at the jaw, but the eyes—they were the same. Pale. Detached. Like he was already halfway out the door even as he stood in the middle of the room.

Terry.

My father.

CHAPTER 22

Natalie

H
e hadn't stayed away. He was here.

And just like that, everything inside me recoiled. My body, once a current of heat and want and the chance of maybe, now felt hollow and tight, like someone had pulled the string too hard and snapped it.

"Natalie," Easton said beside me, quiet and careful, but it didn't reach me.

Not yet.

I couldn't move. Couldn't blink. Couldn't stop staring.

Because even after all these years, even after all the mental gymnastics and well-rehearsed excuses I'd built to keep the past buried, seeing him here felt like being a child again. Like waiting on the front porch in my best dress, trying not to cry when he didn't show. *Again.*

He didn't belong here.

He didn't get to show up now, after staying quiet this whole time— after years of radio silence and nothing else. He didn't get to see Paige glowing with champagne and soft love, or Mom and Steve holding hands like time had made them gentler, not bitter.

He didn't get to ruin this.

Not again.

I moved so fast my chair knocked over.

Someone—my mom, maybe—said my name, soft and gentle, but I didn't stop. I couldn't. I barely felt Easton's hand graze mine, a tether I shook off like it burned.

The lodge doors flew open with a burst of cold air, swallowing me whole.

Outside, snow crunched under my heels as I stumbled across the wrap-around porch. The cold slapped my cheeks, fresh and unforgiving, like it had been waiting for me to lose it. I gripped the wooden railing with frozen fingers and gasped. One breath. Then another. And another. Each one shallow and useless.

My chest felt too tight. My dress too thin. My thoughts too loud.

I stared out at the trees, their branches heavy with snow, a postcard scene that didn't belong to me. It belonged to other people. To fairy tales. To people who didn't feel like a cracked ornament being taped back together for the hundredth time.

Fuck.

I had been seconds from going back to the suite with Easton. From letting him take me somewhere dark and quiet, where the world could fall away. From giving in to the fire between us and letting it mean exactly what it already did. That maybe I was okay. That maybe I was finally free from the part of me that still flinched from the fear of being left behind.

And then *he* showed up.

I pressed a hand to my mouth, squeezing my eyes shut as if I could hold it all in. But the ache was sharp, pressing against my ribs like it had claws.

I wanted to scream. To rip the world apart like he always did.

But I couldn't.

I couldn't ruin this for Paige. I couldn't just leave and miss her day.

So, I just stood there.

Breathing. Trembling. Hating the way old wounds didn't stay gone. Hating that the second I saw him, something in me shrank.

I hated that I could still feel Easton's hand on my thigh and all the ways I had felt wanted. Desired. Chosen.

And I hated that I didn't feel that way anymore.

Not right now. Not with the past staring at me like a bad punch line.

Behind me, the door creaked, and warm light spilled out onto the snow. Footsteps landed softly on the wooden planks . . . but I still didn't turn around. I stared straight ahead, locking my spine in place.

"Natalie."

Just one word. Just my name.

And still, it scraped down my spine like sandpaper.

I let the silence stretch between us. I wanted to see if it would make him squirm. I wanted him to feel just a fraction of what I'd carried.

The footsteps stopped beside me, a few feet away. Not close enough to be familiar. Not far enough to feel safe.

After another breath, cold and sharp, I asked, without looking at him, "Why did you come?"

The words hung there, frozen between us.

He exhaled through his nose. "I wasn't going to. I—" His voice caught. "I didn't want to make anything worse."

A bitter laugh slipped from me before I could stop it. "Well. Nailed it."

He flinched. I could hear it. The sound of someone realizing too late that they walked into the wrong conversation without a map.

"I thought maybe," he said slowly, like the words hurt his mouth. "Just maybe . . . if I showed up, it would mean something."

I turned then.

And maybe I shouldn't have—maybe I should've stayed with the trees and the snow and the version of me that didn't have to look him in the face—but I did.

"Mean something to who?" I asked, my voice sharper than I meant it to be. "To me? To Paige?"

He smiled weakly as if he weren't actually sure.

I crossed my arms, not because I was cold, but because it was the only thing keeping my hands from shaking. "Why now?"

His mouth opened. Closed. His jaw clenched.

And then he said something I wasn't ready for.

"Because I'm sick."

My spine went rigid. My lungs squeezed tight, like his words had knocked the air out of them.

I blinked at him, studying him closer now, seeing how he kind of looked like a ghost trying to remember how to be solid again. Or maybe that was just my hatred, twisting the picture.

"Sick?" I repeated, barely recognizing my own voice.

He nodded, his jaw tight. "Leukemia. They caught it late. I didn't . . . I didn't know how to tell you."

My stomach twisted. Not out of sympathy. Not yet. It was too tangled for that. I didn't know if I felt sad or angry or nothing at all. Maybe all three.

"So, you decided to crash Paige's wedding?" I asked sharply. "Thought you'd just drop the bomb and then blend in with the hors d'oeuvres?"

He winced. "I didn't mean for it to be like this."

"But it is," I said, cutting him off. "It always is with you."

He nodded slowly, lips pressed together like he couldn't argue. Because he couldn't. Because he knew.

I looked away, out into the trees, the world too quiet. The cold burned in my lungs.

"I didn't come to cause trouble," he said softly. "I swear. I just wanted to see you. Once. Before . . ."

He didn't finish.

Didn't have to.

And I hated the part of me that still cracked down the middle at the thought of him dying. Of this being real. Of it being too late, again.

Because no matter how many years had passed, no matter how many times I'd told myself I didn't care—there was still a small, stubborn ember inside me that had wanted *something*. An apology. An explanation. A clean ending, maybe. Closure.

But this? Him showing up now, dragging all those old fractures back into the light like we were unfinished business?

No.

I straightened, spine stiffening like I was snapping a shield back into place.

"Well," I said, lifting my chin, "you're here. But let's get something straight."

He blinked.

"You don't get to ruin this."

His brows drew together. "I didn't come to ruin anything. I tried to call you this week, to talk about everything . . ."

Ah, so I'd been right. That unknown number had been him. I didn't know how he'd even gotten my number in the first place, but I was glad as fuck that I hadn't picked up. Hadn't had his voice ruin the whole week instead of just now.

I stepped closer, my voice low, steady. "Good. Because you won't. Paige gets her day. She gets the magic, and the cake, and the teary vows, and every single ounce of joy without you dragging your history into it."

I paused, letting the weight of my words settle. "And you're not going to tell her you're sick. Not tonight. Not tomorrow. Not until she's back from her honeymoon and all her wedding glow has faded. She doesn't need that in her head when she walks down the aisle. You don't get to ruin this for her."

He didn't speak. Just nodded, something wounded flickering behind his eyes.

"As for me . . ." I shook my head. "We're not doing this. Not now. Maybe not ever."

"I know," he said quietly. "But I hoped maybe—"

"No." I cut him off before the hope in his voice could do any real damage. "You don't get to hope. Not after years of silence. Not after all the missed birthdays and holidays and graduations and broken promises. You don't get to *hope* you still fit somewhere in this story just because you showed up with a tie and a guilty conscience."

His eyes glistened. I didn't care.

"I'm not that little girl who used to wait on the porch in her best dress," I said. "And I'm not going to pretend you get a second chance just because you finally remembered we exist."

A long silence stretched between us. Thick. Cold. Heavy with everything we weren't saying.

"I just wanted to see you," he murmured. "Even if you didn't want to see me."

I took a long breath, let it sear through my lungs.

"Well," I said, my voice firm as I turned toward the door, "now you have."

And I stepped back inside.

The warmth of the lodge wrapped around me, too sudden, too bright. Conversation swirled in half-heard fragments, the flicker of candles catching on sequins and champagne flutes. My heels scuffed softly against the floorboards, but I couldn't quite hear them over the rush in my ears.

Then Easton was there.

He didn't say anything. He didn't ask what happened or press his luck with some charming joke to break the tension. He just wrapped his arms around me, solid and strong, and pulled me into his chest like he'd been waiting to do it all night.

And I let him. Completely.

I sank into him, my hands curling into the fabric of his suit coat. Let his steady heartbeat anchor mine. Let myself be held, because it had been a long time since anyone had seen the cracks and wrapped themselves around me anyway.

I felt the weight of his chin rest lightly on top of my head. His hands slid up and down my back in slow, grounding strokes.

"I've got you," he murmured.

I closed my eyes. Soaked it in. Let it hold me up, just for a minute.

But then . . . I looked past his shoulder.

The room had changed. The golden hum from earlier, the soft laughter, the easy clink of glasses, the sparkle Paige had worked so damn hard for . . . it was gone. Swallowed whole. Replaced by this awful, stretched-out silence that tasted like dread and watched like a car crash. The kind that made people speak softer, like a higher volume might make it worse.

Like everyone in the room had just remembered something ugly.

And the cause of it—of course—was him.

My fists curled before I even realized it, the rage rising fast and hot.

And then I saw her.

Near the fireplace, a girl in a soft green dress stood talking to Paige. She looked polished, quiet, pretty in that catalog-perfect way—glossy brown hair tucked neatly behind her ears, gold necklace resting at her collarbone, her posture just a little too graceful to be accidental. Her smile was small, controlled, like it had been trained.

I leaned toward Easton, barely moving my lips. "Do you know who that is?"

He didn't look away. "That's Brittany," he said quietly. "Your half sister."

The name hit like a crack across glass.

Brittany.

I blinked. Stared harder, like I hadn't really seen her until just now.

Because that was her. The daughter he'd stayed for.

The one he chose.

She wasn't doing anything wrong. Of course she wasn't. She held her cranberry spritzer like someone who'd never spilled anything in her life. She laughed, soft and practiced, at something Paige said. Not cruel. Not warm. Just . . . comfortable. At ease.

And Paige—

Fuck.

She looked like she was barely breathing. She stood stiffly, her shoulders hunched the way they used to when she heard Mom crying after he'd left, and she thought if she made herself small enough, she might disappear. Her arms were folded tightly across her chest, her body tilted just slightly away from the girl. Her eyes flicked around the room like she was searching for an exit . . . or maybe for me.

I couldn't hear what they were saying. Couldn't catch a single word. But I didn't need to.

Just the sight of it—of *Brittany*, smiling like she belonged in this moment Paige had been dreaming about—made something cold and hollow rip through my chest.

Paige didn't look like a bride-to-be anymore. She looked like a kid again. Cornered.

And I hated that I couldn't fix it. I hated that we'd been twisted into this shape, that our emotional wreckage ran so deep Paige thought inviting him might fill something in.

I glanced toward my mom, hoping, stupidly, for some sign that this wasn't unraveling as fast as it felt like it was.

Her lips were pursed into a tight line, eyes trained on Paige and Brittany like she couldn't decide if she wanted to cry or throw something. Steve's hand was wrapped around hers, firm and grounding, his thumb brushing slow circles against her knuckles like he was the only thing keeping her upright.

I knew that look. I'd worn it myself.

The look of a woman holding it together—for everyone but herself.

My grip on Easton's hand tightened, and I didn't even realize I was holding my breath until I felt it lodge hard in my throat.

"I can't," I whispered.

He turned toward me instantly, brow furrowing. "Say the word," he murmured.

And I did.

"Can we go?"

He didn't blink. Just squeezed my hand and started walking—pulling me gently, purposefully, out of the room and into the night.

CHAPTER 23

Easton

I woke before the sun, the sky outside still curled in that soft pre-dawn blue—the kind that made the world feel hushed and waiting.

She was still in my arms.

Natalie.

She was curled toward me, her cheek pressed to my chest, one hand tucked between us like she needed to feel my heartbeat to keep her own steady. Her lashes rested dark against her cheeks, still damp at the corners, and the tip of her nose was pink from crying.

She had cried for hours.

Quiet at first, then loud enough to crack me in half. The kind of crying that didn't ask for comfort, but still begged for it. All I could do was hold her and hope she didn't push me away. Hope I was enough.

And I didn't mean enough to stop her tears—I knew better than that. I meant enough to be there. To stay. To matter when the pieces finally settled again.

I was scared her father had undone everything we'd rebuilt this week.

That the weight of it all—the memory of what he hadn't been, the shame she still carried, the hurt she tried so hard to keep tucked under that sharp wit—was going to swallow us whole. That she'd decide this, *us*, was too much. Too messy. Too close to the pain.

And the thing was, I got it.

But I loved her.

God, I loved her.

It wasn't clean or patient or poetic. It was unhinged. Raw. The kind of love that made my ribs hurt, like my heart was too big for the cage it was in.

She shifted in her sleep, her leg brushing mine under the covers, and I held my breath like she might vanish if I moved too fast.

I had stayed up most of the night just watching her. Not in a creepy way—okay, maybe in a slightly creepy way—but mostly in that reverent I-can't-believe-she's-here kind of way. The way you watch a sunrise and know it's going to be the best part of your whole damn day.

She didn't know.

How much I had wanted this. How much I had wanted *her*—not just the version she gave the world, but the one who had looked at me last night with tear-streaked cheeks and let herself fall apart in my arms.

I would've taken all the pieces. Every single one. Glued them back together with my bare hands if that was what it took.

And if she changed her mind now?

If she woke up and decided this week hadn't meant what I thought it had—what I *felt* it had—I wouldn't go back to California. Not really.

Sure, I'd pack my things. I'd get on a plane. But I'd follow her.

Quietly, at first. A respectable distance, obviously. But I'd find ways to be near. To keep her laughing. To scare off every guy who looked at her sideways. To remind her every damn day that I was the guy who knew her middle name and her go-to drive-through order, and how she talked to paintings when she thought no one was watching.

I'd try to change her mind for the rest of my life if I had to.

Yeah, it sounded dramatic. Borderline pathetic, maybe. But it was true.

She stirred again, her nose nuzzling against my chest. Then, slowly, her lashes fluttered open.

And she looked up at me.

There was a beat—one breathless, suspended second—where her eyes were soft with sleep and the shadow of dreams. Then I saw it. The shift. The flash of awareness behind her eyes as everything came back. The lodge. The porch. Her father. The tears. The way she'd fallen apart in my arms and let me hold every broken piece.

I braced.

Tensed, ready for her to pull away, to roll over, to say something sharp and self-protective like she had so many times before.

But she didn't.

She didn't move. Didn't retreat.

Instead, her brow smoothed slightly. Her shoulders rose and fell with one long, heavy sigh.

"It's the big day," she whispered, her voice scratchy and soft, her breath warm against my skin.

I nodded, careful not to move too much. "Yeah. It is."

Her eyes searched mine for a moment longer, like she was checking to see if I was still the same. Still safe. Still here.

Then without a word, she leaned up . . . and she kissed me.

Slow and quiet and full of things she hadn't said yet.

I kissed her back, my hand cradling the back of her head like she was something fragile and holy and real, and I wasn't about to let her slip through my fingers.

She pulled away with a small, reluctant sigh and reached toward the nightstand, grabbing her phone. The screen lit her face with a soft glow, and I saw the exact moment her expression crumpled.

"Ugh," she groaned. "I have to start getting ready soon."

I brushed a strand of hair away from her cheek, my hand lingering. "Cold reality setting in?"

She tilted her head, eyes narrowing slightly as something mischievous sparked behind them. "Maybe . . ."

Then she looked back at me, lips twitching. "Or maybe I just need a little . . . delay."

My heart skipped. "A delay?"

"A very specific, very hands-on delay," she said sweetly—too sweetly. And then her hand slid beneath the sheets, fingers trailing fire down my abs, slow and deliberate, until they curled around my cock, gripping me with a bold, possessive squeeze.

"Fuck," I hissed, my muscles tensing as I throbbed against her palm.

"Natalie," I cautioned, the word less a warning and more like a plea.

She leaned in, her lips brushing my chest with a slow, sinful graze that stole the air from my lungs. Every muscle in my body coiled tight under her touch, my skin blazing where her mouth lingered, teasing me into a frenzy. Her tongue flicked out, tracing the hard lines of my pecs, and I sucked in a sharp breath, my hips twitching involuntarily.

"Are you saying what I think you're saying?" I rasped, my voice already rough, already hopeful.

She didn't answer with words. Instead, her tongue carved a torturously slow path down my chest, her hot breath ghosting over my skin as she slid lower, her fingers loosening just enough to drag her nails lightly along my length.

The sensation sent a violent shudder through me, and my hands fisted the sheets, twisting them as I fought to keep from begging. Her lips followed her tongue, pressing open-mouthed kisses down my abs, each one wet and deliberate, her teeth grazing just enough to make me curse under my breath.

She paused just above my cock, her breath teasing the sensitive skin, so close I could feel the heat of her mouth but not the relief I was dying for.

"Fuck, Natalie," I groaned, my head falling back against the pillow, eyes slamming shut as my body thrummed with need. Her tongue darted out again, flicking against the taut skin just below my navel, and my cock twitched, aching for her to close the distance. She hummed softly, the vibration of her voice against my skin sending another wave of heat through me, and I swore my brain was short-circuiting, one nerve at a time.

"Are you . . ." I managed, my voice a little strangled. "Trying to use my dick as a distraction?"

She looked up at me, a wicked smile curling at the corners of her mouth. "Do you have a problem with that?"

I pretended to think it over, which was damn near impossible with her mouth so close to where I needed it, her fingers now tracing featherlight patterns along my inner thighs, keeping me on the edge of insanity.

"Hmm," I said, forcing a thoughtful tone as her tongue made another slow, deliberate pass across my skin, this time dangerously close to the base of my cock. My hips bucked slightly, and she smirked, knowing exactly what she was doing to me. "Nope. Not a fucking one."

Her grin deepened, pleased. "I didn't think so."

And then, finally, she lowered her mouth to the head of my dick, her lips grazing the tip with a slow, deliberate swirl of her tongue, teasing the sensitive slit before parting to take me in, and I stopped pretending I had any control left at all.

Natalie

Snow fell like whispers.

It drifted outside the wide frosted windows of the reception hall, turning the whole world soft and white and still. It was the kind of snowfall that asked for silence. Reverence. Like the sky itself had paused to bear witness to my big sister's day.

Inside, the place looked like something straight out of a winter wedding catalog. Twinkle lights wrapped around the old timber beams, low-lit
and tangled in pine boughs, casting everything in that soft, flattering glow
people pretend isn't on purpose. Real candles lined the aisle—flickering,
steady, like even they knew not to screw this up.

I stood at the far end of the aisle, bouquet in hand, my dress pressed
and perfect. But my chest?

It felt tight. Too tight. Like my ribs had lost the memo on how to
stretch. Like if I breathed too deep, everything I was holding together
might finally . . . not.

He was here somewhere. My father.

And just the thought of that made something inside me curl with tension. A quiet kind of dread. Like I was still waiting to be picked, to be seen,
to be enough.

I hated that he was here. I hated that his presence was pushing up
against all my edges like he had a right to be part of this day. Like he
hadn't missed every important thing leading up to it. Like showing up now
earned him a seat at the table and a warm welcome and a neatly folded
name card that didn't say *Liar*.

And yet, somewhere between the sobbing and the sleeping, some-
time around the moment I stopped shaking in Easton's arms and instead
decided to suck his dick, I'd decided something.

He wasn't going to ruin this.

Not for Paige. Not for me.

And I wasn't going to use it as an excuse. Not this time. Not to shut
down. Not to run. And especially not to put more distance between myself
and the man who'd held me through the worst night I'd had in years. The
man who made me laugh when I was still shaking. The man who watched
me like I was something precious.

I wasn't going to run from Easton.

I was so tired of that part of myself.

The part that always braced for the leaving. That read love like a ticking
clock—one I couldn't see but always heard, just waiting for time to run
out. The part of me that flinched when things got too good, that called it
self-preservation when it was really just fear in a prettier dress.

But not today.

Today, I wasn't going to run. I wasn't going to sabotage something
just because it felt like it might matter too much. I'd already wasted

too much time pushing away the very things I wanted most. And I was done.

The music swelled, a single violin, warm and aching, and I took one steady breath before stepping forward.

I wasn't the bride.

But fuck, it sure felt like something was beginning.

My heels clicked softly against the polished wood floor. One step. Another. The hem of my dress swished around my ankles like it had something dramatic to say. The bouquet in my hands—white roses and holly leaves with pinecones tucked in like secrets—trembled just enough to give me away.

But I barely saw anything. I barely noticed the rows of smiling faces, the blur of twinkle lights and flickering candles. Because my head? My heart? Every part of me was already tangled up in one person.

Easton.

The boy I never really stopped loving.

The man I was slowly, terrifyingly letting back in.

He stood at the front like some kind of cinematic fever dream—tall, still, terrifyingly composed in a suit that looked custom-cut to ruin my life. The fabric hugged his shoulders like it had personal feelings about him, narrowed at the waist in a way that should've been illegal, and honestly? It made breathing a whole situation.

His dark hair was a little damp still, like he'd barely made it inside before the music started. His hands were clasped in front of him, fingers tight, like he needed something to hold on to. And that face—fuck. He looked calm, unreadable, like he was keeping every emotion locked behind those stupidly green eyes.

But I knew him.

I knew that jaw. That tension. That look that meant he was feeling everything all at once and had no idea where to put it.

Then his eyes found me.

And the world stopped spinning.

He didn't smile. Not right away. He didn't do anything showy or dramatic. He just . . . looked. Like I was the only person in the room. Like I was something precious and impossible, standing there in borrowed heels with trembling fingers and a bouquet that suddenly felt too small to carry the weight of my chest.

The look in his eyes wasn't playful, or teasing, or flirty like it usually was. It was reverent. Like he was seeing me for the very first time and still somehow recognizing everything he already knew. Like I was a prayer he hadn't realized he'd been whispering all his life.

Like I was a hymn he didn't know he still believed in.

My breath caught in my throat, and for a second I swore I forgot how to move. My knees wobbled. My stomach flipped. That fragile place in my chest, the one that had been locked up since I'd left him, cracked open just a little more.

The guests rose behind me—a soft rustle of fabric and shifting feet, a symphony of murmurs and program pages fluttering like wings. They were standing for the bride.

But Easton didn't glance down the aisle. He didn't blink.

He watched *me*.

As if I were the one walking toward him.

As if I were the moment. The vow. The finish line and the beginning, all wrapped into one girl in a satin dress and shaking heels.

And it wrecked me.

Because in that gaze . . . steady and unwavering and impossibly full, there was no room for fear. No space left for old wounds. Not even the hollow ache that had lived in my chest since yesterday when my father stepped through that door like a ghost given form.

There was no room for him.

Not when Easton was in my life.

The music swelled again, fuller now, warm and orchestral and brimming with joy.

The back doors opened—and there she was.

Paige.

Radiant. Graceful. The picture of a bride in winter—long-sleeved lace, a delicate veil trailing like breath behind her. She smiled, and my throat tightened.

And on her arm?

Steve.

Shoulders squared, chin lifted, pride written in every step. The man who'd shown up. Who'd stayed. Who'd driven us to school in snowstorms and taught us how to change a tire and made pancakes shaped like our initials on birthdays.

The dad who deserved to be there.

The crowd turned as one to face her.

Phones rose. Gasps rippled. Someone near the front dabbed at tears with a crumpled tissue. I heard my mom whisper something to MeMaw as she clutched her pearls like they were holding her together.

And Easton?

He didn't shift or blink or do a single thing that would've meant he wasn't exactly where he wanted to be.

He just kept looking at me.

Like I was still the only one in the room.

Like nothing in the world—not wedding vows or falling snow or the slow march of time—could turn his attention away.

My heart thudded wildly, painfully, beating against my ribs like it wanted out. Like it wanted to hurl itself into his hands and trust him to catch it.

Paige's steps echoed down the aisle, slow and certain. Levi's smile looked like it might split his face in half. People sniffled. My aunt clutched her husband's hand. Paige's veil fluttered slightly behind her like a promise.

And Easton kept watching me.

My breath came shallow. My throat felt tight. My eyes found his again without meaning to.

He still wasn't smiling—but his eyes weren't empty.

They were packed. With awe. With hunger. With a kind of aching devotion that settled deep into my bones and made everything that had ever come before it seem dull by comparison.

I was his beginning.

And maybe . . . maybe. He could be my end.

The thought landed soft and sharp at once, like rose petals on a bruise.

I blinked against the pressure building behind my eyes, willing myself to stay present, to stay steady. For Paige. For the moment. For the version of me that had finally started to believe in more.

But Easton.

Fuck . . . Easton.

He looked at me like I was the vow. The prayer. The last page in a book he'd been reading in secret for years.

And I'd barely done anything.

I was just standing there, bouquet in hand, pretending my heart wasn't a kaleidoscope of cracked pieces finally turning toward the light.

Paige reached the front of the room. Levi took her hand, his eyes glassy, his lips already trembling with whatever vows were about to come pouring out of him.

The officiant welcomed everyone with a calm, pastoral warmth.

I barely heard him.

Easton's eyes still hadn't left mine.

Not when Paige handed off her bouquet to me with a soft squeeze.

Not when she turned to Levi, glowing, ready.

This was it—this thing between Easton and me. It was bigger than the room, louder than the violin that had returned with a gentle refrain. It pulsed under my skin, made my knees feel too soft and my heart feel too full.

And still, he didn't smile.

That's what undid me.

He didn't need to.

Because everything I needed was in his eyes.

That he was here. That he'd stayed. That he was holding the space around me like a promise no one else had ever dared to make.

He was choosing me.

Not in some performative, poetic way.

Not for a night or a weekend or a week in a snowy town with string lights and sleigh rides.

But now. Here. In the middle of my sister's wedding. In the aftermath of the worst day I'd had in years.

In front of the father who had never stayed.

He was still choosing me.

The officiant's voice rose again, warm and certain. "Marriage begins in the quiet spaces. In the stolen glances. In the hands that reach out even when the world is loud and complicated and messy."

My throat tightened.

I understood that line. I understood what it meant to be chosen in the mess.

Because Easton had found me there.

Not in the glossy versions.

Not in the Natalie I played at when things were shiny and effortless.

He'd seen every version of me . . . long before this week. All the years growing up, all the cracks I tried to patch with sarcasm and distance. He'd loved me anyway.

I'd broken up with him. Broken his heart. Walked away like it was the only option. And he still hadn't let me go.

Not when I cried into his shirt. Not when I avoided his eyes for almost two whole years. Not when I stood in front of him yesterday, barely holding myself together.

He hadn't turned away. He hadn't stopped choosing me.

I glanced down, fiddling with Paige's bouquet. Pine needles scraped at my wrist—unsubtle, unapologetic. A little bite of reality when I needed it most.

Easton shifted just slightly across from me.

I bit the inside of my cheek to keep from falling apart, and when I looked back at him, I saw it.

The change.

The smile was there now.

Barely. Soft and reverent. A smile that didn't ask anything of me but gave everything in return.

It undid me.

But I wouldn't cry.

Even though I could feel it in my throat . . . that dangerous, wobbly feeling like my tears might spill over. I wouldn't cry through my sister's wedding. No way. Not after the week we'd had. Not after what I'd promised myself this morning in the mirror.

No matter how utterly undone I was by the man standing across from me, looking at me like I was his beginning.

But I didn't look away, either.

And slowly, my lips tipped up, and I smiled softly back at him. The two of us, sharing this silent moment, full of so many words.

Because he was still mine. And I was finally, finally letting myself believe I could be his, too.

The vows began. Paige's voice rang out clear and steady, each word wrapped in love. Levi answered with his own, his voice breaking once before he laughed and caught it.

It was beautiful. It was everything a wedding should be.

But for me, for the girl still holding her breath under a thousand stars' worth of grief and hope . . .

It felt like the beginning of something else entirely. Something wilder. Something more dangerous.

Something I wanted.

Easton.

His name pressed against my ribs like it belonged there.

My beginning *and* my end.

Finally.

CHAPTER 24

Natalie

The kiss came, soft and sure, and everyone clapped.

My hands ached from holding the bouquets too tightly, but I was smiling . . . really smiling. The kind that started in my chest and spilled out without permission, light and full and unshakable.

Because in the middle of all the lace and candlelight and promises spoken out loud, something had shifted inside me.

And it wasn't grief.

It wasn't fear.

It was something softer.

Brighter.

Hope.

We funneled out into the courtyard for photos, the sound of champagne flutes clinking somewhere behind us. The air was sharp with pine and laughter, a thousand details blurring together like a snow globe turned upside down. My cheeks were still pink from smiling, my fingers aching slightly around the bouquet stems . . . but I didn't care.

And then I felt him.

Easton brushed past me, shoulder to shoulder, warm and solid in a way that made something in me settle. His hand skimmed against mine—casual, easy—and then stayed. A soft press. A silent ask.

He didn't look at me. Just left his hand there, open beside mine.

So I took it.

No hesitation. No drama. Just . . . yes.

Our fingers slid together like they knew the way, like they'd been waiting for this quiet confirmation.

"Always the prettiest girl in the room," he murmured, his voice pitched just for me, warm and steady and utterly disarming.

I almost dropped the damn bouquet.

"You're biased," I whispered, my voice caught somewhere between breathless and beaming. "And that line is still corny."

He leaned in, close enough that I felt his breath on my cheek, his grin lazy and laced with affection. "Sure, but it's my brand of corny. And you love it because it comes with my devastating charm."

"Debatable," I shot back, but it came out softer than I meant.

Snowflakes clung to the ends of his hair, and the corners of his smile crinkled just enough to remind me why I used to stare at him for entire class periods without catching a single word the teacher said.

The courtyard had transformed into a winter painting. Twinkle lights tangled above us. The snow glowed gold. The photographer shouted directions like she was wrangling caffeinated goats, and MeMaw, bless her, flat-out refused to be wrangled.

"I'm not standing next to that shrub," she announced, pointing at a perfectly innocent pine bush. "I have better things to do than blend in with landscaping."

"Mom," my mother hissed, red-faced.

"I'm seventy-eight and fabulous," MeMaw said, flipping her faux fur stole over one shoulder with flair. "Put me center frame or cut me out entirely."

The photographer wisely went with center frame.

Somehow, I ended up next to Easton for the "fun" shot—sandwiched between MeMaw, who was still muttering something about hoping the photographer caught her good side, and Easton, who looked like the kind of man who didn't know how to take a bad photo. Or even a mediocre one. I was dangerously close to looking like a human thumb in comparison.

Then it happened.

The photographer squinted at Easton. Tilted her head. Froze.

"Oh my gosh," she blurted, nearly dropping her camera. "You're— you're *Easton Maddox*."

A beat of silence followed. Easton smiled, charming and just a little sheepish. "Guilty."

Her eyes went saucer-wide. "Oh no. You need to be front and center."

Easton gestured to the bridal party with a diplomatic shrug. "Pretty sure it's not my big day."

The photographer blinked, clearly not computing. "Right. Of course. But maybe . . . just to the left of the bride? Or, wait! What if we do a shot of you solo?"

"I don't even *go* here," he murmured under his breath to me, grinning like this was his personal hell and he loved every second of it.

The photographer finally got everyone positioned—Easton suspiciously near the middle—and clapped her hands. "Okay! Let's get everyone in tighter!"

Before I could even blink, Easton's arm slipped around my waist. Casual. Confident. Like he'd been waiting for an excuse.

And instead of tensing, instead of offering a joke to cover the soft chaos in my chest, I leaned in. On purpose.

His grip tightened. And everything in me just . . . settled. Like a breath finally exhaled.

Easton's whole body froze.

His arm stilled against my back, his fingers paused ever so slightly on my waist . . . like he didn't quite believe it. Like this tiny, quiet moment, a lean, a touch, meant more than all the sex we'd been having this week.

When I risked a glance at him, his head was already tipped toward me, eyes bright with something almost boyish. Hopeful. Disbelieving. He looked like he might actually burst into a grin, but was trying really, *really* hard to play it cool.

Spoiler alert: he was failing.

"You good?" he murmured, his voice low enough to stay just between us.

I nodded, my smile tilting. "Yeah. I'm good."

And the way he looked at me after that—like I'd just handed him the moon—nearly knocked the air out of me.

Out of the corner of my eye, I caught movement by the reception hall doors.

A figure stood half in the shadow—broad shouldered, stiff backed. Familiar in the way a phantom might be. The kind of familiar that made my stomach twist, not from grief this time, but from muscle memory. From years of flinching at shadows that never stayed.

Terry.

He wasn't close enough to hear the laughter. Not close enough to be part of anything. But not far enough to pretend he wasn't watching.

And he *was* watching.

Like a man who didn't know how to step into a world he once chose to abandon. Like he'd missed every invitation until there weren't any left—and now wasn't sure if he should forge one himself.

Beside him stood Brittany. She hovered, looking uncertain, hands clasped in front of her like she wasn't quite sure if she belonged here, either.

Paige's voice rang out, clear and kind. "Hey! Come on in for a picture!"

I turned just in time to see her waving them both over, her veil fluttering gently behind her. She smiled. One of those practiced, diplomatic smiles I'd seen her use at baby showers and awkward brunches.

She was letting them in for the photos.

Because of course she was.

I watched as Paige positioned him near the edge of the group, not too close to Mom and Steve, but not too far from Levi. Brittany stepped in beside him, smoothing her dress. He smiled awkwardly, like he wasn't quite sure what to do with his hands.

I braced.

Waited for the burn.

Waited for the twist in my gut, the old, familiar ache that said *This is what you could've had.* The one that whispered *He chose her, he stayed for her, he made room in his life for everything except you.*

But it didn't come.

That sharp, piercing pain I'd carried like a second spine? It was gone. Or dulled. Or maybe—just maybe—it had finally unraveled into something I could hold without bleeding.

I still remembered. I always would.

But this time, it didn't hurt the same.

Because I'd already broken. I'd already stitched myself back together again on the suite's floor with Easton's arms around me like a promise, his voice in my ear like a lullaby I didn't know I needed.

I'd already faced the wreckage. And I'd chosen to rise from it.

So I didn't flinch.

I didn't cry.

I didn't storm across the courtyard to demand answers I knew I'd never get.

I just stood there—bouquet still in hand, Easton beside me, our fingers loosely intertwined—and I watched him pose with his other daughter. The one he *hadn't* left behind.

And it was fine.

Not good. Not great. But fine.

Because this wasn't his story anymore. It wasn't about what he did or didn't do. It was about me.

It was about the girl who used to sit by the window on her birthday waiting for a phone call that never came, who used to make up stories in her head to explain why he didn't show. Who used to think if she were funnier or smarter or quieter or louder, he might've stayed.

That girl didn't live here anymore.

I looked up at Easton.

He didn't say anything . . . he didn't have to. But the second his thumb brushed over the back of my hand, my breath evened out.

He was here. *He would stay.*

And I wasn't going to run from that.

From him. From us. From our future.

I wasn't going to let a man on the edge of a photo frame undo what we'd built in the quiet hours and breathless moments and kisses that meant something more than promises whispered too late.

Paige stood tall in the center of the group, radiant and glowing and brave in her own way. And I was proud of her. For making peace in the way she needed to.

But I didn't need that anymore.

My peace had come in other forms. In the steady hum of Easton's voice. In the soft weight of his palm. In the way he looked at me like I was something he'd never stop waiting for.

So I smiled, really smiled, and I looked forward. Toward the lens. Toward the light.

And let them take the picture without me looking back.

CHAPTER 25

Natalie

Later, after the speeches were done and Paige got frosting on her nose and Levi kissed it off without hesitation, the two of them obviously trying to secure a spot as the cutest couple around . . . the DJ dimmed the lights. The mood in the room shifted.

Gone was the high-energy buzz of clinking glasses and cake-cutting chaos. In its place was something softer. More serene. The fireplace crackled, throwing shadows up the stone like they were dancing to their own secret beat. The music changed. Something smooth and swoony.

I made a quick exit to the edge of the room and sank into one of the velvet chairs lining the wall. My heels—gorgeous, strappy little devils—had officially declared war on my feet. They made me look hot . . . but they also were trying to kill me. So, I tugged one off with a muffled groan, then the other, tossing both under the chair with zero remorse.

"Don't move," Easton murmured beside me, brushing a kiss to my temple before heading off toward the bar. "I'm getting us champagne."

I smiled as I watched his gorgeous ass walk away, my feet already sighing in relief.

Then I pulled out my phone. Time to give my girls an update.

> Me: If I get pulled into one more photo, I'm faking a sprained ankle and crawling out the back window.

> Riley: Please do. Bonus points if you scream "MY TIME HERE IS DONE" on the way out.

Casey: Wait . . . you're still taking pictures?? There's cake. There's a hot man. What are you doing?

Me: First of all, the cake is gone. MeMaw took the last slice and said, "I birthed the bride's mother—I've earned this frosting." Second of all . . . the man is currently fetching me more champagne like the good boy he is.

Riley: STOP! Did you decide on that satin dress? The one that makes men forget their middle names . . .

Me: Confirmed. It's doing 80% of the flirting for me right now.

Casey: And the other 20% is what? Your soulful glances across the dance floor?

Me: Obviously. Also I may have just winked. WHO AM I?

Casey: YOU'RE THE MAIN CHARACTER, BABY.

Riley: Go get him. Grab his hand. Pull a full Jane Austen moment. We expect a dramatic slow dance and at least one moment of tension so thick you could cut it with MeMaw's salad fork.

Me: Funny you mention that. MeMaw did threaten someone with a salad fork earlier. Her waiter tried to grab her soup before the bowl was empty.

Me: Also, Easton's walking over right now.

Me: And . . . I think it's time for me to say the four letter word.

Me: And I don't mean "fuck".

I hit send and continued watching Easton walk toward me. Like some kind of slow-motion heart attack in his suit and loosened tie, looking at me like I was the only thing in the room worth noticing.

Okay. Okay. Breathe.

I was going to say it.

Not *You look nice* or *Thanks for not letting me emotionally combust this week* or even something safe like *I like you*. No. I was going to say *it*. The big one. The one that had been sitting in my chest like a champagne cork waiting to pop.

I was going to say *I love you*.

My thumb hovered over the keyboard like it was waiting for a better idea, but I'd already sent the last message. I shoved my phone into the pocket of my dress—and yes, God bless this dress for having pockets—and felt it immediately start buzzing like a taser in my hip.

Casey and Riley were clearly losing their minds.

The vibrations came in frantic bursts—three in a row, then two more. I didn't even need to check to know that the group chat was a full-blown emotional crime scene. Caps lock. Emojis. Possibly one or both of them threatening to haunt me if I didn't deliver details within the hour.

I didn't check. Not yet.

Because he was almost here.

I had to check my mouth for drool when he finally got to me because he was looking too good for words tonight. His tie was loosened just enough to be criminal. He looked—ridiculous. And devastating.

"For the girl everyone's pretending not to stare at," he said, handing me the champagne flute, his fingers brushing mine with just enough pressure to make my pulse stutter.

I took the glass and raised an eyebrow. "If this is another butter-me-up move, it's working."

He grinned, that crooked thing that never failed to turn my insides to soup. "You owe me a dance."

"Oh, I do?" I said, lounging back in the chair like I was entirely unimpressed—even though my pulse was sprinting like it was training for a 5K.

He stepped forward, offering his hand. "Absolutely. For surviving your family. For not pulling a MeMaw and throwing a fork at your half sister. And"—his gaze swept down, then back up to my face—"for looking like that and expecting me to carry on like a functioning human."

I snorted. "You're so dramatic."

"And you're dodging," he said, offering his hand. "Come on. Don't make me beg."

I sipped my champagne, letting it fizz against my lips before setting it down. "Fine. But only because you brought me bubbles . . ."

"Bubbles and charm. I'm an overachiever."

He pulled me to my feet, and I wobbled slightly on bare toes before finding my balance. "Maybe I should've kept the shoes on just so I could step on you."

He leaned in with a wicked glint in his eye. "Kinky."

"Maddox," I warned, trying not to laugh as he tugged me toward the dance floor. "You're lucky I like you."

He twirled me once, dramatically, then pulled me in close. One hand rested on my lower back, the other curled through mine, steady and warm. The song was soft—Sinatra, I think. Or maybe something that just wanted to sound like Sinatra. Something swoony and slow and built for exactly this kind of moment.

The fireplace crackled behind us, shadows climbing the stone like they had somewhere to be. Snow kept falling outside the fogged windows, and inside, it felt like time had slowed just for us.

"You looked beautiful today," he said, his voice low, his mouth so close to my temple it sent a shiver down my neck.

I huffed a laugh. "I was full of windblown hair and stress sweat."

"Still beautiful," he murmured. "Especially now."

"Now I've got blisters and wine teeth," I muttered, half into his chest.

He smiled. "And somehow still the most radiant person in the room."

My heart did something embarrassing. Something fluttery and dramatic and definitely *not* sanctioned by my better judgment.

"Just so you know," he murmured, his hand brushing a piece of hair behind my ear, like he couldn't help it. "I love this."

"This?" I echoed.

He nodded, eyes locked on mine. "You. This moment. *Us.* The way it feels like I'm exactly where I'm supposed to be."

I let out a breathy laugh, then stepped closer, resting my head against his shoulder. "You're being charming again."

"You keep saying that like it's a surprise."

"It is," I said, smiling into his suit jacket. "Every single time."

"Natalie . . ." he whispered, an ache in his voice.

"Yes . . ." I whispered back.

It came out as a sigh. A full-body exhale. Like I'd been holding something in for too long, and he was the first person I trusted to see it.

He pulled back just enough to look at me. His fingers found a piece of hair near my ear and tucked it gently behind it. "I can't wait until our wedding."

The only reason I didn't trip over my own feet was because his arms were holding me up.

My heart kicked. My lungs stopped. My brain flatlined.

A weird laugh burst from my lips, the kind you let out when your chest is tight and your eyes sting and you're not sure if you're about to kiss someone or cry on their shirt.

And I might have done both. If he hadn't stiffened.

If a voice behind me hadn't broken through the music like a splinter in silk.

"Mind if I cut in?"

I turned—and there he was. Terry. Again. Hands folded, expression earnest, like he was auditioning for the role of Regret in a toothpaste commercial.

Of course it was him. The human equivalent of a record scratch. Two for two on ruining perfectly good moments with Easton. At this rate, I was going to need hazard pay.

"Remember how we used to dance in the living room?" he said, his voice low. "Your feet on top of mine. You were what—five?" He gave a faint smile. "I could try to pull it off again."

My breath caught. Not because of the offer—but because I did remember.

The worn edges of the carpet under my toes. The scratchy voice of some old crooner on the radio, tinny and soft. The way my tiny fingers had curled around his, trusting. Certain. My giggle bouncing off the walls like it had somewhere important to be.

I remembered all of it. Vivid, like it had happened just last week instead of a lifetime ago.

But I didn't think *he* would.

"I'd rather not," I said. My voice came out steady, calm. Like I hadn't just been sucker punched by a memory I didn't know still had claws.

But inside?

Everything trembled.

The music swelled between us. My fingers still tingled where Easton had touched them.

My father's face didn't shift much. Barely a flicker. Just a tightening at the jaw, a tiny twitch at the corner of his mouth like the smile he'd worn had never quite belonged there. He nodded.

A small, quiet nod.

"I understand," he said.

I hated how calm he sounded. Hated how polite he was. Like he'd turned into a ghost with manners. A man who had spent years disappearing only to reappear with soft words and softened edges and nothing close to an apology.

I could feel Easton beside me, his presence warm and grounding and still watching me with something that looked a lot like permission. Like I didn't owe anyone anything. Like I could say no and walk away and still be whole.

But something—some stupid thing—inside me cracked.

Something small. Some old, splintered part of me that still remembered the sound of his shoes on the kitchen floor. The way he used to whistle under his breath when he thought no one was listening. The way he'd once let me stand on his feet like it meant something.

Maybe it was the hope I thought I saw in his eyes. The fragile, breakable hope of a man who didn't deserve it but carried it anyway.

Maybe it was just the weight of too many years of not saying anything at all.

Or maybe it was that this moment, awkward and aching as it was, felt like something I'd been holding underwater for years—and suddenly, I was too tired to keep it from surfacing.

"Just one," I said, my voice quiet, brittle as ice and just as likely to crack. "One dance."

My father nodded. He didn't push. Didn't speak. Just took the single step forward that closed the space between us and reached for my hand like he thought I might vanish if he touched me too hard. Like I was still small, still five years old with socked feet on top of his dress shoes, not this grown woman in satin and stubbornness who'd learned to stop waiting.

Easton's touch slipped away.

His fingertips grazed mine for half a second, and then he was gone—his warmth retreating like the tide. But I could feel his gaze, hot and steady on my back. I didn't have to turn around to know what it held.

Not judgment. Not pressure.

Just . . . presence. Unflinching. Safe.

I stepped into the slow rhythm of the music like I was walking across thin ice—careful, breath tight, every movement deliberate. My father's palm hovered at my waist, hesitant, like he wasn't sure he had the right to touch his daughter. Like he expected me to pull away. And honestly? Part of me wanted to.

We moved awkwardly at first, like strangers in a scene we'd never rehearsed.

He smelled like aftershave and something faintly medicinal. Different from how I remembered.

"You grew up," he said finally. His voice was soft. Not shaky. Just worn around the edges, like an old shirt that had seen too many wash cycles.

"People do that." My reply was flat. Smooth. The kind of response that sounded casual but hit with the precision of a scalpel.

His throat worked, and he tried again. "You look like your mom."

I stared over his shoulder. Focused on a flickering candle in the far corner of the room. "She looked tired a lot."

That silenced him.

The music played on, too romantic for the moment, some instrumental version of a song that probably played at weddings all the time. I heard the steady swell of strings, the way they held the silence between us like it mattered.

His hand didn't grip mine fully. His fingers rested there, unsure. They didn't know how to hold me anymore, and I didn't offer a map.

He kept trying to look at me.

And I kept looking past him.

It was a whole thing.

He cleared his throat. "I'm not asking you to forgive me."

"Good." My voice stayed steady this time, firm like a fence post in hard earth. "Because I'm not ready."

He nodded again, like he'd been expecting that. Maybe he had.

My jaw clenched until my molars ached. My hand, still loosely held in his, felt foreign. Like it belonged to someone else. Someone younger. Someone who used to believe.

And still—

I let the song finish.

Not because I forgave him.

Not because I needed the closure he was trying to script.

But because this was my sister's wedding. Because people were watching. Because my dress was beautiful, the lights were soft, the music was sweet and aching, and I was tired of being the girl who always bolted.

So I stayed.

One slow, painful dance.

That's all it was.

A minute and a half of shared space. Of ghosts. Of silence that stretched between us like a rope worn thin.

I didn't say another word. Didn't give him anything else. No absolution. No promises. No second chances tucked into a whispered goodbye.

When the music swelled toward its final note, I gently stepped back.

His hand dropped from my waist like it knew better than to try to linger.

"Thank you," he said quietly.

I didn't respond.

I simply turned and walked away, back toward the man whose arms had never let me fall.

CHAPTER 26

Natalie

A ll right, ladies!" Paige called from the front of the room, her veil slightly askew and her lipstick looking way too good for someone who'd just had her tongue down Levi's throat. "It's time!"

Groans and laughter echoed as chairs scraped and women reluctantly shuffled toward the dance floor like it was *The Hunger Games*.

"Oh no," I muttered, grabbing Ellie's arm. "She's really doing this."

"I will *not* be a cliché tonight," someone muttered behind me like they were trying to manifest it into existence . . . while holding a bouquet of roses, a heart-shaped balloon, and what was definitely a ring box.

"Speak for yourself," MeMaw said, cracking her knuckles. "I didn't wear orthopedic heels just to *not* body-slam a bridesmaid."

I side-eyed my mother, silently asking if she was going to step in, but she just rolled her eyes. Judging by the state of her rosy cheeks and glassy eyes, someone had drank a little too much champagne . . .

Up front, Paige clutched her bouquet like it was a glitter-drenched grenade. She grinned, tossed her curls over her shoulder, and yelled, "Who wants to be next?!"

A few cheers. Mostly groaning. Someone made the sign of the cross.

Easton was lounging at a nearby table with a champagne glass in hand, and he caught my eye and winked. "Catch it," he mouthed, and I rolled my eyes, my lips twitching, even if the idea of marriage wasn't seeming nearly as awful nowadays.

The DJ hit play on some upbeat, aggressively sparkly anthem, and Paige turned her back to the crowd, knees bent like a quarterback, the bouquet held high.

"On three!" she yelled. "One . . . two . . ."

"I swear, if this flower carcass hits me in the face—" someone hissed.

"THREE!"

She launched the bouquet over her head with the power of a woman fueled by mimosas and marital bliss.

Gasps. Screams. A full-on scramble.

Arms flailed. Shoes skidded. Someone fell.

And then—

"I got it, you heathens!" a voice shrieked.

We all turned to see—

MeMaw.

Standing center floor, victorious, bouquet in one hand, cane in the other, and smug as a cat in cream.

A stunned silence fell.

"Damn right, I caught it," she declared, adjusting her sequined bolero with flair. "I may be seventy-blessed-and-fabulous, but I still got the reflexes of a teenage cheerleader and the hips of a disco queen, and I'm feeling frisky for some whiskey if you know what I mean."

Laughter erupted. Levi doubled over wheezing. Someone whistled. Because yes . . . we did all know what that meant.

MeMaw tucked the bouquet under her arm like a football and blew kisses to the crowd. "Don't be jealous. I'm taking applications."

"She's unstoppable," I whispered, half in awe.

"Honestly," Ellie said. "I aspire to that level of amazingness."

As the crowd slowly dispersed, Paige was doubled over laughing, and MeMaw was already telling someone she "preferred diamonds over daisies, but she'd make it work." I slipped out the side door and into the hallway.

I needed a bathroom. And then I needed Easton.

Preferably in that order. Though, depending on how long the line was, I could be persuaded to rearrange.

The laughter faded behind me as I padded down the dim corridor, the music muffled now, heels swinging from one hand because I wasn't about to go into a public bathroom with bare feet even if they were wrecked.

I turned the corner and . . . stopped dead.

Terry.

Easton.

And *her*.

Brittany was standing there in her pretty blue dress, staring at Easton like she wanted to eat him.

I didn't love that.

"I'm not asking for charity," Terry was saying, his hand laid dramatically over his chest like he was onstage. "Just a little help. It's prostate cancer. Stage four. Doctor says it's slow-growing, but the bills sure aren't. You know how it is—specialists, scans, medications, and that's *after* insurance takes their sweet little cut."

He gave a strained chuckle, like he expected Easton to laugh, too. He didn't.

"I wouldn't even be here if it wasn't serious," Terry added quickly, sensing the silence. "I don't want pity. I just need a couple grand to stay ahead of the hospital. That's nothing to a guy like you, right?"

Easton said nothing.

Nothing at all.

But his silence was loud. Final. Like a slammed door.

Terry must've felt it, too, because the sympathy-drip dried up fast. He pivoted so fast it gave me secondhand whiplash.

"I mean . . ." His eyes flicked toward Brittany, and suddenly his voice turned slick again. "Look, I've got three beautiful girls. Natalie's always been a little . . . prickly. High-strung. Never did know how to relax."

I would have snorted if the situation wasn't so surreal . . . because how the fuck would he know what I'd always been like?

Terry smiled like that was an endearing quirk. Like he hadn't just dismissed every wound I wore as a personality flaw.

"But this one," he said, motioning lazily to Brittany like she was a car he was trying to unload. "She's fun. Real easy to be around. Wouldn't give you any trouble."

Brittany didn't blink. She didn't look confused or insulted. She smiled like the world owed her something and she'd finally found the cashier.

And then she arched her back—pushed out her chest like she was on a reality show, and the rose ceremony was about to begin.

I gagged a little in my throat. I didn't mean to. But it was either that or let my stomach heave up the steak dinner I'd managed to choke down earlier.

Which was not something these people deserved.

"She could keep you company tonight," Terry added, the words dripping out like oil. "Make the money worth your while."

My heart didn't just drop. It detonated.

Every molecule in my body stilled. Froze. Burned.

I couldn't hear anything—not the music, not the distant *clink* of silverware, not even my own pulse. Just a high-pitched, white-hot static of *Are you fucking kidding me?*

This man—the man who had shown up out of nowhere claiming he wanted to *fix* things—wasn't here for closure or forgiveness.

He was here to barter. To beg. To sell.

Had he really just asked my *boyfriend* for a loan while pimping out his other daughter like some blackjack table bonus?

Was this his idea of *rebuilding a relationship?*

I felt something hot and acidic surge in my throat. I wasn't sad. I wasn't hurt.

I was *furious.*

The kind of fury that came from every scraped knee he never kissed, every birthday he missed, every night I stared at the door wondering if maybe—*maybe*—he'd show up this time.

I wanted to scream. I wanted to claw the smirk off his face and throw Brittany's six-hundred-dollar shoes into the nearest punch bowl.

Easton's voice cut through the quiet like a blade wrapped in thunder.

"You should walk away. Right now."

"Come on," Terry chuckled, but it was dry, brittle. The kind of laugh people fake when they've just been caught stealing from the offering plate. "You're acting like I offended you."

Easton stepped forward, the air around him suddenly ten degrees colder. "You did. Not for my own sake . . . I've had people try to con money out of me since the moment my face hit a billboard. But you just insulted your daughter. The woman I love. The woman I'm going to marry as soon as I can convince her."

I don't know what stunned me more, how calm he sounded, or how much it shook me.

As soon as I can convince her.

Something hot and fizzy lit up inside me, as if a soda can had exploded beneath my ribs.

But I didn't pause to savor it, I couldn't. Not with what I was hearing.

I stepped out from around the corner, my bare feet soundless against the worn wood, my eyes locked on the man who helped create me—who now stood there like he hadn't just tried to auction off my half sister for a check and a pat on the back.

Terry's head jerked up.

"Natalie—" he started, his tone pitched somewhere between innocent and oh-shit.

But he didn't get another syllable out.

Because I punched him. Right across the jaw. A clean, snapping, bone-deep punch that came from years of swallowed pain and everything he had *not* been.

He stumbled sideways into the wall with a grunt, hand clutching his face like I'd just committed treason instead of self-defense. Brittany let out a tiny gasp, one hand fluttering to her chest like someone had spilled red wine on her Birkin.

More offended than concerned. Of course.

"What the hell is wrong with you?" I shouted, fists trembling at my sides. "You show up after years—*years*—give some Oscar-worthy mono-logue about being sick and full of regret, and then I catch you here, asking my boyfriend for money like some back-alley grifter in a Men's Wearhouse clearance suit?! And . . . *offering her up* like she's part of the damn deal?!"

"Natalie—"

"No," I snapped. "Don't speak. Don't say my name. Don't *look* at me."

My voice shook. My hands, too. But my spine? It had never felt straighter.

"She's not a consolation prize," I hissed. "I'm not some missed invest-ment. And Easton sure as hell isn't your personal ATM."

His mouth opened again, but I wasn't done. Not by a mile. Because something had just struck me . . . something he'd said.

"You told me you had *leukemia*."

He froze.

"I stood there while you tried to make me feel bad for you, and now I hear you spinning some sob story about *prostate cancer*?"

His mouth opened, shut, then opened again like a fish yanked out of water. "It—it's both."

"Oh really?" I barked out a laugh, half wild. "You're just collecting cancers now, huh? Like Pokémon cards?"

"That's not—I just didn't think—"

"No, you *didn't*. You didn't think I'd catch you. You didn't think I'd hear. And you definitely didn't think I'd *remember* what you said. You're not even sick, are you?"

Silence fell like glass shattering in the air.

His jaw worked, but nothing came out. His eyes skittered sideways. The corner of his mouth twitched. And there it was—truth, plain as day, smeared all over his face like a bad toupee and even worse lies.

My stomach flipped, but this time it was from clarity, not pain.

"You lied," I whispered. "To *me*. About *cancer*."

"I didn't think you'd talk to me otherwise—" he started.

"Save it."

His eyes darted to Brittany like she might save him, but she was too busy inspecting her nails and pretending the floor was *fascinating*.

I stepped closer.

"Do you know what it cost me just to let you *touch* me today? What I had to *swallow* to say yes to that dance?" My voice cracked. "And this is who you are?"

His eyes flickered . . . guilt, shame, something close to fear.

Good.

Easton stepped in then, his hand brushing my back like a tether. "Let's go."

But I wasn't quite finished. I turned to Brittany.

"And you?" I said, my voice slicing clean. "You let him use you like that?"

Her lips parted like she might gasp or speak or pretend she hadn't just stood there letting herself be offered like a party favor with a pulse.

But nothing came out.

"No," I snapped. "You don't get to be speechless now. You don't get to play innocent when you *smiled* while he bartered you like a fucking accessory."

Color flushed her cheeks, but I didn't care.

"He may have forgotten what being a father means," I said, my words low and cutting. "But you don't have to let him keep treating you like you're a pawn in some cheap, rigged game. Grow a spine, Brittany. Or at the very least, grow up."

Then I turned back to the man I used to wish would come home.

The man who once lived in my daydreams, always stepping through the door with apologies and promises and the miracle of being different this time.

"You never deserved me," I said, voice like frost, sharp and final. "And you never will."

I turned and walked away, Easton close behind.

And I didn't cry.

I didn't even look back.

Because this time, I wasn't the girl anymore. The one waiting for her father . . . hoping that he would change.

I was the woman walking away from him.

Forever.

CHAPTER 27

Natalie

We didn't speak until we were outside.

The cold slapped my cheeks the second the door swung shut behind us, sharp and unrelenting . . . the kind of cold that made your breath visible and your feelings harder to hide. Snow was falling again, slow and delicate, like the sky had the audacity to be gentle when everything inside me was loud and frayed and *raw*.

Easton didn't speak.

He just walked beside me, close enough that his hand brushed the small of my back. Not a guide. Not a claim. Just there. Like a punctuation mark. Like he knew I was unraveling and was quietly volunteering to be the thread that held me together.

We stepped through a second door that led to the covered wraparound patio, strung with soft white lights that glowed like sleepy stars overhead. A few empty chairs faced the mountains, now just jagged shadows against a bruised horizon of snow and pine.

I sank into one of the chairs with the weight of someone who wasn't sure if she'd ever stand up again. The wood creaked beneath me, and the cold from the seat bled through my dress, but I didn't care.

My breath came in short, shallow bursts—tight and high, like my ribs hadn't caught up to the rest of me. Like part of me was still *back there*, frozen in that hallway. Staring at the man who'd once made me believe I wasn't enough. Who'd almost made me believe it again.

Easton sat beside me, knees wide, elbows on them as I stared out at the snow. Watched it fall like tiny ghosts. "He didn't even flinch when I punched him."

Easton was quiet for a moment, his breath clouding in front of him.

"Maybe he's used to being hit," he said finally.

I let out a bitter laugh, sharp and small. "Yeah. Or maybe he just doesn't *feel* anything. Maybe he never did."

I shook my head. "I shouldn't have done it." My voice cracked. "I shouldn't have given him the satisfaction of seeing how much he still gets to me."

He turned his head. "No, Nat. You gave *yourself* the satisfaction. Of not staying quiet. Of not swallowing it down again. You were the one with power back there. You stood there, told the truth, and let him fucking choke on it."

I wiped at my cheek, annoyed to find it damp. "I hate that he made me feel like I was a kid again. Like I was the one being dramatic. Like I was just too emotional to be loved."

"You're not too emotional," he said, voice low and even. "You're not dramatic. You're not difficult."

I side-eyed him. Hard.

He exhaled a short breath through his nose. "Okay, I mean, you *can* be dramatic."

My brow arched higher.

"But not about this," he amended quickly, holding up a hand like a man begging for mercy. "This was righteous fury. Very noble. Would've looked great in slow motion."

Despite myself, my lips twitched.

"Slow motion, huh?"

"Yep. Black and white. Epic swelling music. Maybe a wind machine."

I scoffed and then waggled my eyebrows. "It was kind of epic."

He grinned, looking a little relieved that I wasn't falling to the ground in hysterics at the moment—even though the situation really did call for it.

"It was definitely epic," he told me proudly.

We sat for a beat longer, the silence between us softening around the edges. The snow kept falling. The air stayed cold.

But something inside me had unclenched.

I let my head fall against his shoulder.

"I used to imagine him showing up," I said, quieter now. "Not like this. Not with lies and manipulation and . . . her. But the version I needed when I was a kid. I used to make up conversations in my head. I'd sit at the window and picture him getting out of the car with flowers, or a letter, or just an *apology*. Something real."

"I'd even rehearse what I'd say back. Like it was a scene I could control. Like if I got the lines right, it would fix something. Make him stay."

I pulled in a breath that stung all the way down, the kind of inhale that scraped through your chest like glass.

"But after a while, I stopped. I told myself he was gone. That I'd never see him again. That it was safer to grieve someone alive than keep hoping for something that would never happen."

My voice thinned, raw at the edges. "I never thought he'd actually come back. And now that he did . . ." My throat burned. "I wish he fucking hadn't."

Easton didn't try to fill the silence. He didn't try to fix it. He just reached for my hand and found it easily, his fingers threading through mine. His thumb grazed over my knuckles—lingering on the one that still throbbed from the punch, like he knew exactly where it hurt.

"You could hit him again if you want. I'll hold him down."

That made me laugh, breathless and teary. "Tempting."

"I'm just saying, I have no moral objections to vigilante justice. Especially when the guy deserves it."

"He does deserve it," I whispered back.

The wind shifted, blowing snow across the patio like confetti meant for some other kind of celebration. One I hadn't been invited to. One I wasn't going to miss.

And for a while, we sat like that.

Silent.

Breathing.

Healing, maybe.

The door creaked open again, letting out a burst of warm air and music . . . and Ellie.

She squinted into the dark like she wasn't entirely sure what she was walking into.

"There you are," she said, wrapping her arms around herself against the cold. "Everything okay out here?"

I nodded once. "Yeah. Just needed a minute."

"Are you two coming back in, or what? Paige sent me to look for you. Whataburger just arrived, and MeMaw is officially getting *freaky* on the dance floor. Like, dangerously freaky. We might need to form a perimeter."

Easton huffed a laugh beside me.

I blinked up at Ellie. The cold had numbed my face, but not enough to keep a smile from tugging at the corner of my mouth. "See, this is why we can't have nice things. She was banned from body rolls after that Valentine's dance at the community center where she dislocated her hip trying to drop it to Ginuwine and took down the entire punch table like a domino."

"She swiveled into the garter toss like a backup dancer on tour. I'm scared," Ellie said, deadpan. "And, if we're talking about punch . . . I'm pretty sure someone spiked the one that was *specifically* labeled nonalcoholic. Like, big bold letters. And by *someone*, I mean *Levi*."

I snorted, the laugh catching me off guard, rising up in my chest like something lighter than what I'd been carrying. "We'll be right in," I said.

She nodded, then gave us both a weird little salute before disappearing back inside, her heels clicking and her hips already moving to whatever song was blasting through the speakers.

I stood slowly, Easton rising beside me. My fingers tightened in his for just a second. "You sure you're up for it?" he asked, his voice low, just for me.

I nodded once, firm. "He doesn't get another second of my life," I said. "Not another sliver of space in my head. This day? This week? It belongs to Paige. And you. And me."

His gaze held mine for a beat, steady and sure. "When are you going to tell her?"

I exhaled, the cold biting at my lungs. "I'll tell her later," I murmured. "But not today."

Today didn't belong to Terry.

And neither did I.

Easton led me inside.

Not reluctantly.

Not because I was pretending everything was fine.

But because it *wasn't* fine—and I was walking in anyway.

The music hit me first . . . loud, joyful, chaotic. Then the smell of warm fries and too many candles, someone laughing too hard, the thrum of a beat I didn't recognize but already loved.

I spotted Paige spinning in her dress, a half-eaten burger in one hand, a champagne flute in the other. MeMaw was doing the worm. Someone had given her sunglasses. It was unclear who was in charge anymore.

Easton leaned down. "Sure this isn't too much?"

"It's too much in all the right ways," I muttered. "Let's go party."

We stepped into the whirlwind together—laughter, fries, and questionable dance moves waiting for us.

And I didn't look back.

CHAPTER 28

Natalie

The bed-and-breakfast glowed like a Christmas Eve dream.

The wedding was over. Paige and Levi had been sent off in a flurry of sparklers and champagne-fueled whooping, disappearing into the snowy night like a story that knew exactly how it should end. And now, just a handful of us were left—stray groomsmen, and tipsy cousins still half buttoned into their formalwear—humming with leftover champagne and sentiment, crammed into the parlor for the last tradition of the night.

The fire crackled in the hearth, casting light over the mismatched armchairs draped in plaid throws. Garlands of pine and holly framed the windows, and fairy lights twinkled from the beams overhead. In the corner stood the tree—massive, unapologetically extra, dripping in ornaments from every era. Some sparkled, some leaned a little to the left, and at least three looked like they'd been made by sticky-fingered toddlers with glitter vendettas. But somehow, it worked. It all worked.

The mug was warm in my hands as I stood near the fire, heart thudding quietly in my chest. People laughed around me. Someone spilled something. MeMaw was still holding court in the armchair like the Queen of Christmas Chaos.

And I was just . . . waiting.

Not for a sign. Not for clarity.

Just for five uninterrupted minutes with Easton.

Because I was already all in.

And I was done letting timing get in the way of telling him.

Across the room, Easton stood near the tree, talking to my cousin Jake, his hand curled around a glass of whiskey. He laughed at something, his head tipping back, and the sound sent a flutter through me—because I could picture it echoing through a future kitchen, or beside a summer campfire, or Milan . . . because, you know, he was a movie star.

But really? Anywhere we ended up together.

I could see it.

So clearly, it almost hurt.

He was beautiful. Not just in the movie-star way that made heads turn, but in the way he *was*. Steady. Loyal. Kind. Mine.

He looked up suddenly, like he'd felt me watching, and our eyes locked across the room. My breath hitched. He smiled, just slightly, and my heart answered in kind.

Shit. I was so fucking in love with him.

Before I could respond, Margaret clapped her hands together to get everyone's attention. "All right, everyone!" she called, her voice bright and enthusiastic. "It's time for our Christmas Eve tradition! We're going to write our wishes on these paper stars and hang them on the tree. It's a little bit of holiday magic to bring good luck for the new year. Grab a star and a pen, and let's get started."

People began to shuffle toward the little table set up by the fire, already laughing and teasing as they picked through pens and glittered paper stars.

I set my mug down on the mantel, fingers tingling with nerves and something steadier. I knew what I wanted.

Easton was already there, his brow furrowed as he wrote something carefully onto his star. He looked so focused, so sure, it made my chest ache in the best way.

"Go on, girl," MeMaw said as she passed by, giving me a knowing nudge with her elbow. "Wish for what you really want. And none of that vague 'peace on Earth' crap."

I snorted. "You're terrifying."

She winked, the reindeer ears on her glasses bouncing as she moved toward the snack table.

I grabbed a star and a pen, my fingers steady now. No second-guessing. No overthinking.

I wrote one sentence.

To never lose him again.

The wish felt raw, vulnerable, like I was laying my heart bare for the universe to see, but it was the truth.

I folded the star carefully and moved to the tree, hanging it near the top, where the light caught the gold just right.

The moment I turned, he was there.

Easton.

Watching me with that soft, steady look like I was the only thing in the world that mattered.

He glanced at my star. "What'd you wish for?"

"If I tell you, it won't come true," I said, my lips curving.

"You really believe that?"

"I believe in hedging my bets."

He grinned, then leaned past me and tied his own star to the branch right beside mine. Our wishes spun slowly together, dancing in the twinkle of the tree lights, as though they were already bound by fate.

"What about you?" I teased, fighting to keep my voice steady. "Want to share yours?"

Easton smiled, softer this time, his eyes lingering on mine just a second too long. "Maybe later."

I bit my lip, smiling helplessly as I watched him.

Eventually the evening wound down. Guests began to drift toward their rooms, murmuring soft goodnights and Merry Christmases. Easton touched my elbow lightly as I started toward the staircase, drawing my attention back to him.

"Hey," he said, his voice low and warm, sending a shiver down my spine. "Want to walk together?"

I nodded, my throat tight with emotion. "Yeah," I said, my voice barely above a whisper. "I'd like that."

We climbed the stairs slowly, quietly, in comfortable silence, shoulders occasionally brushing. My heart raced, caught in the tension between wanting to say something—anything—and wanting to just enjoy the quiet closeness.

Then Easton paused by the door that led out into the courtyard. He glanced through the frosted glass, then looked back at me with a mischievous grin.

"Come outside with me."

"It's freezing out there."

"I'll keep you warm."

I raised an eyebrow but couldn't fight my own smile as I followed him into the snowy courtyard. The moment we stepped outside, the chill hit me, crisp and sharp, but the air smelled fresh, like clean snow and possibility.

Easton took my hand without hesitation, and we walked slowly down the winding stone path, snow crunching softly beneath our feet. Overhead, a thousand stars glittered faintly through the soft haze of frost, quiet sentinels to our private moment.

I happened to glance through a window into the bed-and-breakfast and almost fell on my face when I saw MeMaw air-humping as she watched us leave.

That was an image I'd never be able to get rid of.

"Natalie?"

I turned to face him, my breath stuttering for a moment because nowhere in the history of the world had such a pretty man existed.

"Okay," he said. "I'm ready."

"Ready for what?"

He turned to face me fully, pulling me gently to a stop in front of him. His eyes glowed warm beneath the frost beading his lashes, his gaze so tender it stole my breath.

"To tell you my wish," he murmured.

My pulse quickened, my voice barely a whisper. "Yeah?"

He nodded slowly, eyes steady on mine. "I wished to spend every Christmas with you."

The words landed softly, melting through me like snowflakes against my skin. I exhaled shakily, smiling despite the way my heart felt dangerously close to cracking open.

"That's a big wish," I teased softly, even as my throat tightened. "You sure about that?"

"I've never been more sure of anything." He stepped closer, reaching up to brush a fleck of ice from my cheek, his thumb lingering, warm and gentle against my skin. "Every Christmas. Every day in between. I want it all with you, Trouble."

My eyes stung, emotion swelling suddenly . . . fiercely. "Easton . . ."

"I've never stopped loving you," he said quietly, his voice thick and raw, eyes locked intently on mine. "And I never will."

My heart stumbled, the truth so raw, so real, it felt like a gift, perfectly wrapped and placed right in my hands.

"I love you, too," I whispered. "I just got a little lost for a while. But it was always you."

His eyes widened slightly, something wild and bright breaking across his face.

"Say it again," he breathed.

"I love you," I repeated softly, tears clinging stubbornly to my lashes. "I always have."

Easton cupped my face in both his hands, thumbs tracing softly along my jawline. His lips curved into a soft smile—aching, raw, impossibly beautiful—and he drew me in slowly, as if we had all the time in the world.

Snow glittered gently around us, catching the soft, golden glow from the windows, painting the courtyard in a dreamlike haze. The stars above shone clear and bright, as if they, too, held their breath, watching this moment unfold.

But when Easton kissed me, the world disappeared.

There was no lodge, no snow, no noise . . . just him. Just *us*. The kiss deepened gently, with all the emotion we'd been holding inside. Every missed chance, every unspoken word, every sleepless night and whispered dream condensed into the space between our lips.

When we finally pulled apart, breath mingling in the cold night air, he pressed his forehead to mine, eyes closed like he was holding on to the moment with both hands.

"I've loved you for half my life," he said, his voice barely above a whisper. "And I'm going to love you for all the rest of it."

The words hit something deep. Something old and aching and sacred.

"Promise?" I whispered, not because I didn't believe him—but because once, under a sky full of invented constellations and teenage bravado, we'd made that same vow. Said we'd find each other, no matter what.

His eyes softened, something flickering behind them—memory, emotion, the weight of everything we'd been.

"Still do," he said quietly. "Always will."

A laugh broke from me, wet and quiet. "You said you'd come back to me."

He stepped closer, brushing his fingers along my jaw, reverent. "And you said you'd find me. No matter what."

I nodded, tears catching in the corners of my eyes as I whispered the only thing that felt true enough.

"I love you."

"Forever," he said, pulling me in, his voice fierce and full. "Every sky. Every season. Every version of us."

And when he kissed me, I felt the stars shift.

Our star. Our promise.

Finally found again.

CHAPTER 29

Natalie

ONE WEEK LATER

The late afternoon sunlight slanted through the smudged window of my college apartment, casting everything in a soft, honey-colored glow. It made even the mess look charming.

Textbooks were scattered across my desk, sticky notes clinging to their pages like desperate leaves. A half-dead succulent leaned pathetically toward the light, and my lavender candle burned unevenly, valiantly trying to cover the lingering scent of last night's sesame chicken.

The radiator clanked in the corner, loud, stubborn, familiar. Usually, the noise grounded me.

Today, it made the room feel hollow.

My suitcase lay open on the floor, stuffed with clothes and the remnants of a week that had turned everything upside down—in the best, most terrifying way.

Easton had flown back to LA yesterday morning for a few last-minute reshoots. Just a week, we'd promised. We could do a week.

It had felt manageable when he kissed me goodbye at the airport, when he whispered *I'll be counting down every second until I'm back to you* against my ear.

But now?

The silence in my apartment pressed in around me, thick and constant. Like I'd built a space shaped perfectly for him . . . and then he'd left.

I missed him more than I thought possible. Fiercely. Suddenly. Like my body was still trying to calibrate to the space he'd filled and left behind.

We hadn't figured everything out yet. There were still questions. How we'd handle the distance. How we'd juggle our lives on opposite coasts. I still had years of school ahead of me. Papers. Practicums. Late nights and internships and exams.

And he had a career exploding faster than either of us could have predicted.

We didn't have a perfect plan.

But we had each other.

And we were both determined to make it work.

I sighed and ran a hand through my travel-messy hair, then dropped to my knees beside the suitcase. Might as well unpack. Try to return to something that resembled normal before classes started.

I pulled out a red sweater—*the* red sweater—the one that would forever be linked to Christmas brunch and crimes against public decency.

A smile tugged at my lips as I folded it, remembering Easton's hand creeping up my leg while MeMaw delivered an unhinged speech about soulmates and how they created superior children, totally oblivious to the fact that her granddaughter was one rogue gasp away from scandalizing the entire waffle station.

Apparently, Easton and tables and my thigh were a combination I was going to have to watch out for in the future.

Fuck. I missed him.

I kept unpacking. Jeans. Scarves. My toiletry bag. Socks.

Then my fingers brushed against something soft and unfamiliar.

I paused.

There, tucked in the side pocket, hidden beneath a balled-up scarf . . . was a small velvet box.

Deep blue. Elegant.

And definitely not mine.

A tremble worked its way through me as I pulled it out. I turned it over in my hands, my heart thudding, trying to make sense of it. The hinge creaked softly as I opened it.

Inside sat a delicate silver necklace, the pendant shaped like a constellation.

Our constellation.

The one we'd imagined on a summer night with too many mosquitoes and not enough sense. The same one we'd been thinking of just last week, when everything came full circle beneath the snow and starlight and everything we couldn't say until we finally did.

The pendant shimmered in the light—quiet, certain, sacred.

My throat tightened. Because tucked beneath the necklace was a small, folded note.

The paper was slightly crumpled, the edges soft like it had been carried for a while before being placed there with quiet intention.

Easton's handwriting sprawled across it in thick, black ink—messy, rushed, familiar, and my heart thudded as I unfolded it, my breath catching as I read the words.

A thousand lifetimes wouldn't be enough. Come find me under our stars. —E.

I stared at the note, the words sinking in like a stone dropped into water, rippling through every part of me.

A thousand lifetimes.

My throat tightened.

Tears blurred the ink, and I pressed the necklace to my chest, the pendant cool and sharp against my skin. A steady ache settled just beneath my heart—not from fear, not from walls—I didn't have those anymore.

Just the weight of everything we'd survived.

Everything we'd found again.

And the impossible bigness of finally having it.

He must have slipped it into my suitcase before he left.

A quiet gesture. No theatrics. No fanfare. Just this—his heart, folded into velvet and ink.

My knees buckled, and I sank to the floor. The note trembled in my hand, the box still resting in my lap. The room buzzed with silence, just the *clank* of the radiator and the sound of my own breath, uneven and thick with emotion.

I missed him.

But more than that—I *loved* him.

And I was done waiting.

I thought of the week we'd just had. The way we came together in stolen moments—hungry, quiet, desperate. The laughter spilling from our lips during MeMaw's chaotic toasts. The way his hand never left my knee at dinner, like he couldn't bear to not touch me for even a second.

The sound of his voice—low, warm—when he whispered *I've never stopped loving you.*

Every touch, every look, had been a reminder of what we'd once had and what we could have again, if I could just find the courage to let go of my fears.

A slow, steady rekindling of something I thought we'd lost.

But it had never been lost.

It had just been waiting.

And I wasn't waiting anymore.

Tears slipped down my cheeks—quiet, relieved tears—and my breath came in shaky, uneven bursts. I didn't even try to stop them.

Sitting here in my cluttered, little apartment with a constellation in my hands and his love still echoing in my chest, I knew the truth.

Easton had chosen me.

Again and again.

Through the explosion of his career. Through the miles. Through every single excuse I'd hidden behind.

Come find me under our stars.

The words weren't just sweet. They were a challenge. A promise. A plea.

And I was ready to accept it.

He was in LA, filming, living in that shiny world I'd always felt too small for. But he'd left this—this beautiful, quiet, perfect gift—just to show me that the most important part of his life wasn't on set or behind a camera.

It was *me*.

And I wasn't going to make him wait another second to know I felt the same.

I didn't want to wait a week. I didn't even want to wait a day.

I wanted to go to him. To stand under our stars and tell him I loved him. That I was his. Entirely. Eternally.

I wanted to propose to *him*. To ask him to be mine, forever. To build the life we'd whispered about under summer skies, young and in love and dreaming way too big.

I stood slowly, my hands still trembling as I clasped the necklace around my neck.

The pendant settled just above my heart, the weight of it somehow comforting . . . like he was already with me.

I wiped the tears from my cheeks, drew in a deep breath, and grabbed my phone.

The screen glowed softly in the fading light as I pulled up the airline app, fingers hovering.

Los Angeles.
I typed it in without hesitating.
Because I wasn't running anymore.
I was chasing.
Chasing *him*. Chasing *us*.
And this time, I wasn't going to stop.

CHAPTER 30

Easton

The studio lights were still brutal.

Hot, relentless, and way too close. They beat down on the soundstage like twin suns, turning the space into a makeshift furnace.

Fake rain fell from the sprinkler rig above, soaking through my costume and plastering my drenched button-up to my skin. It clung to me like a second layer—cold and slick—while the heat from the lights made sweat bead along my brow and trail down my spine.

December in California meant the air outside was crisp, even cool. But inside, under this synthetic storm and those scorching lights, the contrast was maddening. I was freezing and sweating all at once. Wet, uncomfortable, and barely present.

We were reshooting one of the film's biggest scenes—the big emotional climax.

The one where my character confesses everything in the pouring rain. His love. His regrets. The whole heart-on-his-sleeve moment that was supposed to leave the audience breathless.

Paul, our director, wasn't convinced it was working.

"More raw emotion!" he shouted through his megaphone, his voice slicing through the low hum of the crew like a whip. "You're in *love*, Easton. I need to *feel* it."

I bet he was going to be glad when shooting was over and he didn't have to remind me of that anymore.

Paul was standing near the monitors, waving one arm like a conductor, scowling like this entire production personally offended him.

Around him, the crew moved in fluid, practiced chaos—adjusting lights, refocusing lenses, rolling out cables, mopping up puddles. Efficient. Mechanical.

I barely noticed.

Because I wasn't here. Not really.

My body was on set. My mouth was delivering lines. My clothes were clinging to me like they were part of the performance.

But my mind?

My mind was a thousand miles away.

In a snowy bed-and-breakfast.

With *her*.

It had only been a day since I'd left her. A day since I'd held her in my arms, since she'd whispered goodbye against my collarbone, her voice steady but her hands trembling.

I'll see you in a week, she'd said.

She'd tried to smile as she pulled back, but her bottom lip had wobbled. I'd tucked a piece of her blonde hair behind her ear and kissed her like I wasn't about to leave her at all.

It had felt manageable at the time. A week. Just seven days.

A small price to pay for a final reshoot.

But now, standing under artificial rain with scalding lights melting the edges of my focus, that week felt like an eternity.

I missed her.

Not just in the abstract way you miss someone when they're far away—but in the sharp, aching way that digs under your skin and makes everything else feel wrong.

I missed waking up with her head on my chest, her hair brushing my collarbone, smelling like morning and her. I missed her laugh during MeMaw's wildly inappropriate antics. I missed the sound of her voice catching in her throat when she moaned my name—specifically in the family restroom at the mall.

I missed her hand in mine. I missed her breath against my neck.

I missed *her*.

We'd found something again. At the wedding. Something I thought we'd lost forever.

If I could just prove that I was all in—that I always had been—then maybe, just maybe, we wouldn't lose this thing a second time.

I'd been texting her all morning.

Little messages, nothing intense—just reminders that she was still running laps in my fucking mind.

> Me: Miss you already, Nat. Can't stop thinking about you.

> Me: This rain scene is a mess, but all I can think about is you in that dress.

> Me: I miss the taste of your perfect pussy.

No response.

Not even to that last one.

The silence was starting to eat at me, slow and steady, like water wearing down stone. Maybe she was busy. Maybe she was just tired. Or maybe the magic had faded the second I stepped onto that plane.

I shifted my weight, my drenched costume sticking to my skin, the fake rain continuing its downpour from the rig above like it had something to prove.

Had she found it? The necklace—the note—I'd tucked it deep in the side pocket of her suitcase before I left.

Had she read it? Had she understood what I was trying to say?

She hadn't mentioned it, and the uncertainty gnawed at the edges of everything—my lines, my focus, the scene I was supposed to be pouring my soul into.

"Easton! Let's go!"

Paul's voice cracked like thunder through the megaphone, his tone pure frustration. He waved me forward with a dramatic gesture, clearly on the verge of combusting.

"We need more *intensity* in this take. You're supposed to be *heartbroken*, not distracted. Reset!"

I lifted a hand in acknowledgment, running it back through my rain-soaked hair, droplets trailing down my temple and jaw. The water was cold. The lights were hot. My patience was nonexistent.

All I could think about was being *done*.

Done with the scene. Done with this shoot. Done with being anywhere that wasn't wrapped around Natalie.

I rolled my shoulders and started back toward my mark when I heard the unmistakable *click* of heels behind me.

Vanessa.

Of course.

She sauntered up slowly, her black dress clinging to her like it had been painted on. Her dark hair was slicked back from the rain, and her lips were curved in that same slow smile that always made me want to roll my eyes.

"Drenched looks good on you," she purred.

She stepped in close, too close, her hand sliding down my chest— slow, deliberate—before pressing against the front of my pants, her fingers brushing over me like it was hers to touch.

"Bet you'd feel even better out of those wet clothes," she murmured. "My trailer's waiting."

My hand snapped out and gripped her wrist in a flash, yanking it away with enough force to make her gasp.

From the crew's angle, it probably looked like nothing. Just another costar interaction. But I was done letting her get away with this shit.

"Touch me again," I growled, "and let's see if you can hold a pen after."

Her eyes flicked wide for a second, but I didn't stop.

"I've told you . . . *don't* touch me. Don't talk to me. Don't even fucking look at me unless we're rolling."

She started to speak, lips parting in some feigned confusion or come-back, but I stepped in—close enough for her to see I wasn't bluffing.

"I love someone. And you?" I snorted. "You're not even in the same *league*. Pull that shit again, and I'll report you so fast you'll be lucky to land a toothpaste commercial."

Vanessa froze, stunned silent.

"Now back the fuck off," I snapped, turning away without another glance.

Silence stretched behind me—a pause thick with disbelief.

Then her voice floated after me, light but cracked at the edges. "Your loss."

She turned on her heel and stalked off, back to her mark with her spine a little too straight, her shoulders a little too tense.

Good.

I didn't care if she was embarrassed. I didn't care if she was mad.

Because she wasn't Natalie.

She never would be.

And I wasn't going to let anyone—especially not Vanessa—sabotage what I was rebuilding.

"All right, let's roll!"

Paul's voice echoed across the soundstage, too loud, too sharp.

I dragged myself into position, blinking through the fake rain as it pelted my face, cold against skin already flushed from the heat of the lights.

Focus.

I gritted my teeth and hit my mark.

Every word of the scene came out raw—my voice cracking on the lines that weren't supposed to crack, my jaw clenched so tight I thought I'd splinter something. I didn't even care.

I poured every ounce of missing her into it. Every second of silence. Every unread text.

The rain soaked through me, clinging to my skin, plastering my shirt to my ribs. It blurred with the heat, the pressure, the ache in my chest.

"Cut!" Paul shouted finally. "That's a wrap for today!"

I didn't move for a second.

Then my breath rushed out in a heavy exhale, and my shoulders slumped like I'd been carrying the weight of the entire set.

A PA passed me a towel. I dragged it across my face, not bothering to respond.

I was done. Not just with the scene—but with the pretending. The waiting. The silence.

I stepped off set, boots squeaking on the slick floor, and made my way to the folding chair where I'd left my phone.

Still nothing.

No text. No call. Not even a read receipt.

It had only been a few hours. I knew that. I knew I was being dramatic.

But when something means everything, even a few hours of nothing can feel like the start of the end.

And I couldn't breathe through the fear that maybe . . . maybe she'd changed her mind.

I sat down slowly, fingers already tapping her contact, the phone pressed to my ear before I had time to think better of it.

It rang. And rang. And rang.

Then her voice—bright and warm, a punch straight to the chest.

"Hey, it's Natalie! Leave a message—"

I hung up.

My throat tightened as I shoved the phone into my pocket and stalked back to my trailer, my teeth clenched, my jaw aching.

The clothes I'd worn for the scene were still soaked, sticking to my skin like regret. I stripped them off quickly, tugging on a dry hoodie and sweats, my movements sharp and unsteady. My fingers fumbled with the zipper like they couldn't keep up with my thoughts.

I grabbed my keys and slammed the door behind me.

I had to get out of here.

Back to my apartment. Back to . . . something. A message. Her voice. Anything to prove I hadn't just imagined everything we'd rebuilt.

I slung my bag over my shoulder and pushed toward the exit. Outside the studio, the sound hit first—shouts, laughter, camera shutters clicking in rapid bursts.

It had become routine now.

Fans gathered outside almost every day. Word had spread about our shooting schedule, and they camped out near the barriers hoping for a photo, a wave, anything. Normally, I'd offer a quick smile, maybe stop for a selfie or two. Tonight?

I didn't even look at them.

The crowd blurred into noise and color, voices overlapping in a frenzied chorus—"Easton! Over here!"—but none of it cut through.

I just wanted to reach my car. Call her again. Maybe leave a message this time.

Tell her I missed her. Tell her I wasn't okay. Tell her—

I froze.

My breath caught mid-step.

And suddenly, everything else fell away.

Because right there, just behind the barrier, half hidden in the sea of fans—

I saw her.

Natalie.

Standing in the crowd like it was the most natural thing in the world, like she hadn't just turned my entire reality inside out. Her blonde hair shimmered in the late afternoon light spilling through the studio gates, and her blue eyes—locked on mine—held the kind of intensity that knocked the breath clean out of my lungs.

And then I saw the sign.

A giant, glittery thing held high above her head, sparkling like it had been crafted by a lovestruck middle schooler on a sugar high. The words blazed in bold, sparkling letters.

MARRY ME, EASTON!

For a second, I just stared . . . jaw slack, heart pounding, brain trying to catch up. Then a laugh burst out of me, sharp and full and so stunned it made a few heads turn.

Because Natalie hated glittery signs.

She *mocked* glittery signs.

She had once said they were the handwriting of emotional chaos.

And now she was holding one. For me.

Shock and disbelief and relief tangled in my chest, but so did something warmer and wilder . . . because I knew exactly what this meant.

This wasn't just a grand gesture.

This was *her* grand gesture.

The woman I loved was standing in a crowd of strangers, holding up everything she usually rolled her eyes at, choosing me in the loudest, most gloriously Natalie way possible.

I'd never seen anything more perfect.

Natalie

Here's what I knew about grand romantic gestures.

One: They look a lot easier in movies.

Two: They involve a deeply concerning amount of public humiliation.

Three: TSA is not amused when you try to smuggle glitter into an airport.

But I wasn't thinking about those things as I clutched a glitter-covered sign with shaking hands, and I burst through the airport doors with heart palpitations and a cardigan that I instantly regretted wearing in seventy-degree weather.

The sign read MARRY ME, EASTON!

And it was bedazzled within an inch of its life.

People were staring.

A little boy had already pointed and said, "Mom, is that lady okay?"

I wasn't. Not even a little.

But when you break up with your movie-star boyfriend at eighteen because you're scared and then spend almost two years pretending you're over him only to have him walk back into your life at your sister's Christmas wedding looking like a wet dream and saying things like *I've never stopped loving you*—you make the sign. You board the flight. You risk arrest by carrying a glitter bomb.

I hopped in a cab and nervously told him to head to the film studio where Easton was finishing up today.

"You one of those movie-star 'stans,'" he drawled as he eyed me and my pink dress like I was about to lunge over the console and . . . well, do something.

"Something like that," I mused.

We drove to the lot where a small crowd was gathered, something that Easton told me he was annoyed to deal with after long days on set.

It was warmer than I'd anticipated. I mean California cold wasn't real cold, but the combination of nerves and sweating wasn't doing me any favors.

A security barricade cut a crooked line through the sea of screaming girls and grinning paparazzi, all pressed against it like salvation lived on the other side. I stood near the back—my hands gripped around the sign.

I could feel people staring.

I could hear them whispering.

"That girl with the sign . . . She looks unhinged."

"Who does she think she is?"

"Like he'd notice her."

Maybe I was unhinged.

Or maybe I was in love with a boy I'd let go too soon—a boy who became a movie star, then walked back into my life and kissed me like I still belonged to him.

The sound of production crews shifting filled the air—equipment rolling, assistants barking orders, someone yelling about a drone shot.

The crowd pushed closer.

People cheered, and the doors opened.

And then he stepped out.

My Easton.

Wearing sweats that hugged his frame like it had a personal vendetta against my self-control, his hair a mess . . . He looked equal parts wrecked and godlike. His face was tired. There were smudges under his eyes. But even exhausted, he was stupidly beautiful.

Screams went up around me.

People surged forward, shouting his name.

You could see him take a deep breath and turn on the movie-star smile, even though it must have been killing him.

He started walking, his eyes scanning the crowd half-heartedly.

And then . . .

He saw me.

His gaze landed on mine like a magnet snapping into place, and I watched as his eyes widened and he gaped at the fact that I was such a glorious, sweaty, nervous, beautiful mess.

Or at least that's what I was imagining was going through his head at the moment.

It took half a second.

Then his eyes went up to the sign I was holding above my head.

Slowly, his face broke into a wide grin. Not the practiced, charming one he'd been giving a second before.

The smile he'd only ever given me. Realer. Like a secret he was thrilled to keep.

The noise around me began to shift. The fans closest to me turned, eyebrows raised.

"Wait . . . is he looking at—"

"Who is that?"

"Why does she look familiar?"

"Wait . . . is that the girl he was photographed with over Christmas?"

More heads turned.

More eyes landed on me.

But I didn't move. I'd suddenly forgotten how to breathe, and my whole life suddenly hinged on Easton taking one step forward.

Then another.

And another.

Making his way through the crowd . . . straight to me.

His eyes were soft.

They stayed locked on me like I was the only one here. Not the swarm of fans. Not the paparazzi. Not the guy with an *I Love Easton* shirt standing awkwardly to the left.

Just me.

He moved past the velvet ropes. Past security, who opened the barricade without question because, apparently, being Easton Maddox came with Jedi-level authority.

And then . . . he was standing right in front of me.

Up close, he smelled like stage makeup, sweat, and the cologne he always wore that made me lose IQ points. Not the worst combo, actually.

"You're a menace. I'm just saying," Easton said.

"You're just saying that because I'm better at making sparkly proposal posters."

He eyed the sign. "It's objectively horrifying."

"I went through three glue sticks."

"Of course you did."

We stared at each other.

"Hi," I whispered. My voice cracked like a middle school trumpet.

His smile softened. "Hey, Nat."

He said it like it was only ever going to be me. Like he'd walked off a movie set and into his actual happy ending.

Glancing at my sign, he raised an eyebrow. "You stole my thunder, Trouble."

"I . . . What?"

"I was going to propose to you." He crossed his arms. "I had a whole plan. A ring. Lights. A scripted monologue. And you have the audacity to show up with a glitter poster."

"Oh my gosh," I whispered.

"You ruined my dramatic return," he said, mock stern. "You realize that, right?"

A few fans were filming now. I could feel a camera lens trained on my right cheekbone, but I didn't care.

Plus, that happened to be my good side, so that was helpful.

"You were going to propose?" I asked, my heartbeat going at full throttle.

"You don't seem to have been listening very well to what I've been saying over the last few weeks, baby."

I stuck out my tongue. "Well, listening is pretty difficult sometimes, Maddox."

"I even practiced my speech on the flight out here," he said, his voice getting softer.

"Oh my gosh," someone whispered from the crowd. "It's like *Notting Hill* but hotter."

"Okay," I managed, breathless, as I lowered the sign and tried to find my voice. "Tell me about this supposed proposal."

He stepped closer, his sweatshirt stretching just enough over his chest to make my brain malfunction, his hair damp and messy, like he'd run his hands through it a few too many times. Every inch of him radiated unfairly hot.

And then he *smirked*. Like he knew he was about to ruin me.

"Well," he said, his voice full of smug affection. "There was going to be a snow machine. Possibly a string quartet. Definitely champagne. The ring was going to be inside one of those ridiculous oversized champagne poppers, and when it exploded, confetti would rain down, and the ring would land perfectly in your glass. Very subtle."

I raised an eyebrow. "Let me guess. You were wearing the sweater."

He nodded solemnly. "The one that makes me look like a cable-knit Viking."

I lifted a brow. "That sweater should come with a warning label. It's unfair to the general population."

Easton smirked. "I know."

He leaned in slightly, his voice dipping. "Picture it—snow falling, soft music, you standing under the lights trying to pretend you didn't put effort into your outfit when you very obviously did. And me, about to completely ruin your life in the best way."

I felt myself swooning. *Actually swooning.* In public. But I obviously didn't care.

"I had a speech, too," he added, and there was a sudden seriousness in his tone that made my chest squeeze.

My breath caught. "Do I get to hear this speech of yours?"

He glanced at the crowd, still hovering, still watching. Then he looked back at me, and the rest of the world may as well have vanished.

"You really want me to give you *the* speech right here?" he asked, his voice just for me. "With half of Los Angeles filming it and someone in the back crying like this is the season finale of *The Bachelor*?"

I snorted—not the most romantic sound. But fitting. And very us.

"Yeah," I whispered, smiling through the sudden lump in my throat. "I'm holding a glitter sign in front of a hundred strangers. I think the bar for dignity's already gone. Give me the speech, Hollywood."

He laughed once, then nodded. "Fair enough."

Then he inhaled, his chest rising like the moment had finally settled into him.

"You once told me love was just a chemical reaction," Easton said, his voice low and steady. "That it faded or burned out or exploded. That it wouldn't last."

My throat went tight. My heart was beating far too fast.

Because I remembered saying that. I remembered believing it.

"And maybe back then," he continued, "you were too young to believe in forever. Maybe you needed to protect your heart more than I needed to convince you otherwise. So I let you believe it."

His hand reached out, slow and reverent, and his fingers brushed the silver chain at my neck—the tiny constellation pendant now resting over my heart.

My breath caught.

"But, Nat," he whispered, his thumb tracing the stars, "if love really is a reaction, then you've been the spark in every single one of mine. Every laugh. Every fight. Every godforsaken moment I've missed you."

He took a shaky breath, and when his eyes met mine, they held galaxies.

"I used to wish for this," he said quietly. "When I thought I'd lost you for good. I'd lie awake and picture you—older, somewhere out in the world—and wonder if you still remembered that night in the truck."

My throat tightened. Because of course I remembered. Every second.

"You looked up at the stars like they were the only thing that made sense," he went on. "And when I told you I thought you were my one . . . you didn't say anything."

His smile flickered. Familiar and aching. With something deeper than memory.

"But I meant it. I still mean it. And I don't need stars or fate or anything else to tell me. I just need you."

The lights, the noise, the crowd—gone. Just him and me and the echo of everything we'd survived to get here.

He took one step closer, his eyes steady. "Just in case you're still wondering whether soulmates exist after all this time . . . I know they do. But not in the perfect, easy way people talk about. I think they're rare. Messy. Stubborn as hell."

His voice softened, tugging at something deep inside me.

"They fight. They break. They find their way back, sometimes more than once." He shook his head, his eyes never leaving mine.

"You're my soulmate, Natalie Bennett."

A pause. A breath.

"And I was made to never stop loving you."

A tear slipped down my cheek, and I had to laugh because I was dangerously close to ugly-crying in front of a crowd of strangers.

He exhaled, blinking like his own throat was tight. "So. What do you think?"

I wiped at my eyes, breathing hard. "It was fine."

He blinked again. "Fine?"

"You're gonna need to get on one knee if you want to propose properly."

He tilted his head. "You're literally holding a glitter sign. Glitter, Nat. That's how you were proposing."

"Glitter is the emotional equivalent of being on one knee, Easton. Everyone knows that. You gotta meet me halfway."

He huffed out a laugh—low, incredulous, completely wrecked. "Unbelievable."

But then, slowly, without looking away from me, he dropped to one knee. The crowd gasped, but he barely seemed to hear them. His gaze was steady, soft, shining.

"Natalie Bennett," he said, his voice steadier than mine would ever be, "will you marry me?"

I didn't hesitate. Didn't breathe.

"Yes," I whispered.

And the second I said it, the crowd *erupted*—cheers, clapping, camera flashes—but all I saw was him, still kneeling, looking up at me like I held the stars in my hands.

I dropped the glitter sign and dove straight into his arms, and I felt the universe finally exhale around us.

And right there, tangled against him and the aftershock of everything, I whispered the only thing that mattered.

"I'm yours."

EPILOGUE

Natalie

ONE YEAR LATER

The limo smelled like new leather, champagne, and the kind of over-priced cologne Easton swore wasn't "too much," even though I caught two makeup artists swooning as we passed. I sat beside him in a floor-length black satin gown with a slit that made him lose his train of thought every time I shifted my leg.

Not that I minded.

"You're staring," I said as the car crept down the press gauntlet outside the theater.

"I'm married to the most beautiful woman in the world," he said, shrugging, like it was just a fact. "I'm legally allowed to stare. It's in our vows."

"I don't remember that part."

"You were too busy crying because I said you were my miracle," he said with a wink, reaching over to tuck a piece of hair behind my ear. "Also, you look like sin tonight. Like I should take you home before the press get a look at you."

I arched a brow. "You really want to deprive the world of this?" I motioned to my whole vibe like a game-show girl showcasing a luxury yacht.

He leaned close, his mouth brushing the shell of my ear. "I'd rather unwrap my present in private, Mrs. Maddox."

My breath hitched.

"Behave," I whispered.

"Never," he whispered back.

The car slowed. Through the tinted glass, the red carpet lit up under the flashes of cameras and a sea of shining voices. His name was already echoing from reporters, fans, someone with a glittery sign that said EASTON, MARRY ME—which, frankly, felt a bit late, and was definitely copying me.

"You ready for this?" he asked.

I smirked. "I've survived worse."

"Like?"

"Like the time your mom gave me a detailed lecture on your childhood rashes over brunch."

He grimaced. "Fair."

The driver opened the door, and the night exploded into sound and color and heat.

The moment my heels hit the carpet, the crowd roared. For him, obviously. But I held my head high like it was for me, too.

Because maybe, in a way, it was.

I wasn't just his *date*. I wasn't the girl who'd almost let fear write the ending of her story. I was Natalie Maddox now. Confident. In love. Whole.

And entirely uninterested in pretending otherwise.

Easton came around to take my hand like we were the only two people in the world. "Ready to cause a tabloid scandal, Trouble?"

"Always."

We posed, turned, smiled. I pretended to fix his bow tie while he whispered things entirely inappropriate for public consumption, and I whispered back that I was going to make him pay for it later.

"Easton! Natalie! Over here!"

"Give us a kiss!"

He turned to me with a grin and dipped me dramatically, pressing a slow, movie-worthy kiss to my mouth that had half the crowd cheering and the other half probably fainting.

"You're such a show-off," I murmured as he helped me upright.

"Only when the prize is this good."

Interviewers stopped us with bright lights and flashcards. One of them leaned in with a grin, mic angled toward Easton.

"So, what was it like working with Vanessa Blake? You two had insane chemistry on screen."

Easton gave a practiced smile, the kind that was perfectly measured but meant nothing. "Vanessa's a pro," he said, his tone smooth and polite. "She knows how to make a scene work."

The interviewer's eyes flicked to me—just for a second. A sly little glance, like he thought he was being subtle. Like I wasn't standing *right there*, hand locked with Easton's.

And then, with all the grace of a man who'd definitely watched too many gossip reels, he leaned in. "Any truth to those romance rumors from the set?"

I didn't flinch. Didn't move. Just smiled sweetly, envisioning MeMaw popping out of the crowd with a salad fork and throwing it right at this guy's head.

Easton laughed lightly, but his hand never left mine. "People love to talk," he said, noncommittal, easy. "I save my real-life romance for off-camera."

Then he looked at me—just me—and gave a small, secret smile that made my heart melt right through my dress.

"Oh my gosh," I muttered under my breath, fanning my face like a flustered fangirl. "You're ridiculous."

"You love it."

"Yeah," I said softly, "I really do."

After the last photo op, we slipped inside the velvet-roped lobby where champagne flowed, heels clicked, and the stars looked only slightly less intimidating than marble pillars.

I leaned into Easton's side as we stepped toward the theater entrance, my arm looped through his. "Did I tell you how good you look tonight?" I murmured, my lips brushing his ear.

He grinned. "You did. Repeatedly. With tongue."

"Well," I said, lowering my voice just enough. "Then I should probably also tell you . . . I'm not wearing panties."

He stopped walking.

Just—stopped, mid-stride. His whole body went still like I'd yanked the emergency brake on his brain.

I smiled and kept going.

"Natalie," he said, catching up with a growl so low I felt it more than heard it.

"Yes, Mr. Maddox?"

He stepped in behind me, his hand landing low on my waist, his breath warm against my ear as he leaned in close—close enough that no one else could hear what he said.

"You're evil."

I felt the slight shift of his hips, the unmistakable press of his bulge against my back—hard, solid, undeniable.

My knees nearly buckled.

"Feel that?" he murmured, his voice thick with hunger.

I swallowed. "You seem . . . enthusiastic."

"That's what you do to me."

I didn't even try to hide my smile. "Sometimes I forget how much you've got going on down there until it tries to introduce itself."

"I'm dying," he said, his voice a rough rasp of barely restrained desire as he adjusted himself behind me with an exhale that was practically a prayer. "Give me five minutes. One of those marble-tiled premiere bathrooms. I'll remind you."

I turned to face him, arching a brow. "Oh? But that would make me miss the movie," I said innocently. "And as you know . . . I've been so excited about it."

He stared at me like he was seconds away from hauling me off right then and there. "I'll make it worth your while," he tried to say, all charming-like.

I brushed my lips across his jaw and winked. "The show's about to start, Hollywood. Can't upstage yourself."

He groaned softly, and adjusted his tux jacket—less for fashion, more for survival's sake. "You're going to kill me."

I smiled sweetly and tugged him toward the theater doors. "Better make it through the premiere, Mr. Maddox. You've got a very long night ahead of you."

The theater doors opened, and instantly a hush fell over the room as the two of us walked in. Red velvet seats stretched in perfect symmetry before us, and the low hum of conversation dimmed into a curious quiet.

The kind of quiet that came with recognition.

With star power.

Easton Maddox didn't just *walk* into rooms—he shifted gravity.

And now, I was the one at his side, gown whispering against my legs, hand tucked confidently into his. Heads turned. Cameras flashed one last time as we stepped down the aisle, headed for the front row where *Reserved* tags with our names waited.

"Still with me?" he asked, his voice low, eyes scanning the room like a wolf making sure no one else even *thought* about touching what was his.

I smiled. "Always."

An older gentleman with glasses and a clipboard stepped up to Easton just as we reached our seats and gave a little nod. "They're ready for you, Mr. Maddox."

Easton looked at me, kissed the back of my hand, and whispered, "Don't go anywhere."

"Not a chance," I said, settling in and watching as he walked onto the small, spotlighted stage before the massive screen. He paused for a moment, adjusting the microphone, then gave the crowd a sexy, humble smile that made half the theater sigh.

"Hey, everyone. Thanks for coming. I'll try to be quick—my wife promised me a reward if I don't cry or overshare."

Cue polite laughter, a few whistles, and my entire face catching fire.

He looked right at me.

And he softened.

"This film was special for a lot of reasons . . . the cast, the crew, the story we got to tell. But if I'm honest, what made it unforgettable was what was happening when the cameras weren't rolling. Somewhere between the chaos and the quiet . . . I got her back. The girl who's always been it for me. The one who saw all of me before any of this mattered. And somehow still wanted me after. That's what made this one different. That's what made it everything."

I swallowed hard.

"She's in the front row tonight," he said, his voice softer now. "And every time a scene pushed me to the edge—when I wasn't sure I could pull it off—I thought about her. Because if I could reach her, if I could make *her* feel something . . . then I knew it meant something."

My eyes stung.

"I married the love of my life this year," he finished. "And this film is for her."

Thunderous applause erupted.

He gave a short, humble bow and returned to his seat, slipping into the plush velvet beside me like he hadn't just shattered every woman in the room.

I leaned over and whispered, "That's definitely gonna get you laid, Hollywood."

He grinned and kissed the corner of my mouth. "Just wanted to remind you that you're stuck with me."

The lights dimmed.

The audience hushed in that sacred, anticipatory breath that lives just before the opening shot of a film. The screen flickered to life, and within seconds, there he was. Gritty. Bleeding. Desperate.

Brilliant.

He wasn't just good.

He was *magnificent.*

And I would've had a religious experience watching it, if his fingers weren't inching up my thigh like he had a completely different film in mind. This had become a habit, apparently. Breaking PG-13 ratings in public.

And honestly? I wasn't even mad about it.

His thumb brushed the inside of my leg, slow and lazy, as though he had all the time in the world to ruin me. The silk of my gown shifted as he found bare skin, and my breath hitched.

On screen, his character was delivering a raw monologue, voice wrecked and shaking, tears in his eyes as he fell to his knees in the pouring rain.

Beside me?

The real Easton was smirking like a devil.

I shifted slightly in my seat, the cool press of velvet brushing my thighs.

"You're not even watching," I whispered out the side of my mouth, barely daring to move.

"Oh, I'm watching," he murmured, his voice like a caress. "I've seen that scene a hundred times. But this view . . ." His fingers brushed higher, just grazing the edge of heat and sin. "Is entirely exclusive."

My legs tensed. My pulse pounded.

"Easton," I hissed.

"Shh," he murmured, his lips ghosting along my temple. "You'll miss my best scene."

On screen, a war-torn village crumbled in slow motion. Ash fell like snow as Easton's character emerged from the ruins, bloodied and desperate, jaw clenched with anguish.

The entire theater leaned forward, breathless.

Except me.

I was trying not to *moan.*

His fingertips were unforgivable. Gentle, torturous, claiming. He never pushed—just lingered. Let the barest hint of promise whisper between us. His knuckles brushed so high I thought I'd combust right there in the Dolby Theatre.

"You're unbelievable," I managed, gripping the armrest hard enough to leave fingerprints.

He hadn't even reached the danger zone yet. He was toying with me, aware of every small twitch, every inhale. He knew exactly what he was doing.

His lips brushed my ear. "You're tense," he whispered, his voice a low, wicked murmur. "Should I help you relax?"

I clenched the armrest with my left hand and grabbed his wrist with my right. "You are not going to finger me during your own premiere," I hissed.

His grin touched his voice. "Technically, I wasn't planning to go that far. But now that you've said it . . ."

"Easton."

"You started this, baby."

The woman beside me sniffled. She was crying.

Fucking hell, I thought. People are in actual emotional distress because of the man on the screen, and the man beside me is trying to get me to come apart without making a sound.

His fingers crept higher.

On screen, his character was continuing to break down, sobbing in the arms of another actor, the musical score soaring in a way that would have given me chills if I wasn't already drowning in them for an entirely different reason.

"I can't focus," I whispered through clenched teeth.

"Exactly."

A soft gasp escaped me as his thumb brushed along my inner thigh, his movements infuriatingly slow. Teasing. Gentle. Nothing overt. But intentional enough that every nerve ending in my body flared to life.

I squirmed in my seat, completely regretting the whole no-underwear thing.

He stilled his hand and chuckled softly. "Behave," he whispered. "You're going to get us kicked out."

"I swear on Ari Lancaster's ass," I muttered. "If I black out during your Oscar-winning scene because you're playing the piano on my thighs, I'm going to murder you."

"Just for the fact that you said another man's name, I'm going to be even worse."

He shifted slightly closer, tucking his shoulder into mine. To everyone else, we looked like any other couple watching a movie—maybe whispering about the scene, maybe sharing a sweet moment.

But beneath the shadows, he was completely unraveling me.

My breath caught as his knuckles brushed impossibly close to where I was aching for him. So, so close.

It was official, I was going to go mad.

"This is your fault, you know," he murmured, his breath warm against my ear. "I'm only a man, Trouble. What did you think was going to happen when you told me what you forgot to wear tonight?"

"I hate you," I muttered. But it came out annoyingly breathy.

"No, you don't."

And then . . . because mercy had never been his style, his hand slid just a fraction higher, brushing over my clit with the kind of teasing pressure that ignited every nerve ending like a spark to dry tinder.

My pussy clenched, already slick with arousal, and I bit down hard on my bottom lip to keep from making a sound, my hands gripping the armrests so tightly my knuckles turned white. The theater was packed with industry bigwigs, critics, and fans, and gosh dammit—I was not going to give them a show.

On screen, his character was confessing love . . . raw, broken, poetic. The words echoed through the theater, and women were sniffling all around us, their tissues rustling as they dabbed at their eyes. "Losing her was like forgetting how to breathe," Easton's character said, his voice cracking with vulnerability, the kind of performance that would have Oscar buzz written all over it. "But I'd do it again if it meant I got one more day loving her."

Tears welled in my eyes . . . but it wasn't because of the film. No, it was the unbearable contradiction of what I was hearing and what I was feeling—his character's heartfelt declaration clashing with the wicked, teasing pressure of his fingers against my throbbing clit. I was soaked. There was probably going to be a wet spot on the back of my dress, and my thighs were literally throbbing as I fought to keep my composure.

"You're a problem," I hissed, my breath hitching as his fingers pressed a little harder, circling my clit with a slow, desperate rhythm that made my hips twitch involuntarily. "A big problem."

He smiled, so faintly I might've imagined it, his green eyes glinting with mischief in the dim light of the theater. "And you're hot," he murmured, his voice low and smug, his fingers never stopping their torment as he watched me squirm.

"Yeah, I am sweating. Thanks for noticing," I hissed, my entire body on fire as he pushed me closer to the edge. I could feel the slickness literally dripping down my thighs.

He leaned in closer, his lips brushing my ear as he whispered, "You're so fucking wet for me, Nat. You're dripping all over my fingers like such a good girl. You love this, don't you—knowing I can make you come right here, with everyone watching my face on that screen."

I whimpered softly, forcing myself not to glance to the chair next to me, and just hoping desperately that the movie would be too enthralling for anyone to pay me attention like that.

"Please," I hissed at him, my voice wrecked, my hips rocking slightly against his hand, chasing the release I was so desperate for. "You'd better make me come if we've made it this far."

"I always give you what you want, don't I?" he teased, his voice a low growl as his fingers slid lower, parting my folds, his thumb circling my clit while his middle finger slipped inside me, curling to hit that spot that made my vision blur. "Let them hear you, Nat. Let them know how good I make you feel. Let them know you're mine."

I shook my head frantically, my breath coming in short, ragged gasps as I fought to stay silent, my body trembling on the edge of release. His finger thrust slowly in and out, his thumb never stopping its assault on my clit, and I could feel my orgasm building, a tight coil of pleasure that was about to snap.

"If I make a sound," I panted, "you're explaining it to MeMaw during her prayer circle." My voice broke as the pressure became unbearable, my core clenching around his finger, my thighs shaking as I teetered on the brink.

"Come, Trouble," he murmured, his voice a low, amused command as he added a second finger, stretching me, fucking me with his hand right there in the theater, his thumb pressing harder against my clit, sending me spiraling. "Come all over my fingers, Nat. Give it to me. Show me how much you need me."

I came like a woman possessed, hips twitching, breath hitching, like he'd found the exact button marked "ruin her." I clenched around his fingers, my thighs tightening, slick pouring over his hand while I bit my lip hard enough to bleed . . . desperate to smother the moan clawing its way up my throat.

I was vaguely aware of the film still playing, of the audience's soft sniffles and the dramatic music swelling, but all I could focus on was the way Easton's fingers were still moving, drawing out every last shudder of my climax, his touch relentless even as I came down from the high.

His fingers gave one last, lazy stroke, dragging through my slick folds and grazing my oversensitive clit, making me twitch. Then he pulled his hand back, and I saw it—my arousal glistening on his fingers, catching the light from the flickering screen in front of us. His eyes stayed locked on mine as he lifted them to his mouth and slipped them past his lips, slow and deliberate.

"Sweetest fucking thing I've ever tasted," he murmured, licking them clean like he was making a point.

"Fucking hell," I whispered, my voice wrecked, my chest heaving as I tried to catch my breath, my pussy still throbbing with the memory of his touch.

"I—" I hissed, turning to glare at him. Or at least I tried. Words were hard when your entire body had just been rearranged. I was flushed, slick with sweat, every muscle humming. I probably looked wrecked—and I was sitting in a puddle of my own arousal. This would be fun to explain when the lights came back on.

"That was fun," he murmured, smug as hell.

His green eyes glinted with wicked satisfaction as he laced our fingers together, the gesture suddenly sweet—deceptively innocent—like those fingers hadn't just been inside me . . . like he hadn't just dragged me to the brink and shoved me over it in the middle of a premiere.

I shook my head, a breathless laugh slipping from my lips despite myself. He was impossible. Dangerous. And utterly mine.

The credits rolled across the screen, a soft white scroll fading over black. The applause came next—a tidal wave of it—filling the theater like thunder.

People stood. Clapped. Chanted his name.

A chorus of praise rising like a standing ovation for the man seated beside me, who somehow managed to deliver the performance of a lifetime *and* dismantle my ability to form coherent thought.

I just sat there. Flushed. Shaking.

Wrecked.

My body still thrummed with aftershocks, every subtle shift setting off a fresh ripple between my thighs. My dress clung to me in places it definitely hadn't when we sat down, like it knew things now. Intimate things.

I couldn't remember half the movie—only flashes. His character bleeding and beautiful. A line that cracked open the whole theater emotionally. And then me, unraveling in real time while his hand moved like it had a PhD in bad decisions and a personal vendetta against my self-control.

Performance of a lifetime, they'd say.

Yeah. No kidding.

People were turning now, faces lit with admiration. Wide eyes, big smiles, whispers of *Brilliant* and *He's a lock for the Oscar* floating like confetti in the air.

He leaned in.

Voice low. Breath warm against my ear.

"Still think you can make it through the after-party?" he asked, his tone laced with a promise of more to come.

I turned to him, my gaze narrowing as a smirk tugged at my lips. "As long as you fuck me in the limo on the way," I said, my voice low and dangerous and daring.

Easton's head snapped toward me, his emerald eyes darkening with a hunger that made my breath catch, his polite smile faltering for a moment as he registered my words. "Nat," he growled, his voice a low warning, his hand tightening around mine so hard I thought he might crush my fingers. "You know you're playing with fire."

"Good," I shot back, my smirk widening as I squeezed his hand in return, my voice a sultry purr as I leaned in closer, my lips brushing his earlobe. "I want to burn."

His jaw clenched, a faint grimace flickering across his face before he quickly masked it with his Hollywood smile, his eyes tightening at the corners as he nodded at the first wave of well-wishers.

"Easton, that was incredible," a producer in a sleek tuxedo said, clapping him on the shoulder as he leaned in, his voice booming over the lingering applause. "You've got a real shot at the awards this year, my man. That scene in the rain—pure magic!"

"Thanks, Greg," Easton said, his voice smooth and professional to anyone who was listening.

But I knew Easton better than anyone. I could hear the strain in it, the way his words were clipped as he forced a smile, his hand tightening around mine. He shifted slightly in his seat, and that's when I saw it, the huge bulge in his tailored black pants, straining against the fabric. That was probably uncomfortable.

It gave me a little thrill that teasing me to orgasm had turned him on just as much as it had me . . . maybe more. He was in pain, his cock throbbing with need, and yet he had to sit there, smiling and nodding as more people approached, their voices overlapping with praise and congratulations.

The limo ride was going to be a good time.

"Easton, darling, you were phenomenal!" a woman in a glittering gown gushed, her hands clasped together as she leaned in, her perfume overwhelming as she air-kissed his cheek. "That monologue at the end—I was in tears! You're a genius!"

"Thank you, Marissa," he said, his smile tight, his free hand adjusting his jacket in a futile attempt to hide his arousal.

I slid my hand into his lap, my fingers brushing against the anaconda currently straining to escape his pants.

A sharp cough came out of his mouth, his jaw clenching again as he grabbed my hand and yanked it away, all while trying to smile at well-wishers. His eyes flicked to me for a brief moment, a promise of retribution in his gaze that had my pussy clenching all over again.

I winked at him.

The theater finally started to empty out, people filing toward the exits, their voices buzzing with excitement as they headed to the after-party. Easton stood, pulling me with him, his hand firm on mine as he led me through the crowd, his other hand still holding his tuxedo jacket over his situation in his pants. His posture was stiff, his movements careful as he focused on keeping covered, but his eyes kept darting to me, dark and hungry, and I knew he was counting the seconds until we were alone.

"Easton, you coming to the after-party?" another producer called, raising his champagne glass in salute as the crowd buzzed around us.

Easton didn't even blink. "Yeah, we'll be there," he said, voice tight, jaw set.

His hand closed around mine like a man seconds from losing his damn mind, and before I could even catch my breath, he was pulling me toward the exit with single-minded focus—like nothing else mattered. Not the party. Not the cameras. Just us.

He opened the limo door and practically pushed me inside.

The second it clicked shut behind us, the mask dropped.

His hands were on me in an instant, hot and demanding, yanking up my dress with a roughness that made me gasp.

"Fuck, Natalie," he breathed, his voice wrecked as his mouth crashed against mine.

He fumbled with his belt, the sharp *clink* of the buckle lost in the messy rhythm of our kiss. I barely had time to register the slick sound of his zipper, the desperation in his hands, before he freed himself, grabbed my hips, and thrust into me in one fluid, starving motion.

I cried out into his mouth, clinging to his shoulders as my back hit the leather seat, the stretch of him stealing the breath straight from my lungs.

"Mine," he growled, thrusting again—harder this time. "You feel that?"

My laugh was a gasp, wild and dizzy. "How could I not?"

His mouth found mine again, slower now, deeper, as he rocked into me like we had all the time in the world, like this wasn't the back of a limo after a premiere, but the place he was always meant to be.

Fuck, I love being this man's wife.

As he thrust into me again—slow, deep, claiming every inch like he had the rest of forever to worship me—I wrapped my legs around him and whispered against his mouth, "You really couldn't make it one more hour?"

He smirked.

"Next time, I'm not even waiting for the movie."

And just like that, we missed the after-party.

Again.

Because being married to Easton Maddox?

Was a full-time, thoroughly satisfying job.

And I never wanted a day off.

Rudolph Rum Punch

 ## ALCOHOLIC VERSION

Ingredients

- 1 sprig fresh rosemary
- 1 maraschino cherry
- Ice
- 4 oz. Coca-Cola
- 2 oz. White or dark rum
- 1½ oz. tart cherry juice

Instructions

1. *Garnish First:* Place the maraschino cherry and rosemary sprig in a highball or rocks glass. Gently muddle them together just enough to release the oils and aroma—no need to annihilate the rosemary like it owes you money.
2. *Add Ice:* Fill the glass with ice. All the way up. We want this cold and refreshing.
3. *Pour the Party:* Add the rum and tart cherry juice. Give it a swirl to let the flavors meet and flirt.
4. *Top It Off:* Slowly pour in the Coca-Cola. Stir once or twice, gently, to avoid losing the fizz.

Optional flair: If you're feeling extra, add a second rosemary sprig or a cocktail pick with an extra cherry.

 ## NON-ALCOHOLIC VERSION

Ingredients

- Ginger ale
- Cranberry juice
- Green sanding sugar

Instructions

1. *Garnish First:* Dip the top edge of the serving glasses in water and then dip it into the sanding sugar.
2. *Pour It Up:* Fill each glass about half full of cranberry juice. Then fill it to the rim with ginger ale.

ACKNOWLEDGMENTS

Dear Reader,

If you're reading this, we made it. Through every page and kiss and sleigh crash, through the laughter and the longing and maybe even a few tears. And now you're here at the end with me, and I want to thank you with every piece of my writer-heart.

This story began as a spark. A what-if. A girl who swore she'd never fall for the boy again. A boy who never stopped loving her. I wanted to write about second chances . . .not the neat, easy kind, but the messy, beautiful ones. The kind that requires vulnerability, bravery, and a little Christmas chaos.

Natalie and Easton found their way back to each other in snowstorms and silence, in shared glances and stolen kisses, in the moments that felt too small to matter until they were everything. And maybe, if you've ever loved someone and let them go . . .or hoped someone would come back to you . . .you saw a little of yourself in them too.

Writing this book felt like stepping into warmth after the cold. It reminded me that even the most complicated relationships can carry love at their core. That healing doesn't always look like closure. Sometimes it looks like finally saying *I love you* when it counts.

To every reader who's ever rooted for a happy ending even when the middle was a mess—thank you. For trusting me with your time, your hearts, your book hangovers. For believing in love that circles back around and says, *I'm still here.*

And to the ones who feel like they're still waiting on their miracle . . .I hope you find it. I hope it finds you. Maybe in someone's arms. Maybe in a quiet moment with a cup of cocoa. Maybe in a book like this one.

XOXOXO,
C.R.

P.S. MeMaw says thank you for letting her body roll her way into your hearts. She's already planning a spin-off.

A few thank you's . . .

To Raven: You are magic, Moon. A thousand kinds of light. Equal parts hype squad and therapist and creative genius. You keep me grounded when my head is in the clouds, and shove me off cliffs (with love) when I need to leap. Every plot twist, every laugh-until-we-cry voice memo, every "you've got this" at exactly the right time . . .I carry them all like charms on a bracelet I didn't know I needed. You make the hard days easier. The good days *shine*. ILY.

To my beta readers, Crystal, Blair, and Lisa: Thank you for reading with your hearts wide open. Your insight made this story sharper. Your encouragement made me braver. And your late-night messages, inside jokes, and real-time reactions made the whole process that much better. You didn't just help shape this book . . .you helped *me* keep going.

To Stephanie, my editor: Thank you for being the late-night voice of reason when I was spiraling over sentence structure and emotional arcs. Your notes always push the story (and me) to be better, sharper, more honest. You somehow manage to rein me in *and* let me fly—and I'm endlessly grateful for both. From plot holes to late-night panics to final read-throughs, this book is what it is because of you. Thank you for being in my corner. I'm so lucky to have you.

To my PAs and bffs, Caitlin & Sarah. You already know how much I adore you. How much I *depend* on you. How this chaotic book world of mine would crumble without you holding the glitter-covered pieces together. You are my constants. You make everything brighter, smoother, and way more fun (even the panic edits). There aren't enough words to express my gratitude but just know: I'd be lost without you.

And to my readers who make this dream possible:

Who pick up these books and fall in love with the chaos. Who cry with my characters, scream at the red flags, and laugh in the margins. You are the reason these stories live beyond my laptop. You're the magic, the momentum, the miracle.

I am grateful for you.

Every single day, every single page.

Thank you for being here. Thank you for believing.

ABOUT THE AUTHOR

C.R. Jane is a *USA Today*–bestselling author of romance, fantasy, and whatever else she feels like writing. Her stories are designed to make readers cry, scream, and eventually . . . swoon. Welcome to her world, where heartbreak and happy endings rule.

Podium

FOR A GOOD TIME
follow us on our socials

 podiumentertainment.com

 @podiumentertainment

 /podiumentertainment

 @podium_ent

 @podiumentertainment